TALES OF MYSTERY AND IMAGINATION

Edgar Allan Poe was born in Boston, Massachusetts, on January 19th, 1809; educated at Stoke Newington, England, and the University of Virginia; and died in Baltimore on October 7th, 1849. His poems, stories, and critical essays appeared separately and in various collections between 1827 and 1848, and after his death.

TALES OF MYSTERY AND IMAGINATION

EDGAR ALLAN POE

With an Introduction by John Buchan

NELSON

THOMAS NELSON AND SONS LTD
36 Park Street London W1
P.O. Box 336 Apapa Lagos
P.O. Box 25012 Nairobi
77 Coffee Street San Fernando Trinidad

THOMAS NELSON (AUSTRALIA) LTD
597 Little Collins Street Melbourne

THOMAS NELSON & SONS (SOUTH AFRICA) (PROPRIETARY) LTD
P.O. Box 9881 Johannesburg

THOMAS NELSON AND SONS (CANADA) LTD
81 Curlew Drive Don Mills Ontario

THOMAS NELSON AND SONS
Copewood and Davis Streets Camden 3, N.J.

Printed in Great Britain by
Thomas Nelson (Printers) Ltd, London and Edinburgh

INTRODUCTION

LAST year a selection of Emerson's writings was issued in this series, and it seems desirable to follow it with a collection of the best work of that American writer who, morally and intellectually, was Emerson's extreme antitype. There could be no harsher contrast than between the careers of the two men. One came early to recognition, and lived his simple, blameless, prosperous life amid the plaudits of the world. The other died young after a career of bitter drudgery, and left little behind him but a legacy of hate. In Edgar Allan Poe genius burned with no "hard, gem-like flame," but with a murky intensity that scandalised his contemporaries. In the orderly *bourgeois* world of young America he moved like a panther among polar-bears. No nation—least of all a young, self-satisfied nation—likes to be told that it is "one vast perambulating humbug," and he spoke his opinions equally plainly of his colleagues in literature.

The natural result followed. Every species of literary vulture battened on his reputation, the scandals of his life were magnified, and his genius was hidden by a cloud of vulgar abuse. No man was less fortunate in his epoch and his country. He found an America, middle-class, prosaic, still half Puritan and indomitably respectable, and he ran his head against the stone walls which hemmed him in. He wrote his great stories for starvation wages, since the taste which could value them had largely to be created. Had he lived to-day, we can well imagine that a more cosmopolitan America would have made him a hero almost beyond his deserts. Had he fared less hardly at the world's hands, there might have been no gall in his pen and fewer dark places in his life.

His posthumous reward has been great, for to no other American writer has it been given to exercise so profound an influence at once on English and French literature. For myself, I should rank him, in the hierarchy of American prose, below Hawthorne, who seems to me to have combined a profounder moral insight with an equal sense of form and an equal imaginative force; but certainly, save for Hawthorne, he has no rival.

The tragic story of his life has been often written: one of the best short biographies is that by Professor Harrison of Virginia, which is prefixed to the recent *Virginia Edition* of his works. He was born in 1809, the same year which gave to the world Tennyson, Gladstone, Lincoln, Darwin, Mendelssohn, and Chopin. It is part of the irony of his fate that Boston, the city which he hated like the plague, should have had the honour of giving him birth. He came of good stock, originally from Ulster; his parents were on the stage, and lived a roving, unhappy, impecunious life, both dying shortly after he was born. He was adopted by an elderly Scotsman called Allan, a merchant in Richmond, Virginia; and till his adopted father's second marriage regarded himself, and was regarded by others, as his heir. He spent some years at school in England, where he imbibed the romance of an older country, and then went at an early age to the University of Virginia. He did not greatly distinguish himself there in scholarship, but became noted as a *bon vivant* and an athlete.

He next went to the famous West Point Academy, and afterwards, Allan having died without leaving him anything, turned to journalism as a profession. For the rest of his days he was tied to the drudgery of the pen, and wrote for his bread tales, poems, reviews, essays, any kind of work, much of it strangely bad, but some of an excellence which no contemporary could claim. He made many enemies, and his wild neurotic nature kept him always in a state of white-heat, a fury either of affection or dislike. He took to drink and drugs, though he was never an ordinary drunkard, seeking a stimulant or a narcotic to relieve the misery of his daily life.

His end was as tragic and strange as his life. Passing through Baltimore, he seems to have been drinking in a tavern, where he was drugged by some electioneering roughs and carried round in their custody to the different voting-booths. He never recovered from the treatment, and a few days later died in hospital.

To most people Poe is best known as a poet, and the poems which have the widest vogue are unfortunately his worst productions. " The Raven " was, in his own words, to be composed of " equal proportions of Beauty and Quaintness intermingled with Melancholy." The result was a parody of his peculiar qualities, and the parody, as in the similar case of "The Bells," has been accepted for the original. That sinister fowl has stood between him and the highest kind of poetic fame. "The vagueness of exaltation," he wrote, "aroused by a sweet air (which should be strictly indefinite and never too strongly suggestive) is precisely what we should aim at in poetry." It is a narrow definition, but in his small body of verse he repeatedly reaches the ideal. "To Helen," "The City in the Sea," "The Haunted Palace," "To One in Paradise," "The Sleeper," "For Annie," "Annabel Lee," and even beautiful nonsense like "Ulalume," have all the strange haunting sweetness of music.

On his own definition Poe is a master-singer, and on any definition he is a true lyric poet. But his real medium was prose, for, apart from gifts of style and melody, he had in the highest degree the constructive imagination which can reproduce a realm of fancy with the minute realism of everyday life. He reveals all around us the shadowy domain of the back-world, and behind our smug complacency the shrieking horror of the unknown. There is no humour in him, none of that wise detachment. which makes *Wandering Willie's Tale* immortal, for every nerve, as he writes, quivers at the terrors he is conjuring. To this imaginative intensity he added a style of singular flexibility and grace. He has, to be sure, appalling lapses into the banal, but at his best he has a store of apt and jewelled words in which to clothe his recondite thoughts. It is this combination which endeared him to Théophile Gautier and his school, and gave him Baudelaire and Mallarmé as his translators.

But style and imagination, if left alone, might have landed him in an unprofitable mysticism. What gives him his unique power is the mathematical accuracy of his mind. All his life he had a passion for cryptographs, and maintained that human ingenuity could create no cypher which human ingenuity could not unravel. His mind worked on data with the most logical precision and he once startled Dickens by predicting the whole plot of *Barnaby Rudge* from the material furnished in the earlier chapters. Hence in all his tales there is a clear sequence of cause and effect which gives them an imaginative coherence and verisimilitude. Without this gift his fancy would have lost itself in vague flights and barren splendours.

The conjunction of such very different talents gives him a right to a high place among the masters of the short story, in his own *genre* perhaps to the highest place, for I know no French imitator who can produce the haunting sense of fate which we get from "The Fall of the House of Usher," or the devilish horror of "The Cask of Amontillado." How admirable, too, are his mystifications, "The Murders in the Rue Morgue" or "The Gold-Bug." Sometimes, as in "Berenice," his "mortuary turn of mind" carries him too far for serious art; but he makes amends in tales like "The Narrative of A. Gordon Pym," where his imagination works soberly and convincingly among realities.

It is a fascinating but barren game which critics sometimes indulge in to discuss which is the best

short story in the world. If I were put on oath I
should decide for Scott's *Wandering Willie's Tale*,
and give the second place to Mr. Kipling's *Man who
would be King*.

But such a classification, like the Cambridge Senior
Wranglership, is captious and unintelligent. A more
sensible form of the game is to create a small first-
class, say of a dozen. Here it is possible to get something nearer a general agreement. Most people would
give one place to Scott (*Wandering Willie's Tale*) ;
one to Stevenson (*Thrawn Janet*, perhaps) ; one to
Hawthorne (the choice is large) ; one place each to
Tourgeniev, Balzac, Guy de Maupassant, Daudet,
Anatole France, and Mr. Kipling. In the remaining
three I should include Mr. Joseph Conrad's *Youth*,
and the two other places I should leave to Poe. The
truth seems to be that while Poe wrote nothing that
wholly transcends his rivals in his own sphere, he
wrote more stories that reach the level of the very
best. He deserves two places in a roll of honour where
the others have only one.

In an excellent recent essay Mr. Hamilton W.
Mabie discusses Poe's place in American literature,
and finds in his complete aloofness from vulgar ideals,
his exquisite craftsmanship, and his devotion to an
austere art for its own sake the example which was
especially needed by his generation. He sought above
all things distinction, and to a nation which was apt
to content itself with the gods of the market-place
he preached in his strange way a wholesome lesson.
" The final justification of a democracy lies in its
ability to clear the way for superiority." The

democracy which suffered under his lash is at last beginning to realise the superiority of its critic. So far he is the one great surprise of American letters. A shrewd observer, after the Revolution, might have predicted Longfellow and Emerson and Holmes and Hawthorne, but it would have passed the wit of man to foretell Poe.

J. B.

1909

CONTENTS

TALES OF MYSTERY AND IMAGINATION

I

THE GOLD-BUG

What ho ! what ho ! this fellow is dancing mad !
He hath been bitten by the Tarantula.

All in the Wrong

MANY years ago I contracted an intimacy with a Mr. William Legrand. He was of an ancient Huguenot family, and had once been wealthy ; but a series of misfortunes had reduced him to want. To avoid the mortification consequent upon his disasters, he left New Orleans, the city of his forefathers, and took up his residence at Sullivan's Island, near Charleston, South Carolina.

This island is a very singular one. It consists of little else than the sea sand, and is about three miles long. Its breadth at no point exceeds a quarter of a mile. It is separated from the mainland by a scarcely perceptible creek, oozing its way through a wilderness of reeds and slime, a favourite resort of the marsh-hen. The vegetation, as might be supposed, is scant, or at least dwarfish. No trees of any magnitude are to be seen. Near the western extremity, where Fort Moultrie stands, and where are some miserable frame buildings, tenanted, during summer, by the fugitives from Charleston dust and fever, may be found, indeed, the bristly palmetto ; but the whole island, with the exception of this western point, and a line of hard, white beach on the sea coast, is covered with a dense undergrowth of the sweet myrtle, so much prized by the horticulturists of England. The shrub here often attains the height of fifteen or twenty feet, and forms an almost impenetrable coppice, burthening the air with its fragrance.

In the inmost recesses of this coppice, not far from the eastern or more remote end of the island, Legrand had built himself a small hut, which he occupied when I first, by mere accident, made his acquaintance. This soon ripened into friendship—for there was much in the recluse to excite interest and esteem. I found him well educated, with unusual powers of mind, but infected with misanthropy, and subject to perverse moods of alternate enthusiasm and melancholy. He had with him many books, but rarely employed them. His chief amusements were gunning and fishing, or sauntering along the beach and through the myrtles, in quest of shells or entomological specimens ;—his collection of the latter might have been envied by a Swammerdamm. In these excursions he was usually accompanied by an old negro, called Jupiter, who had been manumitted before the reverses of the family, but who could be induced, neither by threats nor by promises, to abandon what he considered his right of attendance upon the footsteps of his young " Massa Will." It is not improbable that the relatives of Legrand, conceiving him to be somewhat unsettled in intellect, had contrived to instil this obstinacy into Jupiter, with a view to the supervision and guardianship of the wanderer.

The winters in the latitude of Sullivan's Island are seldom very severe, and in the fall of the year it is a rare event indeed when a fire is considered necessary. About the middle of October, 18—, there occurred, however, a day of remarkable chilliness. Just before sunset I scrambled my way through the evergreens to the hut of my friend, whom I had not visited for several weeks—my residence being at that time in Charleston, a distance of nine miles from the island, while the facilities of passage and re-passage were very far behind those of the present day. Upon reaching the hut I rapped, as was my custom, and getting no reply, sought for the key where I knew it was secreted, unlocked the door and went in. A fine fire was blazing upon the hearth. It was a novelty, and by no means an ungrateful one. I threw off an overcoat, took an arm-chair by the crackling logs, and awaited patiently the arrival of my hosts.

Soon after dark they arrived, and gave me a most cordial welcome. Jupiter, grinning from ear to ear, bustled about to prepare some marsh-hens for supper. Legrand was in one of his fits—how else shall I term them?—of enthusiasm. He had found an unknown bivalve, forming a new genus, and, more than this, he had hunted down and secured, with Jupiter's assistance, a *scarabæus* which he believed to be totally new, but in respect to which he wished to have my opinion on the morrow.

"And why not to-night?" I asked, rubbing my hands over the blaze, and wishing the whole tribe of *scarabæi* at the devil.

"Ah, if I had only known you were here!" said Legrand, "but it's so long since I saw you; and how could I foresee that you would pay me a visit this very night of all others? As I was coming home I met Lieutenant G——, from the fort, and, very foolishly, I lent him the bug; so it will be impossible for you to see it until the morning. Stay here to-night, and I will send Jup down for it at sunrise. It is the loveliest thing in creation!"

"What!—sunrise?"

"Nonsense! no!—the bug. If is of a brilliant gold colour—about the size of a large hickory-nut— with two jet black spots near one extremity of the back, and another, somewhat longer, at the other. The *antennæ* are——"

"Dey aint *no* tin in him, Massa Will, I keep a tellin on you," here interrupted Jupiter; "de bug is a goole-bug, solid, ebery bit of him, inside and all, sep him wing—neber feel half so hebby a bug in my life."

"Well, suppose it is, Jup," replied Legrand, some-what more earnestly, it seemed to me, than the case demanded, "is that any reason for your letting the birds burn? The colour"—here he turned to me— "is really almost enough to warrant Jupiter's idea. You never saw a more brilliant metallic lustre than the scales emit—but of this you cannot judge till to-morrow. In the meantime I can give you some idea of the shape." Saying this, he seated himself at a small table, on which were a pen and ink, but no paper. He looked for some in a drawer, but found none.

"Never mind," said he at length, "this will answer;" and he drew from his waistcoat pocket a scrap of what I took to be very dirty foolscap, and made upon it a rough drawing with the pen. While he did this, I retained my seat by the fire, for I was still chilly. When the design was complete, he handed it to me without rising. As I received it, a loud growl was heard, succeeded by a scratching at the door. Jupiter opened it, and a large New-foundland, belonging to Legrand, rushed in, leaped upon my shoulders, and loaded me with caresses; for I had shown him much attention during previous visits. When his gambols were over, I looked at the paper, and, to speak the truth, found myself not a little puzzled at what my friend had depicted.

"Well!" I said, after contemplating it for some minutes, "this *is* a strange *scarabæus*, I must con-fess: new to me: never saw anything like it before —unless it was a skull, or a death's head—which it more nearly resembles than anything else that has come under *my* observation."

"A death's-head!" echoed Legrand—"Oh—yes— well, it has something of that appearance upon paper, no doubt. The two upper black spots look like eyes, eh? and the longer one at the bottom like a mouth —and then the shape of the whole is oval."

"Perhaps so," said I; "but, Legrand, I fear you

are no artist. I must wait until I see the beetle
itself, if I am to form any idea of its personal appearance.''

"Well, I don't know," said he, a little nettled.
"I draw tolerably—*should* do it at least—have had
good masters, and flatter myself that I am not quite
a blockhead.''

"But, my dear fellow, you are joking then,'' said
I; "this is a very passable *skull*—indeed, I may
say that it is a very *excellent* skull, according to the
vulgar notions about such specimens of physiology—
and your *scarabæus* must be the queerest *scarabæus*
in the world if it resembles it. Why, we may get up
a very thrilling bit of superstition upon this hint.
I presume you will call the bug *scarabæus caput
hominis*, or something of that kind—there are many
similar titles in the Natural Histories. But where
are the *antennæ* you spoke of ? ''

"The *antennæ* ! '' said Legrand, who seemed to be
getting unaccountably warm upon the subject ; "I
am sure you must see the *antennæ*. I made them as
distinct as they are in the original insect, and I presume that is sufficient.''

"Well, well," I said, "perhaps you have—still I
don't see them ; '' and I handed him the paper without additional remark, not wishing to ruffle his
temper ; but I was much surprised at the turn
affairs had taken ; his ill-humour puzzled me—and,
as for the drawing of the beetle, there were positively
no antennæ visible, and the whole *did* bear a very
close resemblance to the ordinary cuts of a death's-
head.

He received the paper very peevishly, and was about to crumple it, apparently to throw it in the fire, when a casual glance at the design seemed suddenly to rivet his attention. In an instant his face grew violently red—in another as excessively pale. For some minutes he continued to scrutinise the drawing minutely where he sat. At length he arose, took a candle from the table, and proceeded to seat himself upon a sea-chest in the farthest corner of the room. Here again he made an anxious examination of the paper ; turning it in all directions. He said nothing, however, and his conduct greatly astonished me ; yet I thought it prudent not to exacerbate the growing moodiness of his temper by any comment. Presently he took from his coat pocket a wallet, placed the paper carefully in it, and deposited both in a writing-desk, which he locked. He now grew more composed in his demeanour ; but his original air of enthusiasm had quite disappeared. Yet he seemed not so much sulky as abstracted. As the evening wore away he became more and more absorbed in reverie, from which no sallies of mine could arouse him. It had been my intention to pass the night at the hut, as I had frequently done before, but, seeing my host in this mood, I deemed it proper to take leave. He did not press me to remain, but, as I departed, he shook my hand with even more than his usual cordiality.

It was about a month after this (and during the interval I had seen nothing of Legrand) when I received a visit, at Charleston, from his man, Jupiter. I had never seen the good old negro look so dispirited and I feared that some serious disaster had befallen my friend.

"Well, Jup," said I, "what is the matter now? —how is your master?"

"Why, to speak de troof, massa, him not so berry well as mought be."

"Not well! I am truly sorry to hear it. What does he complain of?"

"Dar! dat's it!—him nebber plain of notin—but him berry sick for all dat."

"*Very* sick, Jupiter!—why didn't you say so at once? Is he confined to bed?"

"No dat he aint!—he aint find nowhar—dat's just whar de shoe pinch—my mind is got to be berry hebby bout poor Massa Will."

"Jupiter, I should like to understand what it is you are talking about. You say your master is sick. Hasn't he told you what ails him?"

"Why, massa, taint worf while for to git mad about de matter—Massa Will say noffin at all aint de matter wid him—but den what make him go about looking dis here way, wid he head down and he soldiers up, and as white as a gose? And den he keep a syphon all de time——"

"Keeps a what, Jupiter?"

"Keeps a syphon wid de figgurs on de slate—de queerest figgurs I ebber did see. Ise gittin to be skeered, I tell you. Hab for to keep mighty tight eye pon him noovers. Todder day he gib me slip fore de sun up, and was gone de whole ob de blessed day. I had a big stick ready cut for to gib him deuced good beating when he did come—but Ise sich

a fool dat I hadn't de heart arter all—he look so
berry poorly."

"Eh ?—what ?—ah yes !—upon the whole I think
you had better not be too severe with the poor fellow
—don't flog him, Jupiter—he can't very well stand
it—but can you form no idea of what has occasioned
this illness, or rather this change of conduct ? Has
anything unpleasant happened since I saw you ? "

"No, massa, dey aint bin noffin onpleasant *since*
den—'twas *fore* den I'm feared—'twas de berry day
you was dare."

"How ? What do you mean ? "

"Why, massa, I mean de bug—dare now."

"The what ? "

"De bug—I'm berry sartain dat Massa Will bin bit
somewhere bout de head by dat goole-bug."

"And what cause have you, Jupiter, for such a
supposition ? "

"Claws enuff, massa, and mouff too. I nebber did
see sich a deuced bug—he kick and he bite ebery ting
what cum near him. Massa Will cotch him fuss, but
had for to let him go gin mighty quick, I tell you—
den was de time he must ha got de bite. I didn't
like de look ob de bug mouff, myself, no how, so I
wouldn't take hold ob him wid my finger, but I cotch
him wid a piece ob paper dat I found. I rap him up
in de paper and stuff piece ob it in he mouff—dat was
de way."

"And you think, then, that your master was really
bitten by the beetle, and that the bite made him
sick ? "

"I don't tink noffin about it—I nose it. What

make him dream bout de goole so much, if taint cause he bit by de goole-bug ? Ise heerd bout dem goole-bugs fore dis.''

" But how do you know he dreams about gold ? "

" How I know ? Why, cause he talk about it in he sleep—dat's how I nose."

" Well, Jup, perhaps you are right ; but to what fortunate circumstance am I to attribute the honour of a visit from you to-day ? "

" What de matter, massa ? "

" Did you bring any message from Mr. Legrand ? "

" No, massa, I bring dis here pissel ; " and here Jupiter handed me a note which ran thus :

" My Dear ——

" Why have I not seen you for so long a time ? I hope you have not been so foolish as to take offence at any little *brusquerie* of mine ; but no, that is improbable.

" Since I saw you I have had great cause for anxiety. I have something to tell you, yet scarcely know how to tell it, or whether I should tell it at all.

" I have not been quite well for some days past, and poor old Jup annoys me, almost beyond endurance, by his well-meant attentions. Would you believe it ?—he had prepared a huge stick, the other day, with which to chastise me for giving him the slip, and spending the day, *solus*, among the hills on the mainland. I verily believe that my ill looks alone saved me a flogging.

" I have made no addition to my cabinet since we met.

"If you can, in any way, make it convenient, come over with Jupiter. *Do* come. I wish to see you *to-night*, upon business of importance. I assure you that it is of the *highest* importance,—Ever yours,

"WILLIAM LEGRAND."

There was something in the tone of this note which gave me great uneasiness. Its whole style differed materially from that of Legrand. What could he be dreaming of? What new crotchet possessed his excitable brain? What "business of the highest importance" could *he* possibly have to transact? Jupiter's account of him boded no good. I dreaded lest the continued pressure of misfortune had, at length, fairly unsettled the reason of my friend. Without a moment's hesitation, therefore, I prepared to accompany the negro.

Upon reaching the wharf, I noticed a scythe and three spades, all apparently new, lying in the bottom of the boat in which we were to embark.

"What is the meaning of all this, Jup?" I inquired.

"Him syfe, massa, and spade."

"Very true; but what are they doing here?"

"Him de syfe and de spade what Massa Will sis pon my buying for him in de town, and de debbil's own lot of money I had to gib for em."

"But what, in the name of all that is mysterious, is your 'Massa Will' going to do with scythes and spades?"

"Dat's more dan *I* know, and debbil take me if I don't blieve 'tis more dan he know too. But it's all cum ob de bug."

Finding that no satisfaction was to be obtained of Jupiter, whose whole intellect seemed to be absorbed by " de bug," I now stepped into the boat and made sail. With a fair and strong breeze we soon ran into the little cove to the northward of Fort Moultrie, and a walk of some two miles brought us to the hut. It was about three in the afternoon when we arrived. Legrand had been awaiting us in eager expectation. He grasped my hand with a nervous *empressement* which alarmed me and strengthened the suspicions already entertained. His countenance was pale even to ghastliness, and his deep-set eyes glared with unnatural lustre. After some inquiries respecting his health, I asked him, not knowing what better to say, if he had yet obtained the *scarabæus* from Lieutenant G——.

" Oh, yes," he replied, colouring violently, " I got it from him the next morning. Nothing should tempt me to part with that *scarabæus*. Do you know that Jupiter is quite right about it ! "

" In what way ? " I asked, with a sad foreboding at heart.

" In supposing it to be a bug of *real gold*." He said this with an air of profound seriousness, and I felt inexpressibly shocked.

" This bug is to make my fortune," he continued, with a triumphant smile, " to reinstate me in my family possessions. Is it any wonder, then, that I prize it ? Since Fortune has thought fit to bestow it upon me, I have only to use it properly and I shall arrive at the gold of which it is the index. Jupiter, bring me that *scarabæus !* "

" What ! de bug, massa ? I'd rudder not go fer trubble dat bug—you mus git him for your own self." Hereupon Legrand arose, with a grave and stately air, and brought me the beetle from a glass case in which it was enclosed. It was a beautiful *scarabæus*, and, at that time, unknown to naturalists—of course a great prize in a scientific point of view. There were two round black spots near one extremity of the back, and a long one near the other. The scales were exceedingly hard and glossy, with all the appearance of burnished gold. The weight of the insect was very remarkable, and, taking all things into consideration, I could hardly blame Jupiter for his opinion respecting it ; but what to make of Legrand's concordance with that opinion, I could not, for the life of me, tell.

" I sent for you," said he, in a grandiloquent tone, when I had completed my examination of the beetle, " I sent for you, that I might have your counsel and assistance in furthering the views of Fate and of the bug——"

" My dear Legrand," I cried, interrupting him, " you are certainly unwell, and had better use some little precautions. You shall go to bed, and I will remain with you a few days, until you get over this. You are feverish and——"

" Feel my pulse," said he.

I felt it, and, to say the truth, found not the slightest indication of fever.

" But you may be ill and yet have no fever. Allow me this once to prescribe for you. In the first place, go to bed. In the next——"

" You are mistaken," he interposed ; " I am as

well as I can expect to be under the excitement which I suffer. If you really wish me well, you will relieve this excitement.''

" And how is this to be done ? "

" Very easily. Jupiter and myself are going upon an expedition into the hills, upon the mainland, and, in this expedition, we shall need the aid of some person in whom we can confide. You are the only one we can trust. Whether we succeed or fail, the excitement which you now perceive in me will be equally allayed.''

" I am anxious to oblige you in any way," I replied ; " but do you mean to say that this infernal beetle has any connection with your expedition into the hills ? "

" It has.''

" Then, Legrand, I can become a party to no such absurd proceeding.''

" I am sorry—very sorry—for we shall have to try it by ourselves.''

" Try it by yourselves ! The man is surely mad !— but stay !—how long do you propose to be absent ? "

" Probably all night. We shall start immediately, and be back, at all events, by sunrise.''

" And will you promise me upon your honour, that when this freak of yours is over, and the bug business (good God !) settled to your satisfaction, you will then return home and follow my advice implicitly, as that of your physician ? "

" Yes ; I promise ; and now let us be off, for we have no time to lose.''

With a heavy heart I accompanied my friend. We

started about four o'clock—Legrand, Jupiter, the dog, and myself. Jupiter had with him the scythe and spades—the whole of which he insisted upon carrying —more through fear, it seemed to me, of trusting either of the implements within reach of his master, than from any excess of industry or complaisance. His demeanour was dogged in the extreme, and " dat deuced bug " were the sole words which escaped his lips during the journey. For my own part, I had charge of a couple of dark lanterns, while Legrand contented himself with the *scarabæus*, which he carried attached to the end of a bit of whip-cord ; twirling it to and fro, with the air of a conjuror, as he went. When I observed this last plain evidence of my friend's aberration of mind I could scarcely refrain from tears. I thought it best, however, to humour his fancy, at least for the present, or until I could adopt some more energetic measures with a chance of success. In the meantime I endeavoured, but all in vain, to sound him in regard to the object of the expedition. Having succeeded in inducing me to accompany him, he seemed unwilling to hold conversation upon any topic of minor importance, and to all my questions vouchsafed no other reply than " We shall see ! "

We crossed the creek at the head of the island by means of a skiff, and, ascending the high grounds on the shore of the mainland, proceeded in a north-westerly direction, through a tract of country excessively wild and desolate, where no trace of a human footstep was to be seen. Legrand led the way with decision ; pausing only for an instant, here and there, to consult what appeared to be certain landmarks of his own contrivance upon a former occasion.

In this manner we journeyed for about two hours, and the sun was just setting when we entered a region infinitely more dreary than any yet seen. It was a species of tableland, near the summit of an almost inaccessible hill, densely wooded from base to pinnacle, and interspersed with huge crags that appeared to lie loosely upon the soil, and in many cases were prevented from precipitating themselves into the valleys below, merely by the support of the trees against which they reclined. Deep ravines, in various directions, gave an air of still sterner solemnity to the scene.

The natural platform to which we had clambered was thickly overgrown with brambles, through which we soon discovered that it would have been impossible to force our way but for the scythe ; and Jupiter, by direction of his master, proceeded to clear for us a path to the foot of an enormously tall tulip-tree, which stood, with some eight or ten oaks, upon the level, and far surpassed them all, and all other trees which I had then ever seen, in the beauty of its foliage and form, in the wide spread of its branches, and in the general majesty of its appearance. When we reached this tree, Legrand turned to Jupiter, and asked him if he thought he could climb it. The old man seemed a little staggered by the question, and for some moments made no reply. At length he approached the huge trunk, walked slowly around it, and examined it with minute attention. When he had completed his scrutiny, he merely said,

"Yes, massa, Jup climb any tree he ebber see in he life."

"Then up with you as soon as possible, for it will soon be too dark to see what we are about."

"How far mus go up, massa?" inquired Jupiter.

"Get up to the main trunk first, and then I will tell you which way to go—and here—stop! take this beetle with you."

"De bug, Massa Will!—de goole-bug!" cried the negro, drawing back in dismay—"what for mus tote de bug way up de tree?—d——n if I do!"

"If you are afraid, Jup, a great big negro like you, to take hold of a harmless little dead beetle, why you can carry it up by this string—but if you do not take it up with you in some way, I shall be under the necessity of breaking your head with this shovel."

"What de matter now, massa?" said Jup, evidently shamed into compliance; "always want for to raise fuss wid old nigger. Was only funnin any how. *Me* feered de bug! what I keer for de bug?" Here he took cautiously hold of the extreme end of the string, and, maintaining the insect as far from his person as circumstances would permit, prepared to ascend the tree.

In youth, the tulip-tree, or *Liriodendron tulipi-ferum*, the most magnificent of American foresters, has a trunk peculiarly smooth, and often rises to a great height without lateral branches; but, in its riper age, the bark becomes gnarled and uneven, while many short limbs make their appearance on the stem. Thus the difficulty of ascension, in the present case, lay more in semblance than in reality. Embracing the huge cylinder, as closely as possible, with his arms and knees, seizing with his hands some projections, and resting his naked toes upon others, Jupiter, after one or two narrow escapes from falling, at length wriggled himself into the first great fork, and seemed to consider the whole business as virtually accomplished. The *risk* of the achievement was, in fact, now over, although the climber was some sixty or seventy feet from the ground.

" Which way mus go now, Massa Will ? " he asked.

" Keep up the largest branch—the one on this side," said Legrand. The negro obeyed him promptly, and apparently with but little trouble ; ascending higher and higher, until no glimpse of his squat figure could be obtained through the dense foliage which enveloped it. Presently his voice was heard in a sort of halloo.

" How much fudder is got for go ? "

" How high up are you ? " asked Legrand.

" Ebber so fur," replied the negro ; " can see de sky fru de top ob de tree."

" Never mind the sky, but attend to what I say. Look down the trunk and count the limbs below you on this side. How many limbs have you passed ? "

" One, two, tree, four, fibe—I done pass fibe big limb, massa, pon dis side."

" Then go one limb higher."

In a few minutes the voice was heard again, announcing that the seventh limb was attained.

" Now, Jup," cried Legrand, evidently much excited, " I want you to work your way out upon that limb as far as you can. If you see anything strange, let me know."

By this time what little doubt I might have entertained of my poor friend's insanity was put finally at rest. I had no alternative but to conclude him stricken with lunacy, and I became seriously anxious about getting him home. While I was pondering upon what was best to be done, Jupiter's voice was again heard.

"Mos feerd for to ventur pon dis limb berry far—tis dead limb putty much all de way."

"Did you say it was a *dead* limb, Jupiter?" cried Legrand in a quavering voice.

"Yes, massa, him dead as de door-nail—done up for sartain—done departed dis here life."

"What in the name of heaven shall I do?" asked Legrand, seemingly in the greatest distress.

"Do!" said I, glad of an opportunity to interpose a word, "why come home and go to bed. Come now!—that's a fine fellow. It's getting late, and, besides, you remember your promise."

"Jupiter," cried he, without heeding me in the least, "do you hear me?"

"Yes, Massa Will, hear you ebber so plain."

"Try the wood well, then, with your knife, and see if you think it *very* rotten."

"Him rotten, massa, sure nuff," replied the negro in a few moments, "but not so berry rotten as mought be. Mought ventur out leetle way pon de limb by myself, dat's true."

"By yourself!—What do you mean?"

"Why, I mean de bug. 'Tis *berry* hebby bug. Spose I drop him down fuss, and den de limb won't break wid just de weight ob one nigger."

" You infernal scoundrel ! " cried Legrand, apparently much relieved, " what do you mean by telling me such nonsense as that ? As sure as you drop that beetle I'll break your neck. Look here, Jupiter, do you hear me ? "

" Yes, massa, needn't hollo at poor nigger dat style."

" Well ! now listen !—if you will venture out on the limb as far as you think safe, and not let go the beetle, I'll make you a present of a silver dollar as soon as you get down."

" I'm gwine, Massa Will—deed I is," replied the negro very promptly—" mos out to the eend now."

" *Out to the end !* " here fairly screamed Legrand, " do you say you are out to the end of that limb ? "

" Soon be to de eend, massa,—o-o-o-o-oh ! Lor-gol-a-marcy ! what *is* dis here pon de tree ? "

" Well," cried Legrand, highly delighted, " what is it ? "

" Why, taint nuffin but a skull—somebody bin let him head up de tree, and de crows done gobble ebery bit ob de meat off."

" A skull, you say !—very well !—how is it fastened to the limb ?—what holds it on ? "

" Sure nuff, massa ; mus look. Why dis berry curous sarcumstance, pon my word—dare's a great big nail in de skull, what fastens ob it on to de tree."

" Well now, Jupiter, do exactly as I tell you—do you hear ? "

" Yes, massa."

" Pay attention, then !—find the left eye of the skull."

"Hum! hoo! dat's good! why dare aint no eye lef at all."

"Curse your stupidity! do you know your right hand from your left?"

"Yes, I nose dat—nose all bout dat—tis my lef hand what I chops de wood wid."

"To be sure! you are left-handed; and your left eye is on the same side as your left hand. Now, I suppose, you can find the left eye of the skull, or the place where the left eye has been. Have you found it?"

Here was a long pause. At length the negro asked,

"Is de lef eye of de skull pon de same side as de lef hand of de skull, too?—cause de skull aint got not a bit ob a hand at all—nebber mind! I got de lef eye now—here de lef eye! what mus do wid it?"

"Let the beetle drop through it, as far as the string will reach—but be careful and not let go your hold of the string."

"All dat done, Massa Will; mighty easy ting for to put de bug fru de hole—look out for him dare below!"

During this colloquy no portion of Jupiter's person could be seen; but the beetle, which he had suffered to descend, was now visible at the end of the string, and glistened, like a globe of burnished gold, in the last rays of the setting sun, some of which still faintly illumined the eminence upon which we stood. The *scarabæus* hung quite clear of any branches, and, if allowed to fall, would have fallen at our feet. Legrand immediately took the scythe, and cleared with it a circular space, three or four yards in diameter, just beneath the insect, and, having accomplished this, ordered Jupiter to let go the string and come down from the tree.

Driving a peg, with great nicety, into the ground, at the precise spot where the beetle fell, my friend now produced from his pocket a tape-measure. Fastening one end of this at that point of the trunk of the tree which was nearest the peg, he unrolled it till it reached the peg, and thence farther unrolled it, in the direction already established by the two points of the tree and the peg, for the distance of fifty feet—Jupiter clearing away the brambles with the scythe. At the spot thus attained a second peg was driven, and about this, as a centre, a rude circle, about four feet in diameter, described. Taking now a spade himself, and giving one to Jupiter and one to me, Legrand begged us to set about digging as quickly as possible.

To speak the truth, I had no especial relish for such amusement at any time, and, at that particular moment, would most willingly have declined it; for the night was coming on, and I felt much fatigued with the exercise already taken; but I saw no mode of escape, and was fearful of disturbing my poor friend's equanimity by a refusal. Could I have depended, indeed, upon Jupiter's aid, I would have had no hesitation in attempting to get the lunatic home by force; but I was too well assured of the old negro's disposition, to hope that he would assist me, under any circumstances, in a personal contest with his master. I made no doubt that the latter had been infected with some of the innumerable Southern superstitions about money buried, and that his fantasy had received confirmation by the finding of the *scarabæus*, or, perhaps, by Jupiter's obstinacy in maintaining it to be "a bug of real gold." A mind disposed to lunacy would readily be led away by such suggestions—especially if chiming in with favourite preconceived ideas—and then I called to mind the poor fellow's speech about the beetle's being "the index of his fortune." Upon the whole, I was sadly vexed and puzzled, but, at length, I concluded to make a virtue of necessity—to dig with a good will, and thus the sooner to convince the visionary, by ocular demonstration, of the fallacy of the opinions he entertained.

The lanterns having been lit, we all fell to work with a zeal worthy a more rational cause; and, as the glare fell upon our persons and implements, I could not help thinking how picturesque a group we composed, and how strange and suspicious our labours must have appeared to any interloper who, by chance, might have stumbled upon our whereabouts.

We dug very steadily for two hours. Little was said; and our chief embarrassment lay in the yelpings of the dog, who took exceeding interest in our proceedings. He at length became so obstreperous, that we grew fearful of his giving the alarm to some stragglers in the vicinity; or, rather, this was the apprehension of Legrand;—for myself, I should have rejoiced at any interruption which might have enabled me to get the wanderer home. The noise was, at length, very effectually silenced by Jupiter, who, getting out of the hole with a dogged air of deliberation, tied the brute's mouth up with one of his suspenders, and then returned, with a grave chuckle, to his task.

When the time mentioned had expired, we had reached a depth of five feet, and yet no signs of any treasure became manifest. A general pause ensued, and I began to hope that the farce was at an end. Legrand, however, although evidently much disconcerted, wiped his brow thoughtfully and recommenced. We had excavated the entire circle of four feet diameter, and now we slightly enlarged the limit, and went to the farther depth of two feet. Still nothing appeared. The gold-seeker, whom I sincerely pitied, at length clambered from the pit, with the bitterest disappointment imprinted upon every feature, and proceeded, slowly and reluctantly, to put on his coat, which he had thrown off at the beginning of his labour. In the meantime I made no remark. Jupiter, at a signal from his master, began to gather up his tools. This done, and the dog having been unmuzzled, we turned in profound silence towards home.

We had taken, perhaps, a dozen steps in this direction, when, with a loud oath, Legrand strode up to Jupiter, and seized him by the collar. The astonished negro opened his eyes and mouth to the fullest extent, let fall the spades, and fell upon his knees.

"You scoundrel," said Legrand, hissing out the syllables from between his clenched teeth—"you infernal black villain!—speak, I tell you!—answer me this instant, without prevarication!—which—which is your left eye?"

"Oh, my golly, Massa Will! aint dis here my lef

eye for sartain ? " roared the terrified Jupiter, placing his hand upon his *right* organ of vision, and holding it there with a desperate pertinacity, as if in immediate dread of his master's attempt at a gouge.

" I thought so !—I knew it ! hurrah ! " vociferated Legrand, letting the negro go, and executing a series of curvets and caracols, much to the astonishment of his valet, who, arising from his knees, looked, mutely, from his master to myself, and then from myself to his master.

" Come ! we must go back," said the latter ; " the game's not up yet ; " and he again led the way to the tulip-tree.

" Jupiter," said he, when he reached its foot, " come here ! was the skull nailed to the limb with the face outwards, or with the face to the limb ? "

" De face was out, massa, so dat de crows could get at de eyes good, widout any trouble."

" Well, then, was it this eye or that through which you dropped the beetle ? "—here Legrand touched each of Jupiter's eyes.

" 'Twas dis eye, massa—de lef eye—jis as you tell me," and here it was his right eye that the negro indicated.

" That will do—we must try it again."

Here my friend, about whose madness I now saw, or fancied that I saw, certain indications of method, removed the peg which marked the spot where the beetle fell, to a spot about three inches to the westward of its former position. Taking, now, the tape-measure from the nearest point of the trunk to the peg, as before, and continuing the extension in a straight line to the distance of fifty feet, a spot was indicated, removed by several yards from the point at which we had been digging.

Around the new position a circle, somewhat larger than in the former instance, was now described, and we again set to work with the spades. I was dreadfully weary, but scarcely understanding what had occasioned the change in my thoughts, I felt no longer any great aversion from the labour imposed. I had become most unaccountably interested—nay, even excited. Perhaps there was something, amid all the extravagant demeanour of Legrand—some air of forethought, or of deliberation, which impressed me. I dug eagerly, and now and then caught myself actually looking, with something that very much resembled expectation, for the fancied treasure, the vision of which had demented my unfortunate companion. At a period when such vagaries of thought most fully possessed me, and when we had been at work perhaps an hour and a half, we were again interrupted by the violent howlings of the dog. His uneasiness, in the first instance, had been, evidently, but the result of playfulness or caprice, but he now assumed a bitter and serious tone. Upon Jupiter's again attempting to muzzle him, he made furious resistance, and, leaping into the hole, tore up the mould frantically with his claws. In a few seconds he had uncovered a mass of human bones, forming two complete skeletons, intermingled with several buttons of metal, and what appeared to be the dust of decayed woollen. One or two strokes of a spade upturned the blade of a large Spanish knife, and, as we dug farther, three or four loose pieces of gold and silver coin came to light.

At the sight of these the joy of Jupiter could scarcely be restrained, but the countenance of his master wore an air of extreme disappointment. He urged us, however, to continue our exertions, and the words were hardly uttered when I stumbled and fell forward, having caught the toe of my boot in a large ring of iron that lay half-buried in the loose earth.

We now worked in earnest, and never did I pass ten minutes of more intense excitement. During this interval we had fairly unearthed an oblong chest of wood, which, from its perfect preservation and wonderful hardness, had plainly been subjected to some mineralising process perhaps that of the bichloride of mercury. This box was three feet and a half long, three feet broad, and two and a half feet deep. It was firmly secured by bands of wrought iron, riveted, and forming a kind of open trellis-work over the whole. On each side of the chest, near the top, were three rings of iron—six in all—by means of which a firm hold could be obtained by six persons. Our utmost united endeavours served only to disturb the coffer very slightly in its bed. We at once saw the impossibility of removing so great a weight. Luckily, the sole fastenings of the lid consisted of two sliding bolts. These we drew back—trembling and panting with anxiety. In an instant, a treasure of incalculable value lay gleaming before us. As the rays of the lanterns fell within the pit, there flashed upwards a glow and a glare, from a confused heap of gold and of jewels, that absolutely dazzled our eyes.

I shall not pretend to describe the feelings with which I gazed. Amazement was, of course, predominant. Legrand appeared exhausted with excitement, and spoke very few words. Jupiter's countenance wore, for some minutes, as deadly a pallor as it is possible, in the nature of things, for any negro's visage to assume. He seemed stupefied—thunderstricken. Presently he fell upon his knees in the pit, and, burying his naked arms up to the elbows in gold, let them there remain, as if enjoying the luxury of a bath. At length, with a deep sigh, he exclaimed, as if in a soliloquy,

" And dis all cum ob de goole-bug ! de putty goole-bug ! de poor little goole-bug, what I boosed in dat sabage kind ob style ! Aint you shamed ob yourself, nigger ?—answer me dat ! "

It became necessary, at last, that I should arouse both master and valet to the expediency of removing the treasure. It was growing late, and it behoved us to make exertion, that we might get everything housed before daylight. It was difficult to say what should be done, and much time was spent in deliberation—so confused were the ideas of all. We, finally, lightened the box by removing two-thirds of its contents, when we were enabled, with some trouble, to raise it from the hole. The articles taken out were deposited among the brambles, and the dog left to guard them, with strict orders from Jupiter neither, upon any pretence, to stir from the spot, nor to open his mouth until our return. We then hurriedly made for home with the chest ; reaching the hut in safety, but after excessive toil, at one o'clock in the morning.

Worn out as we were, it was not in human nature to do more immediately. We rested until two, and had supper ; starting for the hills immediately afterwards, armed with three stout sacks, which, by good luck, were upon the premises. A little before four we arrived at the pit, divided the remainder of the booty, as equally as might be, among us, and, leaving the holes unfilled, again set out for the hut, at which, for the second time, we deposited our golden burthens, just as the first faint streaks of the dawn gleamed from over the tree-tops in the East.

We were now thoroughly broken down ; but the intense excitement of the time denied us repose. After an unquiet slumber of some three or four hours' duration, we arose, as if by preconcert, to make examination of our treasure.

The chest had been full to the brim, and we spent the whole day, and the greater part of the next night, in a scrutiny of its contents. There had been nothing like order or arrangement. Everything had been heaped in promiscuously. Having assorted all with care, we found ourselves possessed of even vaster wealth than we had at first supposed. In coin there was rather more than four hundred and fifty thousand dollars—estimating the value of the pieces, as accurately as we could, by the tables of the period. There was not a particle of silver. All was gold of antique date and of great variety—French, Spanish, and German money, with a few English guineas, and some counters, of which we had never seen specimens before. There were several very large and heavy coins, so worn that we could make nothing of their inscriptions. There was no American money. The value of the jewels we found more difficulty in estimating. There were diamonds—some of them exceedingly large and fine—a hundred and ten in all, and not one of them small ; eighteen rubies of remarkable brilliancy ; three hundred and ten emeralds, all very beautiful ; and twenty-one sapphires, with an opal. These stones had all been broken from their settings and thrown loose in the chest. The settings themselves, which we picked out from among the other gold, appeared to have been beaten up with hammers, as if to prevent identification. Besides all this, there was a vast quantity of solid gold ornaments ;—nearly two hundred massive finger and ear rings ; rich chains —thirty of these, if I remember ; eighty-three very large and heavy crucifixes ; five gold censers of great value ; a prodigious golden punch-bowl, ornamented with richly chased vine-leaves and Bacchanalian figures ; with two sword-handles exquisitely embossed, and many other smaller articles which I cannot recollect. The weight of these valuables exceeded three hundred and fifty pounds avoirdupois ; and in this estimate I have not included one hundred and ninety-seven superb gold watches ; three of the number being worth each five hundred dollars, if one. Many of them were very old, and as time-keepers valueless ; the works having suffered, more or less, from corrosion—but all were richly jewelled and in cases of great worth. We estimated the entire contents of the chest, that night, at a million and a half of dollars ; and, upon the subsequent disposal of the trinkets and jewels (a few being retained for our own use), it was found that we had greatly undervalued the treasure.

When, at length, we had concluded our examination, and the intense excitement of the time had in some measure subsided, Legrand, who saw that I was dying with impatience for a solution of this most extraordinary riddle, entered into a full detail of all the circumstances connected with it.

"You remember," said he, "the night when I handed you the rough sketch I had made of the *scarabæus*. You recollect also, that I became quite vexed at you for insisting that my drawing resembled a death's-head. When you first made this assertion I thought you were jesting ; but afterwards I called to mind the peculiar spots on the back of the insect, and admitted to myself that your remark had some little foundation in fact. Still, the sneer at my graphic powers irritated me—for I am considered a good artist—and, therefore, when you handed me the scrap of parchment, I was about to crumple it up and throw it angrily into the fire."

"The scrap of paper, you mean," said I.

"No ; it had much of the appearance of paper, and at first I supposed it to be such, but when I came to draw upon it, I discovered it, at once, to be a piece of very thin parchment. It was quite dirty, you remember. Well, as I was in the very act of crumpling it up, my glance fell upon the sketch at which you had been looking, and you may imagine my astonishment when I perceived, in fact, the figure of a death's-head just where, it seemed to me, I had made the drawing of the beetle. For a moment I was too much amazed to think with accuracy. I knew that my design was very different in detail from this—although there was a certain similarity in general outline. Presently I took a candle, and seating myself at the other end of the room, proceeded to scrutinise the parchment more closely. Upon turning it over, I saw my own sketch upon the reverse, just as I had made it. My first idea, now, was mere surprise at the really remarkable similarity of outline—at the singular coincidence involved in the fact, that unknown to me, there should have been a skull upon the other side of the parchment, immediately beneath my figure of the *scarabæus*, and that this skull, not only in outline, but in size, should so closely resemble my drawing. I say the singularity of this coincidence absolutely stupefied me for a time. This is the usual effect of such coincidences. The mind struggles to establish a connection—a sequence of cause and effect—and, being unable to do so, suffers a species of temporary paralysis. But when I recovered from this stupor, there dawned upon me gradually a conviction which startled me even far more than the coincidence. I began distinctly, positively, to remember that there had been *no* drawing upon the parchment when I made my sketch of the *scarabæus*. I became perfectly certain of this; for I recollected turning up first one side and then the other, in search of the cleanest spot. Had the skull been then there, of course I could not have failed to notice it. Here was indeed a mystery which I felt it impossible to explain; but, even at that early moment, there seemed to glimmer, faintly, within the most remote and secret chambers of my intellect, a glowworm-like conception of that truth which last night's adventure brought to so magnificent a demonstration. I arose at once, and putting the parchment securely away, dismissed all further reflection until I should be alone.

"When you had gone, and when Jupiter was fast asleep, I betook myself to a more methodical investigation of the affair. In the first place I considered the manner in which the parchment had come into my possession. The spot where we discovered the *scarabæus* was on the coast of the mainland, about a mile eastward of the island, and but a short distance above high-water mark. Upon my taking hold of it, it gave me a sharp bite, which caused me to let it drop. Jupiter, with his accustomed caution, before seizing the insect, which had flown towards him, looked about him for a leaf, or something of that nature, by which to take hold of it. It was at this moment that his eyes, and mine also, fell upon the scrap of parchment, which I then supposed to be paper. It was lying half buried in the sand, a corner sticking up. Near the spot where we found it, I observed the remnants of the hull of what appeared to have been a ship's long-boat. The wreck seemed to have been there for a very great while ; for the resemblance to boat timbers could scarcely be traced.

"Well, Jupiter picked up the parchment, wrapped the beetle in it, and gave it to me. Soon afterwards we turned to go home, and on the way met Lieutenant G——. I showed him the insect, and he begged me to let him take it to the fort. Upon my consenting, he thrust it forthwith into his waistcoat pocket, without the parchment in which it had been wrapped, and which I had continued to hold in my hand during his inspection. Perhaps he dreaded my changing my mind, and thought it best to make sure of the prize at once—you know how enthusiastic he is in all subjects connected with Natural History. At the same time, without being conscious of it, I must have deposited the parchment in my own pocket.

" You remember that when I went to the table, for the purpose of making a sketch of the beetle, I found no paper where it was usually kept. I looked in the drawer, and found none there. I searched my pockets, hoping to find an old letter, when my hand fell upon the parchment. I thus detail the precise mode in which it came into my possession ; for the circumstances impressed me with peculiar force.

" No doubt you will think me fanciful—but I had already established a kind of *connection*. I had put together two links of a great chain. There was a boat lying upon a sea-coast, and not far from the boat was a parchment—*not a paper*—with a skull depicted upon it. You will, of course, ask " Where is the connection ? " I reply that the skull, or death's-head, is the well-known emblem of the pirate. The flag of the death's-head is hoisted in all engagements.

" I have said that the scrap was parchment, and not paper. Parchment is durable—almost imperishable. Matters of little moment are rarely consigned to parchment ; since, for the mere ordinary purposes of drawing or writing, it is not nearly so well adapted as paper. This reflection suggested some meaning—

some relevancy—in the death's-head. I did not fail
to observe, also, the *form* of the parchment. Although
one of its corners had been, by some accident,
destroyed, it could be seen that the original form
was oblong. It was just such a slip, indeed, as might
have been chosen for a memorandum—for a record
of something to be long remembered and carefully
preserved."

" But," I interposed, " you say that the skull was
not upon the parchment when you made the drawing
of the beetle. How then do you trace any connection
between the boat and the skull—since this latter,
according to your own admission, must have been
designed (God only knows how or by whom) at some
period subsequent to your sketching the *scarabæus ?* "

" Ah, hereupon turns the whole mystery ; although
the secret, at this point, I had comparatively little
difficulty in solving. My steps were sure, and could
afford but a single result. I reasoned, for example,
thus : When I drew the *scarabæus*, there was no skull
apparent upon the parchment. When I had completed the drawing I gave it to you, and observed you
narrowly until you returned it. *You*, therefore, did
not design the skull, and no one else was present to
do it. Then it was not done by human agency. And
nevertheless it was done.

" At this stage of my reflections I endeavoured to
remember, and *did* remember, with entire distinctness, every incident which occurred about the period
in question. The weather was chilly (oh rare and
happy accident !), and a fire was blazing upon the
hearth. I was heated with exercise and sat near the

table. You, however, had drawn a chair close to the chimney. Just as I placed the parchment in your hand, and as you were in the act of inspecting it, Wolf, the Newfoundland, entered, and leaped upon your shoulders. With your left hand you caressed him and kept him off, while your right, holding the parchment, was permitted to fall listlessly between your knees, and in close proximity to the fire. At one moment I thought the blaze had caught it, and was about to caution you, but, before I could speak, you had withdrawn it, and were engaged in its examination. When I considered all these particulars, I doubted not for a moment that *heat* had been the agent in bringing to light, upon the parchment, the skull which I saw designed upon it. You are well aware that chemical preparations exist, and have existed time out of mind, by means of which it is possible to write upon either paper or vellum, so that the characters shall become visible only when subjected to the action of fire. Zaffre, digested in *aqua regia*, and diluted with four times its weight of water, is sometimes employed; a green tint results. The regulus of cobalt, dissolved in spirit of nitre, gives a red. These colours disappear at longer or shorter intervals after the material written upon cools, but again become apparent upon the re-application of heat.

" I now scrutinised the death's-head with care. Its outer edges—the edges of the drawing nearest the edge of the vellum—were far more *distinct* than the others. It was clear that the action of the caloric had been imperfect or unequal. I immediately kindled a fire, and subjected every portion of the parchment to a glowing heat. At first, the only effect was the strengthening of the faint lines in the skull; but, upon persevering in the experiment, there became visible, at the corner of the slip, diagonally opposite to the spot in which the death's-head was delineated, the figure of what I at first supposed to be a goat. A closer scrutiny, however, satisfied me that it was intended for a kid."

" Ha ! ha ! " said I, " to be sure I have no right to laugh at you—a million and a half of money is too serious a matter for mirth—but you are not about to establish a third link in your chain—you will not find any especial connection between your pirates and a goat—pirates, you know, have nothing to do with goats ; they appertain to the farming interest."

" But I have said that the figure was *not* that of a goat."

" Well, a kid then—pretty much the same thing."

" Pretty much, but not altogether," said Legrand. " You may have heard of one *Captain* Kidd. I at once looked upon the figure of the animal as a kind of punning or hieroglyphical signature. I say signature ; because its position upon the vellum suggested this idea. The death's-head at the corner diagonally opposite had, in the same manner, the air of a stamp, or seal. But I was sorely put out by the absence of all else—of the body to my imagined instrument—of the text for my context."

" I presume you expected to find a letter between the stamp and the signature."

" Something of that kind. The fact is, I felt irresistibly impressed with a presentiment of some vast good fortune impending. I can scarcely say why. Perhaps, after all, it was rather a desire than an actual belief ; but do you know that Jupiter's silly words, about the bug being of solid gold, had a remarkable effect upon my fancy ? And then the series of accidents and coincidences—these were so *very* extraordinary. Do you observe how mere an accident it was that these events should have occurred upon the *sole* day of all the year in which it has been, or may be, sufficiently cool for fire, and that without the fire, or without the intervention of the dog at the precise moment in which he appeared, I should never have become aware of the death's-head, and so never the possessor of the treasure ? "

" But proceed—I am all impatience."

" Well ; you have heard, of course, the many stories current—the thousand vague rumours afloat about money buried, somewhere upon the Atlantic coast, by Kidd and his associates. These rumours must have had some foundation in fact. And that the rumours have existed so long and so continuous, could have resulted, it appeared to me, only from the circumstance of the buried treasure still *remaining* entombed. Had Kidd concealed his plunder for a time, and afterwards reclaimed it, the rumours would scarcely have reached us in their present unvarying form. You will observe that the stories told are all about money-seekers, not about money-finders. Had the pirate recovered his money, there the affair would have dropped. It seemed to me that some accident —say the loss of a memorandum indicating its locality

—had deprived him of the means of recovering it, and that this accident had become known to his followers, who otherwise might never have heard that treasure had been concealed at all, and who, busying themselves in vain, because unguided attempts, to regain it, had given first birth, and then universal currency, to the reports which are now so common. Have you ever heard of any important treasure being unearthed along the coast ? "

" Never."

" But that Kidd's accumulations were immense is well known. I took it for granted, therefore, that the earth still held them ; and you will scarcely be surprised when I tell you that I felt a hope, nearly amounting to certainty, that the parchment so strangely found, involved a lost record of the place of deposit."

" But how did you proceed ? "

" I held the vellum again to the fire, after increasing the heat ; but nothing appeared. I now thought it possible that the coating of dirt might have something to do with the failure ; so I carefully rinsed the parchment by pouring warm water over it, and, having done this, I placed it in a tin pan, with the skull downwards, and put the pan upon a furnace of lighted charcoal. In a few minutes, the pan having become thoroughly heated, I removed the slip, and, to my inexpressible joy, found it spotted, in several places, with what appeared to be figures arranged in lines. Again I placed it in the pan, and suffered it to remain another minute. Upon taking it off, the whole was just as you see it now."

Here, Legrand, having re-heated the parchment, submitted it to my inspection. The following characters were rudely traced, in a red tint, between the death's-head and the goat :

53‡‡†305))6*;4826)4‡.)4‡);806*;48†8¶60))85;1‡(;:‡*
8†83(88)5*†;46(;88*96*?;8)*‡(;485);5*†2:*‡(;4956*2(5
—4)8¶8;4069285);)6†8)4‡‡;1(‡9;48081;8:8‡1;48†85;
4)485†528806*81(‡9;48;(88;4(‡?34;48)4‡;161;:188;‡?;

" But," said I, returning him the slip, " I am as much in the dark as ever. Were all the jewels of Golconda awaiting me upon my solution of this enigma, I am quite sure that I should be unable to earn them."

" And yet," said Legrand, " the solution is by no means so difficult as you might be led to imagine from the first hasty inspection of the characters. These characters, as any one might readily guess, form a cipher—that is to say, they convey a meaning : but then, from what is known of Kidd, I could not suppose him capable of constructing any of the more abstruse cryptographs. I made up my mind, at once, that this was of a simple species—such, however, as would appear, to the crude intellect of the sailor, absolutely insoluble without the key."

" And you really solved it ? "

" Readily ; I have solved others of an abstruseness ten thousand times greater. Circumstances, a certain bias of mind, have led me to take interest in such riddles, and it may well be doubted whether human ingenuity can construct an enigma of the kind which human ingenuity may not, by proper application, resolve. In fact, having once established connected and legible characters, I scarcely gave a thought to the mere difficulty of developing their import.

" In the present case—indeed in all cases of secret writing—the first question regards the *language* of the cipher ; for the principles of solution, so far, especially, as the more simple ciphers are concerned, depend upon, and are varied by, the genius of the particular idiom. In general, there is no alternative but experiment (directed by probabilities) of every tongue known to him who attempts the solution, until the true one be attained. But, with the cipher now before us, all difficulty was removed by the signature. The pun upon the word ' Kidd ' is appreciable in no other language than the English. But for this consideration I should have begun my attempts with the Spanish and French, as the tongues in which a secret of this kind would most naturally have been written by a pirate of the Spanish main. As it was, I assumed the cryptograph to be English.

" You observe there are no divisions between the words. Had there been divisions, the task would have been comparatively easy. In such case I should have commenced with a collation and analysis of the shorter words, and had a word of a single letter occurred, as is most likely (*a* or *I*, for example), I should have considered the solution as assured. But, there being no division, my first step was to ascertain the predominant letters, as well as the least frequent. Counting all, I constructed a table thus :

Of the character 8 there are 33

;	,,	26
4	,,	19
‡)	,,	16
*	,,	13
5	,,	12
6	,,	11
†1	,,	8
0	,,	6
92	,,	5
:3	,,	4
?	,,	3
¶	,,	2
—.	,,	1

" Now, in English, the letter which most frequently occurs is *e*. Afterwards, the succession runs thus : *a o i d h n r s t u y c f g l m w b k p q x z*. E predominates so remarkably that an individual sentence of any length is rarely seen, in which it is not the prevailing character.

" Here, then, we have, in the very beginning, the groundwork for something more than a mere guess. The general use which may be made of the table is obvious—but in this particular cipher we shall only very partially require its aid. As our predominant character is 8, we will commence by assuming it as the *e* of the natural alphabet. To verify the supposition, let us observe if the 8 be seen often in couples —for *e* is doubled with great frequency in English— in such words, for example, as ' meet,' ' fleet,' ' speed,' ' seen,' ' been,' ' agree,' etc. In the present instance we see it doubled no less than five times, although the cryptograph is brief.

" Let us assume 8 then, as *e*. Now, of all *words* in the language, ' the ' is most usual ; let us see, therefore, whether there are not repetitions of any three characters, in the same order of collocation, the last of them being 8. If we discover repetitions of such letters, so arranged, they will most probably represent the word ' the.' Upon inspection, we find no less than seven such arrangements, the characters being ;48. We may, therefore, assume that ; represents *t*, 4 represents *h*, and 8 represents *e*—the last being now well confirmed. Thus a great step has been taken.

" But, having established a single word, we are enabled to establish a vastly important point ; that is to say, several commencements and terminations of other words. Let us refer, for example, to the last instance but one, in which the combination ;48 occurs —not far from the end of the cipher. We know that the ; immediately ensuing is the commencement of a word, and, of the six characters succeeding this ' the,' we are cognisant of no less than five. Let us set these characters down, thus, by the letters we know them to represent, leaving a space for the unknown—

t eeth.

" Here we are enabled, at once, to discard the ' *th*,' as forming no portion of the word commencing with the first *t* ; since, by experiment of the entire alphabet for a letter adapted to the vacancy, we perceive that no word can be formed of which this *th* can be a part. We are thus narrowed into

t ee,

and, going through the alphabet, if necessary, as
before, we arrive at the word ' tree,' as the sole
possible reading. We thus gain another letter, *r*,
represented by (, with the words ' the tree ' in juxtaposition.

" Looking beyond these words, for a short distance,
we again see the combination ;48, and employ it by
way of *termination* to what immediately precedes. We
have thus this arrangement :

the tree ;4(‡?34 the,

or, substituting the natural letters, where known, it
reads thus :

the tree thr‡?3h the.

" Now, if, in place of the unknown characters, we
leave blank spaces, or substitute dots, we read thus :

the tree thr....h the,

when the word ' *through* ' makes itself evident at once.
But this discovery gives us three new letters, *o*, *u* and *g*,
represented by ‡ ? and 3.

" Looking now, narrowly, through the cipher for
combinations of known characters, we find, not very
far from the beginning, this arrangement,

83(88, or egree,

which, plainly, is the conclusion of the word ' degree,'
and gives us another letter, *d*, represented by †.

" Four letters beyond the word ' degree,' we perceive the combination

;48(;88.

" Translating the known characters, and represent-
ing the unknown by dots, as before, we read thus :

th rtee,

an arrangement immediately suggestive of the word

' thirteen,' and again furnishing us with two new characters *i* and *n*, represented by 6 and *.

" Referring, now, to the beginning of the cryptograph, we find the combination

53‡‡†.

" Translating, as before, we obtain

. good,

which assures us that the first letter is *A*, and that the first two words are ' A good.'

" It is now time that we arrange our key, as far as discovered, in a tabular form, to avoid confusion. It will stand thus :

5	represents	a
†	,,	d
8	,,	e
3	,,	g
4	,,	h
6	,,	i
*	,,	n
‡	,,	o
(	,,	r
;	,,	t

" We have, therefore, no less than ten of the most important letters represented, and it will be unnecessary to proceed with the details of the solution. I have said enough to convince you that ciphers of this nature are readily soluble, and to give you some insight into the *rationale* of their development. But be assured that the specimen before us appertains to the very simplest species of cryptograph. It now only remains to give you the full translation of the characters upon the parchment, as unriddled. Here it is :

" '*A good glass in the bishop's hostel in the devil's seat forty-one degrees and thirteen minutes northeast and by north main branch seventh limb east side shoot from the left eye of the death's-head a bee line from the tree through the shot fifty feet out.*' "

" But," said I, " the enigma seems still in as bad a condition as ever. How is it possible to extort a meaning from all this jargon about ' devil's seats,' ' death's-heads,' and ' bishop's hotels ? ' "

" I confess," replied Legrand, " that the matter still wears a serious aspect, when regarded with a casual glance. My first endeavour was to divide the sentence into the natural division intended by the cryptographist."

" You mean to punctuate it ? "

" Something of that kind."

" But how was it possible to effect this ? "

" I reflected that it had been a *point* with the writer to run his words together without division, so as to increase the difficulty of solution. Now, a not over-acute man, in pursuing such an object, would be nearly certain to overdo the matter. When, in the course of his composition, he arrived at a break in his subject which would naturally require a pause, or a point, he would be exceedingly apt to run his characters, at this place, more than usually close together. If you will observe the MS. in the present instance you will easily detect five such cases of unusual crowding. Acting upon this hint, I made the division thus :

" '*A good glass in the bishop's hostel in the devil's seat —forty-one degrees and thirteen minutes—northeast and by north—main branch seventh limb east side—shoot from the left eye of the death's-head—a bee line from the tree through the shot fifty feet out.'* "

" Even this division," said I, " leaves me still in the dark."

" It left me also in the dark," replied Legrand, " for a few days ; during which I made diligent inquiry, in the neighbourhood of Sullivan's Island, for any building which went by the name of the ' Bishop's Hotel ' ; for, of course, I dropped the obsolete word ' hostel.' Gaining no information on the subject, I was on the point of extending my sphere of search, and proceeding in a more systematic manner, when, one morning, it entered into my head, quite suddenly, that this ' Bishop's Hostel ' might have some reference to an old family, of the name of Bessop, which, time out of mind, had held possession of an ancient manor-house, about four miles to the northward of the Island. I accordingly went over to the plantation, and re-instituted my inquiries among the older negroes of the place. At length one of the most aged of the women said that she had heard of such a place as *Bessop's Castle*, and thought that she could guide me to it, but that it was not a castle, nor a tavern, but a high rock.

" I offered to pay her well for her trouble, and, after some demur, she consented to accompany me to the spot. We found it without much difficulty, when, dismissing her, I proceeded to examine the place. The ' castle ' consisted of an irregular assemblage of cliffs and rocks—one of the latter being quite remarkable for its height as well as for its insulated and artificial appearance. I clambered to its apex, and then felt much at a loss as to what should be next done.

"While I was busied in reflection, my eyes fell upon a narrow ledge in the eastern face of the rock, perhaps a yard below the summit upon which I stood. This ledge projected about eighteen inches, and was not more than a foot wide, while a niche in the cliff just above it gave it a rude resemblance to one of the hollow-backed chairs used by our ancestors. I made no doubt that here was the 'devil's seat' alluded to in the MS., and now I seemed to grasp the full secret of the riddle.

"The 'good glass,' I knew, could have reference to nothing but a telescope; for the word 'glass' is rarely employed in any other sense by seamen. Now here, I at once saw, was a telescope to be used, and a definite point of view, *admitting no variation*, from which to use it. Nor did I hesitate to believe that the phrases, 'forty-one degrees and thirteen minutes,' and 'northeast and by north,' were intended as directions for the levelling of the glass. Greatly excited by these discoveries, I hurried home, procured a telescope, and returned to the rock.

"I let myself down to the ledge, and found that it was impossible to retain a seat upon it except in one particular position. This fact confirmed my preconceived idea. I proceeded to use the glass. Of course, the 'forty-one degrees and thirteen minutes' could allude to nothing but elevation above the visible horizon, since the horizontal direction was clearly indicated by the words, 'northeast and by north.' This latter direction I at once established by means of a pocket-compass; then, pointing the glass as nearly at an angle of forty-one degrees of elevation as I could do it by guess, I moved it cautiously up or down, until my attention was arrested by a circular rift or opening in the foliage of a large tree that over-topped its fellows in the distance. In the centre of this rift I perceived a white spot, but could not, at first, distinguish what it was. Adjusting the focus of the telescope, I again looked, and now made it out to be a human skull.

"Upon this discovery I was so sanguine as to con-sider the enigma solved; for the phrase 'main branch, seventh limb, east side,' could refer only to the posi-tion of the skull upon the tree, while 'shoot from the left eye of the death's head,' admitted also of but one interpretation, in regard to a search for buried treasure. I perceived that the design was to drop a bullet from the left eye of the skull, and that a bee-line, or, in other words, a straight line, drawn from the nearest point of the trunk through "the shot' (or the spot where the bullet fell), and thence extended to a dis-tance of fifty feet, would indicate a definite point—and beneath this point I thought it at least *possible* that a deposit of value lay concealed."

"All this," I said, "is exceedingly clear, and, although ingenious, still simple and explicit. When you left the Bishop's Hotel, what then?"

"Why, having carefully taken the bearings of the tree, I turned homewards. The instant that I left the 'devil's seat,' however, the circular rift vanished; nor could I get a glimpse of it afterwards, turn as I would. What seems to me the chief ingenuity in this whole business is the fact (for repeated experiment has convinced me it *is* a fact) that the circular opening in question is visible from no other attainable point of view than that afforded by the narrow ledge upon the face of the rock.

" In this expedition to the ' Bishop's Hotel ' I had been attended by Jupiter, who had no doubt observed for some weeks past the abstraction of my demeanour, and took especial care not to leave me alone. But on the next day, getting up very early, I contrived to give him the slip, and went into the hills in search of the tree. After much toil I found it. When I came home at night my valet proposed to give me a flogging. With the rest of the adventure I believe you are as well acquainted as myself."

" I suppose," said I, " you missed the spot, in the first attempt at digging, through Jupiter's stupidity in letting the bug fall through the right instead of through the left eye of the skull."

" Precisely. This mistake made a difference of about two inches and a half in the ' shot '—that is to say, in the position of the peg nearest the tree ; and had the treasure been *beneath* the ' shot,' the error would have been of little moment ; but the ' shot,' together with the nearest point of the tree, were merely two points for the establishment of a line of direction ; of course the error, however trivial in the beginning, increased as we proceeded with the line, and, by the time we had gone fifty feet, threw us quite off the scent. But for my deep-seated impressions that treasure was here somewhere actually buried, we might have had all our labour in vain."

" But your grandiloquence, and your conduct in swinging the beetle—how excessively odd ! I was sure you were mad. And why did you insist upon letting fall the bug, instead of a bullet, from the skull ? "

" Why, to be frank, I felt somewhat annoyed by your evident suspicions touching my sanity, and so resolved to punish you quietly, in my own way, by a little bit of sober mystification. For this reason I swung the beetle, and for this reason I let it fall from the tree. An observation of yours about its great weight suggested the latter idea."

" Yes, I perceive ; and now there is only one point which puzzles me. What are we to make of the skeletons found in the hole ? "

" That is a question I am no more able to answer than yourself. There seems, however, only one plausible way of accounting for them—and yet it is dreadful to believe in such atrocity as my suggestion would imply. It is clear that Kidd—if Kidd indeed secreted this treasure, which I doubt not—it is clear that he must have had assistance in the labour. But this labour concluded, he may have thought it expedient to remove all participants in his secret. Perhaps a couple of blows with a mattock were sufficient, while his coadjutors were busy in the pit : perhaps it required a dozen—who shall tell ? "

II

MS. FOUND IN A BOTTLE

Qui n'a plus qu'un moment à vivre
N'a plus rien à dissimuler.   *Quinault—Atys*

OF my country and of my family I have little to say.
Ill-usage and length of years have driven me from the
one, and estranged me from the other. Hereditary
wealth afforded me an education of no common order
and a contemplative turn of mind enabled me to
methodise the stores which early study very diligently
garnered up. Beyond all things, the works of the
German moralists gave me great delight ; not from
any ill-advised admiration of their eloquent madness,
but from the ease with which my habits of rigid
thought enabled me to detect their falsities. I have
often been reproached with the aridity of my genius ;
a deficiency of imagination has been imputed to me
as a crime ; and the Pyrrhonism of my opinions has
at all times rendered me notorious. Indeed, a strong
relish for physical philosophy has, I fear, tinctured
my mind with a very common error of this age—I
mean the habit of referring occurrences, even the least
susceptible of such reference, to the principles of that
science. Upon the whole, no person could be less
liable than myself to be led away from the severe
precincts of truth by the *ignes fatui* of superstition.
I have thought proper to premise thus much, lest the
incredible tale I have to tell should be considered

rather the raving of a crude imagination than the positive experience of a mind to which the reveries of fancy have been a dead letter and a nullity.

After many years spent in foreign travel, I sailed in the year 18—, from the port of Batavia, in the rich and populous island of Java, on a voyage to the Archipelago of the Sunda Islands. I went as passenger —having no other inducement than a kind of nervous restlessness which haunted me as a fiend.

Our vessel was a beautiful ship of about four hundred tons, copper-fastened, and built at Bombay of Malabar teak. She was freighted with cotton-wool and oil, from the Lachadive Islands. We had also on board coir, jaggeree, ghee, cocoa-nuts, and a few cases of opium. The stowage was clumsily done, and the vessel consequently crank.

We got under way with a mere breath of wind, and for many days stood along the eastern coast of Java, without any other incident to beguile the monotony of our course than the occasional meeting with some of the small grabs of the Archipelago to which we were bound.

One evening, leaning over the taffrail, I observed a very singular isolated cloud to the N.W. It was remarkable, as well for its colour as from its being the first we had seen since our departure from Batavia. I watched it attentively until sunset, when it spread all at once to the eastward and westward, girting in the horizon with a narrow strip of vapour, and looking like a long line of low beach. My notice was soon afterwards attracted by the dusky-red appearance of the moon, and the peculiar character of the sea. The latter was undergoing a rapid change, and the water seemed more than usually transparent. Although I could distinctly see the bottom, yet heaving the lead, I found the ship in fifteen fathoms. The air now became intolerably hot, and was loaded with spiral exhalations similar to those arising from heated iron. As night came on, every breath of wind died away, and a more entire calm it is impossible to conceive. The flame of a candle burned upon the poop without the least perceptible motion, and a long hair, held between the finger and thumb, hung without the possibility of detecting a vibration. However, as the captain said he could perceive no indication of danger, and as we were drifting in bodily to shore, he ordered the sails to be furled, and the anchor let go. No watch was set, and the crew, consisting principally of Malays, stretched themselves deliberately upon deck. I went below—not without a full presentiment of evil. Indeed, every appearance warranted me in apprehending a simoom. I told the captain my fears; but he paid no attention to what I said, and left me without deigning to give a reply. My uneasiness, however, prevented me from sleeping, and about midnight I went upon deck. As I placed my foot upon the upper step of the companion-ladder, I was startled by a loud, humming noise like that occasioned by the rapid revolution of a mill-wheel, and before I could ascertain its meaning, I found the ship quivering to its centre. In the next instant, a wilderness of foam hurled up upon our beam-ends, and, rushing over us fore and aft, swept the entire decks from stem to stern.

The extreme fury of the blast proved, in a great

measure, the salvation of the ship. Although completely water-logged, yet, as her masts had gone by the board, she rose, after a minute, heavily from the sea, and, staggering awhile beneath the immense pressure of the tempest, finally righted.

By what miracle I escaped destruction it is impossible to say. Stunned by the shock of the water, I found myself, upon recovery, jammed in between the stern-post and rudder. With great difficulty I gained my feet, and, looking dizzily around, was at first struck with the idea of our being among breakers ; so terrific, beyond the wildest imagination, was the whirlpool of mountainous and foaming ocean within which we were engulfed. After a while, I heard the voice of an old Swede, who had shipped with us at the moment of our leaving port. I hallooed to him with all my strength, and presently he came reeling aft. We soon discovered that we were the sole survivors of the accident. All on deck, with the exception of ourselves, had been swept overboard ; the captain and mates must have perished as they slept, for the cabins were deluged with water. Without assistance, we could expect to do little for the security of the ship, and our exertions were at first paralyzed by the momentary expectation of going down. Our cable had, of course, parted like pack-thread at the first breath of the hurricane, or we should have been instantaneously overwhelmed. We scudded with frightful velocity before the sea, and the water made clear breaches over us. The framework of our stern was shattered excessively, and in almost every respect we had received considerable injury ; but to our extreme joy we found the pumps unchoked, and that we had made no great shifting of our ballast. The main fury of the blast had already blown over, and we apprehended little danger from the violence of the wind ; but we looked forward to its total cessation with dismay ; well believing, that in our shattered condition, we should inevitably perish in the tremendous swell which would ensue. But this very just apprehension seemed by no means likely to be soon verified. For five entire days and nights—during which our only subsistence was a small quantity of jaggeree, procured with great difficulty from the forecastle—the hulk flew at a rate defying computation, before rapidly succeeding flaws of wind, which, without equalling the first violence of the simoom, were still more terrific than any tempest I had before encountered. Our course for the first four days was, with trifling variations, S.E. and by S. ; and we must have run down the coast of New Holland. On the fifth day the cold became extreme, although the wind had hauled round a point more to the northward. The sun arose with a sickly yellow lustre, and clambered a very few degrees above the horizon—emitting no decisive light. There were no clouds apparent, yet the wind was upon the increase, and blew with a fitful and unsteady fury. About noon, as nearly as we could guess, our attention was again arrested by the appearance of the sun. It gave out no light, properly so called, but a dull and sullen glow without reflection, as if all its rays were polarised. Just before sinking within the turgid sea, its central fires suddenly went out, as if hurriedly extinguished by some unaccountable power. It was a dim, silver-like rim, alone, as it rushed down the unfathomable ocean.

We waited in vain for the arrival of the sixth day—that day to me has not arrived—to the Swede never did arrive. Thenceforward we were enshrouded in pitchy darkness, so that we could not have seen an object at twenty paces from the ship. Eternal night continued to envelope us, all unrelieved by the phosphoric sea-brilliancy to which we had been accustomed in the tropics. We observed, too, that although the tempest continued to rage with unabated violence, there was no longer to be discovered the usual appearance of surf, or foam, which had hitherto attended us. All around were horror, and thick gloom, and a black sweltering desert of ebony. Superstitious terror crept by degrees into the spirit of the old Swede, and my own soul was wrapped up in silent wonder. We neglected all care of the ship as worse than useless, and securing ourselves, as well as possible, to the stump of the mizen-mast, looked out bitterly into the world of ocean. We had no means of calculating time, nor could we form any guess of our situation. We were, however, well aware of having made farther to the southward than any previous navigators, and felt great amazement at not meeting with the usual impediments of ice. In the meantime every moment threatened to be our last—every mountainous billow hurried to overwhelm us. The swell surpassed anything I had imagined possible, and that we were not instantly buried is a miracle. My companion spoke of the lightness of our cargo, and reminded me of the excellent qualities of our ship ; but I could not help feeling the utter hopelessness of hope itself, and prepared myself gloomily for that death which I thought nothing could defer beyond an hour, as, with every knot of way the ship made, the swelling of the black stupendous seas became more dismally appalling. At times we gasped for breath at an elevation beyond the albatross—at times became dizzy with the velocity of our descent into some watery hell, where the air grew stagnant, and no sound disturbed the slumbers of the kraken.

We were at the bottom of one of the abysses, when a quick scream from my companion broke fearfully upon the night. " See ! see ! " cried he, shrieking in my ears, " Almighty God ! see ! see ! " As he spoke, I became aware of a dull, sullen glare of red light which streamed down the sides of the vast chasm where we lay, and threw a fitful brilliancy upon our deck. Casting my eyes upwards, I beheld a spectacle which froze the current of my blood. At a terrific height directly above us, and upon the very verge of the precipitous descent, hovered a gigantic ship, of perhaps four thousand tons. Although upreared upon the summit of a wave more than a hundred times her own altitude, her apparent size still exceeded that of any ship of the line or East Indiaman in existence. Her huge hull was of a deep dingy black, unrelieved by any of the customary carvings of a ship. A single row of brass cannon protruded from her open ports, and dashed from their polished surfaces the fires of innumerable battle-lanterns, which swung to and fro about her rigging. But what mainly inspired us with horror and astonishment was, that she bore up under a press of sail in the very teeth of that supernatural sea, and of that ungovernable hurricane. When we first discovered her, her bows were alone to be seen, as she rose slowly from the dim and horrible gulf beyond her. For a moment of intense terror she paused upon the giddy pinnacle, as if in contemplation of her own sublimity, then trembled and tottered, and—came down.

At this instant, I know not what sudden self-possession came over my spirit. Staggering as far aft as I could, I awaited fearlessly the ruin that was to overwhelm. Our own vessel was at length ceasing from her struggles, and sinking with her head to the sea. The shock of the descending mass struck her, consequently, in that portion of her frame which was already under water, and the inevitable result was to hurl me, with irresistible violence, upon the rigging of the stranger.

As I fell, the ship hove in stays, and went about; and to the confusion ensuing I attributed my escape from the notice of the crew. With little difficulty I made my way unperceived, to the main hatchway, which was partially open, and soon found an opportunity of secreting myself in the hold. Why I did so I can hardly tell. An indefinite sense of awe, which at first sight of the navigators of the ship had taken hold of my mind, was perhaps the principle of my concealment. I was unwilling to trust myself with a race of people who had offered, to the cursory glance I had taken, so many points of vague novelty, doubt, and apprehension. I therefore thought proper to contrive a hiding-place in the hold. This I did by removing a small portion of the shifting-boards, in such a manner as to afford me a convenient retreat between the huge timbers of the ship.

I had scarcely completed my work, when a footstep in the hold forced me to make use of it. A man passed by my place of concealment with a feeble and unsteady gait. I could not see his face, but had an opportunity of observing his general appearance. There was about it an evidence of great age and infirmity. His knees tottered beneath a load of years, and his entire frame quivered under the burden. He muttered to himself in a low broken tone, some words of a language which I could not understand, and groped in a corner among a pile of singular-looking instruments, and decayed charts of navigation. His manner was a wild mixture of the peevishness of second childhood and the solemn dignity of a God. He at length went on deck, and I saw him no more.

*　　　*　　　*　　　*　　　*

A feeling, for which I have no name, has taken possession of my soul—a sensation which will admit of no analysis, to which the lessons of bygone time are inadequate, and for which I fear futurity itself will offer me no key. To a mind constituted like my own, the latter consideration is an evil. I shall never —I know that I shall never—be satisfied with regard to the nature of my conceptions. Yet it is not wonderful that these conceptions are indefinite, since they have their origin in sources so utterly novel. A new sense—a new entity is added to my soul.

*　　　*　　　*　　　*　　　*

It is long since I first trod the deck of this terrible ship, and the rays of my destiny are, I think, gathering to a focus. Incomprehensible men! Wrapped up in meditations of a kind which I cannot divine, they pass me by unnoticed. Concealment is utter folly on my part, for the people *will not* see. It was but just now that I passed directly before the eyes of the mate; it was no long while ago that I ventured into the Captain's own private cabin and took thence the materials with which I write, and have written. I shall from time to time continue this journal. It is true that I may not find an opportunity of transmitting it to the world, but I will not fail to make the endeavour. At the last moment I will enclose the MS. in a bottle and cast it within the sea.

*   *   *   *   *

An incident has occurred which has given me new room for meditation. Are such things the operation of ungoverned chance? I had ventured upon deck and thrown myself down, without attracting any notice, among a pile of ratline-stuff and old sails, in the bottom of the yawl. While musing upon the singularity of my fate, I unwittingly daubed with a tar-brush the edges of a neatly-folded studding-sail which lay near me on a barrel. The studding-sail is now bent upon the ship, and the thoughtless touches of the brush are spread out into the word DISCOVERY.

I have made many observations lately upon the structure of the vessel. Although well armed, she is not, I think, a ship of war. Her rigging, build, and general equipment all negative a supposition of this kind. What she *is not*, I can easily perceive; what she *is*, I fear it is impossible to say. I know not how it is, but in scrutinising her strange model and singular cast of spars, her huge size and overgrown suits of canvas, her severely simple bow and antiquated stern, there will occasionally flash across my mind a sensation of familiar things, and there is always mixed up with such indistinct shadows of recollection an unaccountable memory of old foreign chronicles and ages long ago.

*   *   *   *   *

I have been looking at the timbers of the ship. She is built of a material to which I am a stranger. There is a peculiar character about the wood which strikes me as rendering it unfit for the purpose to which it has been applied. I mean its extreme *porousness*, considered independently of the worm-eaten condition which is a consequence of navigation in these seas, and apart from the rottenness attendant upon age. It will appear perhaps an observation somewhat over-curious, but this wood would have every characteristic of Spanish oak, if Spanish oak were distended by any unnatural means.

In reading the above sentence, a curious apothegm of an old weather-beaten Dutch navigator comes full upon my recollection. " It is as sure," he was wont to say, when any doubt was entertained of his veracity, " as sure as there is a sea where the ship itself will grow in bulk like the living body of the seaman." *

About an hour ago, I made bold to thrust myself among a group of the crew. They paid me no manner of attention, and, although I stood in the very midst of them all, seemed utterly unconscious of my presence. Like the one I had first seen in the hold, they all bore about them the marks of a hoary old age. Their knees trembled with infirmity ; their shoulders were bent double with decrepitude ; their shrivelled skins rattled in the wind ; their voices were low, tremulous, and broken ; their eyes glistened with the rheum of years ; and their grey hairs streamed terribly in the tempest. Around them, on every part of the deck, lay scattered mathematical instruments of the most quaint and obsolete construction.   *   *   *   *

I mentioned some time ago the bending of a studding-sail. From that period, the ship, being thrown dead off the wind, has continued her terrific course due south, with every rag of canvas packed upon her, from her trucks to her lower studding-sail booms, and rolling every moment her top-gallant yard-arms into the most appalling hell of water which it can enter into the mind of man to imagine. I have just left the deck, where I find it impossible to maintain a footing, although the crew seem to experience little inconvenience. It appears to me a miracle of miracles that our enormous bulk is not swallowed up at once and for ever. We are surely doomed to hover continually upon the brink of eternity, without taking a final plunge into the abyss. From billows a thousand times more stupendous than any I have ever seen, we glide away with the facility of the arrowy sea-gull ; and the colossal waters rear their heads above us like demons of the deep, but like demons confined to simple threats, and forbidden to destroy. I am led to attribute these frequent escapes to the only natural cause which can account for such effect. I must suppose the ship to be within the influence of some strong current, or impetuous undertow.   *   *   *   *

I have seen the captain face to face, and in his own cabin—but, as I expected, he paid me no attention. Although in his appearance there is, to a casual observer, nothing which might bespeak him more or less than man, still a feeling of irrepressible reverence and awe mingled with the sensation of wonder with which I regarded him. In stature, he is nearly my own height ; that is, about five feet eight inches. He is of a well-knit and compact frame of body, neither robust nor remarkable otherwise. But it is the singularity of the expression which reigns upon the face—it is the intense, the wonderful, the thrilling evidence of old age, so utter, so extreme, which excites within my spirit a sense—a sentiment ineffable. His forehead although little wrinkled, seems to bear upon it the stamp of a myriad of years. His grey hairs are records of the past, and his greyer eyes are sybils of the future. The cabin floor was thickly strewn with strange, iron-clasped folios, and mouldering instruments of science, and obsolete long-forgotten charts. His head was bowed down upon his hands, and he pored with a fiery unquiet eye over a paper which I took to be a commission, and which, at all events, bore the signature of a monarch. He muttered to himself—as did the first seaman whom I saw in the hold—some low peevish syllables of a foreign tongue ; and although the speaker was close at my elbow, his voice seemed to reach my ears from the distance of a mile.   *   *   *   *

The ship and all in it are imbued with the spirit of Eld. The crew glide to and fro like the ghosts of buried centuries ; their eyes have an eager and uneasy meaning ; and when their figures fall athwart my path in the wild glare of the battle-lanterns, I feel as I have never felt before, although I have been all my life a dealer in antiquities, and have imbibed the shadows of fallen columns at Balbec, and Tadmor, and Persepolis, until my very soul has become a ruin.   *   *   *   *

When I look around me I feel ashamed of my former apprehensions. If I trembled at the blast which has hitherto attended us, shall I not stand aghast at a warring of wind and ocean, to convey any idea of which the words tornado and simoom are trivial and ineffective ? All in the immediate vicinity of the ship is the blackness of eternal night, and a chaos of foam-less water ; but, about a league on either side of us, may be seen, indistinctly and at intervals, stupendous ramparts of ice towering away into the desolate sky, and looking like the walls of the universe.   *   *

As I imagined, the ship proves to be in a current— if that appellation can properly be given to a tide which, howling and shrieking by the white ice, thunders on to the southward with a velocity like the headlong dashing of a cataract.   *   *   *   *

To conceive the horror of my sensations is, I pre-sume, utterly impossible ; yet a curiosity to penetrate the mysteries of these awful regions predominates even over my despair, and will reconcile me to the most hideous aspect of death. It is evident that we are hurrying onwards to some exciting knowledge—some never-to-be-imparted secret, whose attainment is destruction. Perhaps this current leads us to the southern pole itself. It must be confessed that a supposition apparently so wild has every probability in its favour.

*   *   *   *   *

The crew pace the deck with unquiet and tremulous step ; but there is upon their countenances an expression more of the eagerness of hope than of the apathy of despair.

In the meantime the wind is still in our poop, and as we carry a crowd of canvas the ship is at times lifted bodily from out the sea ! Oh, horror upon horror !—the ice opens suddenly to the right, and to the left, and we are whirling dizzily, in immense concentric circles, round and round the borders of a gigantic amphitheatre, the summit of whose walls is lost in the darkness and the distance. But little time will be left me to ponder upon my destiny ! The circles rapidly grow small—we are plunging madly within the grasp of the whirlpool—and amid a roaring, and bellowing, and thundering of ocean and of tempest, the ship is quivering—Oh God ! and—— going down !

Note.—The " MS. Found in a Bottle " was originally published in 1831, and it was not until many years afterwards that I became acquainted with the maps of Mercator, in which the ocean is represented as rushing, by four mouths, into the (northern) Polar Gulf, to be absorbed into the bowels of the earth ; the Pole itself being represented by a black rock towering to a prodigious height.

III

A DESCENT INTO THE MAELSTRÖM

The ways of God in Nature, as in Providence, are not as *our* ways; nor are the models that we frame any way commensurate to the vastness, profundity, and unsearchableness of His works, *which have a depth in them greater than the well of Democritus*

Joseph Glanville

WE had now reached the summit of the loftiest crag. For some minutes the old man seemed too much exhausted to speak.

"Not long ago," said he at length, "and I could have guided you on this route as well as the youngest of my sons; but, about three years past, there happened to me an event such as never happened before to mortal man—or at least such as no man ever survived to tell of—and the six hours of deadly terror which I then endured have broken me up body and soul. You suppose me a *very* old man—but I am not. It took less than a single day to change these hairs from a jetty black to white, to weaken my limbs, and to unstring my nerves, so that I tremble at the least exertion, and am frightened at a shadow. Do you know I can scarcely look over this little cliff without getting giddy?"

The "little cliff," upon whose edge he had so carelessly thrown himself down to rest that the weightier portion of his body hung over it, while he was only kept from falling by the tenure of his elbow on its extreme and slippery edge—this "little cliff" arose, a sheer unobstructed precipice of black shining rock, some fifteen or sixteen hundred feet from the world of crags beneath us. Nothing would have tempted me to within half-a-dozen yards of its brink. In truth so deeply was I excited by the perilous position of my companion, that I fell at full length upon the ground, clung to the shrubs around me, and dared not even glance upward at the sky—while I struggled in vain to divest myself of the idea that the very foundations of the mountain were in danger from the fury of the winds. It was long before I could reason myself into sufficient courage to sit up and look out into the distance.

"You must get over these fancies," said the guide, "for I have brought you here that you might have the best possible view of the scene of that event I mentioned—and to tell you the whole story with the spot just under your eye."

"We are now," he continued in that particularising manner which distinguished him—"we are now close upon the Norwegian coast—in the sixty-eighth degree of latitude—in the great province of Nordland—and in the dreary district of Lofoden. The mountain upon whose top we sit is Helseggen, the Cloudy. Now raise yourself up a little higher—hold on to the grass if you feel giddy—so—and look out, beyond the belt of vapour beneath us, into the sea."

I looked dizzily, and beheld a wide expanse of ocean, whose waters wore so inky a hue as to bring at once to my mind the Nubian geographer's account of the *Mare Tenebrarum*. A panorama more deplorably desolate

no human imagination can conceive. To the right
and left as far as the eye could reach, there lay outstretched, like ramparts of the world, lines of horridly
black and beetling cliff, whose character of gloom was
but the more forcibly illustrated by the surf which
reared high up against it its white and ghastly crest,
howling and shrieking for ever. Just opposite the pro-
montory upon whose apex we were placed, and at a
distance of some five or six miles out at sea, there was
visible a small, bleak-looking island ; or, more properly, its position was discernible through the wilderness of surge in which it was enveloped. About two
miles nearer the land arose another of smaller size,
hideously craggy and barren, and encompassed at
various intervals by a cluster of dark rocks.

The appearance of the ocean, in the space between
the more distant island and the shore, had something
very unusual about it. Although at the time so strong
a gale was blowing landward that a brig in the remote
offing lay to under a double-reefed trysail, and constantly plunged her whole hull out of sight, still there
was here nothing like a regular swell, but only a short,
quick, angry cross dashing of water in every direction
—as well in the teeth of the wind as otherwise. Of
foam there was little except in the immediate vicinity
of the rocks.

" The island in the distance," resumed the old man,
" is called by the Norwegians Vurrgh. The one mid-
way is Moskoe. That a mile to the northward is
Ambaaren. Yonder are Islesen, Hotholm, Keildhelm,
Suarven, and Buckholm. Farther off—between
Moskoe and Vurrgh—are Otterholm, Flimen, Sand-

flesen, and Stockholm. These are the true names of the places—but why it has been thought necessary to name them at all, is more than either you or I can understand. Do you hear anything? Do you see any change in the water?"

We had now been about ten minutes upon the top of Helseggen, to which we had ascended from the interior of Lofoden, so that we had caught no glimpse of the sea until it had burst upon us from the summit. As the old man spoke, I became aware of a loud and gradually increasing sound, like the moaning of a vast herd of buffaloes upon an American prairie ; and at the same moment I perceived that what seamen term the *chopping* character of the ocean beneath us, was rapidly changing into a current which set to the eastward. Even while I gazed this current acquired a monstrous velocity. Each moment added to its speed —to its headlong impetuosity. In five minutes the whole sea as far as Vurrgh was lashed into ungovernable fury ; but it was between Moskoe and the coast that the main uproar held its sway. Here the vast bed of the waters, seamed and scarred into a thousand conflicting channels, burst suddenly into frenzied convulsion—heaving, boiling, hissing,—gyrating in gigantic and innumerable vortices, and all whirling and plunging on to the eastward with a rapidity which water never elsewhere assumes except in precipitous descents.

In a few minutes more, there came over the scene another radical alteration. The general surface grew somewhat more smooth, and the whirlpools one by one disappeared, while prodigious streaks of foam became apparent where none had been seen before. These streaks, at length, spreading out to a great distance, and entering into combination, took unto themselves the gyratory motion of the subsided vortices, and seemed to form the germ of another more vast. Suddenly—very suddenly—this assumed a distinct and definite existence in a circle of more than a mile in diameter. The edge of the whirl was represented by a broad belt of gleaming spray ; but no particle of this slipped into the mouth of the terrific funnel, whose interior, as far as the eye could fathom it, was a smooth, shining, and jet-black wall of water, inclined to the horizon at an angle of some forty-five degrees, speeding dizzily round and round with a swaying and sweltering motion, and sending forth to the winds an appalling voice, half-shriek, half-roar, such as not even the mighty cataract of Niagara ever lifts up in its agony to Heaven.

The mountain trembled to its very base, and the rock rocked. I threw myself upon my face, and clung to the scant herbage in an excess of nervous agitation.

" This," said I at length, to the old man—" this *can* be nothing else than the great whirlpool of the Maelström."

" So it is sometimes termed," said he. " We Norwegians call it the Moskoe-ström, from the island of Moskoe in the midway."

The ordinary accounts of this vortex had by no means prepared me for what I saw. That of Jonas Ramus, which is perhaps the most circumstantial of any, cannot impart the faintest conception either of the magnificence, or of the horror of the scene—or of the wild bewildering sense of *the novel* which confounds the beholder. I am not sure from what point of view the writer in question surveyed it, nor at what time ; but it could neither have been from the summit of Helseggen, nor during a storm. There are some passages of his description, nevertheless, which may be quoted for their details, although their effect is exceedingly feeble in conveying an impression of the spectacle.

" Between Lofoden and Moskoe," he says, " the depth of the water is between thirty-five and forty fathoms ; but on the other side, toward Ver (Vurrgh) this depth decreases so as not to afford a convenient passage for a vessel, without the risk of splitting on the rocks, which happens even in the calmest weather. When it is flood, the stream runs up the country between Lofoden and Moskoe with a boisterous rapidity, but the roar of its impetuous ebb to the sea is scarce equalled by the loudest and most dreadful cataracts—the noise being heard several leagues off, and the vortices or pits are of such an extent and depth, that if a ship comes within its attraction it is inevitably absorbed and carried down to the bottom, and there beat to pieces against the rocks, and when the water relaxes the fragments thereof are thrown up again. But these intervals of tranquillity are only at the turn of the ebb and flood, and in calm weather, and last but a quarter of an hour, its violence gradually returning. When the stream is most boisterous, and its fury heightened by a storm, it is dangerous to come within a Norway mile of it. Boats, yachts, and

ships have been carried away by not guarding against
it before they were within its reach. It likewise
happens frequently that whales come too near the
stream, and are overpowered by its violence, and then
it is impossible to describe their howlings and bellow-
ings in their fruitless struggles to disengage themselves. A bear once, attempting to swim from
Lofoden to Moskoe, was caught by the stream and
borne down, while he roared terribly, so as to be heard
on shore. Large stocks of firs and pine trees, after
being absorbed by the current, rise again broken and
torn to such a degree as if bristles grew upon them.
This plainly shows the bottom to consist of craggy
rocks, among which they are whirled to and fro. This
stream is regulated by the flux and reflux of the sea
—it being constantly high and low water every six
hours. In the year 1645, early in the morning of
Sexagesima Sunday, it raged with such noise and
impetuosity that the very stones of the houses on
the coast fell to the ground."

In regard to the depth of the water, I could not
see how this could have been ascertained at all in
the immediate vicinity of the vortex. The "forty
fathoms" must have reference only to portions of the
channel close upon the shore either of Moskoe or
Lofoden. The depth in the centre of the Moskoe-
ström must be immeasurably greater; and no better
proof of this fact is necessary than can be obtained
from even the sidelong glance into the abyss of the
whirl which may be had from the highest crag of
Helseggen. Looking down from this pinnacle upon
the howling Phlegethon below, I could not help smiling

at the simplicity with which the honest Jonas Ramus records, as a matter difficult of belief, the anecdotes of the whales and the bears ; for it appeared to me, in fact, a self-evident thing that the largest ship of the line in existence coming within the influence of that deadly attraction could resist it as little as a feather the hurricane, and must disappear bodily and at once.

The attempts to account for the phenomenon—some of which I remember seemed to me sufficiently plausible in perusal—now wore a very different and unsatisfactory aspect. The idea generally received is that this, as well as three smaller vortices among the Ferroe Islands, " have no other cause than the collision of waves rising and falling at flux and reflux against a ridge of rocks and shelves, which confines the water so that it precipitates itself like a cataract ; and thus the higher the flood rises the deeper must the fall be, and the natural result of all is a whirlpool or vortex, the prodigious suction of which is sufficiently known by lesser experiments."—These are the words of the Encyclopædia Britannica. Kircher and others imagine that in the centre of the channel of the Maelström is an abyss penetrating the globe, and issuing in some very remote part—the Gulf of Bothnia being somewhat decidedly named in one instance. This opinion, idle in itself, was the one to which, as I gazed, my imagination most readily assented ; and, mentioning it to the guide, I was rather surprised to hear him say that, although it was the view almost universally entertained of the subject by the Norwegians, it nevertheless was not his own. As to the former notion he confessed his inability to comprehend it ; and here I agreed with him—for, however conclusive on paper, it becomes altogether unintelligible, and even absurd, amid the thunder of the abyss.

" You have had a good look at the whirl now," said the old man, " and if you will creep round this crag so as to get in its lee, and deaden the roar of the water, I will tell you a story that will convince you I ought to know something of the Moskoe-ström."

I placed myself as desired, and he proceeded.

" Myself and my two brothers once owned a schooner-rigged smack of about seventy tons burthen, with which we were in the habit of fishing among the islands beyond Moskoe, nearly to Vurrgh. In all violent eddies at sea there is good fishing at proper opportunities if one has only the courage to attempt it, but among the whole of the Lofoden coastmen, we three were the only ones who made a regular business of going out to the islands, as I tell you. The usual grounds are a great way lower down to the southward. There fish can be got at all hours, without much risk, and therefore these places are preferred. The choice spots over here among the rocks, however, not only yield the finest variety, but in far greater abundance, so that we often got in a single day what the more timid of the craft could not scrape together in a week. In fact, we made it a matter of desperate speculation—the risk of life standing instead of labour, and courage answering for capital.

" We kept the smack in a cove about five miles higher up the coast than this ; and it was our practice, in fine weather, to take advantage of the fifteen

minutes' slack to push across the main channel of the
Moskoe-ström, far above the pool, and then drop
down upon anchorage somewhere near Otterholm, or
Sandflesen, where the eddies are not so violent as
elsewhere. Here we used to remain until nearly time
for slack-water again, when we weighed and made for
home. We never set out upon this expedition without a steady side wind for going and coming—one
that we felt sure would not fail us before our return
—and we seldom made a miscalculation upon this
point. Twice during six years we were forced to stay
all night at anchor on account of a dead calm, which
is a rare thing indeed just about here ; and once we
had to remain on the grounds nearly a week, starving
to death, owing to a gale which blew up shortly after
our arrival, and made the channel too boisterous to
be thought of. Upon this occasion we should have
been driven out to sea in spite of everything (for the
whirlpools threw us round and round so violently that
at length we fouled our anchor and dragged it) if it
had not been that we drifted into one of the innumerable cross currents—here to-day and gone to-morrow
—which drove us under the lee of Flimen, where, by
good luck, we brought up.

" I could not tell you the twentieth part of the
difficulties we encountered ' on the grounds '—it is
a bad spot to be in, even in good weather—but we
made shift always to run the gauntlet of the Moskoe-
ström itself without accident ; although at times my
heart has been in my mouth when we happened to be
a minute or so behind or before the slack. The wind
sometimes was not as strong as we thought it at

starting, and then we made rather less way than we could wish, while the current rendered the smack unmanageable. My eldest brother had a son eighteen years old, and I had two stout boys of my own. These would have been of great assistance at such times in using the sweeps, as well as afterward in fishing, but somehow, although we ran the risk ourselves, we had not the heart to let the young ones get into the danger—for, after all is said and done, it *was* a horrible danger, and that is the truth.

" It is now within a few days of three years since what I am going to tell you occurred. It was on the tenth day of July 18—, a day which the people of this part of the world will never forget—for it was one in which blew the most terrible hurricane that ever came out of the heavens ; and yet all the morning, and indeed until late in the afternoon, there was a gentle and steady breeze from the south-west, while the sun shone brightly, so that the oldest seaman among us could not have foreseen what was to follow.

" The three of us—my two brothers and myself— had crossed over to the islands about 2 o'clock P.M., and had soon nearly loaded the smack with fine fish, which, we all remarked, were more plentiful that day than we had ever known them. It was just seven *by my watch* when we weighed and started for home, so as to make the worst of the Ström at slack water, which we knew would be at eight.

" We set out with a fresh wind in our starboard quarter, and for some time spanked along at a great rate, never dreaming of danger, for indeed we saw not the slightest reason to apprehend it. All at once we were taken aback by a breeze from over Helseggen. This was most unusual—something that had never happened to us before—and I began to feel a little uneasy without exactly knowing why. We put the boat in the wind but could make no headway at all for the eddies, and I was put upon the point of proposing to return to the anchorage, when, looking astern, we saw the whole horizon covered with a singular copper-coloured cloud that rose with the most amazing velocity.

" In the meantime the breeze that had headed us off fell away, and we were dead becalmed, drifting about in every direction. This state of things, however, did not last long enough to give us time to think about it. In less than a minute the storm was upon us—in less than two the sky was entirely overcast— and what with this and the driving spray it became suddenly so dark that we could not see each other in the smack.

" Such a hurricane as then blew it is folly to attempt describing. The oldest seaman in Norway never experienced anything like it. We had let our sails go by the run before it cleverly took us ; but, at the first puff, both our masts went by the board as if they had been sawed off—the mainmast taking with it my youngest brother, who had lashed himself to it for safety.

" Our boat was the lightest feather of a thing that ever sat upon water. It had a complete flush deck, with only a small hatch near the bow, and this hatch it had always been our custom to batten down when about to cross the Ström by way of precaution against the chopping seas. But for this circumstance we should have foundered at once—for we lay entirely buried for some moments. How my elder brother escaped destruction I cannot say, for I never had an opportunity of ascertaining. For my part, as soon as I had let the foresail run, I threw myself flat on deck, with my feet against the narrow gunwale of the bow, and with my hands grasping a ring-bolt near the foot of the foremast. It was mere instinct that prompted me to do this—which was undoubtedly the very best thing I could have done—for I was too much flurried to think.

" For some moments we were completely deluged, as I say, and all this time I held my breath, and clung to the bolt. When I could stand it no longer I raised myself upon my knees, still keeping hold with my hands, and thus got my head clear. Presently our little boat gave herself a shake, just as a dog does in coming out of the water, and thus rid herself in some measure of the seas. I was now trying to get the better of the stupor that had come over me, and to collect my senses so as to see what was to be done, when I felt somebody grasp my arm. It was my elder brother, and my heart leaped for joy, for I had made sure that he was overboard—but the next moment all this joy was turned into horror—for he put his mouth close to my ear, and screamed out the word ' *Moskoe-ström !* '

" No one ever will know what my feelings were at that moment. I shook from head to foot, as if I had had the most violent fit of the ague. I knew what he wished to make me understand. With the wind

that now drove us on we were bound for the whirl
of the Ström, and nothing could save us !

" You perceive that in crossing the Ström *channel*,
we always went a long way up above the whirl, even
in the calmest weather, and then had to wait and
watch carefully for the slack—but now we were
driving right upon the pool itself, and in such a
hurricane as this ! ' To be sure,' I thought, ' we shall
get there just about the slack—there is some little
hope in that '—but in the next moment I cursed
myself for being so great a fool as to dream of hope
at all. I knew very well that we were doomed had
we been ten times a ninety-gun ship.

" By this time the first fury of the tempest had
spent itself, or perhaps we did not feel it so much as
we scudded before it, but at all events the seas, which
at first had been kept down by the wind and lay flat
and frothing now got up into absolute mountains. A
singular change, too, had come over the heavens.
Around in every direction it was still as black as
pitch, but nearly overhead there burst out, all at
once, a circular rift of clear sky—as clear as I ever saw,
and of a deep bright blue—and through it there blazed
forth the full moon with a lustre that I never before
knew her to wear. She lit up everything about us
with the greatest distinctness—but, O God, what a
scene it was to light up !

" I now made one or two attempts to speak to my
brother—but, in some manner which I could not
understand, the din had so increased that I could not
make him hear a single word, although I screamed at
the top of my voice in his ear. Presently he shook

his head, looking as pale as death, and held up one
of his fingers as if to say ' *listen !* '

"At first I could not make out what he meant—but
soon a hideous thought flashed upon me. I dragged
my watch from its fob. It was not going. I glanced
at its face by the moonlight, and then burst into tears
as I flung it far away into the ocean. *It had run down
at seven o'clock ! We were behind the time of the slack,
and the whirl of the Ström was in full fury !*

"When a boat is well built, properly trimmed, and
not deep laden, the waves in a strong gale, when she
is going large, seem always to slip from beneath her
—which appears very strange to a landsman—and
this is what is called *riding*, in sea-phrase. Well, so
far we had ridden the swells very cleverly, but presently a gigantic sea happened to take us right under
the counter, and bore us with it as it rose—up—up
—as if into the sky. I would not have believed that
any wave could rise so high. And then down we came
with a sweep, a slide, and a plunge, that made me
feel sick and dizzy, as if I was falling from some lofty
mountain-top in a dream. But while we were up I
had thrown a quick glance around—and that one
glance was all sufficient. I saw our exact position in
an instant. The Moskoe-ström whirlpool was about
a quarter of a mile dead ahead—but no more like the
every-day Moskoe-ström, than the whirl as you now
see it is like a mill-race. If I had not known where
we were, and what we had to expect, I should not
have recognized the place at all. As it was, I in-
voluntarily closed my eyes in horror. The lids
clenched themselves together as if in a spasm.

" It could not have been more than two minutes afterward until we suddenly felt the waves subside, and were enveloped in foam. The boat made a sharp half turn to larboard, and then shot off in its new direction like a thunderbolt. At the same moment the roaring noise of the water was completely drowned in a kind of shrill shriek—such a sound as you might imagine given out by the waste-pipes of many thousand steam-vessels letting off their steam all together. We were now in the belt of surf that always surrounds the whirl; and I thought of course that another moment would plunge us into the abyss—down which we could only see indistinctly on account of the amazing velocity with which we were borne along. The boat did not seem to sink into the water at all, but to skim like an air-bubble upon the surface of the surge. Her starboard side was next the whirl, and on the larboard arose the world of ocean we had left. It stood like a huge writhing wall between us and the horizon.

" It may appear strange, but now, when we were in the very jaws of the gulf, I felt more composed than when we were only approaching it. Having made up my mind to hope no more, I got rid of a great deal of that terror which unmanned me at first. I suppose it was despair that strung my nerves.

" It may look like boasting—but what I tell you is truth—I began to reflect how magnificent a thing it was to die in such a manner, and how foolish it was in me to think of so paltry a consideration as my own individual life in view of so wonderful a manifestation of God's power. I do believe that I blushed with shame when this idea crossed my mind. After a little while I became possessed with the keenest curiosity about the whirl itself. I positively felt a *wish* to explore its depths, even at the sacrifice I was going to make ; and my principal grief was that I should never be able to tell my old companions on shore about the mysteries I should see. These, no doubt, were singular fancies to occupy a man's mind in such extremity, and I have often thought since that the revolutions of the boat around the pool might have rendered me a little light-headed.

" There was another circumstance which tended to restore my self-possession, and this was the cessation of the wind, which could not reach us in our present situation—for, as you saw yourself, the belt of surf is considerably lower than the general bed of the ocean, and this latter now towered above us, a high, black, mountainous ridge. If you have never been at sea in a heavy gale you can form no idea of the confusion of mind occasioned by the wind and spray together. They blind, deafen, and strangle you, and take away all power of action or reflection. But we were now, in a great measure, rid of these annoyances—just as death-condemned felons in prison are allowed petty indulgences, forbidden them while their doom is yet uncertain.

" How often we made the circuit of the belt it is impossible to say. We careered round and round for perhaps an hour, flying rather than floating, getting gradually more and more into the middle of the surge, and then nearer and nearer to its horrible inner edge. All this time I had never let go of the ring-bolt. My

4

brother was at the stern, holding on to a small empty water-cask which had been securely lashed under the coop of the counter, and was the only thing on deck that had not been swept overboard when the gale first took us. As we approached the brink of the pit he let go his hold upon this, and made for the ring, from which, in the agony of his terror, he endeavoured to force my hands, as it was not large enough to afford us both a secure grasp. I never felt deeper grief than when I saw him attempt this act—although I knew he was a madman when he did it—a raving maniac through sheer fright. I did not care, however, to contest the point with him. I knew it could make no difference whether either of us held on at all, so I let him have the bolt, and went astern to the cask. This there was no great difficulty in doing, for the smack flew round steadily enough, and upon an even keel, only swaying to and fro with the immense sweeps and swelters of the whirl. Scarcely had I secured myself in my new position when we gave a wild lurch to starboard, and rushed headlong into the abyss. I muttered a hurried prayer to God, and thought all was over.

" As I felt the sickening sweep of the descent I had instinctively tightened my hold upon the barrel, and closed my eyes. For some seconds I dared not open them, while I expected instant destruction, and wondered that I was not already in my death-struggles with the water. But moment after moment elapsed. I still lived. The sense of falling had ceased ; and the motion of the vessel seemed much as it had been before while in the belt of foam, with the exception that she now lay more along. I took courage, and looked once again upon the scene.

" Never shall I forget the sensations of awe, horror, and admiration with which I gazed about me. The boat appeared to be hanging, as if by magic, midway down, upon the interior surface of a funnel vast in circumference, prodigious in depth, and whose perfectly smooth sides might have been mistaken for ebony but for the bewildering rapidity with which they spun around, and for the gleaming and ghastly radiance they shot forth, as the rays of the full moon, from that circular rift amid the clouds which I have already described, streamed in a flood of golden glory along the black walls, and far away down into the inmost recesses of the abyss.

" At first I was too much confused to observe anything accurately. The general burst of terrific grandeur was all that I beheld. When I recovered myself a little, however, my gaze fell instinctively downward. In this direction I was able to obtain an unobstructed view from the manner in which the smack hung on the inclined surface of the pool. She was quite upon an even keel—that is to say, her deck lay in a plane parallel with that of the water—but this latter sloped at an angle of more than forty-five degrees, so that we seemed to be lying upon our beam-ends. I could not help observing, nevertheless, that I had scarcely more difficulty in maintaining my hold and footing in this situation than if we had been upon a dead level, and this, I suppose, was owing to the speed at which we revolved.

" The rays of the moon seemed to search the very

bottom of the profound gulf ; but still I could make out nothing distinctly, on account of a thick mist in which everything there was enveloped, and over which there hung a magnificent rainbow, like that narrow and tottering bridge which Mussulmen say is the only pathway between Time and Eternity. This mist or spray was no doubt occasioned by the clashing of the great walls of the funnel as they all met together at the bottom, but the yell that went up to the Heavens from out of that mist I dare not attempt to describe.

" Our first slide into the abyss itself, from the belt of foam above, had carried us a great distance down the slope, but our farther descent was by no means proportionate. Round and round we swept—not with any uniform movement—but in dizzying swings and jerks, that sent us sometimes only a few hundred yards—sometimes nearly the complete circuit of the whirl. Our progress downward at each revolution was slow but very perceptible.

" Looking about me upon the wide waste of liquid ebony on which we were thus borne, I perceived that our boat was not the only object in the embrace of the whirl. Both above and below us were visible fragments of vessels, large masses of building timber and trunks of trees, with many smaller articles, such as pieces of house furniture, broken boxes, barrels, and staves. I have already described the unnatural curiosity which had taken the place of my original terrors. It appeared to grow upon me as I drew nearer and nearer to my dreadful doom. I now began to watch, with a strange interest, the numerous things that floated in our company. I *must* have been delirious, for I even sought *amusement* in speculating upon the relative velocities of their several descents toward the foam below. ' This fir-tree,' I found myself at one time saying, ' will certainly be the next thing that takes the awful plunge and disappears,'—and then I was disappointed to find that the wreck of a Dutch merchant ship overtook it and went down before. At length, after making several guesses of this nature, and being deceived in all, this fact—the fact of my invariable miscalculation—set me upon a train of reflection that made my limbs again tremble, and my heart beat heavily once more.

" It was not a new terror that thus affected me, but the dawn of a more exciting *hope*. This hope arose partly from memory, and partly from present observation. I called to mind the great variety of buoyant matter that strewed the coast of Lofoden, having been absorbed and then thrown forth by the Moskoe-ström. By far the greater number of the articles were shattered in the most extraordinary way—so chafed and roughened as to have the appearance of being stuck full of splinters—but then I distinctly recollected that there were *some* of them which were not disfigured at all. Now I could not account for this difference except by supposing that the roughened fragments were the only ones which had been *completely absorbed*—that the others had entered the whirl at so late a period of the tide, or, for some reason, had descended so slowly after entering, that they did not reach the bottom before the turn of the flood came, or of the ebb, as the case might be. I conceived it possible, in either instance, that they might thus be whirled up again to the level of the ocean, without undergoing the fate of those which had been drawn in more early, or absorbed more rapidly. I made also three important observations. The first was that, as a general rule, the larger the bodies were the more rapid their descent ; the second, that, between two masses of equal extent, the one spherical and the other *of any other shape*, the superiority in speed of descent was with the sphere ; the third, that, between two masses of equal size, the one cylindrical and the other of any other shape, the cylinder was absorbed the more slowly. Since my escape I have had several conversations on this subject with an old schoolmaster of the district, and it was from him that I learned the use of the words ' cylinder ' and ' sphere.' He explained to me—although I have forgotten the explanation—how what I observed was in fact the natural consequence of the forms of the floating fragments, and showed me how it happened that a cylinder swimming in a vortex offered more resistance to its suction, and was drawn in with greater difficulty than an equally bulky body of any form whatever.*

" There was one startling circumstance which went a great way in enforcing these observations and rendering me anxious to turn them to account, and this was that at every revolution we passed something like a barrel, or else the yard or the mast of a vessel, while many of these things which had been on our level when I first opened my eyes upon the wonders of the whirlpool were now high up above us, and

* See Archimedes, " *De Incidentibus in Fluido*," lib. 2.

seemed to have moved but little from their original station.

" I no longer hesitated what to do. I resolved to lash myself securely to the water-cask upon which I now held, to cut it loose from the counter, and to throw myself with it into the water. I attracted my brother's attention by signs, pointed to the floating barrels that came near us, and did everything in my power to make him understand what I was about to do. I thought at length that he comprehended my design, but, whether this was the case or not, he shook his head despairingly, and refused to move from his station by the ring-bolt. It was impossible to reach him, the emergency admitted of no delay, and so, with a bitter struggle, I resigned him to his fate, fastened myself to the cask by means of the lashings which secured it to the counter, and precipitated myself with it into the sea without another moment's hesitation.

" The result was precisely what I had hoped it might be. As it is myself who now tell you this tale —as you see that I *did* escape—and as you are already in possession of the mode in which this escape was effected, and must therefore anticipate all that I have further to say, I will bring my story quickly to conclusion. It might have been an hour or thereabout after my quitting the smack, when, having descended to a vast distance beneath me, it made three or four wild gyrations in rapid succession, and, bearing my loved brother with it, plunged headlong at once and for ever into the chaos of foam below. The barrel to which I was attached sunk very little farther than half the distance between the bottom of the gulf and the spot at which I leaped overboard, before a great change took place in the character of the whirlpool. The slope of the sides of the vast funnel became momently less and less steep. The gyrations of the whirl grew gradually less and less violent. By degrees the froth and the rainbow disappeared, and the bottom of the gulf seemed slowly to uprise. The sky was clear, the winds had gone down, and the full moon was setting radiantly in the west, when I found myself on the surface of the ocean, in full view of the shores of Lofoden, and above the spot where the pool of the Moskoe-ström *had been*. It was the hour of the slack—but the sea still heaved in mountainous waves from the effects of the hurricane. I was borne violently into the channel of the Ström, and in a few minutes was hurried down the coast into the ' grounds ' of the fishermen. A boat picked me up, exhausted from fatigue and (now that the danger was removed) speechless from the memory of its horror. Those who drew me on board were my old mates and daily companions, but they knew me no more than they would have known a traveller from the spirit land. My hair, which had been raven-black the day before, was as white as you see it now. They say, too, that the whole expression of my countenance had changed. I told them my story—they did not believe it. I now tell it to *you*, and I can scarcely expect you to put more faith in it than did the merry fishermen of Lofoden."

IV

THE FALL OF THE HOUSE OF USHER

Son cœur est un luth suspendu ;
Sitôt qu'on le touche il résonne.
De Béranger

DURING the whole of a dull, dark, and soundless day
in the autumn of the year, when the clouds hung
oppressively low in the heavens, I had been passing
alone, on horseback, through a singularly dreary tract
of country, and at length found myself, as the shades
of evening drew on, within view of the melancholy
House of Usher. I know not how it was—but, with
the first glimpse of the building, a sense of insufferable
gloom pervaded my spirit. I say insufferable ; for
the feeling was unrelieved by any of that half-pleasur-
able, because poetic, sentiment, with which the mind
usually receives even the sternest natural images of
the desolate or terrible. I looked upon the scene
before me—upon the mere house, and the simple
landscape features of the domain—upon the bleak
walls—upon the vacant eye-like windows—upon a few
rank sedges—and upon a few white trunks of decayed
trees—with an utter depression of soul which I can
compare to no earthly sensation more properly than
to the after-dream of the reveller upon opium—the
bitter lapse into every-day life—the hideous dropping
of the veil. There was an iciness, a sinking, a sicken-

ing of the heart—an unredeemed dreariness of thought which no goading of the imagination could torture into aught of the sublime. What was it—I paused to think—what was it that so unnerved me in the contemplation of the House of Usher ? It was a mystery all insoluble ; nor could I grapple with the shadowy fancies that crowded upon me as I pondered. I was forced to fall back upon the unsatisfactory conclusion, that while, beyond doubt, there *are* combinations of very simple natural objects which have the power of thus affecting us, still the analysis of this power lies among considerations beyond our depth. It was possible, I reflected, that a mere different arrangement of the particulars of the scene, of the details of the picture, would be sufficient to modify, or perhaps to annihilate its capacity for sorrowful impression ; and, acting upon this idea, I reined my horse to the precipitous brink of a black and lurid tarn that lay in unruffled lustre by the dwelling, and gazed down—but with a shudder more thrilling than before—upon the remodelled and inverted images of the grey sedge, and the ghastly tree-stems, and the vacant and eye-like windows.

Nevertheless, in this mansion of gloom I now proposed to myself a sojourn of some weeks. Its proprietor, Roderick Usher, had been one of my boon companions in boyhood, but many years had elapsed since our last meeting. A letter, however, had lately reached me in a distant part of the country—a letter from him—which, in its wildly importunate nature, had admitted of no other than a personal reply. The MS. gave evidence of nervous agitation. The writer spoke of acute bodily illness—of a mental disorder which oppressed him—and of an earnest desire to see me, as his best, and indeed his only personal friend, with a view of attempting, by the cheerfulness of my society, some alleviation of his malady. It was the manner in which all this, and much more, was said —it was the apparent *heart* that went with his request —which allowed me no room for hesitation, and I accordingly obeyed forthwith what I still considered a very singular summons.

Although, as boys, we had been even intimate associates, yet I really knew little of my friend. His reserve had been always excessive and habitual. I was aware, however, that his very ancient family had been noted, time out of mind, for a peculiar sensibility of temperament, displaying itself through long ages in many works of exalted art, and manifested of late in repeated deeds of munificent yet unobtrusive charity, as well as in a passionate devotion to the intricacies, perhaps even more than to the orthodox and easily-recognisable beauties of musical science. I had learned, too, the very remarkable fact that the stem of the Usher race, all time-honoured as it was, had put forth at no period any enduring branch ; in other words, that the entire family lay in the direct line of descent, and had always, with very trifling and very temporary variation, so lain. It was this deficiency, I considered, while running over in thought the perfect keeping of the character of the premises with the accredited character of the people, and while speculating upon the possible influence which the one, in the long lapse of centuries, might have exercised upon the other—it was this deficiency perhaps of collateral issue, and the consequent undeviating transmission from sire to son of the patrimony with the name, which had at length so identified the two as to merge the original title of the estate in the quaint and equivocal appellation of the " House of Usher " —an appellation which seemed to include, in the minds of the peasantry who used it, both the family and the family mansion.

I have said that the sole effect of my somewhat childish experiment—that of looking down within the tarn—had been to deepen the first singular impression. There can be no doubt that the consciousness of the rapid increase of my superstition—for why should I not so term it ?—served mainly to accelerate the increase itself. Such, I have long known, is the para-doxical law of all sentiments having terror as a basis ; and it might have been for this reason only that, when I again uplifted my eyes to the house itself from its image in the pool, there grew in my mind a strange fancy—a fancy so ridiculous indeed that I but mention it to show the vivid force of the sensations which oppressed me. I had so worked upon my imagination as really to believe that about the whole mansion and domain there hung an atmosphere peculiar to them-selves and their immediate vicinity—an atmosphere which had no affinity with the air of heaven but which had reeked up from the decayed trees, and the grey wall, and the silent tarn—a pestilent and mystic vapour, dull, sluggish, faintly discernible, and leaden-hued.

Shaking off from my spirit what *must* have been

a dream, I scanned more narrowly the real aspect
of the building. Its principal feature seemed to be
that of an excessive antiquity. The discoloration of
ages had been great. Minute fungi overspread the
whole exterior, hanging in a fine tangled web-work
from the eaves. Yet all this was apart from any
extraordinary dilapidation. No portion of the masonry had fallen, and there appeared to be a wild
inconsistency between its still perfect adaptation of
parts, and the crumbling condition of the individual
stones. In this there was much that reminded me of
the specious totality of old woodwork which has rotted
for long years in some neglected vault with no disturbance from the breath of the external air. Beyond this
indication of extensive decay, however, the fabric
gave little token of instability. Perhaps the eye of a
scrutinising observer might have discovered a barely
perceptible fissure, which, extending from the roof
of the building in front, made its way down the wall
in a zigzag direction, until it became lost in the sullen
waters of the tarn.

Noticing these things, I rode over a short causeway
to the house. A servant in waiting took my horse, and
I entered the Gothic archway of the hall. A valet,
of stealthy step, thence conducted me in silence
through many dark and intricate passages in my
progress to the *studio* of his master. Much that I
encountered on the way contributed, I know not how,
to heighten the vague sentiments of which I have
already spoken. While the objects around me—
while the carvings of the ceilings, the sombre tapestries
of the walls, the ebon blackness of the floors, and the

phantasmagoric armorial trophies which rattled as I strode, were but matters to which, or to such as which, I had been accustomed from my infancy— while I hesitated not to acknowledge how familiar was all this—I still wondered to find how unfamiliar were the fancies which ordinary images were stirring up. On one of the staircases I met the physician of the family. His countenance, I thought, wore a mingled expression of low cunning and perplexity. He accosted me with trepidation and passed on. The valet now threw open a door and ushered me into the presence of his master.

The room in which I found myself was very large and lofty. The windows were long, narrow, and pointed, and at so vast a distance from the black oaken floor as to be altogether inaccessible from within. Feeble gleams of encrimsoned light made their way through the trellised panes, and served to render sufficiently distinct the more prominent objects around ; the eye, however, struggled in vain to reach the remoter angles of the chamber, or the recesses of the vaulted and fretted ceiling. Dark draperies hung upon the walls. The general furniture was profuse, comfortless, antique, and tattered. Many books and musical instruments lay scattered about, but failed to give any vitality to the scene. I felt that I breathed an atmosphere of sorrow. An air of stern, deep, and irredeemable gloom hung over and pervaded all.

Upon my entrance, Usher arose from a sofa on which he had been lying at full length, and greeted me with a vicacious warmth which had much in it, I at first thought, of an overdone cordiality—of the

constrained effort of the *ennuyé* man of the world.
A glance, however, at his countenance convinced me
of his perfect sincerity. We sat down ; and for some
moments, while he spoke not, I gazed upon him with
a feeling half of pity, half of awe. Surely, man had
never before so terribly altered, in so brief a period,
as had Roderick Usher ! It was with difficulty that
I could bring myself to admit the identity of the wan
being before me with the companion of my early boyhood. Yet the character of his face had been at all
times remarkable. A cadaverousness of complexion ;
an eye large, liquid, and luminous beyond comparison ;
lips somewhat thin and very pallid, but of a surpass-
ingly beautiful curve ; a nose of a delicate Hebrew
model, but with a breadth of nostril unusual in similar
formations ; a finely moulded chin, speaking, in its
want of prominence, of a want of moral energy ; hair
of a more than web-like softness and tenuity ; these
features, with an inordinate expansion above the
regions of the temple, made up altogether a countenance not easily to be forgotten. And now in the
mere exaggeration of the prevailing character of these
features, and of the expression they were wont to
convey, lay so much of change that I doubted to
whom I spoke. The now ghastly pallor of the skin,
and the now miraculous lustre of the eye, above all
things startled and even awed me. The silken hair,
too, had been suffered to grow all unheeded, and as,
in its wild gossamer texture, it floated rather than
fell about the face, I could not, even with effort,
connect its Arabesque expression with any idea of
simple humanity.

In the manner of my friend I was at once struck with an incoherence—an inconsistency ; and I soon found this to arise from a series of feeble and futile struggles to overcome an habitual trepidancy—an excessive nervous agitation. For something of this nature I had indeed been prepared, no less by his letter than by reminiscences of certain boyish traits, and by conclusions deduced from his peculiar physical conformation and temperament. His action was alternately vivacious and sullen. His voice varied rapidly from a tremulous indecision (when the animal spirits seemed utterly in abeyance) to that species of energetic concision—that abrupt, weighty, unhurried, and hollow-sounding enunciation—that leaden, self-balanced and perfectly modulated guttural utterance which may be observed in the lost drunkard, or the irreclaimable eater of opium, during the periods of his most intense excitement.

It was thus that he spoke of the object of my visit, of his earnest desire to see me, and of the solace he expected me to afford him. He entered at some length into what he conceived to be the nature of his malady. It was, he said, a constitutional and a family evil, and one for which he despaired to find a remedy—a mere nervous affection, he immediately added, which would undoubtedly soon pass off. It displayed itself in a host of unnatural sensations. Some of these, as he detailed them, interested and bewildered me ; although perhaps the terms and the general manner of the narration had their weight. He suffered much from a morbid acuteness of the senses ; the most insipid food was alone endurable ; he could wear only garments of certain texture ; the odours of all flowers were oppressive ; his eyes were tortured by even a faint light ; and there were but peculiar sounds, and these from stringed instruments, which did not inspire him with horror.

To an anomalous species of terror I found him a bounden slave. "I shall perish," said he, "I *must* perish in this deplorable folly. Thus, thus, and not otherwise, shall I be lost. I dread the events of the future, not in themselves, but in their results. I shudder at the thought of any, even the most trivial incident, which may operate upon this intolerable agitation of soul. I have indeed no abhorrence of danger, except in its absolute effect—in terror. In this unnerved—in this pitiable condition—I feel that the period will sooner or later arrive when I must abandon life and reason together in some struggle with the grim phantasm, FEAR."

I learned, moreover, at intervals, and through broken and equivocal hints, another singular feature of his mental condition. He was enchained by certain superstitious impressions in regard to the dwelling which he tenanted, and whence, for many years, he had never ventured forth—in regard to an influence whose supposititious force was conveyed in terms too shadowy here to be re-stated—an influence which some peculiarities in the mere form and substance of his family mansion, had, by dint of long sufferance, he said, obtained over his spirit—an effect which the *physique* of the grey walls and turrets, and of the dim tarn into which they all looked down, had at length brought about upon the *morale* of his existence.

He admitted, however, although with hesitation, that much of the peculiar gloom which thus afflicted him could be traced to a more natural and far more palpable origin—to the severe and long-continued illness—indeed to the evidently approaching dissolution—of a tenderly beloved sister—his sole companion for long years—his last and only relative on earth. " Her decease," he said, with a bitterness which I can never forget, " would leave him (him the hopeless and the frail) the last of the ancient race of the Ushers." While he spoke, the lady Madeline (for so was she called) passed slowly through a remote portion of the apartment, and, without having noticed my presence, disappeared. I regarded her with an utter astonishment not unmingled with dread—and yet I found it impossible to account for such feelings. A sensation of stupor oppressed me as my eyes followed her retreating steps. When a door at length closed upon her, my glance sought instinctively and eagerly the countenance of the brother—but he had buried his face in his hands, and I could only perceive that a far more than ordinary wanness had overspread the emaciated fingers through which trickled many passionate tears.

The disease of the lady Madeline had long baffled the skill of her physicians. A settled apathy, a gradual wasting away of the person, and frequent although transient affections of a partially cataleptical character, were the unusual diagnosis. Hitherto she had steadily borne up against the pressure of her malady, and had not betaken herself finally to bed ; but, on the closing in of the evening of my arrival at the house, she succumbed (as her brother told me at night with inexpressible agitation) to the prostrating power of the destroyer ; and I learned that the glimpse I had obtained of her person would thus probably be the last I should obtain—that the lady at least while living, would be seen by me no more.

For several days ensuing her name was unmentioned by either Usher or myself ; and during this period I was busied in earnest endeavours to alleviate the melancholy of my friend. We painted and read together, or I listened, as if in a dream, to the wild improvisations of his speaking guitar. And thus, as a closer and still closer intimacy admitted me more unreservedly into the recesses of his spirit, the more bitterly did I perceive the futility of all attempts at cheering a mind from which darkness, as if an inherent positive quality, poured forth upon all objects of the moral and physical universe of one unceasing radiation of gloom.

I shall ever bear about me a memory of the many solemn hours I thus spent alone with the master of the House of Usher. Yet I should fail in any attempt to convey an idea of the exact character of the studies, or of the occupations in which he involved me or led me the way. An excited and highly distempered ideality threw a sulphureous lustre over all. His long improvised dirges will ring forever in my ears. Among other things, I hold painfully in mind a certain singular perversion and amplification of the wild air of the last waltz of Von Weber. From the paintings over which his elaborate fancy brooded, and which grew, touch by touch, into vaguenesses at which I shuddered the more thrillingly, because I shuddered knowing not why;—from these paintings (vivid as their images now are before me) I would in vain endeavour to educe more than a small portion which should lie within the compass of merely written words. By the utter simplicity, by the nakedness of his designs, he arrested and overawed attention. If ever mortal painted an idea that mortal was Roderick Usher. For me at least—in the circumstances then surrounding me—there arose out of the pure abstractions which the hypochondriac contrived to throw upon his canvas an intensity of intolerable awe, no shadow of which felt I ever yet in the contemplation of the certainly glowing yet too concrete reveries of Fuseli.

One of the phantasmagoric conceptions of my friend, partaking not so rigidly of the spirit of abstraction, may be shadowed forth, although feebly, in words. A small picture presented the interior of an immensely long and rectangular vault or tunnel, with low walls, smooth, white, and without interruption or device. Certain accessory points of the design served well to convey the idea that this excavation lay at an exceeding depth below the surface of the earth. No outlet was observed in any portion of its vast extent, and no torch, or other artificial source of light, was discernible, yet a flood of intense rays rolled throughout, and bathed the whole in a ghastly and inappropriate splendour.

I have just spoken of that morbid condition of the auditory nerve which rendered all music intolerable to the sufferer, with the exception of certain effects of stringed instruments. It was perhaps the narrow limits to which he thus confined himself upon the guitar which gave birth, in great measure, to the fantastic character of his performances. But the fervid *facility* of his *impromptus* could not be so accounted for. They must have been and were, in the notes, as well as in the words of his wild fantasias (for he not unfrequently accompanied himself with rhymed-verbal improvisations), the result of that intense mental collectedness and concentration to which I have previously alluded as observable only in particular moments of the highest artificial excitement. The words of one of these rhapsodies I have easily remembered. I was perhaps the more forcibly impressed with it as he gave it, because, in the under or mystic current of its meaning, I fancied that I perceived, and for the first time, a full consciousness on the part of Usher, of the tottering of his lofty reason upon her throne. The verses, which were entitled "The Haunted Palace," ran very nearly, if not accurately, thus:

I

In the greenest of our valleys,
　　By good angels tenanted,
Once a fair and stately palace—
　　Radiant palace—reared its head.
In the monarch Thought's dominion—
　　It stood there!
Never seraph spread a pinion
　　Over fabric half so fair.

II

Banners yellow, glorious, golden,
   On its roof did float and flow ;
(This—all this—was in the olden
   Time long ago)
And every gentle air that dallied,
   In that sweet day,
Along the ramparts plumed and pallid,
   A winged odour went away.

III

Wanderers in that happy valley
   Through two luminous windows saw
Spirits moving musically
   To a lute's well-tunèd law,
Round about a throne, where sitting
   (Porphyrogene !)
In state his glory well befitting,
   The ruler of the realm was seen.

IV

And all with pearl and ruby glowing
   Was the fair palace door,
Through which came flowing, flowing, flowing,
   And sparkling evermore,
A troop of Echoes whose sweet duty
   Was but to sing,
In voices of surpassing beauty,
   The wit and wisdom of their king.

V

But evil things, in robes of sorrow,
   Assailed the monarch's high estate ;
(Ah, let us mourn, for never morrow
   Shall dawn upon him, desolate !)

And, round about his home, the glory
    That blushed and bloomed
Is but a dim-remembered story
    Of the old time entombed.

VI

And travellers now within that valley,
    Through the red-litten windows, see
Vast forms that move fantastically
    To a discordant melody ;
While, like a rapid ghastly river,
    Through the pale door,
A hideous throng rush out for ever,
    And laugh—but smile no more.

I well remember that suggestions arising from this ballad led us into a train of thought wherein there became manifest an opinion of Usher's, which I mention not so much on account of its novelty (for other men * have thought thus), as on account of the pertinacity with which he maintained it. This opinion, in its general form, was that of the sentience of all vegetable things. But, in his disordered fancy, the idea had assumed a more daring character, and trespassed, under certain conditions, upon the kingdom of inorganisation. I lack words to express the full extent, or the earnest *abandon* of his persuasion. The belief, however, was connected (as I have previously hinted) with the grey stones of the home of his forefathers. The conditions of the sentience had been here, he imagined, fulfilled in the method of colloca-

* Watson, Dr. Percival, Spallanzani, and especially the Bishop of Llandaff—See " Chemical Essays," vol. v.

tion of these stones—in the order of their arrangement, as well as in that of the many *fungi* which overspread them, and of the decayed trees which stood around—above all, in the long undisturbed endurance of this arrangement, and in its reduplication in the still waters of the tarn. Its evidence— the evidence of the sentience—was to be seen, he said (and I here started as he spoke), in the gradual yet certain condensation of an atmosphere of their own about the waters and the walls. The result was discoverable, he added, in that silent yet importunate and terrible influence which for centuries had moulded the destinies of his family, and which made *him* what I now saw him—what he was. Such opinions need no comment, and I will make none.

Our books—the books which for years had formed no small portion of the mental existence of the invalid —were, as might be supposed, in strict keeping with this character of phantasm. We pored together over such works as the Ververt et Chartreuse of Gresset ; the Belphegor of Machiavelli ; the Heaven and Hell of Swedenborg ; the Subterranean Voyage of Nicholas Klimm by Holberg ; the Chiromancy of Robert Flud, of Jean D'Indaginé, and of De la Chambre ; the Journey into the Blue Distance of Tieck ; and the City of the Sun of Campanella. One favourite volume was a small octavo edition of the *Directorium Inquisitorum*, by the Dominican Eymeric de Gironne ; and there were passages in Pomponius Mela, about the old African Satyrs and Œgipans, over which Usher would sit dreaming for hours. His chief delight, however, was found in the perusal of an exceedingly rare and curious book in quarto Gothic—the manual of a forgotten church—the *Vigiliae Mortuorum secundum Chorum Ecclesiae Maguntinae.*

I could not help thinking of the wild ritual of this work, and of its probable influence upon the hypochondriac, when, one evening, having informed me abruptly that the lady Madeline was no more, he stated his intention of preserving her corpse for a fortnight (previously to its final interment), in one of the numerous vaults within the main walls of the building. The worldly reason, however, assigned for this singular proceeding was one which I did not feel at liberty to dispute. The brother had been led to his resolution (so he told me) by consideration of the unusual character of the malady of the deceased, of certain obtrusive and eager inquiries on the part of her medical man, and of the remote and exposed situation of the burial-ground of the family. I will not deny that when I called to mind the sinister countenance of the person whom I met upon the staircase on the day of my arrival at the house, I had no desire to oppose what I regarded as at best but a harmless and by no means an unnatural precaution.

At the request of Usher, I personally aided him in the arrangements for the temporary entombment. The body having been encoffined, we two alone bore it to its rest. The vault in which we placed it (and which had been so long unopened that our torches, half smothered in its oppressive atmosphere, gave us little opportunity for investigation) was small, damp, and entirely without means of admission for light, lying at great depth immediately beneath that portion of the building in which was my own sleeping apartment. It had been used apparently in remote feudal times for the worst purposes of a donjon-keep, and in later days as a place of deposit for powder or some other highly combustible substance, as a portion of its floor, and the whole interior of a long archway through which we reached it, were carefully sheathed with copper. The door, of massive iron, had been also similarly protected. Its immense weight caused an unusually sharp grating sound as it moved upon its hinges.

Having deposited our mournful burden upon tressels within this region of horror, we partially turned aside the yet unscrewed lid of the coffin and looked upon the face of the tenant. A striking similitude between the brother and sister now first arrested my attention, and Usher, divining perhaps my thoughts, murmured out some few words from which I learned that the deceased and himself had been twins and that sympathies of a scarcely intelligible nature had always existed between them. Our glances, however, rested not long upon the dead—for we could not regard her unawed. The disease which had thus entombed the lady in the maturity of youth had left, as usual in all maladies of a strictly cataleptical character, the mockery of a faint blush upon the bosom and the face, and that suspiciously lingering smile upon the lip which is so terrible in death. We replaced and screwed down the lid, and having secured the door of iron, made our way with toil into the scarcely less gloomy apartments of the upper portion of the house.

And now, some days of bitter grief having elapsed, an observable change came over the features of the mental disorder of my friend. His ordinary manner had vanished. His ordinary occupations were neglected or forgotten. He roamed from chamber to chamber with hurried, unequal, and objectless step. The pallor of his countenance had assumed if possible a more ghastly hue—but the luminousness of his eye had utterly gone out. The once occasional huskiness of his tone was heard no more, and a tremulous quaver, as if of extreme terror, habitually characterised his utterance. There were times indeed when I thought his unceasingly agitated mind was labouring with some oppressive secret, to divulge which he struggled for the necessary courage. At times again I was obliged to resolve all into the mere inexplicable vagaries of madness, for I beheld him gazing upon vacancy for long hours in an attitude of the profoundest attention, as if listening to some imaginary sound. It was no wonder that his condition terrified —that it infected me. I felt creeping upon me, by slow yet certain degrees, the wild influences of his own fantastic yet impressive superstitions.

It was especially upon retiring to bed late in the night of the seventh or eighth day after the placing of the lady Madeline within the donjon that I experienced the full power of such feelings. Sleep came not near my couch—while the hours waned and waned away. I struggled to reason off the nervousness which had dominion over me. I endeavoured to believe that much if not all of what I felt was due to the bewildering influence of the gloomy furniture of the room—of the dark and tattered draperies which, tortured into motion by the breath of a rising tempest, swayed fitfully to and fro upon the walls, and rustled uneasily about the decorations of the bed. But my efforts were fruitless. An irrepressible tremor gradually pervaded my frame, and at length there sat upon my very heart an incubus of utterly causeless alarm. Shaking this off with a gasp and a struggle I uplifted myself upon the pillows, and peering earnestly within the intense darkness of the chamber, hearkened—I know not why, except that an instinctive spirit prompted me—to certain low and indefinite sounds which came, through the pauses of the storm, at long intervals, I knew not whence. Overpowered by an intense sentiment of horror, unaccountable yet unendurable, I threw on my clothes with haste (for I felt that I should sleep no more during the night), and endeavoured to arouse myself from the pitiable condition into which I had fallen, by pacing rapidly to and fro through the apartment.

I had taken but few turns in this manner, when a light step on an adjoining staircase arrested my attention. I presently recognised it as that of Usher. In an instant afterward he rapped with a gentle touch at my door, and entered, bearing a lamp. His countenance was as usual cadaverously wan—but, moreover, there was a species of mad hilarity in his eyes—an evidently restrained *hysteria* in his whole demeanour. His air appalled me—but anything was preferable to the solitude which I had so long endured, and I even welcomed his presence as a relief.

" And you have not seen it ? " he said abruptly,

after having stared about him for some moments in silence—" you have not then seen it ?—but, stay ! you shall." Thus speaking, and having carefully shaded his lamp, he hurried to one of the casements, and threw it freely open to the storm.

The impetuous fury of the entering gust nearly lifted us from our feet. It was indeed a tempestuous yet sternly beautiful night, and one wildly singular in its terror and its beauty. A whirlwind had apparently collected its force in our vicinity, for there were frequent and violent alterations in the direction of the wind, and the exceeding density of the clouds (which hung so low as to press upon the turrets of the house) did not prevent our perceiving the life-like velocity with which they flew careering from all points against each other without passing away into the distance.

I say that even their exceeding density did not prevent our perceiving this—yet we had no glimpse of the moon or stars—nor was there any flashing forth of the lightning. But the under surfaces of the huge masses of agitated vapour, as well as all terrestrial objects immediately around us, were glowing in the unnatural light of a faintly luminous and distinctly visible gaseous exhalation which hung about and en-shrouded the mansion.

" You must not—you shall not behold this ! " said I, shudderingly, to Usher, as I led him with a gentle violence from the window to a seat. " These appear-ances which bewilder you are merely electrical pheno-mena not uncommon, or it may be that they have their ghastly origin in the rank miasma of the tarn.

Let us close this casement; the air is chilling and dangerous to your frame. Here is one of your favourite romances. I will read, and you shall listen; and so we will pass away this terrible night together."

The antique volume which I had taken up was the "Mad Trist" of Sir Launcelot Canning, but I had called it a favourite of Usher's more in sad jest than in earnest; for in truth, there is little in its uncouth and unimaginative prolixity which could have had interest for the lofty and spiritual ideality of my friend. It was, however, the only book immediately at hand, and I indulged a vague hope that the excitement which now agitated the hypochondriac might find relief (for the history of mental disorder is full of similar anomalies) even in the extremeness of the folly which I should read. Could I have judged, indeed, by the wild overstrained air of vivacity with which he hearkened, or apparently hearkened, to the words of the tale, I might well have congratulated myself upon the success of my design.

I had arrived at that well-known portion of the story where Ethelred, the hero of the Trist, having sought in vain for peaceable admission into the dwelling of the hermit, proceeds to make good an entrance by force. Here, it will be remembered, the words of the narrative run thus:

"And Ethelred, who was by nature of a doughty heart, and who was now mighty withal, on account of the powerfulness of the wine which he had drunken, waited no longer to hold parley with the hermit, who in sooth was of an obstinate and maliceful turn, but feeling the rain upon his shoulders, and fearing the

rising of the tempest, uplifted his mace outright, and
with blows made quickly room in the plankings of the
door for his gauntleted hand; and now pulling therewith sturdily, he so cracked and ripped, and tore all
asunder, that the noise of the dry and hollow-sounding wood alarummed and reverberated throughout
the forest."

At the termination of this sentence I started, and
for a moment paused, for it appeared to me (although
I at once concluded that my excited fancy had
deceived me) that from some very remote portion
of the mansion there came indistinctly to my ears
what might have been, in its exact similarity of
character, the echo (but a stifled and dull one certainly) of the very cracking and ripping sound which
Sir Launcelot had so particularly described. It was
beyond doubt the coincidence alone which had arrested
my attention; for amid the rattling of the sashes of
the casements, and the ordinary commingled noises
of the still increasing storm, the sound in itself had
nothing surely which should have interested or disturbed me. I continued the story:

"But the good champion Ethelred, now entering
within the door, was sore enraged and amazed to
perceive no signal of the maliceful hermit; but in
the stead thereof, a dragon of a scaly and prodigious
demeanour, and of a fiery tongue, which sate in
guard before a palace of gold, with a floor of silver;
and upon the wall there hung a shield of shining
brass with this legend enwritten—

"Who entereth herein, a conqueror hath bin;
Who slayeth the dragon, the shield he shall win.

And Ethelred uplifted his mace, and struck upon the head of the dragon, which fell before him, and gave up his pesty breath, with a shriek so horrid and harsh, and withal so piercing, that Ethelred had fain to close his ears with his hands against the dreadful noise of it, the like whereof was never before heard.''

Here again I paused abruptly, and now with a feeling of wild amazement—for there could be no doubt whatever that in this instance I did actually hear (although from what direction it proceeded I found it impossible to say) a low and apparently distant, but harsh, protracted, and most unusual screaming or grating sound—the exact counterpart of what my fancy had already conjured up for the dragon's unnatural shriek as described by the romancer.

Oppressed, as I certainly was upon the occurrence of this second and most extraordinary coincidence, by a thousand conflicting sensations, in which wonder and extreme terror were predominant, I still retained sufficient presence of mind to avoid exciting by any observation the sensitive nervousness of my companion. I was by no means certain that he had noticed the sounds in question, although, assuredly, a strange alteration had during the last few minutes taken place in his demeanour. From a position fronting my own, he had gradually brought round his chair, so as to sit with his face to the door of the chamber ; and thus I could but partially perceive his features, although I saw that his lips trembled as if he were murmuring inaudibly. His head had dropped upon his breast, yet I knew that he was not asleep, from the wide and rigid opening of the eye as I caught a glance of it in profile. The motion of his body too was at variance with this idea,—for he rocked from side to side with a gentle yet constant and uniform sway. Having rapidly taken notice of all this, I resumed the narrative of Sir Launcelot, which thus proceeded :

" And now, the champion having escaped from the terrible fury of the dragon, bethinking himself of the brazen shield, and of the breaking up of the enchantment which was upon it, removed the carcase from out of the way before him, and approached valorously over the silver pavement of the castle to where the shield was upon the wall ; which in sooth tarried not for his full coming, but fell down at his feet upon the silver floor with a mighty great and terrible ringing sound."

No sooner had these syllables passed my lips, than —as if a shield of brass had indeed at the moment fallen heavily upon a floor of silver—I became aware of a distinct, hollow, metallic, and clangorous, yet apparently muffled, reverberation. Completely unnerved, I leaped to my feet, but the measured rocking movement of Usher was undisturbed. I rushed to the chair in which he sat. His eyes were bent fixedly before him, and throughout his whole countenance there reigned a stony rigidity. But, as I placed my hand upon his shoulder, there came a strong shudder over his whole person ; a sickly smile quivered about his lips, and I saw that he spoke in a low, hurried, and gibbering murmur, as if unconscious of my presence. Bending closely over him, I at length drank in the hideous import of his words.

" Not hear it ?—yes, I hear it, and *have* heard it.
Long—long—long—many minutes, many hours, many
days, have I heard it—yet I dared not—oh, pity me,
miserable wretch that I am !—I dared not—I *dared*
not speak ! *We have put her living in the tomb !* Said
I not that my senses were acute ? I *now* tell you that
I heard her first feeble movements in the hollow coffin.
I heard them—many, many days ago—yet I dared
not—*I dared not speak !* And now—to-night—
Ethelred—ha ! ha !—the breaking of the hermit's
door, and the death-cry of the dragon, and the
clangour of the shield !—say, rather, the rending of
her coffin, and the grating of the iron hinges of her
prison, and her struggles within the coppered archway of the vault. O whither shall I fly ? Will she
not be here anon ? Is she not hurrying to upbraid
me for my haste ? Have I not heard her footstep on
the stair ? Do I not distinguish that heavy and
horrible beating of her heart ? Madman ! " Here
he sprang furiously to his feet, and shrieked out his
syllables, as if in the effort he were giving up his
soul—" *Madman ! I tell you that she now stands
without the door !* "

As if in the superhuman energy of his utterance
there had been found the potency of a spell—the huge
antique panels to which the speaker pointed, threw
slowly back, upon the instant, their ponderous and
ebony jaws. It was the work of the rushing gust—
but then without those doors there *did* stand the lofty
and enshrouded figure of the lady Madeline of Usher.
There was blood upon her white robes, and the
evidence of some bitter struggle upon every portion

of her emaciated frame. For a moment she remained trembling and reeling to and fro upon the threshold —then, with a low moaning cry, fell heavily inward upon the person of her brother, and in her violent and now final death-agonies, bore him to the floor a corpse, and a victim to the terrors he had anticipated.

From that chamber and from that mansion I fled aghast. The storm was still abroad in all its wrath as I found myself crossing the old causeway. Suddenly there shot along the path a wild light, and I turned to see whence a gleam so unusual could have issued, for the vast house and its shadows were alone behind me. The radiance was that of the full, setting, and blood-red moon, which now shone vividly through that once barely-discernible fissure, of which I have before spoken as extending from the roof of the building in a zigzag direction to the base. While I gazed, this fissure rapidly widened ; there came a fierce breath of the whirlwind ; the entire orb of the satellite burst at once upon my sight ; my brain reeled as I saw the mighty walls rushing asunder ; there was a long tumultuous shouting sound like the voice of a thousand waters, and the deep and dark tarn at my feet closed sullenly and silently over the fragments of the " *House of Usher*."

V

WILLIAM WILSON

What say of it ? what says CONSCIENCE grim,
That spectre in my path ?
                        W. Chamberlayn's " Pharonnida "

LET me call myself, for the present, William Wilson.
The fair page now lying before me need not be sullied
with my real appellation. This has been already too
much an object for the scorn, for the horror, for the
detestation of my race. To the uttermost regions of
the globe have not the indignant winds bruited its
unparalleled infamy ? O outcast of all outcasts most
abandoned ! to the earth art thou not for ever dead ?
to its honours, to its flowers, to its golden aspirations ?
—and a cloud, dense, dismal, and limitless, does it
not hang eternally between thy hopes and heaven ?

I would not, if I could, here or to-day, embody a
record of my later years of unspeakable misery and
unpardonable crime. This epoch—these later years
—took unto themselves a sudden elevation in turpi-
tude, whose origin alone it is my present purpose to
assign. Men usually grow base by degrees. From me
in an instant all virtue dropped bodily as a mantle.
From comparatively trivial wickedness I passed, with
the stride of a giant, into more than the enormities
of an Elagabalus. What chance—what one event
brought this evil thing to pass, bear with me while
I relate. Death approaches, and the shadow which

foreruns him has thrown a softening influence over my spirit. I long in passing through the dim valley for the sympathy, I had nearly said for the pity, of my fellow-men. I would fain have them believe that I have been in some measure the slave of circumstances beyond human control. I would wish them to seek out for me, in the details I am about to give, some little oasis of *fatality* amid a wilderness of error. I would have them allow, what they cannot refrain from allowing, that although temptation may have erewhile existed as great, man was never *thus* at least tempted before, certainly never *thus* fell. And is it therefore that he has never thus suffered ? Have I not indeed been living in a dream ? And am I not now dying a victim to the horror and the mystery of the wildest of all sublunary visions ?

I am the descendant of a race whose imaginative and easily excitable temperament has at all times rendered them remarkable ; and in my earliest infancy I gave evidence of having fully inherited the family character. As I advanced in years it was more strongly developed, becoming for many reasons a cause of serious disquietude to my friends, and of positive injury to myself. I grew self-willed, addicted to the wildest caprices, and a prey to the most ungovernable passions. Weak-minded, and beset with constitutional infirmities akin to my own, my parents could do but little to check the evil propensities which distinguished me. Some feeble and ill-directed efforts resulted in complete failure on their part, and of course in total triumph on mine. Thenceforward my voice was a household law, and at an age when few children have abandoned their leading-strings, I was left to the guidance of my own will, and became in all but name the master of my own actions.

My earliest recollections of a school-life are connected with a large rambling Elizabethan house, in a misty-looking village of England, where were a vast number of gigantic and gnarled trees, and where all the houses were excessively ancient. In truth, it was a dream-like and spirit-soothing place that venerable old town. At this moment, in fancy, I feel the refreshing chilliness of its deeply-shadowed avenues, inhale the fragrance of its thousand shrubberies, and thrill anew with indefinable delight at the deep hollow note of the church-bell, breaking each hour with sullen and sudden roar upon the stillness of the dusky atmosphere in which the fretted Gothic steeple lay imbedded and asleep.

It gives me perhaps as much of pleasure as I can now in any manner experience to dwell upon minute recollections of the school and its concerns. Steeped in misery as I am—misery, alas! only too real—I shall be pardoned for seeking relief, however slight and temporary, in the weakness of a few rambling details. These, moreover, utterly trivial, and even ridiculous in themselves, assume to my fancy adventitious importance, as connected with a period and a locality when and where I recognise the first ambiguous monitions of the destiny which afterwards so fully overshadowed me. Let me then remember.

The house, I have said, was old and irregular. The grounds were extensive, and a high and solid brick wall, topped with a bed of mortar and broken glass encompassed the whole. This prison-like rampart formed the limit of our domain : beyond it we saw but thrice a week, once every Saturday afternoon, when, attended by two ushers, we were permitted to take brief walks in a body through some of the neighbouring fields ; and twice during Sunday, when we were paraded in the same formal manner to the morning and evening service in the one church of the village. Of this church the principal of our school was pastor. With how deep a spirit of wonder and perplexity was I wont to regard him from our remote pew in the gallery, as with step solemn and slow he ascended the pulpit ! This reverend man, with countenance so demurely benign, with robes so glossy and so clerically flowing, with wig so minutely powdered, so rigid and so vast—could this be he who, of late, with sour visage, and in snuffy habiliments, administered, ferule in hand, the Draconian laws of the academy ? O gigantic paradox, too utterly monstrous for solution !

At an angle of the ponderous wall frowned a more ponderous gate. It was riveted and studded with iron bolts, and surmounted with jagged iron spikes. What impressions of deep awe did it inspire ! It was never opened save for the three periodical egressions and ingressions already mentioned ; then in every creak of its mighty hinges we found a plenitude of mystery, a world of matter for solemn remark, or for more solemn meditation.

The extensive enclosure was irregular in form, having many capacious recesses. Of these, three or four of the largest constituted the play-ground. It was level, and covered with fine hard gravel. I well remember it had no trees nor benches, nor anything similar within it. Of course it was in the rear of the house. In front lay a small parterre, planted with box and other shrubs, but through this sacred division we passed only upon rare occasions indeed, such as a first advent to school or final departure thence, or perhaps, when a parent, or friend having called for us, we joyfully took our way home for the Christmas or Midsummer holidays.

But the house !—how quaint an old building was this ! to me how veritably a palace of enchantment ! There was really no end to its windings, to its incomprehensible sub-divisions. It was difficult, at any given time, to say with certainty upon which of its two stories one happened to be. From each room to every other there were sure to be found three or four steps either in ascent or descent. Then the lateral branches were innumerable, inconceivable, and so returning in upon themselves that our most exact ideas in regard to the whole mansion were not very far different from those with which we pondered upon infinity. During the five years of my residence here I was never able to ascertain with precision in what remote locality lay the little sleeping apartment assigned to myself and some eighteeen or twenty other scholars.

The school-room was the largest in the house, I could not help thinking, in the world. It was very long, narrow, and dismally low, with pointed Gothic windows and a ceiling of oak. In a remote and terror-inspiring angle was a square enclosure of eight or ten feet, comprising the *sanctum*, " during hours," of our principal, the Reverend Dr. Bransby. It was a solid structure, with massy door, sooner than open which in the absence of the " dominie " we would all have willingly perished by the *peine forte et dure*. In other angles were two other similar boxes, far less reverenced, indeed, but still greatly matters of awe. One of these was the pulpit of the " classical " usher, one of the " English and mathematical." Interspersed about the room, crossing and re-crossing in endless irregularity, were innumerable benches and desks, black, ancient, and time-worn, piled desperately with much-bethumbed books, and so beseamed with initial letters, names at full length, grotesque figures, and other multiplied efforts of the knife, as to have entirely lost what little of original form might have been their portion in days long departed. A huge bucket with water stood at one extremity of the room, and a clock of stupendous dimensions at the other.

Encompassed by the massy walls of this venerable academy, I passed, yet not in a tedium or disgust, the years of the third lustrum of my life. The teeming brain of childhood requires no external world of incident to occupy or amuse it ; and the apparently dismal monotony of a school was replete with more intense excitement than my riper youth has derived from luxury, or my full manhood from crime. Yet I must believe that my first mental development had in it much of the uncommon—even much of the *outré*. Upon mankind at large the events of very early existence rarely leave in mature age any definite impression. All is grey shadow—a weak and irregular remembrance —an indistinct regathering of feeble pleasures and phantasmagoric pains. With me this is not so. In childhood I must have felt with the energy of a man what I now find stamped upon memory in lines as vivid, as deep, and as durable as the *exergues* of the Carthaginian medals.

Yet in fact—in the fact of the world's view—how little was there to remember! The morning's awakening, the nightly summons to bed; the connings, the recitations; the periodical half-holidays, and perambulations; the playground, with its broils, its pastimes, its intrigues;—these, by a mental sorcery long forgotten, were made to involve a wilderness of sensation, a world of rich incident, a universe of varied emotion, of excitement the most passionate and spirit-stirring. "*O le bon temps, que ce siècle de fer!*"

In truth, the ardour, the enthusiasm, and the imperiousness of my disposition, soon rendered me a marked character among my schoolmates, and by slow but natural gradations gave me an ascendency over all not greatly older than myself—over all with a single exception. This exception was found in the person of a scholar, who, although no relation, bore the same christian and surname as myself, a circumstance, in fact, little remarkable; for notwithstanding a noble descent, mine was one of those every-day appellations which seem, by prescriptive right, to have been, time out of mind, the common property of the mob. In this narrative I have therefore designated myself as William Wilson—a fictitious title not very dissimilar to the real. My namesake alone, of those who in school phraseology constituted "our set," presumed to compete with me in the studies of the class—in the sports and

broils of the playground—to refuse implicit belief in
my assertions, and submission to my will—indeed, to
interfere with my arbitrary dictation in any respect
whatsoever. If there is on earth a supreme and unqualified despotism, it is the despotism of a master-
mind in boyhood over the less energetic spirits of its
companions.

Wilson's rebellion was to me a source of the greatest
embarrassment : the more so as, in spite of the bravado
with which in public I made a point of treating him
and his pretensions, I secretly felt that I feared him,
and could not help thinking the equality which he
maintained so easily with myself a proof of his true
superiority, since not to be overcome cost me a perpetual struggle. Yet this superiority—even this
equality—was in truth acknowledged by no one but
myself ; our associates, by some unaccountable blind-
ness, seemed not even to suspect it. Indeed, his com-
petition, his resistance, and especially his impertinent
and dogged interference with my purposes, were not
more pointed than private. He appeared to be
destitute alike of the ambition which urged, and of the
passionate energy of mind which enabled me to excel.
In his rivalry he might have been supposed actuated
solely by a whimsical desire to thwart, astonish, or
mortify myself ; although there were times when I
could not help observing, with a feeling made up of
wonder, abasement, and pique, that he mingled with
his injuries, his insults, or his contradictions, a certain
most inappropriate, and assuredly most unwelcome
affectionateness of manner. I could only conceive this
singular behaviour to arise from a consummate self-

conceit assuming the vulgar airs of patronage and protection.

Perhaps it was this latter trait in Wilson's conduct, conjoined with our identity of name, and the mere accident of our having entered the school upon the same day, which set afloat the notion that we were brothers among the senior classes in the academy. These do not usually inquire with much strictness into the affairs of their juniors. I have before said, or should have said, that Wilson was not, in the most remote degree, connected with my family. But assuredly if we *had* been brothers we must have been twins ; for, after leaving Dr. Bransby's, I casually learned that my namesake was born on the nineteenth of January 1813—and this is a somewhat remarkable coincidence, for the day is precisely that of my own nativity.

It may seem strange that in spite of the continual anxiety occasioned me by the rivalry of Wilson, and his intolerable spirit of contradiction, I could not bring myself to hate him altogether. We had, to be sure, nearly every day a quarrel, in which, yielding me publicly the palm of victory, he in some manner contrived to make me feel that it was he who had deserved it, yet a sense of pride on my part and a veritable dignity on his own, kept us always upon what are called " speaking terms," while there were many points of strong congeniality in our tempers, operating to awake in me a sentiment which our position alone, perhaps, prevented from ripening into friendship. It is difficult indeed to define or even to describe my real feelings towards him. They formed a motley and heterogeneous admixture ; some petulant animosity, which was not yet hatred, some esteem, more respect, much fear, with a world of uneasy curiosity. To the moralist it will be unnecessary to say in addition that Wilson and myself were the most inseparable of companions.

It was no doubt the anomalous state of affairs existing between us which turned all my attacks upon him (and they were many, either open or covert) into the channel of banter or practical joke (giving pain while assuming the aspect of mere fun), rather than into a more serious and determined hostility. But my endeavours on this head were by no means uniformly successful, even when my plans were the most wittily concocted ; for my namesake had much about him in character of that unassuming and quiet austerity which, while enjoying the poignancy of its own jokes, has no heel of Achilles in itself, and absolutely refuses to be laughed at. I could find indeed but one vulnerable point, and that lying in a personal peculiarity, arising perhaps from constitutional disease, would have been spared by any antagonist less at his wit's end than myself ; my rival had a weakness in the faucial or guttural organs which precluded him from raising his voice at any time *above a very low whisper*. Of this defect I did not fail to take what poor advantage lay in my power.

Wilson's retaliations in kind were many ; and there was one form of his practical wit that disturbed me beyond measure. How his sagacity first discovered at all that so petty a thing would vex me is a question I never could solve, but having discovered, he habitu-

ally practised the annoyance. I had always felt aversion to my uncourtly patronymic and its very common,
if not plebeian prænomen. The words were venom in
my ears ; and when, upon the day of my arrival, a
second William Wilson came also to the academy, I
felt angry with him for bearing the name, and doubly
disgusted with the name because a stranger bore it,
who would be the cause of its twofold repetition, who
would be constantly in my presence, and whose concerns, in the ordinary routine of the school business,
must inevitably, on account of the detestable coincidence, be often confounded with my own.

The feeling of vexation thus engendered grew
stronger with every circumstance tending to show
resemblance, moral or physical, between my rival and
myself. I had not then discovered the remarkable fact
that we were of the same age ; but I saw that we were
of the same height, and I perceived that we were even
singularly alike in general contour of person and outline of feature. I was galled, too, by the rumour touching a relationship, which had grown current in the
upper forms. In a word, nothing could more seriously
disturb me (although I scrupulously concealed such
disturbance), than any allusion to a similarity of mind,
person, or condition existing between us. But, in
truth, I had no reason to believe that (with the exception of the matter of relationship, and in the case
of Wilson himself) this similarity had ever been made
a subject of comment or even observed at all by our
school-fellows. That *he* observed it in all its bearings,
and as fixedly as I, was apparent ; but that he could
discover in such circumstances so fruitful a field of

annoyance can only be attributed, as I said before, to his more than ordinary penetration.

His cue, which was to perfect an imitation of myself, lay both in words and in actions, and most admirably did he play his part. My dress it was an easy matter to copy ; my gait and general manner were without difficulty appropriated ; in spite of his constitutional defect, even my voice did not escape him. My louder tones were of course unattempted, but then the key, it was identical ; *and his singular whisper, it grew the very echo of my own.*

How greatly this most exquisite portraiture harassed me (for it could not justly be termed a caricature), I will not now venture to describe. I had but one consolation—in the fact that the imitation, apparently, was noticed by myself alone, and that I had to endure only the knowing and strangely sarcastic smiles of my namesake himself. Satisfied with having produced in my bosom the intended effect he seemed to chuckle in secret over the sting he had inflicted, and was characteristically disregardful of the public applause which the success of his witty endeavours might have so easily elicited. That the school, indeed, did not feel his design, perceive its accomplishment, and participate in his sneer, was for many anxious months a riddle I could not resolve. Perhaps the *gradation* of his copy rendered it not so readily perceptible, or more possibly I owed my security to the masterly air of the copyist, who, disdaining the letter (which in a painting is all the obtuse can see), gave but the full spirit of his original for my individual contemplation and chagrin.

I have already more than once spoken of the disgusting air of patronage which he assumed toward me, and of his frequent officious interference with my will. This interference often took the ungracious character of advice—advice not openly given but hinted or insinuated. I received it with a repugnance which gained strength as I grew in years. Yet at this distant day, let me do him the simple justice to acknowledge that I can recall no occasion when the suggestions of my rival were on the side of those errors or follies so usual to his immature age and seeming inexperience; that his moral sense, at least, if not his general talents and worldly wisdom, was far keener than my own; and that I might to-day have been a better, and thus a happier man, had I less frequently rejected the counsels embodied in those meaning whispers which I then but too cordially hated and too bitterly despised.

As it was, I at length grew restive in the extreme under his distasteful supervision, and daily resented more and more openly what I considered his intolerable arrogance. I have said that in the first years of our connection as schoolmates, my feelings in regard to him might have been easily ripened into friendship; but, in the latter months of my residence at the academy, although the intrusion of his ordinary manner had, beyond doubt, in some measure abated, my sentiments in nearly similar proportion partook very much of positive hatred. Upon one occasion he saw this, I think, and afterwards avoided, or made a show of avoiding me.

It was about the same period, if I remember aright, that, in an altercation of violence with him, in which he was more than usually thrown off his guard, and spoke and acted with an openness of demeanour rather foreign to his nature, I discovered, or fancied I discovered, in his accent, his air, and general appearance, a something which first startled, and then deeply interested me, by bringing to mind dim visions of my earliest infancy, wild, confused, and thronging memories of a time when memory herself was yet unborn. I cannot better describe the sensation which oppressed me than by saying that I could with difficulty shake off the belief of my having been acquainted with the being who stood before me at some epoch very long ago, some point of the past even infinitely remote. The delusion, however, faded rapidly as it came, and I mention it at all but to define the day of the last conversation I there held with my singular namesake.

The huge old house, with its countless subdivisions, had several large chambers communicating with each other, where slept the greater number of the students. There were, however (as must necessarily happen in a building so awkwardly planned), many little nooks or recesses, the odds and ends of the structure, and these the economic ingenuity of Dr. Bransby had also fitted up as dormitories, although, being the merest closets, they were capable of accommodating but a single individual. One of these small apartments was occupied by Wilson.

One night, about the close of my fifth year at the school, and immediately after the altercation just mentioned, finding every one wrapped in sleep, I arose from bed, and, lamp in hand, stole through a wilderness of narrow passages from my own bedroom to that of my rival. I had long been plotting one of those ill-natured pieces of practical wit at his expense in which I had hitherto been so uniformly unsuccessful. It was my intention now to put my scheme in operation, and I resolved to make him feel the whole extent of the malice with which I was imbued. Having reached his closet I noiselessly entered, leaving the lamp, with a shade over it, on the outside. I advanced a step and listened to the sound of his tranquil breathing. Assured of his being asleep, I returned, took the light, and with it again approached the bed. Close curtains were around it, which, in the prosecution of my plan, I slowly and quietly withdrew, when the bright rays fell vividly upon the sleeper, and my eyes, at the same moment, upon his countenance. I looked, and a numbness, an iciness of feeling, instantly pervaded my frame. My breast heaved, my knees tottered, my whole spirit became possessed with an objectless yet intolerable horror. Gasping for breath I lowered the lamp in still nearer proximity to the face. Were these —*these* the lineaments of William Wilson? I saw, indeed, that they were his, but I shook as if with a fit of the ague in fancying they were not. What *was* there about them to confound me in this manner? I gazed, while my brain reeled with a multitude of incoherent thoughts. Not thus he appeared, assuredly not *thus*, in the vivacity of his waking hours. The same name, the same contour of person, the same day of arrival at the academy; and then his dogged and meaningless imitation of my gait, my voice, my habits, and my manner. Was it, in truth, within the bounds of human possibility that *what I now saw* was the result merely of the habitual practice of this sarcastic imitation. Awe-stricken, and with a creeping shudder, I extinguished the lamp, passed silently from the chamber, and left at once the halls of that old academy, never to enter them again.

After a lapse of some months, spent at home in mere idleness, I found myself a student at Eton. The brief interval had been sufficient to enfeeble my remembrance of the events at Dr. Bransby's, or at least to effect a material change in the nature of the feelings with which I remembered them. The truth, the tragedy, of the drama was no more. I could now find room to doubt the evidence of my senses, and seldom called up the subject at all but with wonder at the extent of human credulity, and a smile at the vivid force of the imagination which I hereditarily possessed. Neither was this species of scepticism likely to be diminished by the character of the life I led at Eton. The vortex of thoughtless folly into which I there so immediately and so recklessly plunged washed away all but the froth of my past hours, engulfed at once every solid or serious impression, and left to memory only the veriest levities of a former existence.

I do not wish, however, to trace the course of my miserable profligacy here—a profligacy which set at defiance the laws, while it eluded the vigilance of the institution. Three years of folly, passed without profit, had but given me rooted habits of vice, and added, in a somewhat unusual degree, to my bodily stature, when, after a week of soulless dissipation, I invited a small party of the most dissolute students to a secret carousal in my chambers. We met at a late hour of the night, for our debaucheries were to be faithfully protracted until morning. The wine flowed freely, and there were not wanting other and perhaps more dangerous seductions, so that the grey dawn had already faintly appeared in the east, while our delirious extravagance was at its height. Madly flushed with cards and intoxication, I was in the act of insisting upon a toast of more than wonted profanity when my attention was suddenly diverted by the violent, although partial, unclosing of the door of the apartment, and by the eager voice of a servant from without. He said that some person, apparently in great haste, demanded to speak with me in the hall.

Wildly excited with wine, the unexpected interruption rather delighted than surprised me. I staggered forward at once, and a few steps brought me to the vestibule of the building. In this low and small room there hung no lamp, and now no light at all was admitted, save that of the exceedingly feeble dawn which made its way through the semi-circular window. As I put my foot over the threshold I became aware of the figure of a youth about my own height, and habited in a white kerseymere morning frock, cut in the novel fashion of the one I myself wore at the moment. This the faint light enabled me to perceive, but the features of his face I could not distinguish. Upon my entering he strode hurriedly up to me, and seizing me by the arm with a gesture of petulant impatience, whispered the words "William Wilson!" in my ear.

I grew perfectly sober in an instant.

There was that in the manner of the stranger, and in the tremulous shake of his uplifted finger, as he held it between my eyes and the light, which filled me with unqualified amazement ; but it was not this which had so violently moved me. It was the pregnancy of solemn admonition in the singular, low, hissing utterance, and, above all, it was the character, the tone, *the key*, of those few, simple, and familiar, yet *whispered* syllables, which came with a thousand thronging memories of by-gone days, and struck upon my soul with the shock of a galvanic battery. Ere I could recover the use of my senses he was gone.

Although this event failed not of a vivid effect upon my disordered imagination, yet was it evanescent as vivid. For some weeks, indeed, I busied myself in earnest inquiry, or was wrapped in a cloud of morbid speculation. I did not pretend to disguise from my perception the identity of the singular individual who thus perseveringly interfered with my affairs, and harassed me with his insinuated counsel. But who and what was this Wilson ?—and whence came he ?—and what were his purposes ? Upon neither of these points could I be satisfied—merely ascertaining in regard to him, that a sudden accident in his family had caused his removal from Dr. Bransby's academy on the afternoon of the day in which I myself had eloped. But in a brief period I ceased to think upon the subject, my attention being all absorbed in a contemplated departure for Oxford. Thither I soon went, the uncalculating vanity of my parents furnishing me with an outfit and annual establishment which would enable me to indulge at will in the luxury already so dear to my heart—to vie in profuseness of expenditure with the haughtiest heirs of the wealthiest earldoms in Great Britain.

Excited by such appliances to vice, my constitutional temperament broke forth with redoubled ardour, and I spurned even the common restraints of decency in the mad infatuation of my revels. But it were absurd to pause in the detail of my extravagance. Let it suffice, that among spendthrifts I out-Heroded Herod, and that giving name to a multitude of novel follies, I added no brief appendix to the long catalogue of vices then usual in the most dissolute university of Europe.

It could hardly be credited, however, that I had, even here, so utterly fallen from the gentlemanly estate as to seek acquaintance with the vilest arts of the gambler by profession, and having become an adept in his despicable science, to practise it habitually as a means of increasing my already enormous income at the expense of the weak-minded among my fellow-collegians. Such, nevertheless, was the fact ; and the very enormity of this offence against all manly and honourable sentiment proved, beyond doubt, the main, if not the sole reason of the impunity with which it was committed. Who, indeed, among my most abandoned associates would not rather have disputed the clearest evidence of his senses than have suspected of such courses the gay, the frank, the generous William Wilson—the noblest and most liberal commoner at Oxford—him whose follies (said his parasites) were but the follies of youth and unbridled fancy—whose errors but inimitable whim—whose darkest vice but a careless and dashing extravagance ?

I had been now two years successfully busied in this way when there came to the university a young *parvenu* nobleman, Glendinning—rich, said report, as Herodes Atticus—his riches, too, as easily acquired. I soon found him of weak intellect, and of course marked him as a fitting subject for my skill. I frequently engaged him in play, and contrived with the gambler's usual art to let him win considerable sums, the more effectually to entangle him in my snares. At length, my schemes being ripe, I met him (with the full intention that this meeting should be final and decisive) at the chambers of a fellow-commoner (Mr. Preston) equally intimate with both, but who, to do him justice, entertained not even a remote suspicion of my design. To give to this a better colouring I had contrived to have assembled a party of some eight or ten, and was solicitously careful that the introduction of cards should appear accidental, and originate in the proposal of my contemplated dupe himself. To be brief upon a vile topic, none of the low finesse was omitted, so customary upon similar occasions, that it is a just matter for wonder how any are still found so besotted as to fall its victim.

We had protracted our sitting far into the night, and I had at length effected the manœuvre of getting Glendinning as my sole antagonist. The game, too, was my favourite *écarté*. The rest of the company, interested in the extent of our play, had abandoned their own cards, and were standing around us as spectators. The *parvenu*, who had been induced by my artifices in the early part of the evening to drink deeply, now shuffled, dealt, or played, with a wild nervousness of manner for which his intoxication I thought might partially but could not altogether account. In a very short period he had become my debtor to a large amount, when, having taken a long draught of port, he did precisely what I had been coolly anticipating—he proposed to double our already extravagant stakes. With a well-feigned show of reluctance, and not until after my repeated refusal had seduced him into some angry words which gave a colour of *pique* to my compliance, did I finally comply. The result of course did but prove how entirely the prey was in my toils : in less than an hour he had quadrupled his debt. For some time his countenance had been losing the florid tinge lent it by the wine, but now to my astonishment I perceived that it had grown to a pallor truly fearful. I say to my astonishment. Glendinning had been represented to my eager inquiries as immeasurably wealthy ; and the sums which he had as yet lost, although in themselves vast, could not, I supposed, very seriously annoy, much less so violently affect him. That he was overcome by the wine just swallowed was the idea which most readily presented itself ; and, rather with a view to the preservation of my own character in the eyes of my associates, than from any less interested motive, I was about to insist peremptorily upon a discontinuance of the play, when some expressions at my elbow from among the company, and an ejaculation evincing utter despair on the part of Glendinning, gave me to understand that I had effected his total ruin under circumstances which, rendering him an object for the pity of all, should have protected him from the ill offices even of a fiend.

What now might have been my conduct it is difficult to say. The pitiable condition of my dupe had thrown an air of embarrassed gloom over all, and for some moments a profound silence was maintained, during which I could not help feeling my cheeks tingle with the many burning glances of scorn or reproach cast upon me by the less abandoned of the party. I will even own that an intolerable weight of anxiety was a brief instant lifted from my bosom by the sudden and extraordinary interruption which ensued. The wide heavy folding-doors of the apartment were all at once thrown open to their full extent, with a vigorous and rushing impetuosity that extinguished, as if by magic, every candle in the room. Their light, in dying, enabled us just to perceive that a stranger had entered, about my own height, and closely muffled in a cloak. The darkness, however, was now total, and we could only *feel* that he was standing in our midst. Before any one of us could recover from the extreme astonishment into which this rudeness had thrown all, we heard the voice of the intruder.

" Gentlemen," he said, in a low, distinct, and never-to-be-forgotten *whisper* which thrilled to the very marrow of my bones, " Gentlemen, I make no apology for this behaviour, because in thus behaving, I am but fulfilling my duty. You are, beyond doubt, uninformed of the true character of the person who has to-night won at *écarté* a large sum of money from Lord Glendinning. I will therefore put you upon an expeditious and decisive plan of obtaining this very necessary information. Please to examine at your leisure the inner linings of the cuff of his left sleeve, and the several little packages which may be found in the somewhat capacious pockets of his embroidered morning wrapper."

While he spoke, so profound was the stillness that one might have heard a pin drop upon the floor. In ceasing, he departed at once, and as abruptly as he had entered. Can I—shall I describe my sensations? Must I say that I felt all the horrors of the damned? Most assuredly I had little time for reflection. Many hands roughly seized me upon the spot, and lights were immediately re-procured. A search ensued. In the lining of my sleeve were found all the court cards essential in *écarté*, and in the pockets of my wrapper a number of packs, fac-similes of those used at our sittings, with the single exception that mine were of the species called, technically, *arrondées*; the honours being slightly convex at the ends, the lower cards slightly convex at the sides. In this disposition, the dupe who cuts, as customary, at the length of the pack, will invariably find that he cuts his antagonist an honour; while the gambler, cutting at the breadth, will as certainly cut nothing for his victim which may count in the records of the game.

Any burst of indignation upon this discovery would have affected me less than the silent contempt, or the sarcastic composure, with which it was received.

"Mr. Wilson," said our host, stooping to remove from beneath his feet an exceedingly luxurious cloak of rare furs, "Mr. Wilson, this is your property." (The weather was cold; and, upon quitting my own room, I had thrown a cloak over my dressing wrapper, putting it off upon reaching the scene of play.) "I

presume it is supererogatory to seek here (eyeing the
folds of the garment with a bitter smile) for any further
evidence of your skill. Indeed, we have had enough.
You will see the necessity, I hope, of quitting Oxford
—at all events, of quitting instantly my chambers."

Abased, humbled to the dust as I then was, it is
probable that I should have resented this galling
language by immediate personal violence, had not my
whole attention been at the moment arrested by a fact
of the most startling character. The cloak which I had
worn was of a rare description of fur ; how rare, how
extravagantly costly, I shall not venture to say. Its
fashion, too, was of my own fantastic invention, for I
was fastidious to an absurd degree of coxcombry in
matters of this frivolous nature. When, therefore, Mr.
Preston reached me that which he had picked up upon
the floor, and near the folding doors of the apartment,
it was with an astonishment nearly bordering upon
terror, that I perceived my own already hanging on
my arm (where I had no doubt unwittingly placed it),
and that the one presented me was but its exact
counterpart in every, in even the minutest possible
particular. The singular being who had so disastrously
exposed me had been muffled, I remembered, in a
cloak, and none had been worn at all by any of the
members of our party with the exception of myself.
Retaining some presence of mind, I took the one offered
me by Preston, placed it unnoticed over my own, left
the apartment with a resolute scowl of defiance, and
next morning, ere dawn of day, commenced a hurried
journey from Oxford to the Continent in a perfect
agony of horror and of shame.

I fled in vain. My evil destiny pursued me as if in exultation, and proved indeed that the exercise of its mysterious dominion had as yet only begun. Scarcely had I set foot in Paris ere I had fresh evidence of the detestable interest taken by this Wilson in my concerns. Years flew while I experienced no relief. Villain !—at Rome, with how untimely, yet with how spectral an officiousness, stepped he in between me and my ambition ! At Vienna, too—at Berlin—and at Moscow ! Where, in truth, had I *not* bitter cause to curse him within my heart ? From his inscrutable tyranny did I at length flee, panic-stricken, as from a pestilence ; and to the very ends of the earth *I fled in vain.*

And again and again, in secret communion with my own spirit, would I demand the questions " Who is he ?—whence came he ?—and what are his objects ? " But no answer was there found. And now I scrutinised, with a minute scrutiny, the forms, and the methods, and the leading traits of his impertinent supervision. But even here there was very little upon which to base a conjecture. It was noticeable, indeed, that in no one of the multiplied instances in which he had of late crossed my path had he so crossed it except to frustrate those schemes, or to disturb those actions, which, if fully carried out, might have resulted in bitter mischief. Poor justification this, in truth, for an authority so imperiously assumed ! Poor indemnity for natural rights of self-agency so pertinaciously, so insultingly denied !

I had also been forced to notice that my tormentor for a very long period of time (while scrupulously and with miraculous dexterity maintaining his whim of an identity of apparel with myself) had so contrived it, in the execution of his varied interference with my will, that I saw not at any moment the features of his face. Be Wilson what he might, *this* at least was but the veriest of affectation or of folly. Could he for an instant have supposed that in my admonisher at Eton—in the destroyer of my honour at Oxford—in him who thwarted my ambition at Rome, my revenge at Paris, my passionate love at Naples, or what he falsely termed my avarice in Egypt,—that in this, my arch-enemy and evil genius, I could fail to recognise the William Wilson of my school-boy days,—the name-sake, the companion, the rival,—the hated and dreaded rival at Dr. Bransby's? Impossible!—But let me hasten to the last eventful scene of the drama.

Thus far I had succumbed supinely to this imperious domination. The sentiment of deep awe with which I habitually regarded the elevated character, the majestic wisdom, the apparent omnipresence and omnipotence of Wilson, added to a feeling of even terror, with which certain other traits in his nature and assumptions inspired me, had operated hitherto to impress me with an idea of my own utter weakness and helplessness, and to suggest an implicit, although bitterly reluctant submission to his arbitrary will. But of late days I had given myself up entirely to wine, and its maddening influence upon my hereditary temper rendered me more and more impatient of control. I began to murmur,—to hesitate,—to resist. And was it only fancy which induced me to believe that, with the increase of my own firmness, that of my tormentor underwent a pro-

portional diminution ?   Be this as it may, I now began
to feel the inspiration of a burning hope, and at length
nurtured in my secret thoughts a stern and desperate
resolution that I would submit no longer to be enslaved.

It was at Rome, during the Carnival of 18—, that I
attended a masquerade in the palazzo of the Neapolitan
Duke Di Broglio.   I had indulged more freely than
usual in the excesses of the wine-table, and now the
suffocating atmosphere of the crowded rooms irritated
me beyond endurance.   The difficulty, too, of forcing
my way through the mazes of the company contributed
not a little to the ruffling of my temper ; for I was
anxiously seeking (let me not say with what unworthy
motive) the young, the gay, the beautiful wife of the
aged and doting Di Broglio.   With a too unscrupulous
confidence she had previously communicated to me
the secret of the costume in which she would be
habited, and now, having caught a glimpse of her
person, I was hurrying to make my way into her
presence.   At this moment I felt a light hand placed
upon my shoulder, and that ever-remembered, low,
damnable *whisper* within my ear.

In an absolute frenzy of wrath I turned at once upon
him who had thus interrupted me, and seized him
violently by the collar.   He was attired, as I had expected, in a costume altogether similar to my own ;
wearing a Spanish cloak of blue velvet, begirt about
the waist with a crimson belt sustaining a rapier.   A
mask of black silk entirely covered his face.

" Scoundrel ! " I said, in a voice husky with rage,
while every syllable I uttered seemed as new fuel to
my fury ; " scoundrel ! impostor ! accursed villain !

you shall not—you *shall not* dog me unto death ! Follow me, or I stab you where you stand ! "—and I broke my way from the ball-room into a small antechamber adjoining, dragging him unresistingly with me as I went.

Upon entering, I thrust him furiously from me. He staggered against the wall, while I closed the door with an oath, and commanded him to draw. He hesitated but for an instant ; then, with a slight sigh, drew in silence, and put himself upon his defence.

The contest was brief indeed. I was frantic with every species of wild excitement, and felt within my single arm the energy and power of a multitude. In a few seconds I forced him by sheer strength against the wainscoting, and thus, getting him at mercy, plunged my sword, with brute ferocity, repeatedly through and through his bosom.

At that instant some person tried the latch of the door. I hastened to prevent an intrusion, and then immediately returned to my dying antagonist. But what human language can adequately portray *that* astonishment, *that* horror which possessed me at the spectacle then presented to view ? The brief moment in which I averted my eyes had been sufficient to produce apparently a material change in the arrangements at the upper or farther end of the room. A large mirror—so at first it seemed to me in my confusion—now stood where none had been perceptible before ; and, as I stepped up to it in extremity of terror, mine own image, but with features all pale and dabbled in blood, advanced to meet me with a feeble and tottering gait.

Thus it appeared, I say, but was not. It was my

antagonist—it was Wilson who then stood before me in the agonies of his dissolution. His mask and cloak lay where he had thrown them upon the floor. Not a thread in all his raiment—not a line in all the marked and singular lineaments of his face which was not, even in the most absolute identity, *mine own!*

It was Wilson ; but he spoke no longer in a whisper, and I could have fancied that I myself was speaking while he said :

"*You have conquered and I yield. Yet, henceforward art thou also dead—dead to the World, to Heaven, and to Hope! In me didst thou exist—and, in my death, see by this image, which is thine own, how utterly thou hast murdered thyself.*"

VI

THE MURDERS IN THE RUE MORGUE

What song the Syrens sang, or what name Achilles assumed when he hid himself among women, although puzzling questions, are not beyond *all* conjecture.   *Sir Thomas Browne*

THE mental features discoursed of as the analytical are, in themselves, but little susceptible of analysis. We appreciate them only in their effects. We know of them, among other things, that they are always to their possessor, when inordinately possessed, a source of the liveliest enjoyment. As the strong man exults in his physical ability, delighting in such exercises as call his muscles into action, so glories the analyst in that moral activity which *disentangles*. He derives pleasure from even the most trivial occupations bringing his talent into play. He is fond of enigmas, of conundrums, of hieroglyphics; exhibiting in his solutions of each a degree of *acumen* which appears to the ordinary apprehension preternatural. His results, brought about by the very soul and essence of method, have, in truth, the whole air of intuition.

The faculty of re-solution is possibly much invigorated by mathematical study, and especially by that highest branch of it which, unjustly, and merely on account of its retrograde operations, has been called, as if *par excellence*, analysis. Yet to calculate is not in itself to analyse. A chess-player, for example, does the one without effort at the other. It follows that the game of chess, in its effects upon mental character, is greatly misunderstood. I am not now writing a treatise, but simply prefacing a somewhat peculiar narrative by observations very much at random ; I will therefore take occasion to assert that the higher powers of the reflective intellect are more decidedly and more usefully tasked by the unostentatious game of draughts than by all the elaborate frivolity of chess. In this latter, where the pieces have different and *bizarre* motions, with various and variable values, what is only complex is mistaken (a not unusual error) for what is profound. The *attention* is here called powerfully into play. If it flag for an instant, an oversight is committed, resulting in injury or defeat. The possible moves being not only manifold but involute, the chances of such oversights are multiplied ; and in nine cases out of ten it is the more concentrative rather than the more acute player who conquers. In draughts, on the contrary, where the moves are *unique* and have but little variation, the probabilities of inadvertence are diminished, and the mere attention being left comparatively unemployed, what advantages are obtained by either party are obtained by superior *acumen*. To be less abstract—let us suppose a game of draughts where the pieces are reduced to four kings, and where, of course, no oversight is to be expected. It is obvious that here the victory can be decided (the players being at all equal) only by some *recherché* movement, the result of some strong exertion of the intellect. Deprived of ordinary resources, the analyst throws himself into the spirit of his opponent, identifies himself therewith, and not unfrequently sees thus, at a glance, the sole methods (sometimes indeed absurdly simple ones) by which he may seduce into error or hurry into miscalculation.

Whist has long been noted for its influence upon what is termed the calculating power ; and men of the highest order of intellect have been known to take an apparently unaccountable delight in it, while eschewing chess as frivolous. Beyond doubt there is nothing of a similar nature so greatly tasking the faculty of analysis. The best chess-player in Christendom *may* be little more than the best player of chess ; but proficiency in whist implies capacity for success in all those more important undertakings where mind struggles with mind. When I say proficiency, I mean that perfection in the game which includes a comprehension of *all* the sources whence legitimate advantage may be derived. These are not only manifold but multiform, and lie frequently among recesses of thought altogether inaccessible to the ordinary understanding. To observe attentively is to remember distinctly; and, so far, the concentrative chess-player will do very well at whist ; while the rules of Hoyle (themselves based upon the mere mechanism of the game) are sufficiently and generally comprehensible. Thus to have a retentive memory, and to proceed by " the book," are points commonly regarded as the sum total of good playing. But it is in matters beyond the limits of mere rule that the skill of the analyst is evinced. He makes, in silence, a host of observations and inferences. So, perhaps, do his companions ; and the difference in the extent of the information obtained lies not so much in the validity of the inference as in the quality of the observation. The necessary knowledge is that of *what* to observe. Our player confines himself not at all ; nor, because the game is the object, does he reject deductions from things external to the game. He examines the countenance of his partner, comparing it carefully with that of each of his opponents. He considers the mode of assorting the cards in each hand ; often counting trump by trump, and honour by honour, through the glances bestowed by their holders upon each. He notes every variation of face as the play progresses, gathering a fund of thought from the differences in the expression of certainty, of surprise, of triumph, or of chagrin. From the manner of gathering up a trick he judges whether the person taking it can make another in the suit. He recognises what is played through feint, by the air with which it is thrown upon the table. A casual or inadvertent word ; the accidental dropping or turning of a card, with the accompanying anxiety or carelessness in regard to its concealment ; the counting of the tricks, with the order of their arrangement ; embarrassment, hesitation, eagerness or trepidation—all afford, to his apparently intuitive perception, indications of the true state of affairs. The first two or three rounds having been played, he is in full possession of the contents of each hand, and thenceforward puts down his cards with as absolute a precision of purpose as if the rest of the party had turned outward the faces of their own.

The analytical power should not be confounded with simple ingenuity ; for while the analyst is necessarily ingenious, the ingenious man is often remarkably incapable of analysis. The constructive or combining power, by which ingenuity is usually manifested, and to which the phrenologists (I believe erroneously) have assigned a separate organ, supposing it a primitive faculty, has been so frequently seen in those whose intellect bordered otherwise upon idiocy, as to have attracted general observation among writers on morals. Between ingenuity and the analytic ability there exists a difference far greater indeed, than that between the fancy and the imagination, but of a character very strictly analogous. It will be found, in fact, that the ingenious are always fanciful, and the *truly* imaginative never otherwise than analytic.

The narrative which follows will appear to the reader somewhat in the light of a commentary upon the propositions just advanced.

Residing in Paris during the spring and part of the summer of 18—, I there became acquainted with a Monsieur C. Auguste Dupin. This young gentleman was of an excellent—indeed of an illustrious family, but, by a variety of untoward events, had been reduced to such poverty that the energy of his character succumbed beneath it, and he ceased to bestir himself in the world, or to care for the retrieval of his fortunes. By courtesy of his creditors, there still remained in his possession a small remnant of his patrimony ; and upon the income arising from this, he managed by means of a rigorous economy to procure the necessaries of life, without troubling himself about its superfluities. Books, indeed, were his sole luxuries, and in Paris these are easily obtained.

Our first meeting was at an obscure library in the

Rue Montmartre, where the accident of our both being in search of the same very rare and very remarkable volume brought us into closer communion. We saw each other again and again. I was deeply interested in the little family history which he detailed to me with all that candour which a Frenchman indulges whenever mere self is his theme. I was astonished, too, at the vast extent of his reading; and, above all, I felt my soul enkindled within me by the wild fervour, and the vivid freshness of his imagination. Seeking in Paris the objects I then sought, I felt that the society of such a man would be to me a treasure beyond price; and this feeling I frankly confided to him. It was at length arranged that we should live together during my stay in the city; and as my worldly circumstances were somewhat less embarrassed than his own, I was permitted to be at the expense of renting and furnishing, in a style which suited the rather fantastic gloom of our common temper, a time-eaten and grotesque mansion, long deserted through superstitions into which we did not inquire, and tottering to its fall in a retired and desolate portion of the Faubourg St. Germain.

Had the routine of our life at this place been known to the world, we should have been regarded as madmen —although, perhaps, as madmen of a harmless nature. Our seclusion was perfect. We admitted no visitors. Indeed the locality of our retirement had been carefully kept a secret from my own former associates; and it had been many years since Dupin had ceased to know or be known in Paris. We existed within ourselves alone.

It was a freak of fancy in my friend (for what else shall I call it ?) to be enamoured of the Night for her own sake ; and into this *bizarrerie*, as into all his others, I quietly fell ; giving myself up to his wild whims with a perfect *abandon*. The sable divinity would not herself dwell with us always ; but we could counterfeit her presence. At the first dawn of the morning we closed all the massive shutters of our old building ; lighting a couple of tapers which, strongly perfumed, threw out only the ghastliest and feeblest of rays. By the aid of these we then busied our souls in dreams— reading, writing, or conversing, until warned by the clock of the advent of the true Darkness. Then we sallied forth into the streets, arm in arm, continuing the topics of the day, or roaming far and wide until a late hour, seeking amid the wild lights and shadows of the populous city that infinity of mental excitement which quiet observation can afford.

At such times I could not help remarking and admiring (although from his rich ideality I had been prepared to expect it) a peculiar analytic ability in Dupin. He seemed, too, to take an eager delight in its exercise—if not exactly in its display—and did not hesitate to confess the pleasure thus derived. He boasted to me, with a low chuckling laugh, that most men, in respect to himself, wore windows in their bosoms, and was wont to follow up such assertions by direct and very startling proofs of his intimate knowledge of my own. His manner at these moments was frigid and abstract ; his eyes were vacant in expression ; while his voice, usually a rich tenor, rose into a treble which would have sounded petulantly but for the deliberateness and entire distinctness of the enunciation. Observing him in these moods, I often dwelt meditatively upon the old philosophy of the Bi-Part Soul, and amused myself with the fancy of a double Dupin—the creative and the resolvent.

Let it not be supposed from what I have just said that I am detailing any mystery, or penning any romance. What I have described in the Frenchman was merely the result of an excited or perhaps of a diseased intelligence. But of the character of his remarks at the periods in question an example will best convey the idea.

We were strolling one night down a long dirty street, in the vicinity of the Palais Royal. Being both apparently occupied with thought, neither of us had spoken a syllable for fifteen minutes at least. All at once Dupin broke forth with these words:

" He is a very little fellow, that's true, and would do better for the *Théâtre des Variétés*."

" There can be no doubt of that," I replied unwittingly, and not at first observing (so much had I been absorbed in reflection) the extraordinary manner in which the speaker had chimed in with my meditations. In an instant afterwards I recollected myself, and my astonishment was profound.

" Dupin," said I gravely, " this is beyond my comprehension. I do not hesitate to say that I am amazed, and can scarcely credit my senses. How was it possible you should know I was thinking of— ? " Here I paused, to ascertain beyond a doubt whether he really knew of whom I thought.

——" of Chantilly," said he ; " why do you pause ?

You were remarking to yourself that his diminutive figure unfitted him for tragedy."

This was precisely what had formed the subject of my reflections. Chantilly was a *quondam* cobbler of the Rue St. Denis, who, becoming stage-mad, had attempted the *rôle* of Xerxes, in Crébillon's tragedy so-called, and been notoriously pasquinaded for his pains.

"Tell me, for Heaven's sake," I exclaimed, "the method—if method there is—by which you have been enabled to fathom my soul in this matter." In fact I was even more startled than I would have been willing to express.

"It was the fruiterer," replied my friend, "who brought you to the conclusion that the mender of soles was not of sufficient height for Xerxes *et id genus omne.*"

"The fruiterer!—you astonish me—I know no fruiterer whomsoever."

"The man who ran up against you as we entered the street—it may have been fifteen minutes ago."

I now remembered that, in fact, a fruiterer, carrying upon his head a large basket of apples, had nearly thrown me down by accident as we passed from the Rue C—— into the thoroughfare where we stood ; but what this had to do with Chantilly I could not possibly understand.

There was not a particle of *charlatanerie* about Dupin. "I will explain," he said, "and that you may comprehend all clearly, we will first retrace the course of your meditations from the moment in which I spoke to you until that of the *rencontre* with the fruiterer in question. The larger links of the chain run thus—Chantilly,

Orion, Dr. Nichols, Epicurus, Stereotomy, the street stones, the fruiterer.''

There are few persons who have not at some period of their lives amused themselves in retracing the steps by which particular conclusions of their own minds have been attained. The occupation is often full of interest ; and he who attempts it for the first time is astonished by the apparently illimitable distance and incoherence between the starting-point and the goal. What then must have been my amazement when I heard the Frenchman speak what he had just spoken, and when I could not help acknowledging that he had spoken the truth. He continued :

" We had been talking of horses, if I remember aright, just before leaving the Ruc C——. This was the last subject we discussed. As we crossed into this street, a fruiterer, with a large basket upon his head, brushing quickly past us, thrust you upon a pile of paving-stones collected at a spot where the causeway is undergoing repair. You stepped upon one of the loose fragments, slipped, slightly strained your ankle, appeared vexed or sulky, muttered a few words, turned to look at the pile, and then proceeded in silence. I was not particularly attentive to what you did ; but observation has become with me, of late, a species of necessity.

" You kept your eyes upon the ground—glancing, with a petulant expression, at the holes and ruts in the pavement (so that I saw you were still thinking of the stones), until we reached the little alley called Lamartine, which has been paved, by way of experiment, with the overlapping and riveted blocks. Here your countenance brightened up, and, perceiving your lips move, I could not doubt that you murmured the word ' stereotomy,' a term very affectedly applied to this species of pavement. I knew that you could not say to yourself ' stereotomy ' without being brought to think of atomies, and thus of the theories of Epicurus; and since, when we discussed this subject not very long ago, I mentioned to you how singularly, yet with how little notice, the vague guesses of that noble Greek had met with confirmation in the late nebular cosmogony, I felt that you could not avoid casting your eyes upward to the great *nebula* in Orion, and I certainly expected that you would do so. You did look up; and I was now assured that I had correctly followed your steps. But in that bitter *tirade* upon Chantilly, which appeared in yesterday's ' *Musée*,' the satirist, making some disgraceful allusions to the cobbler's change of name upon assuming the buskin, quoted a Latin line about which we have often conversed. I mean the line—

Perdidit antiquum litera prima sonum.

I had told you that this was in reference to Orion, formerly written Urion, and from certain pungencies connected with this explanation I was aware that you could not have forgotten it. It was clear, therefore, that you would not fail to combine the two ideas of Orion and Chantilly. That you did combine them I saw by the character of the smile which passed over your lips. You thought of the poor cobbler's immolation. So far you had been stooping in your gait, but now I saw you draw yourself up to your full height. I was then sure that you reflected upon the diminutive figure of Chantilly. At this point I interrupted your meditations to remark that as, in fact, he *was* a very little fellow that Chantilly, he would do better at the *Théâtre des Variétés*."

Not long after this we were looking over an evening edition of the " Gazette des Tribunaux," when the following paragraphs arrested our attention.

" EXTRAORDINARY MURDERS.—This morning about three o'clock the inhabitants of the Quartier St. Roch were aroused from sleep by a succession of terrific shrieks, issuing, apparently, from the fourth storey of a house in the Rue Morgue, known to be in the sole occupancy of one Madame L'Espanaye, and her daughter, Mademoiselle Camille L'Espanaye. After some delay, occasioned by a fruitless attempt to procure admission in the usual manner, the gateway was broken in with a crowbar, and eight or ten of the neighbours entered, accompanied by two *gendarmes*. By this time the cries had ceased, but as the party rushed up the first flight of stairs, two or more rough voices in angry contention were distinguished, and seemed to proceed from the upper part of the house. As the second landing was reached these sounds also had ceased, and everything remained perfectly quiet. The party spread themselves and hurried from room to room. Upon arriving at a large back chamber in the fourth storey (the door of which, being found locked with the key inside, was forced open), a spectacle presented itself which struck every one present not less with horror than with astonishment.

The apartment was in the wildest disorder, the furniture broken and thrown about in all directions. There was only one bedstead, and from this the bed had been removed and thrown into the middle of the floor. On a chair lay a razor besmeared with blood. On the hearth were two or three long and thick tresses of grey human hair, also dabbled in blood, and seeming to have been pulled out by the roots. Upon the floor were found four Napoleons, an earring of topaz, three large silver spoons, three smaller of *métal d'Alger*, and two bags containing nearly four thousand francs in gold. The drawers of a *bureau* which stood in one corner were open, and had been apparently rifled, although many articles still remained in them. A small iron safe was discovered under the *bed* (not under the bedstead). It was open, with the key still in the door. It had no contents beyond a few old letters and other papers of little consequence.

" Of Madame L'Espanaye no traces were here seen, but an unusual quantity of soot being observed in the fireplace, a search was made in the chimney, and (horrible to relate !) the corpse of the daughter, head downward, was dragged therefrom, it having been thus forced up the narrow aperture for a considerable distance. The body was quite warm. Upon examining it many excoriations were perceived, no doubt occasioned by the violence with which it had been thrust up and disengaged. Upon the face were many severe scratches, and upon the throat, dark bruises and deep indentations of finger nails, as if the deceased had been throttled to death.

" After a thorough investigation of every portion of the house, without further discovery, the party made its way into a small paved yard in the rear of the building, where lay the corpse of the old lady, with her throat so entirely cut that, upon an attempt to raise her, the head fell off. The body as well as the head was fearfully mutilated, the former so much so as scarcely to retain any semblance of humanity.

"To this horrible mystery there is not as yet, we believe, the slightest clue."

The next day's paper had these additional particulars.

"*The Tragedy in the Rue Morgue*.—Many individuals have been examined in relation to this most extraordinary and frightful affair" [the word "*affaire*" has not yet in France that levity of import which it conveys with us], "but nothing whatever has transpired to throw light upon it. We give below all the material testimony elicited.

"*Pauline Dubourg*, laundress, deposes that she has known both the deceased for three years, having washed for them during that period. The old lady and her daughter seemed on good terms—very affectionate towards each other. They were excellent pay. Could not speak in regard to their mode or means of living. Believed that Madame L. told fortunes for a living. Was reputed to have money put by. Never met any persons in the house when she called for the clothes or took them home. Was sure that they had no servant in employ. There appeared to be no furniture in any part of the building except in the fourth storey.

"*Pierre Moreau*, tobacconist, deposes that he has been in the habit of selling small quantities of tobacco and snuff to Madame L'Espanaye for nearly four years.

Was born in the neighbourhood, and has always resided there. The deceased and her daughter had occupied the house in which the corpses were found for more than six years. It was formerly occupied by a jeweller, who underlet the upper rooms to various persons. The house was the property of Madame L. She became dissatisfied with the abuse of the premises by her tenant, and moved into them herself, refusing to let any portion. The old lady was childish. Witness had seen the daughter some five or six times during the six years. The two lived an exceedingly retired life— were reputed to have money. Had heard it said among the neighbours that Madame L. told fortunes —did not believe it. Had never seen any person enter the door except the old lady and her daughter, a porter once or twice, and a physician some eight or ten times.

" Many other persons, neighbours, gave evidence to the same effect. No one was spoken of as frequenting the house. It was not known whether there were any living connections of Madame L. and her daughter. The shutters of the front windows were seldom opened. Those in the rear were always closed with the exception of the large back room, fourth storey. The house was a good house, not very old.

" *Isidore Muset, gendarme,* deposes that he was called to the house about three o'clock in the morning, and found some twenty or thirty persons at the gateway endeavouring to gain admittance. Forced it open at length with a bayonet—not with a crowbar. Had but little difficulty in getting it open on account of its being a double or folding gate, and bolted neither at bottom nor top. The shrieks were continued until the gate was forced, and then suddenly ceased. They seemed to be screams of some person (or persons) in great agony, were loud and drawn out, not short and quick. Witness led the way up stairs. Upon reaching the first landing, heard two voices in loud and angry contention—the one a gruff voice, the other much shriller—a very strange voice. Could distinguish some words of the former, which was that of a Frenchman. Was positive that it was not a woman's voice. Could distinguish the words ' sacré ' and ' diable.' The shrill voice was that of a foreigner. Could not be sure whether it was the voice of a man or of a woman. Could not make out what was said, but believed the language to be Spanish. The state of the room and of the bodies was described by this witness as we described them yesterday.

" *Henri Duval*, a neighbour, and by trade a silversmith, deposes that he was one of the party who first entered the house. Corroborates the testimony of Muset in general. As soon as they forced an entrance, they reclosed the door to keep out the crowd, which collected very fast, notwithstanding the lateness of the hour. The shrill voice, this witness thinks, was that of an Italian. Was certain it was not French. Could not be sure that it was a man's voice. It might have been a woman's. Was not acquainted with the Italian language. Could not distinguish the words, but was convinced by the intonation that the speaker was an Italian. Knew Madame L. and her daughter. Had conversed with both frequently. Was sure that the shrill voice was not that of either of the deceased.

" ——*Odenheimer, restaurateur.*—This witness volun-

teered his testimony. Not speaking French, was examined through an interpreter. Is a native of Am-
sterdam. Was passing the house at the time of the
shrieks. They lasted for several minutes—probably
ten. They were long and loud—very awful and distressing. Was one of those who entered the building.
Corroborated the previous evidence in every respect
but one. Was sure that the shrill voice was that of
a man—of a Frenchman. Could not distinguish the
words uttered. They were loud and quick—unequal—
spoken apparently in fear as well as in anger. The
voice was harsh—not so much shrill as harsh. Could
not call it a shrill voice. The gruff voice said repeatedly
' sacré,' ' diable,' and once ' mon Dieu.'

   " *Jules Mignaud*, banker, of the firm of Mignaud et
Fils, Rue Deloraine.—Is the elder Mignaud. Madame
L'Espanaye had some property. Had opened an account with his banking house in the spring of the year
—— (eight years previously). Made frequent deposits
in small sums. Had checked for nothing until the third
day before her death, when she took out in person the
sum of 4000 francs. This sum was paid in gold, and a
clerk sent home with the money.

   " *Adolphe Lebon*, clerk to Mignaud et Fils, deposes
that on the day in question, about noon, he accompanied Madame L'Espanaye to her residence with the
4000 francs put up in two bags. Upon the door being
opened, Mademoiselle L. appeared and took from his
hands one of the bags, while the old lady relieved him
of the other. He then bowed and departed. Did not
see any person in the street at the time. It is a bye-
street—very lonely.

"*William Bird*, tailor, deposes that he was one of the party who entered the house. Is an Englishman. Has lived in Paris two years. Was one of the first to ascend the stairs. Heard the voices in contention. The gruff voice was that of a Frenchman. Could make out several words, but cannot now remember all. Heard distinctly ' *sacré* ' and ' *mon Dieu.*' There was a sound at the moment as if of several persons struggling—a scraping and scuffling sound. The shrill voice was very loud—louder than the gruff one. Is sure that it was not the voice of an Englishman. Appeared to be that of a German. Might have been a woman's voice. Does not understand German.

" Four of the above-named witnesses, being recalled, deposed that the door of the chamber in which was found the body of Mademoiselle L. was locked on the inside when the party reached it. Everything was perfectly silent—no groans or noises of any kind. Upon forcing the door no person was seen. The windows, both of the back and front room, were down and firmly fastened from within. A door between the two rooms was closed, but not locked. The door leading from the front room into the passage was locked, with the key on the inside. A small room in the front of the house, on the fourth storey, at the head of the passage, was open, the door being ajar. This room was crowded with old beds, boxes, and so forth. These were carefully removed and searched. There was not an inch of any portion of the house which was not carefully searched. Sweeps were sent up and down the chimneys. The house was a four storey one, with garrets (*mansardes*). A trap-door on the roof was nailed down very securely—did not appear to have been opened for years. The time elapsing between the hearing of the voices in contention and the breaking open of the room door was variously stated by the witnesses. Some made it as short as three minutes—some as long as five. The door was opened with difficulty.

" *Alfonzo Garcio*, undertaker, deposes that he resides in the Rue Morgue. Is a native of Spain. Was one of the party who entered the house. Did not proceed up stairs. Is nervous, and was apprehensive of the consequences of agitation. Heard the voices in contention. The gruff voice was that of a Frenchman. Could not distinguish what was said. The shrill voice was that of an Englishman—is sure of this. Does not understand the English language, but judges by the intonation.

" *Alberto Montani*, confectioner, deposes that he was among the first to ascend the stairs. Heard the voices in question. The gruff voice was that of a Frenchman. Distinguished several words. The speaker appeared to be expostulating. Could not make out the words of the shrill voice. Spoke quick and unevenly. Thinks it the voice of a Russian. Corroborates the general testimony. Is an Italian. Never conversed with a native of Russia.

" Several witnesses, recalled, here testified that the chimneys of all the rooms on the fourth storey were too narrow to admit the passage of a human being. By ' sweeps ' were meant cylindrical sweeping-brushes, such as are employed by those who clean chimneys. These brushes were passed up and down every flue in the house. There is no back passage by which any one could have descended while the party proceeded up stairs. The body of Mademoiselle L'Espanaye was so firmly wedged in the chimney that it could not be got down until four or five of the party united their strength.

" *Paul Dumas*, physician, deposes that he was called to view the bodies about daybreak. They were both then lying on the sacking of the bedstead in the chamber where Mademoiselle L. was found. The corpse of the young lady was much bruised and excoriated. The fact that it had been thrust up the chimney would sufficiently account for these appearances. The throat was greatly chafed. There were several deep scratches just below the chin, together with a series of livid spots which were evidently the impression of fingers. The face was fearfully discoloured, and the eye-balls protruded. The tongue had been partially bitten through. A large bruise was discovered upon the pit of the stomach, produced apparently by the pressure of a knee. In the opinion of M. Dumas, Mademoiselle L'Espanaye had been throttled to death by some person or persons unknown. The corpse of the mother was horribly mutilated. All the bones of the right leg and arm were more or less shattered. The left *tibia* much splintered, as well as all the ribs of the left side. Whole body dreadfully bruised and discoloured. It was not possible to say how the injuries had been inflicted. A heavy club of wood, or a broad bar of iron—a chair—any large, heavy, and obtuse weapon would have produced such results if wielded by the hands of a very powerful man. No woman could have inflicted the blows with any weapon. The head of the deceased, when seen by witness, was entirely separated from the body, and was also greatly shattered. The throat had evidently been cut with some very sharp instrument—probably with a razor.

"*Alexandre Etienne*, surgeon, was called with M. Dumas to view the bodies. Corroborated the testimony, and the opinions of M. Dumas.

"Nothing further of importance was elicited, although several other persons were examined. A murder so mysterious, and so perplexing in all its particulars, was never before committed in Paris—if indeed a murder has been committed at all. The police are entirely at fault—an unusual occurrence in affairs of this nature. There is not, however, the shadow of a clue apparent."

The evening edition of the paper stated that the greatest excitement still continued in the Quartier St. Roch—that the premises in question had been carefully researched, and fresh examinations of witnesses instituted, but all to no purpose. A postscript, however, mentioned that Adolphe Lebon had been arrested and imprisoned—although nothing appeared to criminate him beyond the facts already detailed.

Dupin seemed singularly interested in the progress of this affair—at least so I judged from his manner, for he made no comments. It was only after the announcement that Lebon had been imprisoned that he asked me my opinion respecting the murders.

I could merely agree with all Paris in considering them an insoluble mystery. I saw no means by which it would be possible to trace the murderer.

" We must not judge of the means," said Dupin,
" by this shell of an examination. The Parisian police,
so much extolled for *acumen*, are cunning, but no more.
There is no method in their proceedings, beyond the
method of the moment. They make a vast parade
of measures ; but, not unfrequently, these are so ill-
adapted to the objects proposed as to put us in mind
of Monsieur Jourdain's calling for his *robe de chambre
—pour mieux entendre la musique*. The results attained
by them are not unfrequently surprising, but for the
most part are brought about by simple diligence and
activity. When these qualities are unavailing, their
schemes fail. Vidocq, for example, was a good guesser,
and a persevering man. But, without educated
thought, he erred continually by the very intensity of
his investigations. He impaired his vision by holding
the object too close. He might see, perhaps, one or
two points with unusual clearness, but in so doing,
he necessarily lost sight of the matter as a whole.
Thus there is such a thing as being too profound.
Truth is not always in a well. In fact, as regards the
more important knowledge, I do believe that she is
invariably superficial. The depth lies in the valleys
where we seek her, and not upon the mountain-top
where she is found. The modes and sources of this
kind of error are well typified in the contemplation
of the heavenly bodies. To look at a star by glances—
to view it in a side-long way, by turning towards it
the exterior portions of the *retina* (more susceptible
of feeble impressions of light than the interior), is to
behold the star distinctly—is to have the best appreciation of its lustre—a lustre which grows dim just in

proportion as we turn our vision *fully* upon it. A greater number of rays actually fall upon the eye in the latter case, but in the former there is the more refined capacity for comprehension. By undue profundity we perplex and enfeeble thought ; and it is possible to make even Venus herself vanish from the firmament by a scrutiny too sustained, too concentrated, or too direct.

" As for these murders, let us enter into some examinations for ourselves before we make up an opinion respecting them. An inquiry will afford us amusement " [I thought this an odd term so applied, but said nothing], " and besides, Lebon once rendered me a service for which I am not ungrateful. We will go and see the premises with our own eyes. I know G——, the Prefect of Police, and shall have no difficulty in obtaining the necessary permission."

The permission was obtained, and we proceeded at once to the Rue Morgue. This is one of those miserable thoroughfares which intervene between the Rue Richelieu and the Rue St. Roch. It was late in the afternoon when we reached it, as this quarter is at a great distance from that in which we resided. The house was readily found ; for there were still many persons gazing up at the closed shutters, with an objectless curiosity, from the opposite side of the way. It was an ordinary Parisian house, with a gateway, on one side of which was a glazed watch-box, with a sliding panel in the window, indicating a *loge du concierge*. Before going in we walked up the street, turned down an alley, and then, again turning, passed in the rear of the building —Dupin, meanwhile, examining the whole neighbourhood, as well as the house, with a minuteness of attention for which I could see no possible object.

Retracing our steps, we came again to the front of the dwelling, rang, and, having shown our credentials, were admitted by the agents in charge. We went upstairs—into the chamber where the body of Mademoiselle L'Espanaye had been found, and where both the deceased still lay. The disorders of the room had, as usual, been suffered to exist. I saw nothing beyond what had been stated in the " Gazette des Tribunaux." Dupin scrutinised everything — not excepting the bodies of the victims. We then went into the other rooms, and into the yard ; a *gendarme* accompanying us throughout. The examination occupied us until dark, when we took our departure. On our way home my companion stepped in for a moment at the office of one of the daily papers.

I have said that the whims of my friend were manifold, and that *Je les ménageais*—for this phrase there is not English equivalent. It was his humour now to decline all conversation on the subject of the murder, until about noon the next day. He then asked me suddenly, if I had observed anything *peculiar* at the scene of the atrocity.

There was something in his manner of emphasising the word " peculiar," which caused me to shudder, without knowing why.

" No, nothing *peculiar*," I said ; " nothing more, at least, than we both saw stated in the paper."

" The ' Gazette,' " he replied, " has not entered, I fear, into the unusual horror of the thing. But dismiss the idle opinions of this print. It appears to me that

this mystery is considered insoluble for the very reason
which should cause it to be regarded as easy of solution
—I mean for the *outré* character of its features. The
police are confounded by the seeming absence of
motive—not for the murder itself, but for the atrocity
of the murder. They are puzzled, too, by the seeming
impossibility of reconciling the voices heard in contention, with the facts that no one was discovered
upstairs but the assassinated Mademoiselle L'Espanaye, and that there were no means of egress
without the notice of the party ascending. The wild
disorder of the room ; the corpse thrust, with the head
downward, up the chimney ; the frightful mutilation
of the body of the old lady ; these considerations, with
those just mentioned, and others which I need not
mention, have sufficed to paralyse the powers, by putting completely at fault the boasted *acumen* of the
government agents. They have fallen into the gross
but common error of confounding the unusual with
the abstruse. But it is by these deviations from the
plane of the ordinary that reason feels its way, if at all,
in its search for the true. In investigations such as
we are now pursuing it should not be so much asked
' what has occurred,' as ' what has occurred that has
never occurred before.' In fact, the facility with which
I shall arrive, or have arrived at the solution of this
mystery, is in the direct ratio of its apparent insolu-
bility in the eyes of the police."

I stared at the speaker in mute astonishment.

" I am now awaiting," continued he, looking towards the door of our apartment—" I am now awaiting
a person who, although perhaps not the perpetrator

of these butcheries, must have been in some measure implicated in their perpetration. Of the worst portion of the crimes committed, it is probable that he is innocent. I hope that I am right in this supposition ; for upon it I build my expectation of reading the entire riddle. I look for the man here—in this room—every moment. It is true that he may not arrive ; but the probability is that he will. Should he come, it will be necessary to detain him. Here are pistols ; and we both know how to use them when occasion demands their use."

I took the pistols, scarcely knowing what I did, or believing what I heard, while Dupin went on, very much as if in a soliloquy. I have already spoken of his abstract manner at such times. His discourse was addressed to myself ; but his voice, although by no means loud, had that intonation which is commonly employed in speaking to some one at a great distance. His eyes, vacant in expression, regarded only the wall.

" That the voices heard in contention," he said, " by the party upon the stairs, were not the voices of the women themselves, was fully proved by the evidence. This relieves us of all doubt upon the question whether the old lady could have first destroyed the daughter, and afterwards have committed suicide. I speak of this point chiefly for the sake of method ; for the strength of Madame L'Espanaye would have been utterly unequal to the task of thrusting her daughter's corpse up the chimney as it was found ; and the nature of the wounds upon her own person entirely precludes the idea of self-destruction. Murder, then, has been committed by some third party ; and the voices of this third party were those heard in contention. Let me now advert—not to the whole testimony respecting these voices—but to what was *peculiar* in that testimony. Did you observe anything peculiar about it ? "

I remarked that, while all the witnesses agreed in supposing that gruff voice to be that of a Frenchman, there was much disagreement in regard to the shrill, or, as one individual termed it, the harsh voice.

" That was the evidence itself," said Dupin, " but it was not the peculiarity of the evidence. You have observed nothing distinctive. Yet there *was* something to be observed. The witnesses, as you remark, agreed about the gruff voice ; they were here unanimous. But in regard to the shrill voice, the peculiarity is—not that they disagreed—but that, while an Italian, an Englishman, a Spaniard, a Hollander, and a Frenchman attempted to describe it, each one spoke of it as that *of a foreigner.* Each is sure that it was not the voice of one of his own countrymen. Each likens it—not to the voice of an individual of any nation with whose language he is conversant—but the converse. The Frenchman supposes it the voice of a Spaniard, and ' might have distinguished some words *had he been acquainted with the Spanish.*' The Dutchman maintains it to have been that of a Frenchman ; but we find it stated that ' *not understanding French this witness was examined through an interpreter.*' The Englishman thinks it the voice of a German, and ' *does not understand German.*' The Spaniard ' is sure ' that it was that of an Englishman, but ' judges by the intonation ' altogether, ' *as he has no knowledge of the English.*'

The Italian believes it the voice of a Russian, but ' *has never conversed with a native of Russia.*' A second Frenchman differs, moreover, with the first, and is positive that the voice was that of an Italian; but, *not being cognisant of that tongue*, is, like the Spaniard, ' convinced by the intonation.' Now, how strangely unusual must that voice have really been, about which such testimony as this *could* have been elicited!—in whose *tones*, even, denizens of the five great divisions of Europe could recognise nothing familiar! You will say that it might have been the voice of an Asiatic— of an African. Neither Asiatics nor Africans abound in Paris; but, without denying the inference, I will now merely call your attention to three points. The voice is termed by one witness ' harsh rather than shrill.' It is represented by two others to have been ' quick and *unequal*.' No words—no sounds resembling words—were by any witness mentioned as distinguishable.

" I know not," continued Dupin, " what impression I may have made, so far, upon your own understanding, but I do not hesitate to say that legitimate deductions even from this portion of the testimony—the portion respecting the gruff and shrill voices—are in themselves sufficient to engender a suspicion which should give direction to all further progress in the investigation of the mystery. I said ' legitimate deductions,' but my meaning is not thus fully expressed. I designed to imply that the deductions are the *sole* proper ones, and that the suspicion arises *inevitably* from them as the single result. What the suspicion is, however, I will not say just yet. I merely wish you to bear in mind that, with myself, it was sufficiently forcible to give a definite form—a certain tendency—to my inquiries in the chamber.

" Let us now transport ourselves, in fancy, to this chamber. What shall we first seek here ? The means of egress employed by the murderers. It is not too much to say that neither of us believe in preternatural events. Madame and Mademoiselle L'Espanaye were not destroyed by spirits. The doers of the deed were material and escaped materially. Then how ? Fortunately there is but one mode of reasoning upon the point, and that mode *must* lead us to a definite decision. Let us examine, each by each, the possible means of egress. It is clear that the assassins were in the room where Mademoiselle L'Espanaye was found, or at least in the room adjoining, when the party ascended the stairs. It is then only from these two apartments that we have to seek issues. The police have laid bare the floors, the ceilings, and the masonry of the walls in every direction. No *secret* issues could have escaped their vigilance. But, not trusting to *their* eyes, I examined with my own. There were, then, *no* secret issues. Both doors leading from the rooms into the passage were securely locked, with the keys inside. Let us turn to the chimneys. These, although of ordinary width for some eight or ten feet above the hearths, will not admit, throughout their extent, the body of a large cat. The impossibility of egress, by means already stated, being thus absolute, we are reduced to the windows. Through those of the front room no one could have escaped without notice from the crowd in the street. The murderers *must* have passed, then, through those of the back room. Now, brought to this conclusion in so unequivocal a manner as we are, it is not our part, as reasoners, to reject it on account of apparent impossibilities. It is only left for us to prove that these apparent ' impossibilities ' are, in reality, not such.

" There are two windows in the chamber. One of them is unobstructed by furniture, and is wholly visible. The lower portion of the other is hidden from view by the head of the unwieldy bedstead which is thrust close up against it. The former was found securely fastened from within. It resisted the utmost force of those who endeavoured to raise it. A large gimlet-hole had been pierced in its frame to the left, and a very stout nail was found fitted therein, nearly to the head. Upon examining the other window a similar nail was seen similarly fitted in it ; and a vigorous attempt to raise this sash failed also. The police were now entirely satisfied that egress had not been in these directions. And, *therefore*, it was thought a matter of supererogation to withdraw the nails and open the windows.

" My own examination was somewhat more particular, and was so for the reason I have just given— because here it was, I knew, that all apparent impossibilities *must* be proved to be not such in reality.

" I proceeded to think thus—*a posteriori*. The murderers *did* escape from one of these windows. This being so, they could not have re-fastened the sashes from the inside, as they were found fastened—the consideration which put a stop, through its obviousness, to the scrutiny of the police in this quarter. Yet the sashes *were* fastened. They *must*, then, have the power of fastening themselves. There was no escape from this conclusion. I stepped to the unobstructed casement, withdrew the nail with some difficulty, and attempted to raise the sash. It resisted all my efforts, as I had anticipated. A concealed spring must, I now knew, exist; and this corroboration of my idea convinced me that my premises, at least, were correct, however mysterious still appeared the circumstances attending the nails. A careful search soon brought to light the hidden spring. I pressed it, and, satisfied with the discovery, forbore to upraise the sash.

" I now replaced the nail and regarded it attentively. A person passing out through this window might have reclosed it, and the spring would have caught; but the nail could not have been replaced. The conclusion was plain, and again narrowed in the field of my investigations. The assassins *must* have escaped through the other window. Supposing, then, the springs upon each sash to be the same, as was probable, there *must* be found a difference between the nails, or at least between the modes of their fixture. Getting upon the sacking of the bedstead, I looked over the headboard minutely at the second casement. Passing my hand down behind the board, I readily discovered and pressed the spring, which was, as I had supposed, identical in character with its neighbour. I now looked at the nail. It was as stout as the other, and apparently fitted in the same manner driven in nearly up to the head.

" You will say that I was puzzled; but if you think so you must have misunderstood the nature of the inductions. To use a sporting phrase, I had not been once ' at fault.' The scent had never for an instant been lost. There was no flaw in any link of the chain. I had traced the secret to its ultimate result ; and that result was *the nail*. It had, I say, in every respect the appearance of its fellow in the other window ; but this fact was an absolute nullity (conclusive as it might seem to be) when compared with the consideration that here at this point terminated the clue. ' There *must* be something wrong,' I said, ' about the nail.' I touched it, and the head, with about a quarter of an inch of the shank, came off in my fingers. The rest of the shank was in the gimlet-hole, where it had been broken off. The fracture was an old one (for its edges were incrusted with rust), and had apparently been accomplished by the blow of a hammer, which had partially imbedded in the top of the bottom sash the head portion of the nail. I now carefully replaced this head portion in the indentation whence I had taken it, and the resemblance to a perfect nail was complete—the fissure was invisible. Pressing the spring, I gently raised the sash for a few inches ; the head went up with it, remaining firm in its bed. I closed the window, and the semblance of the whole nail was again perfect.

" The riddle, so far, was now unriddled. The assassin had escaped through the window which looked upon the bed. Dropping of its own accord upon his exit (or perhaps purposely closed), it had become fastened by the spring ; and it was the retention of this spring which had been mistaken by the police for that of the nail,— further inquiry being thus considered unnecessary.

" The next question is that of the mode of descent. Upon this point I had been satisfied in my walk with you around the building. About five feet and a-half from the casement in question there runs a lightning-rod. From this rod it would have been impossible for any one to reach the window itself, to say nothing of entering it. I observed, however, that the shutters of the fourth storey were of the peculiar kind called by Parisian carpenters *ferrades*—a kind rarely employed at the present day, but frequently seen upon very old mansions at Lyons and Bordeaux. They are in the form of an ordinary door (a single, not a folding door), except that the lower half is latticed or worked in open trellis, thus affording an excellent hold for the hands. In the present instance these shutters are fully three feet and a-half broad. When we saw them from the rear of the house they were both about half-open—that is to say, they stood off at right angles from the wall. It is probable that the police, as well as myself, examined the back of the tenement ; but if so, in looking at these *ferrades* in the line of their breadth (as they must have done), they did not perceive this great breadth itself, or, at all events, failed to take it into due consideration. In fact, having once satisfied themselves that no egress could have been made in this quarter, they would naturally bestow here a very cursory examination. It was clear to me, however, that the shutter belonging to the window at the head of the bed would, if swung fully back to the wall, reach to within two feet of the lightning-rod. It was also evident that by exertion of a very unusual degree of activity and courage an entrance into the window from the rod might have been thus effected. By reaching to the distance of two feet and a-half (we now suppose the shutter open to its whole extent) a robber might have taken a firm grasp upon the trellis-work. Letting go, then, his hold upon the rod, placing his feet securely against the wall, and springing boldly from it, he might have swung the shutter so as to close it, and, if we imagine the window open at the time, might even have swung himself into the room.

" I wish you to bear especially in mind that I have spoken of a *very* unusual degree of activity as requisite to success in so hazardous and so difficult a feat. It is my design to show you, first, that the thing might possibly have been accomplished ; but, secondly and *chiefly*, I wish to impress upon your understanding the *very extraordinary*, the almost preternatural, character of that agility which could have accomplished it.

" You will say, no doubt, using the language of the law, that ' to make out my case,' I should rather under-value than insist upon a full estimation of the activity required in this matter. This may be the practice in law, but it is not the usage of reason. My ultimate object is only the truth. My immediate purpose is to lead you to place in juxtaposition that *very unusual* activity of which I have just spoken with that *very peculiar* shrill (or harsh) and *unequal* voice, about whose nationality no two persons could be found to agree, and in whose utterance no syllabification could be detected."

At these words a vague and half-formed conception of the meaning of Dupin flitted over my mind. I seemed to be upon the verge of comprehension, without power to comprehend, as men at times find themselves upon the brink of remembrance, without being able in the end to remember. My friend went on with his discourse.

" You will see," he said, " that I have shifted the question from the mode of egress to that of ingress. It was my design to convey the idea that both were effected in the same manner at the same point. Let us now revert to the interior of the room. Let us survey the appearances here. The drawers of the bureau, it is said, had been rifled, although many articles of apparel still remained within them. The conclusion here is absurd. It is a mere guess—a very silly one—and no more. How are we to know that the articles found in the drawers were not all these drawers had originally contained ? Madame L'Espanaye and her daughter lived an exceedingly retired life—saw no company—seldom went out—had little use for numerous changes of habiliment. Those found were at least of as good quality as any likely to be possessed by these ladies. If a thief had taken any, why did he not take the best—why did he not take all ? In a word, why did he abandon four thousand francs in gold to encumber himself with a bundle of linen ? The gold *was* abandoned. Nearly the whole sum mentioned by Monsieur Mignaud, the banker, was discovered in bags upon the floor. I wish you, therefore, to discard from your thoughts the blundering idea of *motive*, engendered in the brains of the police by that portion of the evidence which speaks of money delivered at the door of the house. Coincidences ten times as remarkable as this (the delivery of the money, and murder committed within three days upon the party receiving it), happen to all of us every hour of our lives, without attracting even momentary notice. Coincidences, in general, are great stumbling-blocks in the way of that class of thinkers who have been educated to know nothing of the theory of probabilities—that theory to which the most glorious objects of human research are indebted for the most glorious of illustration. In the present instance, had the gold been gone, the fact of its delivery three days before would have formed something more than a coincidence. It would have been corroborative of this idea of motive. But, under the real circumstances of the case, if we are to suppose gold the motive of this outrage, we must also imagine the perpetrator so vacillating an idiot as to have abandoned his gold and his motive together.

" Keeping now steadily in mind the points to which I have drawn your attention—that peculiar voice, that unusual agility, and that startling absence of motive in a murder so singularly atrocious as this—let us glance at the butchery itself. Here is a woman strangled to death by manual strength, and thrust up a chimney, head downward. Ordinary assassins employ no such modes of murder as this. Least of all do they thus dispose of the murdered. In the manner of thrusting the corpse up the chimney, you will admit that there was something *excessively outré*—something altogether irreconcilable with our common notions of human action, even when we suppose the actors the most depraved of men. Think, too, how great must have been that strength which could have thrust the body *up* such an aperture so forcibly that the united vigour of several persons was found barely sufficient to drag it *down !*

" Turn, now, to other indications of the employment of a vigour most marvellous. On the hearth were thick tresses—very thick tresses—of grey human hair. These had been torn out by the roots. You are aware of the great force necessary in tearing thus from the head even twenty or thirty hairs together. You saw the locks in question as well as myself. Their roots (a hideous sight) were clotted with fragments of the flesh of the scalp—sure token of the prodigious power which had been exerted in uprooting perhaps half-a-million of hairs at a time. The throat of the old lady was not merely cut, but the head absolutely severed from the body—the instrument was a mere razor. I wish you also to look at the *brutal* ferocity of these deeds. Of the bruises upon the body of Madame L'Espanaye I do not speak. Monsieur Dumas, and his worthy coadjutor, Monsieur Etienne, have pronounced that they were inflicted by some obtuse instrument ; and so far these gentlemen are very correct. The obtuse instrument was clearly the stone pavement in the yard upon which the victim had fallen from the window which looked in upon the bed. This idea, however simple it may now seem, escaped the police for the same reason that the breadth of the shutters escaped them—because, by the affair of the nails, their perceptions had been hermetically sealed against the possibility of the windows having ever been opened at all.

" If, now, in addition to all these things, you have

properly reflected upon the odd disorder of the chamber, we have gone so far as to combine the ideas of an agility astounding, a strength superhuman, a ferocity brutal, a butchery without motive, a *grotesquerie* in horror absolutely alien from humanity, and a voice foreign in tone to the ears of men of many nations, and devoid of all distinct or intelligible syllabification. What result, then, has ensued ? What impression have I made upon your fancy ? "

I felt a creeping of the flesh as Dupin asked me the question. " A madman," I said, " has done this deed —some raving maniac escaped from a neighbouring *maison de santé*."

" In some respects," he replied, " your idea is not irrelevant ; but the voices of madmen, even in their wildest paroxysms, are never found to tally with that peculiar voice heard upon the stairs. Madmen are of some nation, and their language, however incoherent in its words, has always the coherence of syllabification. Besides, the hair of a madman is not such as I now hold in my hand. I disentangled this little tuft from the rigidly clutched fingers of Madame L'Espanaye. Tell me what you can make of it ? "

" Dupin ! " I said, completely unnerved, " this hair is most unusual—this is no *human* hair."

" I have not asserted that it is," said he ; " but, before we decide this point, I wish you to glance at the little sketch I have here traced upon this paper. It is a *facsimile* drawing of what has been described in one portion of the testimony as ' dark bruises, and deep indentations of finger nails,' upon the throat of Mademoiselle L'Espanaye, and in another (by Messrs.

Dumas and Etienne), as a 'series of livid spots evidently the impression of fingers.'

"You will perceive," continued my friend, spreading out the paper upon the table before us, "that this drawing gives the idea of a firm and fixed hold. There is no *slipping* apparent. Each finger has retained—possibly until the death of the victim—the fearful grasp by which it originally embedded itself. Attempt, now, to place all your fingers, at the same time, in the respective impressions as you see them."

I made the attempt in vain.

"We are possibly not giving this matter a fair trial," he said. "The paper is spread out upon a plane surface ; but the human throat is cylindrical. Here is a billet of wood, the circumference of which is about that of the throat. Wrap the drawing around it, and try the experiment again."

I did so ; but the difficulty was even more obvious than before. "This," I said, "is the mark of no human hand."

"Read now," replied Dupin, "this passage from Cuvier."

It was a minute anatomical and generally descriptive account of the large fulvous Ourang-outang of the East Indian Islands. The gigantic stature, the prodigious strength and activity, the wild ferocity, and the imitative propensities of these mammalia are sufficiently well known to all. I understood the full horrors of the murder at once.

"The description of the digits," said I, as I made an end of reading, "is in exact accordance with this drawing. I see that no animal but an Ourang-outang, of the species here mentioned, could have impressed the indentations as you have traced them. This tuft of tawny hair, too, is identical in character with that of the beast of Cuvier. But I cannot possibly comprehend the particulars of this frightful mystery. Besides, there were *two* voices heard in contention, and one of them was unquestionably the voice of a Frenchman."

"True ; and you will remember an expression attributed almost unanimously, by the evidence, to this voice,—the expression ' *Mon Dieu !* ' This, under the circumstances, has been justly characterised by one of the witnesses (Montani, the confectioner) as an expression of remonstrance or expostulation. Upon these two words, therefore, I have mainly built my hopes of a full solution of the riddle. A Frenchman was cognisant of the murder. It is possible—indeed it is far more than probable—that he was innocent of all participation in the bloody transactions which took place. The Ourang-outang may have escaped from him. He may have traced it to the chamber ; but, under the agitating circumstances which ensued, he could never have recaptured it. It is still at large. I will not pursue these guesses—for I have no right to call them more—since the shades of reflection upon which they are based are scarcely of sufficient depth to be appreciable by my own intellect, and since I could not pretend to make them intelligible to the understanding of another. We will call them guesses, then, and speak of them as such. If the Frenchman in question is indeed, as I suppose, innocent of this atrocity, this advertisement which I left last night upon our return home at the office of ' Le Monde ' (a paper devoted to the shipping interest, and much sought by sailors) will bring him to our residence."

He handed me a paper, and I read thus :

"CAUGHT.—*In the Bois de Boulogne, early in the morning of the* —— *inst.* (the morning of the murder), *a very large, tawny Ourang-outang of the Bornese species. The owner (who is ascertained to be a sailor, belonging to a Maltese vessel) may have the animal again, upon identifying it satisfactorily, and paying a few charges arising from its capture and keeping. Call at No.* —, *Rue* ——, *Faubourg St. Germain—au troisieme.*"

" How was it possible," I asked, " that you should know the man to be a sailor, and belonging to a Maltese vessel ? "

" I do *not* know it," said Dupin. " I am not *sure* of it. Here, however, is a small piece of ribbon, which from its form, and from its greasy appearance, has evidently been used in tying the hair in one of those long *queues* of which sailors are so fond. Moreover, this knot is one which few besides sailors can tie, and is peculiar to the Maltese. I picked the ribbon up at the foot of the lightning-rod. It could not have belonged to either of the deceased. Now if, after all, I am wrong in my induction from this ribbon, that the Frenchman was a sailor belonging to a Maltese vessel, still I can have done no harm in saying what I did in the advertisement. If I am in error, he will merely suppose that I have been misled by some circumstance into which he will not take the trouble to inquire. But if I am right, a great point is gained. Cognisant, although innocent, of the murder, the Frenchman will naturally hesitate about replying to the advertisement—about demanding the Ourang-outang. He will reason thus : —' I am innocent ; I am poor ; my Ourang-outang is of great value—to one in my circumstances a fortune of itself—why should I lose it through idle apprehensions of danger ? Here it is within my grasp. It was found in the Bois de Boulogne—at a vast distance from the scene of that butchery. How can it ever be suspected that a brute beast should have done the deed ? The police are at fault—they have failed to procure the slightest clue. Should they even trace the animal, it would be impossible to prove me cognisant of the murder, or to implicate me in guilt on account of that cognisance. Above all, *I am known*. The advertiser designates me as the possessor of the beast. I am not sure to what limit his knowledge may extend. Should I avoid claiming a property of so great value, which it is known that I possess, I will render the animal at least liable to suspicion. It is not my policy to attract attention either to myself or to the beast. I will answer the advertisement, get the Ourang-outang, and keep it close until this matter has blown over."

At this moment we heard a step upon the stairs.

" Be ready," said Dupin, " with your pistols, but neither use them nor show them until at a signal from myself."

The front door of the house had been left open, and the visitor had entered without ringing, and advanced several steps upon the staircase. Now, however, he seemed to hesitate. Presently we heard him descending. Dupin was moving quickly to the door, when we again heard him coming up. He did not turn back a second time, but stepped up with decision, and rapped at the door of our chamber.

"Come in," said Dupin, in a cheerful and hearty tone.

A man entered. He was a sailor, evidently—a tall, stout, and muscular-looking person, with a certain dare-devil expression of countenance, not altogether unprepossessing. His face, greatly sunburnt, was more than half hidden by whisker and *mustachio*. He had with him a huge oaken cudgel, but appeared to be otherwise unarmed. He bowed awkwardly, and bade us " good evening " in French accents, which, although somewhat Neufchâtelish, were still sufficiently indicative of a Parisian origin.

"Sit down, my friend," said Dupin. " I suppose you have called about the Ourang-outang. Upon my word I almost envy you the possession of him ; a remarkably fine, and no doubt a very valuable animal. How old do you suppose him to be ? "

The sailor drew a long breath, with the air of a man relieved of some intolerable burden, and then replied in an assured tone :

" I have no way of telling—but he can't be more than four or five years old. Have you got him here ? "

" Oh no ; we had no conveniences for keeping him here. He is at a livery stable in the Rue Dubourg, just by. You can get him in the morning. Of course you are prepared to identify the property ? "

" To be sure I am, sir."

" I shall be sorry to part with him," said Dupin.

" I don't mean that you should be at all this trouble for nothing, sir," said the man. " Couldn't expect it.

Am very willing to pay a reward for the finding of the animal—that is to say, anything in reason."

" Well," replied my friend, " that is all very fair, to be sure. Let me think !—what should I have ? Oh ! I will tell you. My reward shall be this. You shall give me all the information in your power about these murders in the Rue Morgue."

Dupin said the last words in a very low tone, and very quietly. Just as quietly, too, he walked towards the door, locked it, and put the key in his pocket. He then drew a pistol from his bosom and placed it, without the least flurry, upon the table.

The sailor's face flushed up as if he were struggling with suffocation. He started to his feet and grasped his cudgel ; but the next moment he fell back into his seat, trembling violently, and with the countenance of death itself. He spoke not a word. I pitied him from the bottom of my heart.

" My friend," said Dupin in a kind tone, " you are alarming yourself unnecessarily—you are indeed. We mean you no harm whatever. I pledge you the honour of a gentleman, and of a Frenchman, that we intend you no injury. I perfectly well know that you are innocent of the atrocities in the Rue Morgue. It will not do, however, to deny that you are in some measure implicated in them. From what I have already said, you must know that I have had means of information about this matter—means of which you could never have dreamed. Now the thing stands thus. You have done nothing which you could have avoided—nothing, certainly, which renders you culpable. You were not even guilty of robbery, when you might have robbed with impunity. You have nothing to conceal. You have no reason for concealment. On the other hand, you are bound by every principle of honour to confess all you know. An innocent man is now imprisoned, charged with that crime of which you can point out the perpetrator."

The sailor had recovered his presence of mind, in a great measure, while Dupin uttered these words ; but his original boldness of bearing was all gone.

" So help me God," said he, after a brief pause, " I *will* tell you all I know about this affair ;—but I do not expect you to believe one-half I say—I would be a fool indeed if I did. Still I *am* innocent, and I will make a clean breast if I die for it."

What he stated was in substance this. He had lately made a voyage to the Indian Archipelago. A party, of which he formed one, landed at Borneo, and passed into the interior on an excursion of pleasure. Himself and a companion had captured the Ourang-outang. This companion dying, the animal fell into his own exclusive possession. After great trouble, occasioned by the intractable ferocity of his captive during the home voyage, he at length succeeded in lodging it safely at his own residence in Paris, where, not to attract towards himself the unpleasant curiosity of his neighbours, he kept it carefully secluded until such time as it should recover from a wound in the foot received from a splinter on board ship. His ultimate design was to sell it.

Returning home from some sailor's frolic on the night, or rather in the morning of the murder, he found the beast occupying his own bed-room, into which it had broken from a closet adjoining, where it had been, as was thought, securely confined. Razor in hand, and fully lathered, it was sitting before a looking-glass attempting the operation of shaving, in which it had no doubt previously watched its master through the key-hole of the closet. Terrified at the sight of so dangerous a weapon in the possession of an animal so ferocious and so well able to use it, the man, for some moments, was at a loss what to do. He had been accustomed, however, to quiet the creature, even in its fiercest moods, by the use of a whip, and to this he now resorted. Upon sight of it, the Ourang-outang sprang at once through the door of the chamber, down the stairs, and then through a window, unfortunately open, into the street.

The Frenchman followed in despair ; the ape, razor still in hand, occasionally stopping to look back and gesticulate at its pursuer, until the latter had nearly come up with it. It then again made off. In this manner the chase continued for a long time. The streets were profoundly quiet, as it was nearly three o'clock in the morning. In passing down an alley in the rear of the Rue Morgue, the fugitive's attention was arrested by a light gleaming from the open window of Madame L'Espanaye's chamber, in the fourth storey of her house. Rushing to the building, it perceived the lightning-rod, clambered up with inconceivable agility, grasped the shutter, which was thrown fully back against the wall, and, by its means, swung itself directly upon the headboard of the bed. The whole feat did not occupy a minute. The shutter was kicked open again by the Ourang-outang as it entered the room.

The sailor, in the meantime, was both rejoiced and perplexed. He had strong hopes of now recapturing the brute, as it could scarcely escape from the trap into which it had ventured except by the rod, where it might be intercepted as it came down. On the other hand, there was much cause for anxiety as to what it might do in the house. This latter reflection urged the man still to follow the fugitive. A lightning-rod is ascended without difficulty, especially by a sailor ; but when he had arrived as high as the window, which lay far to his left, his career was stopped ; the most that he could accomplish was to reach over so as to obtain a glimpse of the interior of the room. At this glimpse he nearly fell from his hold through excess of horror. Now it was that those hideous shrieks arose upon the night which had startled from slumber the inmates of the Rue Morgue. Madame L'Espanaye and her daughter, habited in their night-clothes, had apparently been occupied in arranging some papers in the iron chest already mentioned, which had been wheeled into the middle of the room. It was open, and its contents lay beside it on the floor. The victims must have been sitting with their backs towards the window ; and, from the time elapsing between the ingress of the beast and the screams, it seems probable that it was not immediately perceived. The flapping to of the shutter would naturally have been attributed to the wind.

As the sailor looked in, the gigantic animal had seized Madame L'Espanaye by the hair (which was loose, as she had been combing it), and was flourishing the razor about her face in imitation of the motions

of a barber. The daughter lay prostrate and motionless; she had swooned. The screams and struggles
of the old lady (during which the hair was torn from
her head) had the effect of changing the probably
pacific purposes of the Ourang-outang into those of
wrath. With one determined sweep of its muscular
arm it nearly severed her head from her body. The
sight of blood inflamed its anger into frenzy. Gnash-
ing its teeth and flashing fire from its eyes, it flew upon
the body of the girl, and imbedded its fearful talons
in her throat, retaining its grasp until she expired.
Its wandering and wild glances fell at this moment
upon the head of the bed, over which the face of its
master, rigid with horror, was just discernible. The
fury of the beast, which no doubt bore still in mind
the dreaded whip, was instantly converted into fear.
Conscious of having deserved punishment, it seemed
desirous of concealing its bloody deeds, and skipped
about the chamber in an agony of nervous agitation,
throwing down and breaking the furniture as it moved,
and dragging the bed from the bedstead. In conclusion, it seized first the corpse of the daughter and
thrust it up the chimney, as it was found; then that
of the old lady, which it immediately hurled through
the window headlong.

As the ape approached the casement with its mutilated burden, the sailor shrank aghast to the rod, and,
rather gliding than clambering down it, hurried at once
home—dreading the consequences of the butchery,
and gladly abandoning, in his terror, all solicitude
about the fate of the Ourang-outang. The words
heard by the party upon the staircase were the French-

man's exclamations of horror and affright, commingled with the fiendish jabberings of the brute.

I have scarcely anything to add. The Ourang-outang must have escaped from the chamber by the rod, just before the breaking of the door. It must have closed the window as it passed through it. It was subsequently caught by the owner himself, who obtained for it a very large sum at the *Jardin des Plantes*. Lebon was instantly released, upon our narration of the circumstances (with some comments from Dupin) at the *bureau* of the Prefect of Police. This functionary, however well disposed to my friend, could not altogether conceal his chagrin at the turn which affairs had taken, and was fain to indulge in a sarcasm or two about the propriety of every person minding his own business.

"Let him talk," said Dupin, who had not thought it necessary to reply. "Let him discourse; it will ease his conscience. I am satisfied with having defeated him in his own castle. Nevertheless, that he failed in the solution of this mystery is by no means that matter for wonder which he supposes it; for, in truth, our friend the Prefect is somewhat too cunning to be profound. In his wisdom is no *stamen*. It is all head and no body, like the pictures of the Goddess Laverna, —or, at best, all head and shoulders, like a codfish. But he is a good creature after all. I like him especially for one master-stroke of cant, by which he has attained his reputation for ingenuity. I mean the way he has ' *de nier ce qui est, et d'expliquer ce qui n'est pas.*' " *

* Rousseau—Nouvelle Héloïse.

VII

THE MYSTERY OF MARIE ROGÊT *

A SEQUEL TO " THE MURDERS IN THE RUE MORGUE "

Es giebt eine Reihe idealischer Begebenheiten, die der Wirklich-
keit parallel lauft. Selten fallen sie zusammen. Menschen und
Zufälle modificiren gewöhnlich die idealische Begebenheit, so dass
sie unvollkommen erscheint, und ihre Folgen gleichfalls unvollkommen sind. So bei der Reformation ; statt des Protestantismus
kam das Lutherthum hervor.

There are ideal series of events which run parallel with the real
ones. They rarely coincide. Men and circumstances generally
modify the ideal train of events, so that it seems imperfect, and its
consequences are equally imperfect. Thus with the Reformation ;
instead of Protestantism came Lutheranism.—Novalis, *Moral
Ansichten*

THERE are few persons, even among the calmest
thinkers, who have not occasionally been startled into
a vague yet thrilling half-credence in the supernatural,
by *coincidences* of so seemingly marvellous a character
that, as *mere* coincidences, the intellect has been unable
to receive them. Such sentiments—for the half-

* Upon the original publication of " Marie Rogêt," the foot-notes
now appended were considered unnecessary : but the lapse of several
years since the tragedy upon which the tale is based, renders it expedient to give them, and also to say a few words in explanation of
the general design. A young girl, *Mary Cecilia Rogers*, was murdered
in the vicinity of New York ; and although her death occasioned an
intense and long-enduring excitement, the mystery attending it had
remained unsolved at the period when the present paper was written
and published (November 1842). Herein, under pretence of relating
the fate of a Parisian *grisette*, the author has followed in minute
detail, the essential, while merely paralleling the inessential facts
of the real murder of Mary Rogers. Thus all argument founded

credences of which I speak have never the full force of *thought*—such sentiments are seldom thoroughly stifled unless by reference to the doctrine of chance, or as it is technically termed, the Calculus of Probabilities. Now this Calculus is in its essence purely mathematical ; and thus we have the anomaly of the most rigidly exact in science applied to the shadow and spirituality of the most intangible in speculation.

The extraordinary details which I am now called upon to make public will be found to form, as regards sequence of time, the primary branch of a series of scarcely intelligible *coincidences*, whose secondary or concluding branch will be recognised by all readers in the late murder of MARY CECILIA ROGERS, at New York.

When, in an article entitled "The Murders in the Rue Morgue," I endeavoured, about a year ago, to depict some very remarkable features in the mental character of my friend, the Chevalier C. Auguste Dupin, it did not occur to me that I should ever resume the subject. This depicting of character constituted my

upon the fiction is applicable to the truth ; and the investigation of the truth was the object.

The " Mystery of Marie Rogêt " was composed at a distance from the scene of the atrocity, and with no other means of investigation than the newspapers afforded. Thus much escaped the writer of which he could have availed himself had he been upon the spot, and visited the localities. It may not be improper to record, nevertheless, that the confessions of *two* persons (one of them the Madame Deluc of the narrative), made at different periods, long subsequent to the publication, confirmed in full, not only the general conclusion, but absolutely *all* the chief hypothetical details by which that conclusion was attained.

design ; and this design was thoroughly fulfilled in the wild train of circumstances brought to instance Dupin's idiosyncrasy. I might have adduced other examples, but I should have proved no more. Late events, however, in their surprising development, have startled me into some further details, which will carry with them the air of extorted confession. Hearing what I have lately heard, it would be indeed strange should I remain silent in regard to what I both heard and saw so long ago.

Upon the winding up of the tragedy involved in the deaths of Madame L'Espanaye and her daughter, the Chevalier dismissed the affair at once from his attention, and relapsed into his old habits of moody reverie. Prone, at all times, to abstraction I readily fell in with his humour ; and continuing to occupy our chambers in the Faubourg Saint Germain, we gave the Future to the winds, and slumbered tranquilly in the Present, weaving the dull world around us into dreams.

But these dreams were not altogether uninterrupted. It may readily be supposed that the part played by my friend in the drama at the Rue Morgue, had not failed of its impression upon the fancies of the Parisian police. With its emissaries, the name of Dupin had grown into a household word. The simple character of those inductions by which he had disentangled the mystery never having been explained even to the Prefect, or to any other individual than myself, of course it is not surprising that the affair was regarded as little less than miraculous, or that the Chevalier's analytical abilities acquired for him the credit of intuition. His frankness would have led him to disabuse every inquirer of such prejudice ; but his indolent humour forbade all further agitation of a topic whose interest to himself had long ceased. It thus happened that he found himself the cynosure of the policial eyes ; and the cases were not few in which attempt was made to engage his services at the Prefecture. One of the most remarkable instances was that of the murder of a young girl named Marie Rogêt.

This event occurred about two years after the atrocity in the Rue Morgue. Marie, whose Christian and family name will at once arrest attention from their resemblance to those of the unfortunate " cigar-girl," was the only daughter of the widow Estelle Rogêt. The father had died during the child's infancy, and from the period of his death, until within eighteen months before the assassination which forms the subject of our narrative, the mother and daughter had dwelt together in the Rue Pavée Sainte Andrée ; * Madame there keeping a *pension*, assisted by Marie. Affairs went on thus until the latter had attained her twenty-second year, when her great beauty attracted the notice of a perfumer, who occupied one of the shops in the basement of the Palais Royal, and whose custom lay chiefly among the desperate adventurers infesting that neighbourhood. Monsieur Le Blanc † was not unaware of the advantages to be derived from the attendance of the fair Marie in his perfumery ; and his liberal proposals were accepted eagerly by the girl, although with somewhat more of hesitation by Madame.

* Nassau Street.   † Anderson.

The anticipations of the shopkeeper were realised, and his rooms soon became notorious through the charms of the sprightly *grisette*. She had been in his employ about a year, when her admirers were thrown into confusion by her sudden disappearance from the shop. Monsieur Le Blanc was unable to account for her absence, and Madame Rogêt was distracted with anxiety and terror. The public papers immediately took up the theme, and the police were upon the point of making serious investigations, when, one fine morning, after the lapse of a week, Marie, in good health, but with a somewhat saddened air, made her reappearance at her usual counter in the perfumery. All inquiry, except that of a private character, was of course immediately hushed. Monsieur Le Blanc professed total ignorance, as before. Marie, with Madame, replied to all questions, that the last week had been spent at the house of a relation in the country. Thus the affair died away and was generally forgotten, for the girl, ostensibly to relieve herself from the impertinence of curiosity, soon bade a final adieu to the perfumer, and sought the shelter of her mother's residence in the Rue Pavée Sainte Andrée.

It was about five months after this return home, that her friends were alarmed by her sudden disappearance for the second time. Three days elapsed, and nothing was heard of her. On the fourth her corpse was found floating in the Seine,* near the shore which is opposite the Quartier of the Rue Sainte Andrée, and at a point not very far distant from the secluded neighbourhood of the Barrière du Roule.†

* The Hudson.   † Weehawken.

The atrocity of this murder (for it was at once evident that murder had been committed), the youth and beauty of the victim, and, above all, her previous notoriety, conspired to produce intense excitement in the minds of the sensitive Parisians. I can call to mind no similar occurrence producing so general and so intense an effect. For several weeks, in the discussion of this one absorbing theme, even the momentous political topics of the day were forgotten. The Prefect made unusual exertions ; and the powers of the whole Parisian police were of course tasked to the utmost extent.

Upon the first discovery of the corpse it was not supposed that the murderer would be able to elude for more than a very brief period the inquisition which was immediately set on foot. It was not until the expiration of a week that it was deemed necessary to offer a reward ; and even then this reward was limited to a thousand francs. In the meantime the investigation proceeded with vigour, if not always with judgment, and numerous individuals were examined to no purpose ; while, owing to the continued absence of all clue to the mystery, the popular excitement greatly increased. At the end of the tenth day it was thought advisable to double the sum originally proposed ; and, at length, the second week having elapsed without leading to any discoveries, and the prejudice which always exists in Paris against the Police having given vent to itself in several serious *émeutes*, the Prefect took it upon himself to offer the sum of twenty thousand francs " for the conviction of the assassin," or, if more than one should prove to have been implicated,

" for the conviction of any one of the assassins." In the proclamation setting forth this reward, a full pardon was promised to any accomplice who should come forward in evidence against his fellow ; and to the whole was appended, wherever it appeared, the private placard of a committee of citizens, offering ten thousand francs in addition to the amount proposed by the Prefecture. The entire reward thus stood at no less than thirty thousand francs, which will be regarded as an extraordinary sum when we consider the humble condition of the girl, and the great frequency in large cities of such atrocities as the one described.

No one doubted now that the mystery of this murder would be immediately brought to light. But although, in one or two instances, arrests were made which promised elucidation, yet nothing was elicited which could implicate the parties suspected, and they were discharged forthwith. Strange as it may appear, the third week from the discovery of the body had passed, and passed without any light being thrown upon the subject, before even a rumour of the events which had so agitated the public mind reached the ears of Dupin and myself. Engaged in researches which had absorbed our whole attention, it had been nearly a month since either of us had gone abroad, or received a visitor, or more than glanced at the leading political articles in one of the daily papers. The first intelligence of the murder was brought us by G——, in person. He called upon us early in the afternoon of the thirteenth of July 18—, and remained with us until late in the night. He had been piqued by the failure of all his

endeavours to ferret out the assassins. His reputation
—so he said with a peculiarly Parisian air—was at
stake. Even his honour was concerned. The eyes of
the public were upon him and there was really no
sacrifice which he would not be willing to make for
the development of the mystery. He concluded a
somewhat droll speech with a compliment upon what
he was pleased to term the *tact* of Dupin, and made
him a direct and certainly a liberal proposition, the
precise nature of which I do not feel myself at liberty
to disclose, but which has no bearing upon the proper
subject of my narrative.

The compliment my friend rebutted as best he could,
but the proposition he accepted at once, although its
advantages were altogether provisional. This point
being settled, the Prefect broke forth at once into
explanations of his own views, interspersing them
with long comments upon the evidence ; of which
latter we were not yet in possession. He discoursed
much, and, beyond doubt, learnedly ; while I hazarded
an occasional suggestion as the night wore drowsily
away. Dupin, sitting steadily in his accustomed arm-
chair, was the embodiment of respectful attention.
He wore spectacles during the whole interview, and
an occasional glance beneath their green glasses
sufficed to convince me that he slept not the less
soundly, because silently, throughout the seven or
eight leaden-footed hours which immediately preceded
the departure of the Prefect.

In the morning I procured at the Prefecture a full
report of all the evidence elicited, and, at the various
newspaper offices, a copy of every paper in which,

from first to last, had been published any decisive information in regard to this sad affair. Freed from all that was positively disproved, this mass of information stood thus :—

Marie Rogêt left the residence of her mother, in the Rue Pavée Sainte Andrée, about nine o'clock in the morning of Sunday, June the twenty-second, 18—. In going out, she gave notice to a Monsieur Jacques St. Eustache,* and to him only, of her intention to spend the day with an aunt who resided in the Rue des Drômes. The Rue des Drômes is a short and narrow but populous thoroughfare, not far from the banks of the river, and at a distance of some two miles, in the most direct course possible from the *pension* of Madame Rogêt. St. Eustache was the accepted suitor of Marie, and lodged, as well as took his meals, at the *pension*. He was to have gone for his betrothed at dusk, and to have escorted her home. In the afternoon, however, it came on to rain heavily ; and, supposing that she would remain all night at her aunt's (as she had done under similar circumstances before), he did not think it necessary to keep his promise. As night drew on, Madame Rogêt (who was an infirm old lady, seventy years of age) was heard to express a fear " that she should never see Marie again ; " but this observation attracted little attention at the time.

On Monday it was ascertained that the girl had not been to the Rue des Drômes ; and when the day elapsed without tidings of her, a tardy search was instituted at several points in the city and its environs.

* Payne.

It was not, however, until the fourth day from the period of her disappearance that anything satisfactory was ascertained respecting her. On this day (Wednesday, the twenty-fifth of June), a Monsieur Beauvais,* who, with a friend, had been making inquiries for Marie near the Barrière du Roule, on the shore of the Seine which is opposite the Rue Pavée Sainte Andrée, was informed that a corpse had just been towed ashore by some fishermen, who had found it floating in the river. Upon seeing the body, Beauvais, after some hesitation, identified it as that of the perfumery-girl. His friend recognised it more promptly.

The face was suffused with dark blood, some of which issued from the mouth. No foam was seen, as in the case of the merely drowned. There was no discoloration in the cellular tissue. About the throat were bruises and impressions of fingers. The arms were bent over on the chest and were rigid. The right hand was clenched; the left partially open. On the left wrist were two circular excoriations, apparently the effect of ropes, or of a rope in more than one volution. A part of the right wrist, also, was much chafed, as well as the back throughout its extent, but more especially at the shoulder-blades. In bringing the body to the shore the fishermen had attached to it a rope, but none of the excoriations had been effected by this. The flesh of the neck was much swollen. There were no cuts apparent, or bruises which appeared the effect of blows. A piece of lace was found tied so tightly around the neck as to be hidden from sight; it was completely buried in the

* Crommelin.

flesh, and was fastened by a knot which lay just under the left ear. This alone would have sufficed to produce death. The medical testimony spoke confidently of the virtuous character of the deceased. She had been subjected, it said, to brutal violence. The corpse was in such condition when found that there could have been no difficulty in its recognition by friends.

The dress was much torn and otherwise disordered. In the outer garment a slip, about a foot wide, had been torn upward from the bottom hem to the waist, but not torn off. It was wound three times around the waist, and secured by a sort of hitch in the back. The dress immediately beneath the frock was of fine muslin ; and from this a slip eighteen inches wide had been torn entirely out—torn very evenly and with great care. It was found around her neck, fitting loosely, and secured with a hard knot. Over this muslin slip and the slip of lace, the strings of a bonnet were attached ; the bonnet being appended. The knot by which the strings of the bonnet were fastened was not a lady's, but a slip or sailor's knot.

After the recognition of the corpse, it was not, as usual, taken to the Morgue (this formality being superfluous), but hastily interred not far from the spot at which it was brought ashore. Through the exertions of Beauvais, the matter was industriously hushed up, as far as possible ; and several days had elapsed before any public emotion resulted. A weekly paper,* however, at length, took up the theme ; the corpse was disinterred, and a re-examination instituted, but nothing was elicited beyond what has been already

* " The New York Mercury."

noted. The clothes, however, were now submitted to the mother and friends of the deceased, and fully identified as those worn by the girl upon leaving home.

Meantime the excitement increased hourly. Several individuals were arrested and discharged. St. Eustache fell especially under suspicion ; and he failed at first to give an intelligible account of his whereabouts during the Sunday on which Marie left home. Subsequently, however, he submitted to Monsieur G—— affidavits, accounting satisfactorily for every hour of the day in question. As time passed and no discovery ensued, a thousand contradictory rumours were circulated, and journalists busied themselves in *suggestions*. Among these, the one which attracted the most notice was the idea that Marie Rogêt still lived —that the corpse found in the Seine was that of some other unfortunate. It will be proper that I submit to the reader some passages which embody the suggestion alluded to. These passages are *literal* translations from " L'Etoile," * a paper conducted, in general, with much ability.

" Mademoiselle Rogêt left her mother's house on Sunday morning, June the twenty-second, 18—, with the ostensible purpose of going to see her aunt, or some other connection, in the Rue des Drômes. From that hour nobody is proved to have seen her. There is no trace or tidings of her at all. . . . . There has no person whatever come forward so far, who saw her at all on that day after she left her mother's door. . . . . Now, though we have no evidence that Marie Rogêt was in the land of the living after nine o'clock on Sunday.

* The " New York Brother Jonathan," edited by Mr. Hastings Weld.

June the twenty-second, we have proof that up to that hour she was alive. On Wednesday at noon, a female body was discovered afloat on the shore of the Barrière du Roule. This was, even if we presume that Marie Rogêt was thrown into the river within three hours after she left her mother's house, only three days from the time she left her home—three days to an hour. But it is folly to suppose that the murder, if murder was committed on her body, could have been consummated soon enough to have enabled her murderers to throw the body into the river before midnight. Those who are guilty of such horrid crimes choose darkness rather than light. . . . . Thus we see that if the body found in the river *was* that of Marie Rogêt, it could only have been in the water two and a half days, or three at the outside. All experience has shown that drowned bodies, or bodies thrown into the water immediately after death by violence, require from six to ten days for sufficient decomposition to take place to bring them to the top of the water. Even where a cannon is fired over a corpse, and it rises before at least five or six days' immersion, it sinks again, if let alone. Now, we ask, what was there in this case to cause a departure from the ordinary course of nature ? . . . . If the body had been kept in its mangled state on shore until Tuesday night, some trace would be found on shore of the murderers. It is a doubtful point, also, whether the body would be so soon afloat, even were it thrown in after having been dead two days. And, furthermore, it is exceedingly improbable that any villains who had committed such a murder as is here supposed would have thrown the body in without weight to sink it, when such a precaution could have so easily been taken."

The editor here proceeds to argue that the body must have been in the water " not three days merely, but at least five times three days," because it was so far decomposed that Beauvais had great difficulty in recognising it. This latter point, however, was fully disproved. I continue the translation :

" What, then, are the facts on which M. Beauvais says that he has no doubt the body was that of Marie Rogêt ? He ripped up the gown sleeve, and says he found marks which satisfied him of the identity. The public generally supposed those marks to have consisted of some description of scars. He rubbed the arm and found *hair* upon it—something as indefinite, we think, as can readily be imagined—as little conclusive as finding an arm in the sleeve. M. Beauvais did not return that night, but sent word to Madame Rogêt at seven o'clock on Wednesday evening that an investigation was still in progress respecting her daughter. If we allow that Madame Rogêt from her age and grief could not go over (which is allowing a great deal) there certainly must have been some one who would have thought it worth while to go over and attend the investigation if they thought the body was that of Marie. Nobody went over. There was nothing said or heard about the matter in the Rue Pavée Sainte Andrée that reached even the occupants of the same building. M. St. Eustache, the lover and intended husband of Marie, who boarded in her mother's house, deposes that he did not hear of the discovery of the body of his intended until the next morning, when M. Beauvais came into his chamber and told him of it. For an item of news like this, it strikes us it was very coolly received."

In this way the journal endeavoured to create the impression of an apathy on the part of the relatives of Marie, inconsistent with the supposition that these relatives believed the corpse to be hers. Its insinuations amount to this :—that Marie with the connivance of her friends, had absented herself from the city for reasons involving a charge against her chastity, and that these friends, upon the discovery of a corpse in the Seine, somewhat resembling that of the girl, had availed themselves of the opportunity to impress the public with the belief of her death. But "L'Etoile" was again over-hasty. It was distinctly proved that no apathy, such as was imagined, existed : that the old lady was exceedingly feeble, and so agitated as to be unable to attend to any duty : that St. Eustache, so far from receiving the news cooly, was distracted with grief and bore himself so frantically that M. Beauvais prevailed upon a friend and relative to take charge of him, and prevent his attending the examination at the disinterment. Moreover, although it was stated by " L'Etoile " that the corpse was reinterred at the public expense—that an advantageous offer of private sepulture was absolutely declined by the family—and that no member of the family attended the ceremonial :—although, I say, all this was asserted by " L'Etoile " in furtherance of the impression it designed to convey—yet *all* this was satisfactorily disproved. In a subsequent number of the paper, an attempt was made to throw suspicion upon Beauvais himself. The editor says :

" Now, then, a change comes over the matter. We are told that on one occasion, while a Madame B—— was at Madame Rogêt's house, M. Beauvais, who was going out, told her that a *gendarme* was expected there, and that she, Madame B——, must not say anything to the *gendarme* until he returned, but let the matter be for him. . . . In the present posture of affairs M. Beauvais appears to have the whole matter locked up in his head. A single step cannot be taken without M. Beauvais, for go which way you will you run against him. . . . For some reason he determined that nobody shall have anything to do with the proceedings but himself, and he has elbowed the male relatives out of the way, according to their representations, in a very singular manner. He seems to have been very much averse to permitting the relatives to see the body."

By the following fact some colour was given to the suspicion thus thrown upon Beauvais. A visitor at his office a few days prior to the girl's disappearance, and during the absence of its occupant, had observed a *rose* in the keyhole of the door, and the name " *Marie* " inscribed upon a slate which hung near at hand.

The general impression, so far as we were enabled to glean it from the newspapers, seemed to be that Marie had been the victim of *a gang* of desperadoes— that by these she had been borne across the river, maltreated, and murdered. " Le Commercial," * however, a print of extensive influence, was earnest in combating this popular idea. I quote a passage or two from its columns :—

" We are persuaded that pursuit has hitherto been on a false scent, so far as it has been directed to the Barrière du Roule. It is impossible that a person so well known to thousands as this young woman was should have passed three blocks without some one having seen her ; and any one who saw her would have remembered it,

* New York " Journal of Commerce."

for she interested all who knew her. It was when the streets were full of people that she went out. . . . It is impossible that she could have gone to the Barrière du Roule or to the Rue des Drômes without being recognised by a dozen persons, yet no one has come forward who saw her outside of her mother's door, and there is no evidence, except the testimony concerning her *expressed intentions*, that she did go out at all. Her gown was torn, bound round her, and tied, and by that the body was carried as a bundle. If the murder had been committed at the Barrière du Roule there would have been no necessity for any such arrangement. The fact that the body was found floating near the Barrière is no proof as to where it was thrown into the water. . . . . A piece of one of the unfortunate girl's petticoats, two feet long and one foot wide, was torn out and tied under her chin around the back of her head, probably to prevent screams. This was done by fellows who had no pocket handkerchiefs."

A day or two before the Prefect called upon us, however, some important information reached the police, which seemed to overthrow, at least, the chief portion of " Le Commercial's " argument. Two small boys, sons of a Madame Deluc, while roaming among the woods near the Barrière du Roule, chanced to penetrate a close thicket, within which were three or four large stones, forming a kind of seat, with a back and footstool. On the upper stone lay a white petticoat, on the second a silk scarf. A parasol, gloves, and a pocket handkerchief were also here found. The handkerchief bore the name " Marie Rogêt." Fragments of dress were discovered on the brambles around. The earth was trampled, the bushes were broken, and there was every evidence of a struggle. Between the thicket and the river the fences were found taken down, and the ground bore evidence of some heavy burthen having been dragged along it.

A weekly paper, "Le Soleil," * had the following comments upon this discovery—comments which merely echoed the sentiment of the whole Parisian press:

"The things had all evidently been there at least three or four weeks; they were all mildewed down hard with the action of the rain, and stuck together from mildew. The grass had grown around and over some of them. The silk on the parasol was strong, but the threads of it were run together within. The upper part, where it had been doubled and folded, was all mildewed and rotten, and tore on its being opened. . . . . The pieces of her frock torn out by the bushes were about three inches wide and six inches long. One part was the hem of the frock, and it had been mended; the other piece was part of the skirt, not the hem. They looked like strips torn off, and were on the thorn bush, about a foot from the ground. . . . . There can be no doubt, therefore, that the spot of this appalling outrage has been discovered."

Consequent upon this discovery, new evidence appeared. Madame Deluc testified that she keeps a roadside inn not far from the bank of the river, opposite the Barrière du Roule. The neighbourhood is secluded—particularly so. It is the usual Sunday resort of blackguards from the city, who cross the river in boats. About three o'clock in the afternoon of the Sunday in question a young girl arrived at the inn accompanied by a young man of dark complexion.

* Philadelphia "Saturday Evening Post."

The two remained here for some time. On their departure, they took the road to some thick woods in the vicinity. Madame Deluc's attention was called to the dress worn by the girl on account of its resemblance to one worn by a deceased relative. A scarf was particularly noticed. Soon after the departure of the couple a gang of miscreants made their appearance, behaved boisterously, ate and drank without making payment, followed in the route of the young man and girl, returned to the inn about dusk, and re-crossed the river as if in great haste.

It was soon after dark, upon this same evening, that Madame Deluc, as well as her eldest son, heard the screams of a female in the vicinity of the inn. The screams were violent but brief. Madame D. recognised not only the scarf which was found in the thicket, but the dress which was discovered upon the corpse. An omnibus-driver, Valence,* now also testified that he saw Marie Rogêt cross a ferry on the Seine, on the Sunday in question, in company with a young man of dark complexion. He, Valence, knew Marie, and could not be mistaken in her identity. The articles found in the thicket were fully identified by the relatives of Marie.

The items of evidence and information thus collected by myself from the newspapers, at the suggestion of Dupin, embraced only one more point—but this was a point of seemingly vast consequence. It appears that, immediately after the discovery of the clothes as above described, the lifeless, or nearly lifeless body of St. Eustache, Marie's bethrothed, was found in the

* Adam.

vicinity of what all now supposed the scene of the outrage. A phial labelled " laudanum," and emptied, was found near him. His breath gave evidence of the poison. He died without speaking. Upon his person was found a letter, briefly stating his love for Marie, with his design of self-destruction.

" I need scarcely tell you," said Dupin, as he finished the perusal of my notes, " that this is a far more intricate case than that of the Rue Morgue, from which it differs in one important respect. This is an *ordinary*, although an atrocious instance of crime. There is nothing peculiarly *outré* about it. You will observe that, for this reason, the mystery has been considered easy, when, for this reason, it should have been considered difficult of solution. Thus, at first, it was thought unnecessary to offer a reward. The myrmidons of G—— were able at once to comprehend how and why such an atrocity *might have been* committed. They could picture to their imaginations a mode—many modes—and a motive—many motives ; and because it was not impossible that either of these numerous modes and motives *could* have been the actual one, they have taken it for granted that one of them *must*. But the ease with which these variable fancies were entertained, and the very plausibility which each assumed, should have been understood as indicative rather of the difficulties than of the facilities which must attend elucidation. I have before observed that it is by prominences above the plane of the ordinary, that reason feels her way, if at all, in her search for the true, and that the proper question in cases such as this, is not so much ' what has occurred ? '

as 'what has occurred that has never occurred before?' In the investigations at the house of Madame L'Espanaye,* the agents of G—— were discouraged and confounded by that very *unusualness* which, to a properly regulated intellect, would have afforded the surest omen of success; while this same intellect might have been plunged in despair at the ordinary character of all that met the eye in the case of the perfumery-girl, and yet told of nothing but easy triumph to the functionaries of the Prefecture.

"In the case of Madame L'Espanaye and her daughter there was, even at the beginning of our investigation, no doubt that murder had been committed. The idea of suicide was excluded at once. Here, too, we are freed at the commencement from all supposition of self-murder. The body found at the Barrière du Roule was found under such circumstances as to leave us no room for embarrassment upon this important point. But it has been suggested that the corpse discovered is not that of the Marie Rogêt, for the conviction of whose assassin, or assassins, the reward is offered, and respecting whom, solely, our agreement has been arranged with the Prefect. We both know this gentleman well. It will not do to trust him too far. If, dating our inquiries from the body found, and then tracing a murderer, we yet discover this body to be that of some other individual than Marie; or, if starting from the living Marie, we find her, yet find her unassassinated—in either case we lose our labour, since it is Monsieur —— with whom we have to deal. For our own purpose, therefore, if not for the purpose

* See " Murders in the Rue Morgue."

of justice, it is indispensable that our first step should
be the determination of the identity of the corpse
with the Marie Rogêt who is missing.

" With the public the arguments of ' L'Etoile ' have
had weight ; and that the journal itself is convinced
of their importance would appear from the manner in
which it commences one of its essays upon the subject
—' Several of the morning papers of the day,' it says,
' speak of the *conclusive* article in Monday's " Etoile." '
To me, this article appears conclusive of little beyond
the zeal of its inditer. We should bear in mind, that
in general it is the object of our newspapers rather to
create a sensation—to make a point—than to further
the cause of truth. The latter end is only pursued
when it seems coincident with the former. The print
which merely falls in with ordinary opinion (however
well founded this opinion may be) earns for itself no
credit with the mob. The mass of the people regard
as profound only him who suggests *pungent contradictions* of the general idea. In ratiocination, not less
than in literature, it is the *epigram* which is the most
immediately and the most universally appreciated. In
both, it is of the lowest order of merit.

" What I mean to say is, that it is the mingled
epigram and melodrama of the idea, that Marie Rogêt
still lives, rather than any true plausibility in this
idea, which have suggested it to ' L'Etoile,' and secured
it a favourable reception with the public. Let us
examine the heads of this journal's argument ; endeavouring to avoid the incoherence with which it is
originally set forth.

" The first aim of the writer is to show, from the

brevity of the interval between Marie's disappearance and the finding of the floating corpse, that this corpse cannot be that of Marie. The reduction of this interval to its smallest possible dimension, becomes thus, at once, an object with the reasoner. In the rash pursuit of this object he rushes into mere assumption at the outset. ' It is folly to suppose,' he says, ' that the murder, if murder was committed on her body, could have been consummated soon enough to have enabled her murderers to throw the body into the river before midnight.' We demand at once, and very naturally, *why ?* Why is it folly to suppose that the murder was committed *within five minutes* after the girl's quitting her mother's house ? Why is it folly to suppose that the murder was committed at any given period of the day ? There have been assassinations at all hours. But, had the murder taken place at any moment between nine o'clock in the morning of Sunday, and a quarter before midnight, there would still have been time enough ' to throw the body into the river before midnight.' This assumption, then, amounts precisely to this—that the murder was not committed on Sunday at all ; and, if we allow ' L'Etoile ' to assume this, we may permit it any liberties whatever. The paragraph beginning, ' It is folly to suppose that the murder,' etc., however it appears as printed in ' L'Etoile,' may be imagined to have existed actually *thus* in the brain of its inditer—' It is folly to suppose that the murder, if murder was committed on the body, could have been committed soon enough to have enabled her murderers to throw the body into the river before midnight. It is folly, we say, to suppose all this, and to suppose at the same time (as we are resolved to suppose), that the body was *not* thrown in until *after* midnight '—a sentence sufficiently inconsequential in itself, but not so utterly preposterous as the one printed.

" Were it my purpose," continued Dupin, " merely to *make out a case* against this passage of ' L'Etoile's ' argument, I might safely leave it where it is. It is not, however, with ' L'Etoile ' that we have to do, but with the truth. The sentence in question has but one meaning as it stands, and this meaning I have fairly stated ; but it is material that we go behind the mere words for an idea which these words have obviously intended—and failed—to convey. It was the design of the journalist to say that, at whatever period of the day or night of Sunday this murder was committed, it was improbable that the assassins would have ventured to bear the corpse to the river before midnight. And herein lies, really, the assumption of which I complain. It is assumed that the murder was committed at such a position, and under such circumstances, that *the bearing it* to the river became necessary. Now, the assassination might have taken place upon the river's brink or on the river itself ; and, thus, the throwing the corpse in the water might have been resorted to at any period of the day or night as the most obvious and most immediate mode of disposal. You will understand that I suggest nothing here as probable, or as coincident with my own opinion. My design, so far, has no reference to the *facts* of the case. I wish merely to caution you against the whole tone of ' L'Etoile's ' *suggestion*, by calling your attention to its *ex parte* character at the outset.

"Having prescribed thus a limit to suit its own preconceived notions ; having assumed that, if this were the body of Marie, it could have been in the water but a very brief time ; the journal goes on to say :—

' All experience has shown that drowned bodies, or bodies thrown into the water immediately after death by violence, require from six to ten days for sufficient decomposition to take place to bring them to the top of the water. Even when a cannon is fired over a corpse, and it rises before at least five or six days' immersion, it sinks again if let alone.'

"These assertions have been tacitly received by every paper in Paris with the exception of ' Le Moniteur.' * This latter print endeavours to combat that portion of the paragraph which has reference to ' drowned bodies ' only, by citing some five or six instances in which the bodies of individuals known to be drowned were found floating after the lapse of less time than is insisted upon by ' L'Etoile.' But there is something excessively unphilosophical in the attempt on the part of ' Le Moniteur ' to rebut the general assertion of ' L'Etoile,' by a citation of particular instances militating against that assertion. Had it been possible to adduce fifty instead of five examples of bodies found floating at the end of two or three days, these fifty examples could still have been properly regarded only as exceptions to ' L'Etoile's ' rule until such time as the rule itself

* The New York " Commercial Advertiser."

should be confuted. Admitting the rule (and this ' Le Moniteur ' does not deny, insisting merely upon its exceptions), the argument of ' L'Etoile ' is suffered to remain in full force ; for this argument does not pretend to involve more than a question of the *probability* of the body having risen to the surface in less than three days ; and this probability will be in favour of ' L'Etoile's ' position until the instances so childishly adduced shall be sufficient in number to establish an antagonistical rule.

" You will see at once that all argument upon this head should be urged, if at all, against the rule itself ; and for this end we must examine the *rationale* of the rule. Now the human body, in general, is neither much lighter nor much heavier than the water of the Seine ; that is to say, the specific gravity of the human body, in its natural condition, is about equal to the bulk of fresh water which it displaces. The bodies of fat and fleshy persons, with small bones, and of women generally, are lighter than those of the lean and large-boned, and of men ; and the specific gravity of the water of a river is somewhat influenced by the presence of the tide from sea. But, leaving this tide out of question, it may be said that *very* few human bodies will sink at all, even in fresh water, *of their own accord*. Almost any one, falling into a river, will be enabled to float, if he suffer the specific gravity of the water fairly to be adduced in comparison with his own —that is to say, if he suffer his whole person to be immersed, with as little exception as possible. The proper position for one who cannot swim, is the upright position of the walker on land, with the head thrown fully back and immersed ; the mouth and nostrils alone remaining above the surface. Thus circumstanced, we shall find that we float without difficulty and without exertion. It is evident, however, that the gravities of the body, and of the bulk of water displaced, are very nicely balanced, and that a trifle will cause either to preponderate. An arm, for instance, uplifted from the water, and thus deprived of its support, is an additional weight sufficient to immerse the whole head, while the accidental aid of the smallest piece of timber will enable us to elevate the head so as to look about. Now, in the struggles of one unused to swimming, the arms are invariably thrown upwards, while an attempt is made to keep the head in its usual perpendicular position. The result is the immersion of the mouth and nostrils, and the reception, during efforts to breathe while beneath the surface, of water into the lungs. Much is also received into the stomach, and the whole body becomes heavier by the difference between the weight of the air originally distending these cavities, and that of the fluid which now fills them. This difference is sufficient to cause the body to sink, as a general rule ; but is insufficient in the cases of individuals with small bones and an abnormal quantity of flaccid or fatty matter. Such individuals float even after drowning.

The corpse, being supposed at the bottom of the river, will there remain until, by some means, its specific gravity again becomes less than that of the bulk of water which it displaces. This effect is brought about by decomposition, or otherwise. The result of decomposition is the generation of gas, distending the cellular tissues and all the cavities, and giving the *puffed* appearance which is so horrible. When this distension has so far progressed that the bulk of the corpse is materially increased without a corresponding increase of *mass* or weight, its specific gravity becomes less than that of the water displaced, and it forthwith makes its appearance at the surface. But decomposition is modified by innumerable circumstances—is hastened or retarded by innumerable agencies ; for example, by the heat or cold of the season, by the mineral impregnation or purity of the water, by its depth or shallowness, by its currency or stagnation, by the temperament of the body, by its infection or freedom from disease before death. Thus it is evident that we can assign no period, with anything like accuracy, at which the corpse shall rise through decomposition. Under certain conditions this result would be brought about within an hour ; under others, it might not take place at all. There are chemical infusions by which the animal frame can be preserved *for ever* from corruption ; the bi-chloride of mercury is one. But, apart from decomposition, there may be, and very usually is, a generation of gas within the stomach from the acetous fermentation of vegetable matter (or within other cavities from other causes) sufficient to induce a distension which will bring the body to the surface. The effect produced by the firing of a cannon is that of simple vibration. This may either loosen the corpse from the soft mud or ooze in which it is imbedded, thus permitting it to rise when other agencies have already prepared it for so doing ; or it may overcome the tenacity of some putrescent portions of the cellular tissue, allowing the cavities to distend under the influence of the gas.

" Having thus before us the whole philosophy of this subject, we can easily test by it the assertions of ' L'Etoile.' ' All experience shows,' says this paper, 'that drowned bodies, or bodies thrown into the water immediately after death by violence, require from six to ten days for sufficient decomposition to take place to bring them to the top of the water. Even when a cannon is fired over a corpse, and it rises before at least five or six days' immersion, it sinks again if let alone.'

" The whole of this paragraph must now appear a tissue of inconsequence and incoherence. All experience does *not* show that ' drowned bodies ' *require* from six to ten days for sufficient decomposition to take place to bring them to the surface. Both science and experience show that the period of their rising is, and necessarily must be, indeterminate. If, moreover, a body has risen to the surface through firing a cannon, it will *not* ' sink again if let alone,' until decomposition has so far progressed as to permit the escape of the generated gas. But I wish to call your attention to the distinction which is made between ' drowned bodies ' and ' bodies thrown into the water immediately after death by violence.' Although the writer admits the distinction, he yet includes them all in the same category. I have shown how it is that the body of a drowning man becomes specifically heavier than its bulk of water, and that he would not sink at all, except for the struggles by which he elevates his arms above the surface, and his gasps for breath while beneath the surface—gasps which supply by water the place of the original air in the lungs. But these struggles and these gasps would not occur in the body 'thrown into the water immediately after death by violence.' Thus, in the latter instance, *the body, as a general rule, would not sink at all*—a fact of which ' L'Etoile ' is evidently ignorant. When decomposition had proceeded to a very great extent—when the flesh had in a great measure left the bones—then, indeed, but not *till* then, should we lose sight of the corpse.

" And now what are we to make of the argument that the body found could not be that of Marie Rogêt, because, three days only having elapsed, this body was found floating ? If drowned, being a woman, she might never have sunk ; or, having sunk, might have reappeared in twenty-four hours, or less. But no one supposes her to have been drowned ; and, dying before being thrown into the river, she might have been found floating at any period afterwards whatever.

" ' But,' says ' L'Etoile,' ' if the body had been kept in its mangled state on shore until Tuesday night, some trace would be found on shore of the murderers.' Here it is at first difficult to perceive the intention of the reasoner. He means to anticipate what he imagines would be an objection to his theory—viz., that the body was kept on shore two days, suffering rapid decomposition—*more* rapid than if immersed in water. He supposes that, had this been the case, it *might* have appeared at the surface on the Wednesday, and thinks that *only* under such circumstances it could so have appeared. He is accordingly in haste to show that it *was not* kept on shore ; for, if so, ' some trace would be found on shore of the murderers.' I presume you smile at the *sequitur*. You cannot be made to see how the mere *duration* of the corpse on the shore could operate to *multiply traces* of the assassins. Nor can I.

" ' And, furthermore, it is exceedingly improbable,' continues our journal, ' that any villains who had committed such a murder as is here supposed, would have thrown the body in without weight to sink it, when such a precaution could have so easily been taken.' Observe, here, the laughable confusion of thought. No one—not even ' L'Etoile '—disputes the murder committed *on the body found*. The marks of violence are too obvious. It is our reasoner's object merely to show that this body is not Marie's. He wishes to prove that *Marie* is not assassinated—not that the corpse was not. Yet his observation proves only the latter point. Here is a corpse without weight attached. Murderers, casting it in, would not have failed to attach a weight. Therefore it was not thrown in by murderers. This is all which is proved, if anything is. The question of identity is not even approached, and ' L'Etoile ' has been at great pains merely to gainsay now what it has admitted only a moment before. ' We are perfectly convinced,' it says, ' that the body found was that of a murdered female.'

" Nor is this the sole instance, even in this division of his subject, where our reasoner unwittingly reasons against himself. His evident object, I have already said, is to reduce, as much as possible, the interval between Marie's disappearance and the finding of the corpse. Yet we find him *urging* the point that no person saw the girl from the moment of her leaving her mother's house. ' We have no evidence,' he says, ' that Marie Rogêt was in the land of the living after nine o'clock on Sunday, June the twenty-second.' As his argument is obviously an *ex parte* one, he should, at least, have left this matter out of sight ; for had any one been known to see Marie, say on Monday or on Tuesday, the interval in question would have been much reduced, and by his own ratiocination, the probability much diminished of the corpse being that of the *grisette*. It is, nevertheless, amusing to observe that ' L'Etoile ' insists upon its point in the full belief of its furthering its general argument.

" Reperuse now that portion of this argument which has reference to the identification of the corpse by Beauvais. In regard to the *hair* upon the arm, ' L'Etoile ' has been obviously disingenuous. M. Beauvais, not being an idiot, could never have urged, in identification of the corpse, simply *hair upon its arm*. No arm is *without* hair. The *generality* of the expression of ' L'Etoile ' is a mere perversion of the witness's phraseology. He must have spoken of some *peculiarity* in this hair. It must have been a peculiarity of colour, of quantity, of length, or of situation.

" ' Her foot,' says the journal, ' was small,—so are thousands of feet. Her garter is no proof whatever, nor is her shoe, for shoes and garters are sold in packages. The same may be said of the flowers in her hat. One thing upon which M. Beauvais strongly insists is that the clasp on the garter found had been set back to take it in. This amounts to nothing; for most women find it proper to take a pair of garters home and fit them to the size of the limbs they are to encircle, rather than to try them in the store where they purchase.' Here it is difficult to suppose the reasoner in earnest. Had M. Beauvais, in his search for the body of Marie, discovered a corpse corresponding in general size and appearance to the missing girl, he would have been warranted (without reference to the question of habiliment at all) in forming an opinion that his search had been successful. If, in addition to the point of general size and contour, he had found upon the arm a peculiar hairy appearance which he had observed upon the living Marie, his opinion might have been justly strengthened, and the increase of positiveness might well have been in the ratio of the peculiarity or unusualness of the hairy mark. If the feet of Marie being small, those of the corpse were also small, the increase of probability that the body was that of Marie would not be an increase in a ratio merely arithmetical, but in one highly geometrical, or accumulative. Add to all this shoes such as she had been known to wear upon the day of her disappearance, and although these shoes may be ' sold in packages,' you so far augment the probability as to verge upon the certain. What of itself would be no evidence of identity, becomes, through its corroborative position, proof most sure. Give us, then, flowers in the hat corresponding to those worn by the missing girl, and we seek for nothing further. If only *one* flower, we seek for nothing further—what then if two or three, or more ? Each successive one is multiple evidence

—proof not *added* to proof, but *multiplied* by hundreds or thousands. Let us now discover upon the deceased garters such as the living used, and it is almost folly to proceed. But these garters are found to be tightened by the setting back of a clasp, in just such a manner as her own had been tightened by Marie, shortly previous to her leaving home. It is now madness or hypocrisy to doubt. What ' L'Etoile ' says in respect to this abbreviation of the garter's being a usual occurrence, shows nothing beyond its own pertinacity in error. The elastic nature of the clasp-garter is self-demonstration of the *unusualness* of the abbreviation. What is made to adjust itself must of necessity require foreign adjustment but rarely. It must have been by an accident, in its strictest sense, that these garters of Marie needed the tightening described. They alone would have amply established her identity. But it is not that the corpse was found to have the garters of the missing girl, or found to have her shoes, or her bonnet, or the flowers of her bonnet, or her feet, or a peculiar mark upon the arm, or her general size and appearance—it is that the corpse had each, and *all collectively*. Could it be proved that the editor of ' L'Etoile ' *really* entertained a doubt, under the circumstances, there would be no need, in his case, of a commission *de lunatico inquirendo*. He has thought it sagacious to echo the small talk of the lawyers, who, for the most part, content themselves with echoing the rectangular precepts of the courts. I would here observe that very much of what is rejected as evidence by a court is the best of evidence to the intellect. For the court, guiding itself by the general principles of evidence—the recognised and *booked* principles—is averse from swerving at particular instances. And this steadfast adherence to principle, with rigorous disregard of the conflicting exception, is a sure mode of attaining the *maximum* of attainable truth in any long sequence of time. The practice, *in mass*, is therefore philosophical ; but it is not the less certain that it engenders vast individual error.*

" In respect to the insinuations levelled at Beauvais, you will be willing to dismiss them in a breath. You have already fathomed the true character of this good gentleman. He is a *busybody*, with much of romance and little of wit. Any one so constituted will readily so conduct himself, upon occasion of *real* excitement, as to render himself liable to suspicion on the part of the over-acute or the ill-disposed. M. Beauvais (as it appears from your notes) had some personal interviews with the editor of ' L'Etoile,' and offended him by venturing an opinion that the corpse, notwithstanding the theory of the editor, was in sober fact that of Marie. ' He persists,' says the paper, ' in asserting the corpse to be that of Marie, but cannot give a circumstance, in addition to those which we have commented upon, to make others believe.' Now,

---

* " A theory based on the qualities of an object will prevent its being unfolded according to its objects ; and he who arranges topics in reference to their causes will cease to value them according to their results. Thus the jurisprudence of every nation will show that, when law becomes a science and a system, it ceases to be justice. The errors into which a blind devotion to *principles* of classification has led the common law will be seen by observing how often the legislature has been obliged to come forward to restore the equity its scheme had lost."—*Landor*.

without re-adverting to the fact that stronger evidence ' to make others believe ' could *never* have been adduced, it may be remarked that a man may very well be understood to believe, in a case of this kind, without the ability to advance a single reason for the belief of a second party. Nothing is more vague than impressions of individual identity. Each man recognises his neighbour, yet there are few instances in which any one is prepared to *give a reason* for his recognition. The editor of ' L'Etoile ' had no right to be offended at M. Beauvais' unreasoning belief.

" The suspicious circumstances which invest him, will be found to tally much better with my hypothesis of *romantic busybodyism*, than with the reasoner's suggestion of guilt. Once adapting the more charitable interpretation we shall find no difficulty in comprehending the rose in the key-hole ; the ' Marie ' upon the slate ; the ' elbowing the male relatives out of the way ; ' the ' aversion to permitting them to see the body ; ' the caution given to Madame B——, that she must hold no conversation with the *gendarme* until his return (Beauvais') ; and, lastly, this apparent determination ' that nobody should have anything to do with the proceedings except himself.' It seems to me unquestionable that Beauvais was a suitor of Marie's ; that she coquetted with him ; and that he was ambitious of being thought to enjoy her fullest intimacy and confidence. I shall say nothing more upon this point ; and, as the evidence fully rebuts the assertion of ' L'Etoile,' touching the matter of *apathy* on the part of the mother and other relatives—an apathy inconsistent with the supposition of their

believing the corpse to be that of the perfumery-girl
—we shall now proceed as if the question of *identity*
were settled to our perfect satisfaction."

" And what," I here demanded, " do you think of
the opinions of ' Le Commercial ' ? "

" That, in spirit, they are far more worthy of attention than any which have been promulgated upon the
subject. The deductions from the premises are philosophical and acute ; but the premises, in two instances
at least, are founded in imperfect observation. ' Le
Commercial ' wishes to intimate that Marie was seized
by some gang of low ruffians not far from her mother's
door.

" ' It is impossible,' it urges, ' that a person so well
known to thousands as this young woman was, should
have passed three blocks without some one having
seen her.' This is the idea of a man long resident in
Paris—a public man—and one whose walks to and
fro in the city have been mostly limited to the vicinity
of the public offices. He is aware that *he* seldom
passes so far as a dozen blocks from his own *bureau*
without being recognised and accosted. And, knowing the extent of his personal acquaintance with others,
and of others with him, he compares his notoriety with
that of the perfumery-girl, finds no great difference
between them, and reaches at once the conclusion that
she in her walks would be equally liable to recognition
with himself in his. This could only be the case were
her walks of the same unvarying, methodical character, and within the same *species* of limited region as
are his own. He passes to and fro at regular intervals,
within a confined periphery, abounding in individuals

who are led to observation of her person through
interest in the kindred nature of his occupation with
their own.   But the walks of Marie may, in general,
be supposed discursive.   In this particular instance it
will be understood as most probable, that she proceeded upon a route of more than average diversity
from her accustomed ones.   The parallel which we
imagine to have existed in the mind of ' Le Commercial ' would only be sustained in the event of the
two individuals traversing the whole city.   In this
case, granting the personal acquaintances to be equal,
the chances would be also equal that an equal number
of personal rencounters would be made.   For my own
part, I should hold it not only as possible, but as very
far more than probable, that Marie might have proceeded, at any given period, by any one of the many
routes between her own residence and that of her
aunt, without meeting a single individual whom she
knew, or by whom she was known.   In viewing this
question in its full and proper light, we must hold
steadily in mind the great disproportion between the
personal acquaintances of even the most noted individual in Paris and the entire population of Paris
itself.

" But whatever force there may still appear to be
in the suggestion of ' Le Commercial ' will be much
diminished when we take into consideration *the hour*
at which the girl went abroad.   ' It was when the
streets were full of people,' says ' Le Commercial,'
' that she went out.'   But not so.   It was at nine
o'clock in the morning.   Now at nine o'clock of every
morning in the week, *with the exception of Sunday*, the

streets of the city are, it is true, thronged with people. At nine on Sunday the populace are chiefly within doors, *preparing for church*. No observing person can have failed to notice the peculiarly deserted air of the town from about eight until ten on the morning of every Sabbath. Between ten and eleven the streets are thronged, but not at so early a period as that designated.

"There is another point at which there seems a deficiency of *observation* on the part of ' Le Commercial.' ' A piece,' it says, ' of one of the unfortunate girl's petticoats, two feet long, and one foot wide, was torn out and tied under her chin, and around the back of her head, probably to prevent screams. This was done by fellows who had no pocket-handkerchiefs.' Whether this idea is or is not well founded we will endeavour to see hereafter ; but ' by fellows who have no pocket-handkerchiefs' the editor intends the lowest class of ruffians. These, however, are the very description of people who will always be found to have handkerchiefs even when destitute of shirts. You must have had occasion to observe how absolutely indispensable, of late years, to the thorough blackguard, has become the pocket-handkerchief."

"And what are we to think," I asked, " of the article in ' Le Soleil ' ? "

"That it is a vast pity its inditer was not born a parrot—in which case he would have been the most illustrious parrot of his race. He has merely repeated the individual items of the already published opinion ; collecting them, with a laudable industry, from this paper and from that. ' The things had all *evidently* been there,' he says, ' at least three or four weeks, and there can be *no doubt* that the spot of this appalling outrage has been discovered.' The facts here re-stated by ' Le Soleil ' are very far indeed from removing my own doubts upon this subject, and we will examine them more particularly hereafter in connection with another division of the theme.

" At present we must occupy ourselves with other investigations. You cannot fail to have remarked the extreme laxity of the examination of the corpse. To be sure, the question of identity was readily determined, or should have been, but there were other points to be ascertained. Had the body been in any respect *despoiled ?* Had the deceased any articles of jewellery about her person upon leaving home ? if so, had she any when found ? These are important questions utterly untouched by the evidence ; and there are others of equal moment which have met with no attention. We must endeavour to satisfy ourselves by personal inquiry. The case of St. Eustache must be re-examined. I have no suspicion of this person, but let us proceed methodically. We will ascertain beyond a doubt the validity of the *affidavits* in regard to his whereabouts on the Sunday. Affidavits of this character are readily made matter of mystification. Should there be nothing wrong here, however, we will dismiss St. Eustache from our investigations. His suicide, however corroborative of suspicion, were there found to be deceit in the affidavits, is, without such deceit, in no respect an unaccountable circumstance, or one which need cause us to deflect from the line of ordinary analysis.

" In that which I now propose, we will discard the interior points of this tragedy, and concentrate our attention upon its outskirts. Not the least usual error, in investigations such as this, is the limiting of inquiry to the immediate, with total disregard of the collateral or circumstantial events. It is the malpractice of the courts to confine evidence and discussion to the bounds of apparent relevancy. Yet experience has shown, and a true philosophy will always show, that a vast, perhaps the larger portion of truth, arises from the seemingly irrelevant. It is through the spirit of this principle, if not precisely through its letter, that modern science has resolved to *calculate upon the unforeseen.* But perhaps you do not comprehend me. The history of human knowledge has so uninterruptedly shown that to collateral, or incidental, or accidental events, we are indebted for the most numerous and most valuable discoveries, that it has at length become necessary, in any prospective view of improvement, to make not only large, but the largest allowances for inventions that shall rise by chance, and quite out of the range of ordinary expectation. It is no longer philosophical to base upon what has been a vision of what is to be. *Accident* is admitted as a portion of the substructure. We make chance a matter of absolute calculation. We subject the unlooked for and unimagined to the mathematical *formulæ* of the schools.

" I repeat that it is no more than fact that the *larger* portion of all truth has sprung from the collateral ; and it is but in accordance with the spirit of the principle involved in this fact that I would divert inquiry in the present case, from the trodden and hitherto unfruitful ground of the event itself, to the contemporary circumstances which surround it. While you ascertain the validity of the affidavits, I will examine the newspapers more generally than you have as yet done. So far, we have only reconnoitred the field of investigation ; but it will be strange indeed if a comprehensive survey, such as I propose, of the public prints will not afford us some minute points which shall establish a *direction* for inquiry."

In pursuance of Dupin's suggestion, I made a scrupulous examination of the affair of the affidavits. The result was a firm conviction of their validity, and of the consequent innocence of St. Eustache. In the meantime my friend occupied himself with what seemed to me a minuteness altogether objectless in a scrutiny of the various newspaper files. At the end of a week he placed before me the following extracts :—

" About three years and a half ago a disturbance very similar to the present was caused by the disappearance of this same Marie Rogêt from the *parfumerie* of Monsieur Le Blanc in the Palais Royal. At the end of a week, however, she reappeared at her customary *comptoir* as well as ever, with the exception of a slight paleness not altogether usual. It was given out by Monsieur Le Blanc and her mother that she had merely been on a visit to some friend in the country, and the affair was speedily hushed up. We presume that the present absence is a freak of the same nature, and that, at the expiration of a week, or perhaps a month, we shall have her among us again."—*Evening Paper—Monday, June* 23.*

" An evening journal of yesterday refers to a former

* New York " Express."

mysterious disappearance of Mademoiselle Rogêt. It is well known that during the week of her absence from Le Blanc's *parfumerie* she was in the company of a young naval officer much noted for his debaucheries. A quarrel, it is supposed, providentially led to her return home. We have the name of the Lothario in question, who is at present stationed in Paris, but, for obvious reasons, forbear to make it public."—*Le Mercurie*—*Tuesday Morning, June* 24.*

" An outrage of the most atrocious character was perpetrated near this city the day before yesterday. A gentleman, with his wife and daughter, engaged about dusk the services of six young men, who were idly rowing a boat to and fro near the banks of the Seine, to convey him across the river. Upon reaching the opposite shore, the three passengers stepped out, and had proceeded so far as to be beyond the view of the boat, when the daughter discovered that she had left in it her parasol. She returned for it, was seized by the gang, carried out into the stream, gagged, brutally treated, and finally taken to the shore at a point not far from that at which she had originally entered the boat with her parents. The villains have escaped for the time, but the police are upon their trail, and some of them will soon be taken."
—*Morning Paper*—*June* 25.†

" We have received one or two communications, the object of which is to fasten the crime of the late atrocity upon Mennais ; ‡ but as this gentleman has been fully exonerated by a legal inquiry, and as the arguments of our several correspondents appear to be more zealous than profound, we do not think it advisable to make them public."—*Morning Paper*—*June* 28. §

---

* New York " Herald."   † New York " Courier and Inquirer."

‡ Mennais was one of the parties originally suspected and arrested, but discharged through total lack of evidence.

§ New York " Courier and Inquirer."

" We have received several forcibly written communications, apparently from various sources, and
which go far to render it a matter of certainty that the
unfortunate Marie Rogêt has become a victim of one of
the numerous bands of blackguards which infest the
vicinity of the city upon Sunday. Our own opinion is
decidedly in favour of this supposition. We shall
endeavour to make room for some of these arguments
hereafter."—*Evening Paper—Tuesday, June* 31.*

" On Monday, one of the bargemen connected with
the revenue service saw an empty boat floating down the
Seine. Sails were lying in the bottom of the boat. The
bargeman towed it under the barge office. The next
morning it was taken from thence without the knowledge of any of the officers. The rudder is now at the
barge office." *Le Diligence—Thursday, June* 26. †

Upon reading these various extracts, they not only
seemed to me irrelevant, but I could perceive no
mode in which any one of them could be brought to
bear upon the matter in hand. I waited for some
explanation from Dupin.

" It is not my present design," he said, " to *dwell*
upon the first and second of these extracts. I have
copied them chiefly to show you the extreme remiss-
ness of the police, who, as far as I can understand
from the Prefect, have not troubled themselves in
any respect with an examination of the naval officer
alluded to. Yet it is mere folly to say that between
the first and second disappearance of Marie there is no
supposable connection. Let us admit the first elopement to have resulted in a quarrel between the lovers
and the return home of the betrayed. We are now

* New York " Evening Post."   † New York " Standard."

prepared to view a second *elopement* (if we *know* that an elopement has again taken place) as indicating a renewal of the betrayer's advances, rather than as the result of new proposals by a second individual— we are prepared to regard it as a ' making up ' of the old *amour* rather than as the commencement of a new one. The chances are ten to one that he who had once eloped with Marie would again propose an elopement rather than that she to whom proposals of elopement had been made by one individual should have them made to her by another. And here let me call your attention to the fact that the time elapsing between the first ascertained, and the second supposed elopement, is a few months more than the general period of the cruises of our men-of-war. Had the lover been interrupted in his first villany by the necessity of departure to sea, and had he seized the first moment of his return to renew the base designs not yet altogether accomplished, or not yet altogether accomplished *by him ?* Of all these things we know nothing.

" You will say, however, that, in the second instance, there was *no* elopement as imagined. Certainly not—but are we prepared to say that there was not the frustrated design ? Beyond St. Eustache, and perhaps Beauvais, we find no recognised, no open, no honourable suitors of Marie. Of none other is there anything said. Who, then, is the secret lover of whom the relatives (*at least most of them*) know nothing, but whom Marie meets upon the morning of Sunday, and who is so deeply in her confidence that she hesitates not to remain with him until the shades of the evening descend amid the solitary groves of the Barrière du

Roule? Who is that secret lover, I ask, of whom, at least, *most* of the relatives know nothing? And what means the singular prophecy of Madame Rogêt on the morning of Marie's departure?—' I fear that I shall never see Marie again.'

"But if we cannot imagine Madame Rogêt privy to the design of elopement, may we not at least suppose this design entertained by the girl? Upon quitting home, she gave it to be understood that she was about to visit her aunt in the Rue des Drômes, and St. Eustache was requested to call for her at dark. Now, at first glance, this fact strongly militates against my suggestion, but let us reflect. That she *did* meet some companion, and proceed with him across the river, reaching the Barrière du Roule at so late an hour as three o'clock in the afternoon, is known. But in consenting so to accompany this individual *for whatever purpose—to her mother known or unknown*), she must have thought of her expressed intention when leaving home, and of the surprise and suspicion aroused in the bosom of her affianced suitor, St. Eustache, when, calling for her at the hour appointed in the Rue des Drômes, he should find that she had not been there, and when, moreover, upon returning to the *pension* with this alarming intelligence, he should become aware of her continued absence from home. She must have thought of these things, I say. She must have foreseen the chagrin of St. Eustache, the suspicion of all. She could not have thought of returning to brave this suspicion; but the suspicion becomes a point of trivial importance to her if we suppose her *not* intending to return.

" We may imagine her thinking thus—'I am to meet a certain person for the purpose of elopement, or for certain other purposes known only to myself. It is necessary that there be no chance of interruption—there must be sufficient time given us to elude pursuit—I will give it to be understood that I shall visit and spend the day with my aunt at the Rue des Drômes—I will tell St. Eustache not to call for me until dark—in this way, my absence from home for the longest possible period, without causing suspicion or anxiety, will be accounted for, and I shall gain more time than in any other manner. If I bid St. Eustache call for me at dark, he will be sure not to call before ; but if I wholly neglect to bid him call, my time for escape will be diminished, since it will be expected that I return the earlier, and my absence will the sooner excite anxiety. Now, if it were my design to return *at all*—if I had in contemplation merely a stroll with the individual in question—it would not be my policy to bid St. Eustache call ; for, calling, he will be *sure* to ascertain that I have played him false—a fact of which I might keep him for ever in ignorance, by leaving home without notifying him of my intention, by returning before dark, and by then stating that I had been to visit my aunt in the Rue des Drômes. But, as it is my design *never* to return— or not for some weeks—or not until certain concealments are effected—the gaining of time is the only point about which I need give myself any concern.''

" You have observed, in your notes, that the most general opinion in relation to this sad affair is, and was from the first, that the girl had been the victim of *a gang* of blackguards. Now, the popular opinion, under certain conditions, is not to be disregarded. When arising of itself—when manifesting itself in a strictly spontaneous manner—we should look upon it as analogous with that *intuition* which is the idiosyncrasy of the individual man of genius. In ninety-nine cases from the hundred I would abide by its decision. But it is important that we find no palpable traces of *suggestion*. The opinion must be rigorously *the public's own ;* and the distinction is often exceedingly difficult to perceive and to maintain. In the present instance, it appears to me that this ' public opinion,' in respect to *a gang*, has been superinduced by the collateral event which is detailed in the third of my extracts. All Paris is excited by the discovered corpse of Marie, a girl young, beautiful, and notorious. This corpse is found, bearing marks of violence, and floating in the river. But it is now made known that, at the very period, or about the very period, in which it is supposed that the girl was assassinated, an outrage similar in nature to that endured by the deceased, although less in extent, was perpetrated, by a gang of young ruffians, upon the person of a second young female. Is it wonderful that the one known atrocity should influence the popular judgment in regard to the other unknown ? This judgment awaited direction, and the known outrage seemed so opportunely to afford it ! Marie, too, was found in the river ; and upon this very river was this known outrage committed. The connection of the two events had about it so much of the palpable, that the true wonder would have been a *failure* of the populace to appreciate

9

and to seize it. But, in fact, the one atrocity, known to be so committed, is, if anything, evidence that the other, committed at a time nearly coincident, was *not* so committed. It would have been a miracle indeed, if, while a gang of ruffians were perpetrating, at a given locality, a most unheard-of wrong, there should have been another similar gang, in a similar locality, in the same city, under the same circumstances, with the same means and appliances, engaged in a wrong of precisely the same aspect, at precisely the same period of time! Yet in what, if not in this marvellous train of coincidence, does the accidentally *suggested* opinion of the populace call upon us to believe?

"Before proceeding further, let us consider the supposed scene of the assassination in the thicket at the Barrière du Roule. This thicket, although dense, was in the close vicinity of a public road. Within were three or four large stones, forming a kind of seat with a back and footstool. On the upper stone was discovered a white petticoat; on the second, a silk scarf. A parasol, gloves, and a pocket-handker-chief, were also here found. The handkerchief bore the name, 'Marie Rogêt.' Fragments of dress were seen on the branches around. The earth was trampled, the bushes were broken, and there was every evidence of a violent struggle.

"Notwithstanding the acclamation with which the discovery of this thicket was received by the press, and the unanimity with which it was supposed to indicate the precise scene of the outrage, it must be admitted that there was some very good reason for doubt. That it *was* the scene, I may or I may not believe—but there was excellent reason for doubt. Had the *true* scene been, as ' Le Commercial ' suggested, in the neighbourhood of the Rue Pavée Sainte Andrée, the perpetrators of the crime, supposing them still resident in Paris, would naturally have been stricken with terror at the public attention thus acutely directed into the proper channel ; and in certain classes of minds there would have arisen at once a sense of the necessity of some exertion to redivert this attention. And thus the thicket of the Barrière du Roule having been already suspected, the idea of placing the articles where they were found might have been naturally entertained. There is no real evidence, although ' Le Soleil ' so supposes, that the articles discovered had been more than a very few days in the thicket ; while there is much circumstantial proof that they could not have remained there, without attracting attention, during the twenty days elapsing between the fatal Sunday and the afternoon upon which they were found by the boys. ' They were all *mildewed* down hard,' says ' Le Soleil,' adopting the opinions of its predecessors, ' with the action of the rain, and stuck together from *mildew*. The grass had grown around and over some of them. The silk of the parasol was strong, but the threads of it were run together within. The upper part, where it had been doubled and folded, was all *mildewed* and rotten, and tore on being opened.' In respect to the grass having ' grown around and over some of them,' it is obvious that the fact could only have been ascertained from the words, and thus from the recollections, of two small boys ; for these boys removed the articles and took them home before they had been seen by a third party. But grass will grow, especially in warm and damp weather (such as was that of the period of the murder), as much as two or three inches in a single day. A parasol lying upon a newly-turfed ground might in a single week be entirely concealed from sight by the upspringing grass. And touching that *mildew*, upon which the editor of ' Le Soleil ' so pertinaciously insists, that he employs the word no less than three times in the brief paragraph just quoted, is he really unaware of the nature of this *mildew ?* Is he to be told that it is one of the many classes of *fungus*, of which the most ordinary feature is its upspringing and decadence within twenty-four hours ?

" Thus we see at a glance that what has been most triumphantly adduced in support of the idea that the articles had been ' for at least three or four weeks ' in the thicket is most absurdly null as regards any evidence of that fact. On the other hand, it is exceedingly difficult to believe that these articles could have remained in the thicket specified for a longer period than a single week—for a longer period than from one Sunday to the next. Those who know anything of the vicinity of Paris know the extreme difficulty of finding *seclusion*, unless at a great distance from its suburbs. Such a thing as an unexplored, or even an unfrequently visited recess, amid its woods or groves, is not for a moment to be imagined. Let any one, who, being at heart a lover of nature, is yet chained by duty to the dust and heat of this great metropolis—let any such one attempt, even during the week-days, to slake his thirst for solitude amid the scenes of natural loveliness which immediately surround us—at every second step he will find the growing charm dispelled by the voice and personal intrusion of some ruffian or party of carousing black-guards. He will seek privacy amid the densest foliage all in vain. Here are the very nooks where the un-washed most abound—here are the temples most desecrate. With sickness of the heart the wanderer will flee back to the polluted Paris as to a less odious, because less incongruous, sink of pollution. But if the vicinity of the city is so beset during the working days of the week, how much more so on the Sabbath ! It is now especially that, released from the claims of labour or deprived of the customary opportunities of crime, the town blackguard seeks the precincts of the town, not through love of the rural, which in his heart he despises, but by way of escape from the restraints and conventionalities of society. He desires less the fresh air and the green trees than the utter *license* of the country. Here, at the roadside inn or beneath the foliage of the woods, he indulges, un-checked by any eye except those of his boon com-panions, in all the mad excess of a counterfeit hilarity—the joint offspring of liberty and of rum. I say nothing more than what must be obvious to every dispassion-ate observer, when I repeat that the circumstance of the articles in question having remained undiscovered for a longer period than from one Sunday to another in *any* thicket in the immediate neighbourhood of Paris, is to be looked upon as little less than miraculous.

 " But there are not wanting other grounds for the

suspicion that the articles were placed in the thicket with the view of diverting attention from the real scene of the outrage. And, first, let me direct your notice to the *date* of the discovery of the articles. Collate this with the date of the fifth extract made by myself from the newspapers. You will find that the discovery followed, almost immediately, the urgent communications sent to the evening newspaper. These communications, although various, and apparently from various sources, tended all to the same point—viz., the directing of attention to *a gang* as the perpetrators of the outrage, and to the neighbourhood of the Barrière du Roule as its scene. Now here, of course, the suspicion is not that, in consequence of these communications, or of the public attention by them directed, the articles were found by the boys ; but the suspicion might and may well have been that the articles were not *before* found by the boys for the reason that the articles had not before been in the thicket ; having been deposited there only at so late a period as at the date, or shortly prior to the date of the communications, by the guilty authors of these communications themselves.

" This thicket was a singular—an exceedingly singular one. It was unusually dense. Within its naturally walled enclosure were three extraordinary stones, *forming a seat with a back and footstool*. And this thicket, so full of a natural art, was in the immediate vicinity, *within a few rods*, of the dwelling of Madame Deluc, whose boys were in the habit of closely examining the shrubberies about them in search of the bark of the sassafras. Would it be a

rash wager—a wager of one thousand to one—that
a day never passed over the heads of these boys without finding at least one of them ensconced in the
umbrageous hall, and enthroned upon its natural
throne ? Those who would hesitate at such a wager
have either never been boys themselves or have forgotten the boyish nature. I repeat—it is exceedingly
hard to comprehend how the articles could have
remained in this thicket undiscovered for a longer
period than one or two days ; and that thus there is
good ground for suspicion, in spite of the dogmatic
ignorance of ' Le Soleil,' that they were, at a comparatively late date, deposited where found.

" But there are still other and stronger reasons for
believing them so deposited than any which I have
as yet urged. And, now, let me beg your notice to
the highly artificial arrangement of the articles. On
the *upper* stone lay a white petticoat ; on the *second*
a silk scarf ; scattered around, were a parasol, gloves,
and a pocket-handkerchief bearing the name of
' Marie Rogêt.' Here is just such an arrangement as
would *naturally* be made by a not-over-acute person
wishing to dispose the articles *naturally*. But it is
by no means a *really* natural arrangement. I should
rather have looked to see the things *all* lying on the
ground and trampled under foot. In the narrow
limits of that bower, it would have been scarcely
possible that the petticoat and scarf should have
retained a position upon the stones, when subjected
to the brushing to and fro of many struggling persons.
' There was evidence,' it is said, ' of a struggle ; and
the earth was trampled, the bushes were broken,'—

but the petticoat and scarf are found deposited as if upon shelves. ' The pieces of the frock torn out by the bushes were about three inches wide and six inches long. One part was the hem of the frock, and it had been mended. They *looked* like strips torn off.' Here, inadvertently, ' Le Soleil ' has employed an exceedingly suspicious phrase. The pieces, as described, do indeed ' look like strips torn off,' but purposely and by hand. It is one of the rarest of accidents that a piece is ' torn off ' from any garment such as is now in question, by the agency *of a thorn*. From the very nature of such fabrics, a thorn or nail becoming entangled in them tears them rectangularly —divides them into two longitudinal rents, at right angles—with each other, and meeting at an apex where the thorn enters—but it is scarcely possible to conceive the piece ' torn off.' I never so knew it, nor did you. To tear a piece *off* from such fabric, two distinct forces, in different directions, will be in almost every case required. If there be two edges to the fabric—if, for example, it be a pocket-handkerchief and it is desired to tear from it a slip, then, and then only, will the one force serve the purpose. But in the present case, the question is of a dress presenting but one edge. To tear a piece from the interior, where no edge is presented, could only be effected by a miracle through the agency of thorns, and no *one* thorn could accomplish it. But, even where an edge is presented, two thorns will be necessary, operating the one in two distinct directions, and the other in one. And this in the supposition that the edge is unhemmed. If hemmed, the matter is nearly out of the question. We thus see the numerous and great obstacles in the way of pieces being torn off ' through the simple agency of ' thorns ; ' yet we are required to believe not only that one piece but that many have been so torn. ' And one part,' too, ' *was the hem of the frock !* ' Another piece was ' *part of the skirt not the hem,*'—that is to say, was torn completely out, through the agency of thorns, from the unedged interior of the dress ! These, I say, are things which one may well be pardoned for disbelieving ; yet, taken collectedly, they form, perhaps, less of reasonable ground for suspicion than the one startling circumstance of the articles having been left in this thicket at all by any *murderers* who had enough precaution to think of removing the corpse. You will not have apprehended me rightly, however, if you suppose it my design to *deny* this thicket as the scene of the outrage. There might have been a wrong *here,* or, more possibly, an accident at Madame Deluc's. But, in fact, this is a point of minor importance. We are not engaged in an attempt to discover the scene, but to produce the perpetrators of the murder. What I have adduced, notwithstanding the minuteness with which I have adduced it, has been with the view, first, to show the folly of the positive and headlong assertions of ' Le Soleil,' but secondly and chiefly, to bring you by the most natural route to a further contemplation of the doubt whether this assassination has, or has not been, the work of a *gang*.

" We will resume this question by mere allusion to the revolting details of the surgeon examined at the inquest. It is only necessary to say that his published *inferences*, in regard to the number of the ruffians, have been properly ridiculed as unjust and totally baseless by all the reputable anatomists of Paris. Not that the matter *might not* have been as inferred, but that there was no ground for the inference—was there not much for another ?

" Let us reflect now upon ' the traces of a struggle ; ' and let me ask what these traces have been supposed to demonstrate. A gang. But do they not rather demonstrate the absence of a gang ? What *struggle* could have taken place—what struggle so violent and so enduring as to have left its ' traces ' in all directions—between a weak and defenceless girl and the *gang* of ruffians imagined ? The silent grasp of a few rough arms and all would have been over. The victim must have been absolutely passive at their will. You will here bear in mind that the arguments urged against the thicket as the scene, are applicable, in chief part, only against it as the scene of an outrage committed by *more than a single individual*. If we imagine but *one* violator, we can conceive, and thus only conceive, the struggle of so violent and so obstinate a nature as to have left the ' traces ' apparent.

" And again. I have already mentioned the suspicion to be excited by the fact that the articles in question were suffered to remain at all in the thicket where discovered. It seems almost impossible that these evidences of guilt should have been accidentally left where found. There was sufficient presence of mind (it is supposed) to remove the corpse ; and yet a more positive evidence than the corpse itself (whose features might have been quickly obliterated by decay) is allowed to lie conspicuously in the scene of the outrage—I allude to the handkerchief with the name of the deceased. If this was accident, it was not the accident of a gang. We can imagine it only the accident of an individual. Let us see. An individual has committed the murder. He is alone with the ghost of the departed. He is appalled by what lies motionless before him. The fury of his passion is over, and there is abundant room in his heart for the natural awe of the deed. His is none of that confidence which the presence of numbers inevitably inspires. He is *alone* with the dead. He trembles and is bewildered. Yet there is a necessity for disposing of the corpse. He bears it to the river, but leaves behind him the other evidences of guilt ; for it is difficult, if not impossible, to carry all the burthen at once, and it will be easy to return for what is left. But in his toilsome journey to the water his fears redouble within him. The sounds of life encompass his path. A dozen times he hears or fancies the step of an observer. Even the very lights from the city bewilder him. Yet, in time, and by long and frequent pauses of deep agony, he reaches the river's brink, and disposes of his ghastly charge—perhaps through the medium of a boat. But *now* what treasure does the world hold— what threat of vengeance could it hold out—which would have power to urge the return of that lonely murderer over that toilsome and perilous path, to the thicket and its blood-chilling recollections? He returns *not*, let the consequences be what they may. He *could* not return if he would. His sole thought is immediate escape. He turns his back *for ever* upon those dreadful shrubberies, and flees as from the wrath to come.

"But how with a gang? Their number would have inspired them with confidence; if, indeed, confidence is ever wanting in the breast of the arrant blackguard; and of arrant blackguards alone are the supposed *gangs* ever constituted. Their number, I say, would have prevented the bewildering and unreasoning terror which I have imagined to paralyse the single man. Could we suppose an oversight in one, or two, or three, this oversight would have been remedied by a fourth. They would have left nothing behind them; for their number would have enabled them to carry *all* at once. There would have been no need of *return*.

"Consider now the circumstance that, in the outer garment of the corpse when found, ' a slip, about a foot wide, had been torn upward from the bottom hem to the waist, wound three times round the waist, and secured by a sort of hitch in the back.' This was done with the obvious design of affording *a handle* by which to carry the body. But would any *number* of men have dreamed of resorting to such an expedient? To three or four, the limbs of the corpse would have afforded not only a sufficient, but the best possible hold. The device is that of a single individual; and this brings us to the fact that ' between the thicket and the river, the rails of the fences were found taken down, and the ground bore evident traces of some heavy burden having been dragged along it ! ' But would a *number* of men have put themselves to the superfluous trouble of taking down a fence for the purpose of dragging through it a corpse which they might have *lifted over* any fence in an instant ? Would a *number* of men have so *dragged* a corpse at all as to have left evident *traces* of the dragging ?

"And here we must refer to an observation of ' Le Commercial,' an observation upon which I have already, in some measure, commented. 'A piece,' says this journal, ' of one of the unfortunate girl's petticoats was torn out and tied under her chin, and around the back of her head, probably to prevent screams. This was done by fellows who had no pocket-handkerchiefs.'

" I have before suggested that a genuine black-guard is never *without* a pocket-handkerchief. But it is not to this fact that I now especially advert. That it was not through want of a handkerchief for the purpose imagined by ' Le Commercial ' that this bandage was employed, is rendered apparent by the handkerchief left in the thicket ; and that the object was not ' to prevent screams ' appears, also, from the bandage having been employed in preference to what would so much better have answered the purpose. But the language of the evidence speaks of the strip in question as ' found around the neck, fitting loosely, and secured with a hard knot.' These words are sufficiently vague, but differ materially from those of ' Le Commercial.' The slip was eighteen inches wide, and therefore, although of muslin, would form a strong band when folded or rumpled longitudinally. And thus rumpled it was discovered. My inference is this. The solitary murderer, having borne the corpse for some distance (whether from the thicket or else-where by means of the bandage hitched around its middle), found the weight in this mode of procedure too much for his strength. He resolved to drag the burthen—the evidence goes to show that it *was* dragged. With this object in view, it became necessary to attach something like a rope to one of the extremities. It could be best attached about the neck, where the head would prevent its slipping off. And now the murderer bethought him, unquestionably, of the bandage about the loins. He would have used this, but for its volution about the corpse, the hitch which embarrassed it, and the reflection that it had not been ' torn off ' from the garment. It was easier to tear a new slip from the petticoat. He tore it, made it fast about the neck, and so *dragged* his victim to the brink of the river. That this ' bandage,' only attainable with trouble and delay, and but imperfectly answering its purpose—that this bandage was employed *at all*, demonstrates that the necessity for its employment sprang from circumstances arising at a period when the handkerchief was no longer attainable, that is to say, arising, as we have imagined, after quitting the thicket (if the thicket it was), and on the road between the thicket and the river.

" But the evidence, you will say, of Madame Deluc (!) points especially to the presence of *a gang*, in the vicinity of the thicket, or at about the epoch of the murder. This I grant. I doubt if there were not a *dozen* gangs, such as described by Madame Deluc, in and about the vicinity of the Barrière du Roule, at *or about* the period of this tragedy. But the gang which has drawn upon itself the pointed animadversion, although the somewhat tardy and very suspicious evidence of Madame Deluc, is the *only* gang which is represented by that honest and scrupulous old lady as having eaten her cakes and swallowed her brandy without putting themselves to the trouble of making her payment. *Et hinc illæ iræ ?*

" But what *is* the precise evidence of Madame Deluc ? A gang of miscreants made their appearance, behaved boisterously, ate and drank without making payment, followed in the route of the young man and girl, returned to the inn *about dusk*, and recrossed the river as if in ' great haste.'

" Now this ' great haste ' very possibly seemed *greater* haste in the eyes of Madame Deluc since she dwelt lingeringly and lamentingly upon her violated cakes and ale—cakes and ale for which she might still have entertained a faint hope of compensation. Why, otherwise, since it was *about dusk*, should she make a point of the haste ? It is no cause for wonder, surely, that even a gang of blackguards should make *haste* to get home, when a wide river is to be crossed in small boats, when storm impends, and when night *approaches*.

" I say *approaches ;* for the night had *not yet arrived*. It was only *about dusk* that the indecent haste of these ' miscreants ' offended the sober eyes of Madame Deluc. But we are told that it was upon this very evening that Madame Deluc, as well as her eldest son, ' heard the screams of a female in the vicinity of the inn.' And in what words does Madame Deluc designate the period of the evening at which these screams were heard ? ' It was *soon after dark*,' she says. But ' soon *after dark* ' is, at least, *dark ;* and, ' *about dusk* ' is as certainly daylight. Thus it is abundantly clear that the gang quitted the Barrière

du Roule *prior* to the screams overheard (?) by
Madame Deluc. And although, in all the many reports of the evidence, the relative expressions in
question are distinctly and invariably employed just
as I have employed them in this conversation with
yourself, no notice whatever of the gross discrepancy
has as yet been taken by any of the public journals,
or by any of the myrmidons of police.

"I shall add but one to the arguments against *a
gang;* but this *one* has, to my own understanding
at least, a weight altogether irresistible. Under the
circumstances of large reward offered, and full pardon
to any King's evidence, it is not to be imagined, for
a moment, that some member of *a gang* of low ruffians,
or of any body of men, would not long ago have betrayed his accomplices. Each one of a gang so placed
is not so much greedy of reward, or anxious for escape,
as *fearful of betrayal*. He betrays eagerly and early
that *he may not himself be betrayed*. That the secret has
not been divulged is the very best of proof that it is in
fact a secret. The horrors of this dark deed are known
only to *one* or two living human beings and to God.

"Let us sum up now the meagre yet certain fruits
of our long analysis. We have attained the idea
either of a fatal accident under the roof of Madame
Deluc or of a murder perpetrated in the thicket at
the Barrière du Roule, by a lover, or at least by an
intimate and secret associate of the deceased. This
associate is of swarthy complexion. This complexion,
the 'hitch' in the bandage, and the sailor's 'knot,'
with which the bonnet-ribbon is tied, point to a seaman. His companionship with the deceased, a gay,

but not an abject young girl, designates him as above the grade of the common sailor. Here the well-written and urgent communications to the journals are much in the way of corroboration. The circumstance of the first elopement, as mentioned by ' Le Mercurie,' tends to blend the idea of this seaman with that of the ' naval officer ' who is first known to have led the unfortunate into crime.

" And here most fitly comes the consideration of the continued absence of him of the dark complexion. Let me pause to observe that the complexion of this man is dark and swarthy ; it was no common swarthiness which constituted the *sole* point of remembrance, both as regards Valence and Madame Deluc. But why is this man absent ? Was he murdered by the gang ? If so, why are there only *traces* of the assassinated girl ? The scene of the two outrages will naturally be supposed identical. And where is his corpse ? The assassins would most probably have disposed of both in the same way. But it may be said that this man lives, and is deterred from making himself known through dread of being charged with the murder. This consideration might be supposed to operate upon him now—at this late period—since it has been given in evidence that he was seen with Marie—but it would have had no force at the period of the deed. The first impulse of an innocent man would have been to announce the outrage, and to aid in identifying the ruffians. This *policy* would have suggested. He had been seen with the girl. He had crossed the river with her in an open ferry-boat. The denouncing of the assassins would have appeared, even to an idiot,

the surest and sole means of relieving himself from
suspicion. We cannot suppose him on the night of
the fatal Sunday both innocent himself and incognisant
of an outrage committed. Yet only under such circumstances is it possible to imagine that he would have
failed, if alive, in the denouncement of the assassins.

"And what means are ours of attaining the truth?
We shall find these means multiplying and gathering
distinctness as we proceed. Let us sift to the bottom
this affair of the first elopement. Let us know the
full history of ' the officer,' with his present circumstances, and his whereabouts at the precise period of
the murder. Let us carefully compare with each other
the various communications sent to the evening paper,
in which the object was to inculpate *a gang*. This
done, let us compare these communications, both as
regards style and MS., with those sent to the morning
paper, at a previous period, and insisting so vehemently
upon the guilt of Mennais. And all this done, let us
again compare these various communications with the
known MSS. of the officer. Let us endeavour to
ascertain by repeated questionings of Madame Deluc
and her boys, as well as of the omnibus-driver, Valence,
something more of the personal appearance and bearing of the ' man of dark complexion.' Queries skil-
fully directed will not fail to elicit from some of these
parties information on this particular point (or upon
others)—information which the parties themselves
may not even be aware of possessing. And let us
now trace *the boat* picked up by the bargeman on the
morning of Monday the twenty-third of June, and
which was removed from the barge-office without the

cognisance of the officer in attendance, and *without the rudder*, at some period prior to the discovery of the corpse. With a proper caution and perseverance we shall infallibly trace this boat ; for not only can the bargeman who picked it up identify it, but the *rudder is at hand.* The rudder *of a sail-boat* would not have been abandoned, without inquiry, by one altogether at ease in heart. And here let me pause to insinuate a question. There was no *advertisement* of the picking up of this boat. It was silently taken to the barge-office, and as silently removed. But its owner or employer—how *happened* he, at so early a period as Tuesday morning, to be informed without the agency of advertisement, of the locality of the boat taken up on Monday, unless we imagine some connection with the *navy*—some personal permanent connection leading to cognisance of its minute interests—its petty local news?

" In speaking of the lonely assassin dragging his burden to the shore, I have already suggested the probability of his availing himself *of a boat.* Now we are to understand that Marie Rogêt *was* precipitated from a boat. This would naturally have been the case. The corpse could not have been trusted to the shallow waters of the shore. The peculiar marks on the back and shoulders of the victim tell of the bottom ribs of a boat. That the body was found without weight is also corroborative of the idea. If thrown from the shore a weight would have been attached. We can only account for its absence by supposing the murderer to have neglected the precaution of supplying himself with it before pushing off. In the act of consigning the corpse to the water, he would unquestionably have noticed his oversight ; but then no remedy would have been at hand. Any risk would have been preferred to a return to that accursed shore. Having rid himself of his ghastly charge, the murderer would have hastened to the city. There, at some obscure wharf, he would have leaped on land. But the boat—would he have secured it ? He would have been in too great haste for such things as securing a boat. Moreover, in fastening it to the wharf he would have felt as if securing evidence against himself. His natural thought would have been to cast from him as far as possible all that had held connection with his crime. He would not only have fled from the wharf, but he would not have permitted *the boat* to remain. Assuredly he would have cast it adrift. Let us pursue our fancies.—In the morning the wretch is stricken with unutterable horror at finding that the boat has been picked up and detained at a locality which he is in the daily habit of frequenting—at a locality, perhaps, which his duty compels him to frequent. The next night, *without daring to ask for the rudder* he removes it. Now *where* is that rudderless boat ? Let it be one of our first purposes to discover. With the first glimpse we obtain of it, the dawn of our success shall begin. This boat shall guide us, with a rapidity which will surprise even ourselves, to him who employed it in the midnight of the fatal Sabbath. Corroboration will rise upon corroboration, and the murderer will be traced."

[For reasons which we shall not specify, but which to many readers will appear obvious, we have taken the liberty of here omitting, from the MS. placed in our hands, such portion as details the *following up* of the apparently slight clue obtained by Dupin. We feel it advisable only to state, in brief, that the result desired was brought to pass; and that the Prefect fulfilled punctually, although with reluctance, the terms of his compact with the Chevalier. Mr. Poe's article concludes with the following words.—*Eds.**]

It will be understood that I speak of coincidences *and no more*. What I have said above upon this topic must suffice. In my own heart there dwells no faith in preternature. That nature and its God are two, no man who thinks will deny. That the latter, creating the former, can, at will, control or modify it, is also unquestionable. I say "at will;" for the question is of will, and not, as the insanity of logic has assumed, of power. It is not that the Deity *cannot* modify His laws, but that we insult Him in imagining a possible necessity for modification. In their origin these laws were fashioned to embrace *all* contingencies which *could* lie in the Future. With God all is *Now*.

I repeat, then, that I speak of these things only as of coincidences. And further: in what I relate it will be seen that between the fate of the unhappy Mary Cecilia Rogers, so far as that fate is known, and the fate of one Marie Rogêt up to a certain epoch in her history, there has existed a parallel in the contemplation of whose wonderful exactitude the reason becomes embarrassed. I say all this will be seen. But let it not for a moment be supposed that, in proceeding with the sad narrative of Marie from the epoch just

* Of the Magazine in which the article was originally published.—*Ed.*

mentioned, and in tracing to its *dénouement* the mystery which enshrouded her, it is my covert design to hint at an extension of the parallel, or even to suggest that the measures adopted in Paris for the discovery of the assassin of a grisette, or measures founded in any similar ratiocination, would produce any similar result.

For, in respect to the latter branch of the supposition, it should be considered that the most trifling variation in the facts of the two cases might give rise to the most important miscalculations, by diverting thoroughly the two courses of events ; very much as, in arithmetic, an error which, in its own individuality, may be inappreciable, produces, at length, by dint of multiplication at all points of the process, a result enormously at variance with truth. And, in regard to the former branch, we must not fail to hold in view that the very Calculus of Probabilities to which I have referred, forbids all idea of the extension of the parallel :—forbids it with a positiveness strong and decided just in proportion as this parallel has already been long-drawn and exact. This is one of those anomalous propositions which, seemingly appealing to thought altogether apart from the mathematical, is yet one which only the mathematician can fully entertain. Nothing, for example, is more difficult than to convince the merely general reader that the fact of sixes having been thrown twice in succession by a player at dice is sufficient cause for betting the largest odds that sixes will not be thrown in the third attempt. A suggestion to this effect is usually rejected by the intellect at once. It does not appear that the two throws which have been completed, and which lie now absolutely in the Past, can have influence upon the throw which exists only in the Future. The chance for throwing sixes seems to be precisely as it was at an ordinary time—that is to say, subject only to the influence of the various other throws which may be made by the dice. And this is a reflection which appears so exceedingly obvious that attempts to controvert it are received more frequently with a derisive smile than with anything like respectful attention. The error here involved—a gross error redolent of mischief—I cannot pretend to expose within the limits assigned me at present ; and with the philosophical it needs no exposure. It may be sufficient here to say that it forms one of an infinite series of mistakes which arise in the path of Reason through her propensity for seeking truth *in detail*.

VIII

THE PIT AND THE PENDULUM

Impia tortorum longas hic turba furores
Sanguinis innocui, non satiata, aluit.
Sospite nunc patria, fracto nunc funeris antro,
Mors ubi dira fuit vita salusque patent.

*[Quatrain composed for the gates of a market to be erected upon
the site of the Jacobin Club House at Paris]*

I WAS sick, sick unto death, with that long agony, and
when they at length unbound me, and I was permitted
to sit, I felt that my senses were leaving me. The
sentence, the dread sentence of death, was the last of
distinct accentuation which reached my ears. After
that, the sound of the inquisitorial voices seemed
merged in one dreamy intermediate hum. It conveyed to my soul the idea of *revolution*, perhaps from
its association in fancy with the burr of a mill-wheel.
This only for a brief period, for presently I heard no
more. Yet, for a while, I saw, but with how terrible
an exaggeration ! I saw the lips of the black-robed
judges. They appeared to me white—whiter than the
sheet upon which I trace these words—and thin even
to grotesqueness ; thin with the intensity of their
expression of firmness, of immovable resolution, of
stern contempt of human torture. I saw that the
decrees of what to me was fate were still issuing from
those lips. I saw them writhe with a deadly locution.
I saw them fashion the syllables of my name, and I

shuddered, because no sound succeeded. I saw, too, for a few moments of delirious horror, the soft and nearly imperceptible waving of the sable draperies which enwrapped the walls of the apartment ; and then my vision fell upon the seven tall candles upon the table. At first they wore the aspect of charity, and seemed white slender angels who would save me ; but then all at once there came a most deadly nausea over my spirit, and I felt every fibre in my frame thrill, as if I had touched the wire of a galvanic battery, while the angel forms became meaningless spectres, with heads of flame, and I saw that from them there would be no help. And then there stole into my fancy, like a rich musical note, the thought of what sweet rest there must be in the grave. The thought came gently and stealthily, and it seemed long before it attained full appreciation ; but just as my spirit came at length properly to feel and entertain it, the figures of the judges vanished, as if magically, from before me ; the tall candles sank into nothingness ; their flames went out utterly ; the blackness of darkness supervened ; all sensations appeared swallowed up in a mad rushing descent as of the soul into Hades. Then silence, and stillness, and night were the universe.

I had swooned ; but still will not say that all of consciousness was lost. What of it there remained I will not attempt to define, or even to describe ; yet all was not lost. In the deepest slumber—no ! In delirium— no ! In a swoon—no ! In death—no ! Even in the grave all *is not* lost. Else there is no immortality for man. Arousing from the most profound of slumbers, we break the gossamer web of *some* dream. Yet in a second afterwards (so frail may that web have been) we remember not that we have dreamed. In the return to life from the swoon there are two stages : first, that of the sense of mental or spiritual ; secondly, that of the sense of physical existence. It seems probable that if, upon reaching the second stage, we could recall the impressions of the first, we should find these impressions eloquent in memories of the gulf beyond. And that gulf is—what ? How at least shall we distinguish its shadows from those of the tomb ? But if the impressions of what I have termed the first stage are not at will recalled, yet, after long interval, do they not come unbidden, while we marvel whence they come ? He who has never swooned is not he who finds strange palaces and wildly familiar faces in coals that glow ; is not he who beholds floating in mid-air the sad visions that the many may not view ; is not he who ponders over the perfume of some novel flower ; is not he whose brain grows bewildered with the meaning of some musical cadence which has never before arrested his attention.

Amid frequent and thoughtful endeavours to remember, amid earnest struggles to regather some token of the state of seeming nothingness into which my soul had lapsed, there have been moments when I have dreamed of success ; there have been brief, very brief periods when I have conjured up remembrances which the lucid reason of a later epoch assures me could have had reference only to that condition of seeming unconsciousness. These shadows of memory tell indistinctly of tall figures that lifted and bore me in silence down—down—still down—till a hideous dizziness oppressed me at the mere idea of the interminableness of the descent. They tell also of a vague horror at my heart on account of that heart's unnatural stillness. Then comes a sense of sudden motionlessness throughout all things; as if those who bore me (a ghastly train!) had outrun, in their descent, the limits of the limitless, and paused from the wearisomeness of their toil. After this I call to mind flatness and dampness; and then all is *madness*—the madness of a memory which busies itself among forbidden things.

Very suddenly there came back to my soul motion and sound—the tumultuous motion of the heart, and in my ears the sound of its beating. Then a pause in which all is blank. Then again sound, and motion, and touch, a tingling sensation pervading my frame. Then the mere consciousness of existence, without thought—a condition which lasted long. Then, very suddenly, *thought*, and shuddering terror, and earnest endeavour to comprehend my true state. Then a strong desire to lapse into insensibility. Then a rushing revival of soul and a successful effort to move. And now a full memory of the trial, of the judges, of the sable draperies, of the sentence, of the sickness, of the swoon. Then entire forgetfulness of all that followed; of all that a later day and much earnestness of endeavour have enabled me vaguely to recall.

So far I had not opened my eyes. I felt that I lay upon my back unbound. I reached out my hand, and it fell heavily upon something damp and hard. There I suffered it to remain for many minutes, while I strove to imagine where and *what* I could be. I longed, yet dared not, to employ my vision. I dreaded the first glance at objects around me. It was not that I feared to look upon things horrible, but that I grew aghast lest there should be *nothing* to see. At length, with a wild desperation at heart, I quickly unclosed my eyes. My worst thoughts, then, were confirmed. The blackness of eternal night encompassed me. I struggled for breath. The intensity of the darkness seemed to oppress and stifle me. The atmosphere was intolerably close. I still lay quietly, and made effort to exercise my reason. I brought to mind the inquisitorial proceedings, and attempted from that point to deduce my real condition. The sentence had passed, and it appeared to me that a very long interval of time had since elapsed. Yet not for a moment did I suppose myself actually dead. Such a supposition, notwithstanding what we read in fiction, is altogether inconsistent with real existence;—but where and in what state was I? The condemned to death, I knew, perished usually at the *autos-da-fé*, and one of these had been held on the very night of the day of my trial. Had I been remanded to my dungeon, to await the next sacrifice, which would not take place for many months? This I at once saw could not be. Victims had been in immediate demand. Moreover my dungeon, as well as all the condemned cells at Toledo, had stone floors, and light was not altogether excluded.

A fearful idea now suddenly drove the blood in torrents upon my heart, and for a brief period I once more relapsed into insensibility. Upon recovering, I at once started to my feet, trembling convulsively in every fibre. I thrust my arms wildly above and around me

in all directions. I felt nothing ; yet dreaded to move
a step, lest I should be impeded by the walls of a *tomb*.
Perspiration burst from every pore, and stood in cold
big beads upon my forehead. The agony of suspense
grew at length intolerable, and I cautiously moved
forward, with my arms extended, and my eyes straining from their sockets, in the hope of catching some
faint ray of light. I proceeded for many paces, but
still all was blackness and vacancy. I breathed more
freely. It seemed evident that mine was not, at least,
the most hideous of fates.

And now, as I still continued to step cautiously onward, there came thronging upon my recollection a
thousand vague rumours of the horrors of Toledo. Of
the dungeons there had been strange things narrated
—fables I had always deemed them—but yet strange,
and too ghastly to repeat, save in a whisper. Was I
left to perish of starvation in this subterranean world
of darkness ; or what fate perhaps even more fearful
awaited me ? That the result would be death, and a
death of more than customary bitterness, I knew too
well the character of my judges to doubt. The mode
and the hour were all that occupied or distracted me.

My outstretched hands at length encountered some
solid obstruction. It was a wall, seemingly of stone
masonry—very smooth, slimy, and cold. I followed
it up ; stepping with all the careful distrust with which
certain antique narratives had inspired me. This process, however, afforded me no means of ascertaining
the dimensions of my dungeon ; as I might make its
circuit, and return to the point whence I set out, without being aware of the fact, so perfectly uniform

seemed the wall. I therefore sought the knife which had been in my pocket when led into the inquisitorial chamber, but it was gone; my clothes had been exchanged for a wrapper of coarse serge. I had thought of forcing the blade in some minute crevice of the masonry, so as to identify my point of departure. The difficulty, nevertheless, was but trivial, although, in the disorder of my fancy, it seemed at first insuperable. I tore a part of the hem from the robe, and placed the fragment at full length, and at right angles to the wall. In groping my way around the prison, I could not fail to encounter this rag upon completing the circuit. So, at least, I thought, but I had not counted upon the extent of the dungeon or upon my own weakness. The ground was moist and slippery. I staggered onward for some time, when I stumbled and fell. My excessive fatigue induced me to remain prostrate, and sleep soon overtook me as I lay.

Upon awaking, and stretching forth an arm, I found beside me a loaf and a pitcher with water. I was too much exhausted to reflect upon this circumstance, but ate and drank with avidity. Shortly afterwards I resumed my tour around the prison, and with much toil came at last upon the fragment of the serge. Up to the period when I fell I had counted fifty-two paces, and upon resuming my walk I had counted forty-eight more, when I arrived at the rag. There were in all, then, a hundred paces; and, admitting two paces to the yard, I presumed the dungeon to be fifty yards in circuit. I had met, however, with many angles in the wall, and thus I could form no guess at the shape of the vault, for vault I could not help supposing it to be.

I had little object—certainly no hope—in these researches, but a vague curiosity prompted me to continue them. Quitting the wall, I resolved to cross the area of the enclosure. At first I proceeded with extreme caution, for the floor, although seemingly of solid material, was treacherous with slime. At length, however, I took courage and did not hesitate to step firmly—endeavouring to cross in as direct a line as possible. I had advanced some ten or twelve paces in this manner, when the remnant of the torn hem of my robe became entangled between my legs. I stepped on it, and fell violently on my face.

In the confusion attending my fall, I did not immediately apprehend a somewhat startling circumstance, which yet, in a few seconds afterward, and while I still lay prostrate, arrested my attention. It was this : my chin rested upon the floor of the prison, but my lips, and the upper portion of my head, although seemingly at a less elevation than the chin, touched nothing. At the same time, my forehead seemed bathed in a clammy vapour, and the peculiar smell of decayed fungus arose to my nostrils. I put forward my arm, and shuddered to find that I had fallen at the very brink of a circular pit, whose extent of course I had no means of ascertaining at the moment. Groping about the masonry just below the margin, I succeeded in dislodging a small fragment, and let it fall into the abyss. For many seconds I hearkened to its reverberations as it dashed against the sides of the chasm in its descent ; at length there was a sullen plunge into the water, succeeded by loud echoes. At the same moment there came a sound resembling the quick opening, and as rapid closing, of a door overhead, while a faint gleam of light flashed suddenly through the gloom, and as suddenly faded away.

I saw clearly the doom which had been prepared for me, and congratulated myself upon the timely accident by which I had escaped. Another step before my fall, and the world had seen me no more ; and the death just avoided was of that very character which I had regarded as fabulous and frivolous in the tales respecting the Inquisition. To the victims of its tyranny, there was the choice of death with its direct physical agonies, or death with its most hideous moral horrors. I had been reserved for the latter. By long suffering my nerves had been unstrung, until I trembled at the sound of my own voice, and had become in every respect a fitting subject for the species of torture which awaited me.

Shaking in every limb, I groped my way back to the wall—resolving there to perish rather than risk the terrors of the wells, of which my imagination now pictured many in various positions about the dungeon. In other conditions of mind I might have had courage to end my misery at once by a plunge into one of these abysses ; but now I was the veriest of cowards. Neither could I forget what I had read of these pits—that the *sudden* extinction of life formed no part of their most horrible plan.

Agitation of spirit kept me awake for many long hours ; but at length I again slumbered. Upon arousing, I found by my side, as before, a loaf and a pitcher of water. A burning thirst consumed me, and I emptied the vessel at a draught. It must have been drugged, for scarcely had I drunk before I became irresistibly drowsy. A deep sleep fell upon me—a sleep like that of death. How long it lasted of course I know not ; but when once again I unclosed my eyes the objects around me were visible. By a wild sulphurous lustre, the origin of which I could not at first determine, I was enabled to see the extent and aspect of the prison.

In its size I had been greatly mistaken. The whole circuit of its walls did not exceed twenty-five yards. For some minutes the fact occasioned me a world of vain trouble ; vain indeed—for what could be of less importance, under the terrible circumstances which environed me, than the mere dimensions of my dungeon ? But my soul took a wild interest in trifles, and I busied myself in endeavours to account for the error I had committed in my measurement. The truth at length flashed upon me. In my first attempt at exploration I had counted fifty-two paces up to the period when I fell ; I must then have been within a pace or two of the fragment of serge ; in fact I had nearly performed the circuit of the vault. I then slept, and upon awaking, I must have returned upon my steps, thus supposing the circuit nearly double what it actually was. My confusion of mind prevented me from observing that I began my tour with the wall to the left, and ended it with the wall to the right.

I had been deceived, too, in respect to the shape of the enclosure. In feeling my way I had found many angles, and thus deduced an idea of great irregularity, so potent is the effect of total darkness upon one arousing from lethargy of sleep ! The angles were simply those of a few slight depressions or niches at odd intervals. The general shape of the prison was square. What I had taken for masonry seemed now to be iron, or some other metal, in huge plates, whose sutures or joints occasioned the depression. The entire surface of this metallic enclosure was rudely daubed in all the hideous and repulsive devices to which the charnel superstition of the monks has given rise. The figures of fiends in aspects of menace, with skeleton forms and other more really fearful images, overspread and disfigured the walls. I observed that the outlines of these monstrosities were sufficiently distinct, but that the colours seemed faded and blurred, as if from the effects of a damp atmosphere. I now noticed the floor, too, which was of stone. In the centre yawned the circular pit from whose jaws I had escaped ; but it was the only one in the dungeon.

All this I saw indistinctly and by much effort, for my personal condition had been greatly changed during slumber. I now lay upon my back, and, at full length, on a species of low framework of wood. To this I was securely bound by a long strap resembling a surcingle. It passed in many convolutions about my limbs and body, leaving at liberty only my head, and my left arm to such extent that I could by dint of much exertion supply myself with food from an earthen dish which lay by my side on the floor. I saw to my horror that the pitcher had been removed. I say to my horror, for I was consumed with intolerable thirst. This thirst it appeared to be the design of my persecutors to stimulate, for the food in the dish was meat pungently seasoned.

Looking upward, I surveyed the ceiling of my prison. It was some thirty or forty feet overhead, and constructed much as the side walls. In one of its panels a very singular figure riveted my whole attention. It was the painted figure of Time as he is commonly represented, save that in lieu of a scythe he held what at a casual glance I supposed to be the pictured image of a huge pendulum, such as we see on antique clocks. There was something, however, in the appearance of this machine which caused me to regard it more attentively. While I gazed directly upward at it (for its position was immediately over my own), I fancied that I saw it in motion. In an instant afterward the fancy was confirmed. Its sweep was brief, and of course slow. I watched it for some minutes, somewhat in fear but more in wonder. Wearied at length with observing its dull movement, I turned my eyes upon the other objects in the cell.

A slight noise attracted my notice, and looking to the floor, I saw several enormous rats traversing it. They had issued from the well which lay just within view to my right. Even then while I gazed, they came up in troops, hurriedly, with ravenous eyes, allured by the scent of the meat. From this it required much effort and attention to scare them away.

It might have been half-an-hour, perhaps even an hour (for I could take but imperfect note of time), before I again cast my eyes upward. What I then saw confounded and amazed me. The sweep of the pendulum had increased in extent by nearly a yard. As a natural consequence, its velocity was also much greater. But what mainly disturbed me was the idea that it had perceptibly *descended*. I now observed, with what horror it is needless to say, that its nether extremity was formed of a crescent of glittering steel, about a foot in length from horn to horn ; the horns upward, and the under edge evidently as keen as that of a razor. Like a razor also it seemed massy and heavy, tapering from the edge into a solid and broad structure above. It was appended to a weighty rod of brass, and the whole *hissed* as it swung through the air.

I could no longer doubt the doom prepared for me by monkish ingenuity in torture. My cognisance of the pit had become known to the inquisitorial agents —*the pit*, whose horrors had been destined for so bold a recusant as myself, *the pit*, typical of hell, and regarded by rumour as the Ultima Thule of all their punishments. The plunge into this pit I had avoided by the merest of accidents, and I knew that surprise or entrapment into torment formed an important portion of all the grotesquerie of these dungeon deaths. Having failed to fall, it was no part of the demon plan to hurl me into the abyss, and thus (there being no alternative) a different and a milder destruction awaited me. Milder ! I half smiled in my agony as I thought of such application of such a term.

What boots it to tell of the long, long hours of horror more than mortal, during which I counted the rushing oscillations of the steel ! Inch by inch—line by line— with a descent only appreciable at intervals that seemed ages—down and still down it came ! Days passed—it might have been that many days passed—

ere it swept so closely over me as to fan me with its acrid breath. The odour of the sharp steel forced itself into my nostrils. I prayed—I wearied heaven with my prayer for its more speedy descent. I grew frantically mad, and struggled to force myself upward against the sweep of the fearful scimitar. And then I fell suddenly calm and lay smiling at the glittering death as a child at some rare bauble.

There was another interval of utter insensibility; it was brief, for upon again lapsing into life there had been no perceptible descent in the pendulum. But it might have been long—for I knew there were demons who took note of my swoon, and who could have arrested the vibration at pleasure. Upon my recovery, too, I felt very—oh! inexpressibly—sick and weak, as if through long inanition. Even amid the agonies of that period the human nature craved food. With painful effort I outstretched my left arm as far as my bonds permitted, and took possession of the small remnant which had been spared me by the rats. As I put a portion of it within my lips there rushed to my mind a half-formed thought of joy—of hope. Yet what business had *I* with hope? It was, as I say, a half-formed thought—man has many such, which are never completed. I felt that it was of joy—of hope; but I felt also that it had perished in its formation. In vain I struggled to perfect—to regain it. Long suffering had nearly annihilated all my ordinary powers of mind. I was an imbecile—an idiot.

The vibration of the pendulum was at right angles to my length. I saw that the crescent was designed to cross the region of the heart. It would fray the serge of my robe; it would return and repeat its operations—again—and again. Notwithstanding its terrifically wide sweep (some thirty feet or more) and the hissing vigour of its descent, sufficient to sunder these very walls of iron, still the fraying of my robe would be all that, for several minutes, it would accomplish; and at this thought I paused. I dared not go farther than this reflection. I dwelt upon it with a pertinacity of attention—as if, in so dwelling, I could arrest *here* the descent of the steel. I forced myself to ponder upon the sound of the crescent as it should pass across the garment—upon the peculiar thrilling sensation which the friction of cloth produces on the nerves. I pondered upon all this frivolity until my teeth were on edge.

Down—steadily down it crept. I took a frenzied pleasure in contrasting its downward with its lateral velocity. To the right—to the left—far and wide—with the shriek of a damned spirit! to my heart with the stealthy pace of the tiger! I alternately laughed and howled, as the one or the other idea grew predominant.

Down—certainly, relentlessly, down! It vibrated within three inches of my bosom! I struggled violently—furiously—to free my left arm. This was free only from the elbow to the hand. I could reach the latter, from the platter beside me, to my mouth with great effort, but no farther. Could I have broken the fastenings above the elbow, I would have seized and attempted to arrest the pendulum. I might as well have attempted to arrest an avalanche!

Down—still unceasingly—still inevitably down! I gasped and struggled at each vibration. I shrunk convulsively at its every sweep. My eyes followed its outward or upward whirls with the eagerness of the most unmeaning despair ; they closed themselves spasmodically at the descent, although death would have been a relief, O, how unspeakable ! Still I quivered in every nerve to think how slight a sinking of the machinery would precipitate that keen glistening axe upon my bosom. It was *hope* that prompted the nerve to quiver—the frame to shrink. It was *hope*—the hope that triumphs on the rack—that whispers to the death-condemned even in the dungeons of the Inquisition.

I saw that some ten or twelve vibrations would bring the steel in actual contact with my robe, and with this observation there suddenly came over my spirit all the keen, collected calmness of despair. For the first time during many hours, or perhaps days, I *thought*. It now occurred to me that the bandage or surcingle which enveloped me was *unique*. I was tied by no separate cord. The first stroke of the razor-like crescent athwart any portion of the band would so detach it that it might be unwound from my person by means of my left hand. But how fearful, in that case, the promixity of the steel ! The result of the slightest struggle, how deadly ! Was it likely, moreover, that the minions of the torturer had not foreseen and provided for this possibility ? Was it probable that the bandage crossed my bosom in the track of the pendulum ? Dreading to find my faint, and, as it seemed, my last hope frustrated, I so far elevated my head as to obtain a distinct view of my breast. The surcingle enveloped my limbs and body close in all directions *save in the path of the destroying crescent*.

Scarcely had I dropped my head back into its original position when there flashed upon my mind what I cannot better describe than as the unformed half of that idea of deliverance to which I have previously alluded, and of which a moiety only floated indeterminately through my brain when I raised food to my burning lips. The whole thought was now present—feeble, scarcely sane, scarcely definite, but still entire. I proceeded at once, with the nervous energy of despair, to attempt its execution.

For many hours the immediate vicinity of the low framework upon which I lay had been literally swarming with rats. They were wild, bold, ravenous, their red eyes glaring upon me as if they waited but for motionlessness on my part to make me their prey. " To what food," I thought, " have they been accustomed in the well ? "

They had devoured, in spite of all my efforts to prevent them, all but a small remnant of the contents of the dish. I had fallen into an habitual see-saw or wave of the hand about the platter ; and at length the unconscious uniformity of the movement deprived it of effect. In their voracity the vermin frequently fastened their sharp fangs in my fingers. With the particles of the oily and spicy viand which now remained, I thoroughly rubbed the bandage wherever I could reach it ; then, raising my hand from the floor, I lay breathlessly still.

At first the ravenous animals were startled and terrified at the change—at the cessation of movement. They shrank alarmedly back ; many sought the well. But this was only for a moment. I had not counted in vain upon their voracity. Observing that I remained without motion, one or two of the boldest leaped upon the frame-work and smelt at the surcingle. This seemed the signal for a general rush. Forth from the well they hurried in fresh troops. They clung to the wood, they overran it, and leaped in hundreds upon my person. The measured movement of the pendulum disturbed them not at all. Avoiding its strokes, they busied themselves with the anointed bandage. They pressed, they swarmed upon me in ever accumulating heaps. They writhed upon my throat ; their cold lips sought my own ; I was half stifled by their thronging pressure ; disgust, for which the world has no name, swelled my bosom, and chilled with heavy clamminess my heart. Yet one minute and I felt that the struggle would be over. Plainly I perceived the loosening of the bandage. I knew that in more than one place it must be already severed. With a more than human resolution I lay *still*.

Nor had I erred in my calculations, nor had I endured in vain. I at length felt that I was *free*. The surcingle hung in ribands from my body. But the stroke of the pendulum already pressed upon my bosom. It had divided the serge of the robe. It had cut through the linen beneath. Twice again it swung, and a sharp sense of pain shot through every nerve. But the moment of escape had arrived. At a wave of my hand my deliverers hurried tumultuously away. With a steady movement, cautious, sidelong, shrinking, and slow, I slid from the embrace of the bandage and beyond the reach of the scimitar. For the moment, at least, *I was free*.

Free !—and in the grasp of the Inquisition ! I had scarcely stepped from my wooden bed of horror upon the stone floor of the prison, when the motion of the hellish machine ceased, and I beheld it drawn up by some invisible force through the ceiling. This was a lesson which I took desperately to heart. My every motion was undoubtedly watched. Free !—I had but escaped death in one form of agony to be delivered unto worse than death in some other. With that thought I rolled my eyes nervously around on the barriers of iron that hemmed me in. Something unusual—some change which at first I could not appreciate distinctly—it was obvious had taken place in the apartment. For many minutes of a dreamy and trembling abstraction I busied myself in vain, unconnected conjecture. During this period I became aware, for the first time, of the origin of the sulphurous light which illumined the cell. It proceeded from a fissure about half-an-inch in width extending entirely around the prison at the base of the walls which thus appeared, and were completely separated from the floor. I endeavoured, but of course in vain, to look through the aperture.

As I arose from the attempt the mystery of the alteration in the chamber broke at once upon my understanding. I have observed that although the outlines of the figures upon the walls were sufficiently distinct, yet the colours seemed blurred and indefinite. These colours had now assumed, and were momentarily assuming, a startling and most intense brilliancy, that gave to the spectral and fiendish portraitures an aspect that might have thrilled even firmer nerves than my own. Demon eyes, of a wild and ghastly vivacity, glared upon me in a thousand directions where none had been visible before, and gleamed with the lurid lustre of a fire that I could not force my imagination to regard as unreal.

Unreal !—Even while I breathed there came to my nostrils the breath of the vapour of heated iron ! A suffocating odour pervaded the prison ! A deeper glow settled each moment in the eyes that glared at my agonies ! A richer tint of crimson diffused itself over the pictured horrors of blood. I panted ! I gasped for breath ! There could be no doubt of the design of my tormentors—oh, most unrelenting ! oh, most demoniac of men ! I shrank from the glowing metal to the centre of the cell. Amid the thought of the fiery destruction that impended, the idea of the coolness of the well came over my soul like balm. I rushed to its deadly brink. I threw my straining vision below. The glare from the unkindled roof illumined its inmost recesses. Yet, for a wild moment, did my spirit refuse to comprehend the meaning of what I saw. At length it forced—it wrestled its way into my soul—it burned itself in upon my shuddering reason. O for a voice to speak !—oh, horror !—oh, any horror but this ! With a shriek I rushed from the margin and buried my face in my hands—weeping bitterly.

The heat rapidly increased, and once again I looked up, shuddering as with a fit of the ague. There had been a second change in the cell—and now the change was obviously in the *form*. As before, it was in vain that I at first endeavoured to appreciate or understand what was taking place. But not long was I left in doubt. The Inquisitorial vengeance had been hurried by my two-fold escape, and there was to be no more dallying with the King of Terrors. The room had been square. I saw that two of its iron angles were now acute—two, consequently, obtuse. The fearful difference quickly increased with a low rumbling or moaning sound. In an instant the apartment had shifted its form into that of a lozenge. But the alteration stopped not here—I neither hoped nor desired it to stop. I could have clasped the red walls to my bosom as a garment of eternal peace. "Death," I said, "any death but that of the pit!" Fool! might I not have known that *into the pit* it was the object of the burning iron to urge me? Could I resist its glow? or if even that, could I withstand its pressure? And now, flatter and flatter grew the lozenge, with a rapidity that left me no time for contemplation. Its centre, and, of course, its greatest width, came just over the yawning gulf. I shrank back—but the closing walls pressed me resistlessly onward. At length for my seared and writhing body there was no longer an inch of foothold on the firm floor of the prison. I struggled no more, but the agony of my soul found vent in one loud, long, and final scream of despair. I felt that I tottered upon the brink—I averted my eyes—

There was a discordant hum of human voices! There was a loud blast as of many trumpets! There was a harsh grating as of a thousand thunders! The fiery walls rushed back! An outstretched arm caught my own as I fell fainting into the abyss. It was that of General Lasalle. The French army had entered Toledo. The Inquisition was in the hands of its enemies.

IX

THE TELL-TALE HEART

TRUE! nervous, very, very dreadfully nervous I had been and am; but why *will* you say that I am mad? The disease had sharpened my senses, not destroyed, not dulled them. Above all was the sense of hearing acute. I heard all things in the heaven and in the earth. I heard many things in hell. How then am I mad? Hearken! and observe how healthily, how calmly, I can tell you the whole story.

It is impossible to say how first the idea entered my brain, but, once conceived, it haunted me day and night. Object there was none. Passion there was none. I loved the old man. He had never wronged me. He had never given me insult. For his gold I had no desire. I think it was his eye! Yes, it was this! One of his eyes resembled that of a vulture—a pale blue eye with a film over it. Whenever it fell upon me my blood ran cold, and so by degrees, very gradually, I made up my mind to take the life of the old man, and thus rid myself of the eye for ever.

Now this is the point. You fancy me mad. Madmen know nothing. But you should have seen *me*. You should have seen how wisely I proceeded—with what caution—with what foresight, with what dissimulation, I went to work! I was never kinder to the old man than during the whole week before I killed him. And every night about midnight I turned the latch of his door and opened it—oh, so gently! And then when I had made an opening sufficient for my head I put in a dark lantern all closed, closed so that no light shone out, and then I thrust in my head. Oh, you would have laughed to see how cunningly I thrust it in! I moved it slowly, very, very slowly, so that I might not disturb the old man's sleep. It took me an hour to place my whole head within the opening so far that I could see him as he lay upon his bed. Ha! would a madman have been so wise as this? And then when my head was well in the room I undid the lantern cautiously—oh, so cautiously—cautiously (for the hinges creaked), I undid it just so much that a single thin ray fell upon the vulture eye. And this I did for seven long nights, every night just at midnight, but I found the eye always closed, and so it was impossible to do the work, for it was not the old man who vexed me but his Evil Eye. And every morning, when the day broke, I went boldly into the chamber and spoke courageously to him, calling him by name in a hearty tone, and inquiring how he had passed the night. So you see he would have been a very profound old man, indeed, to suspect that every night, just at twelve, I looked in upon him while he slept.

Upon the eighth night I was more than usually cautious in opening the door. A watch's minute hand moves more quickly than did mine. Never before that night had I *felt* the extent of my own powers, of my sagacity. I could scarcely contain my feeling of triumph. To think that there I was opening the door little by little, and he not even to dream of my secret deeds or thoughts. I fairly chuckled at the idea, and perhaps he heard me, for he moved on the bed suddenly as if startled. Now you may think that I drew back—but no. His room was as black as pitch with the thick darkness (for the shutters were close fastened through fear of robbers), and so I knew that he could not see the opening of the door, and I kept pushing it on steadily, steadily.

I had my head in, and was about to open the lantern, when my thumb slipped upon the tin fastening, and the old man sprang up in the bed, crying out, " Who's there ? "

I kept quite still and said nothing. For a whole hour I did not move a muscle, and in the meantime I did not hear him lie down. He was still sitting up in the bed, listening ; just as I have done night after night hearkening to the death watches in the wall.

Presently I heard a slight groan, and I knew it was the groan of mortal terror. It was not a groan of pain or of grief—oh, no ! it was the low stifled sound that arises from the bottom of the soul when overcharged with awe. I knew the sound well. Many a night, just at midnight, when all the world slept, it has welled up from my own bosom, deepening with its dreadful echo, the terrors that distracted me. I say I knew it well. I knew what the old man felt, and pitied him although I chuckled at heart. I knew that he had been lying awake ever since the first slight noise when he had turned in the bed. His fears had been ever since growing upon him. He had been trying to fancy them causeless, but could not. He had been saying to himself, " It is nothing but the wind in the chimney, it is only a mouse crossing the floor," or " It is merely a cricket which has made a single chirp." Yes, he has been trying to comfort himself with these suppositions; but he had found all in vain. *All in vain,* because Death in approaching him had stalked with his black shadow before him and enveloped the victim. And it was the mournful influence of the unperceived shadow that caused him to feel, although he neither saw nor heard, to *feel* the presence of my head within the room.

When I had waited a long time very patiently without hearing him lie down, I resolved to open a little—a very, very little, crevice in the lantern. So I opened it—you cannot imagine how stealthily, stealthily—until at length a single dim ray like the thread of the spider shot out from the crevice and fell upon the vulture eye.

It was open, wide, wide open, and I grew furious as I gazed upon it. I saw it with perfect distinctness—all a dull blue with a hideous veil over it that chilled the very marrow in my bones, but I could see nothing else of the old man's face or person, for I had directed the ray as if by instinct precisely upon the damned spot.

And now have I not told you that what you mistake for madness is but over-acuteness of the senses? now, I say, there came to my ears a low, dull, quick sound, such as a watch makes when enveloped in cotton. I knew *that* sound well, too. It was the beating of the old man's heart. It increased my fury, as the beating of a drum stimulates the soldier into courage.

But even yet I refrained and kept still. I scarcely

breathed. I held the lantern motionless. I tried how steadily I could maintain the ray upon the eye. Meantime the hellish tattoo of the heart increased. It grew quicker and quicker, and louder and louder, every instant. The old man's terror *must* have been extreme! It grew louder, I say, louder every moment! —do you mark me well? I have told you that I am nervous; so I am. And now at the dead hour of the night, amid the dreadful silence ot that old house, so strange a noise as this excited me to uncontrollable terror. Yet, for some minutes longer I refrained and stood still. But the beating grew louder, louder! I thought the heart must burst. And now a new anxiety seized me—the sound would be heard by a neighbour! The old man's hour had come! With a loud yell, I threw open the lantern and leaped into the room. He shrieked once—once only. In an instant I dragged him to the floor, and pulled the heavy bed over him. I then smiled gaily, to find the deed so far done. But tor many minutes the heart beat on with a muffled sound. This, however, did not vex me; it would not be heard through the wall. At length it ceased. The old man was dead. I removed the bed and examined the corpse. Yes, he was stone, stone dead. I placed my hand upon the heart and held it there many minutes. There was no pulsation. He was stone dead, His eye would trouble me no more.

It still you think me mad, you will think so no longer when I describe the wise precautions I took for the concealment of the body. The night waned, and I worked hastily, but in silence.

I took up three planks from the flooring of the

chamber, and deposited all between the scantlings. I then replaced the boards so cleverly, so cunningly, that no human eye—not even *his*—could have detected anything wrong. There was nothing to wash out—no stain of any kind—no blood-spot whatever. I had been too wary for that.

When I had made an end of these labours, it was four o'clock—still dark as midnight. As the bell sounded the hour, there came a knocking at the street door. I went down to open it with a light heart,—for what had I *now* to fear ? There entered three men, who introduced themselves, with perfect suavity, as officers of the police. A shriek had been heard by a neighbour during the night ; suspicion of foul play had been aroused ; information had been lodged at the police office, and they (the officers) had been deputed to search the premises.

I smiled,—for *what* had I to fear ? I bade the gentlemen welcome. The shriek, I said, was my own in a dream. The old man, I mentioned, was absent in the country. I took my visitors all over the house. I bade them search—search *well*. I led them, at length, to *his* chamber. I showed them his treasures, secure, undisturbed. In the enthusiasm of my confidence, I brought chairs into the room, and desired them *here* to rest from their fatigues, while I myself, in the wild audacity of my perfect triumph, placed my own seat upon the very spot beneath which reposed the corpse of the victim.

The officers were satisfied. My *manner* had convinced them. I was singularly at ease. They sat, and while I answered cheerily, they chatted of familiar things. But, ere long, I felt myself getting pale and wished them gone. My head ached, and I fancied a ringing in my ears ; but still they sat, and still chatted. The ringing became more distinct ;—it continued and became more distinct : I talked more freely to get rid of the feeling : but it continued and gained definitiveness—until, at length, I found that the noise was *not* within my ears.

No doubt I now grew *very* pale ;—but I talked more fluently, and with a heightened voice. Yet the sound increased—and what could I do ? It was *a low, dull, quick sound—much such a sound as a watch makes when enveloped in cotton.* I gasped for breath—and yet the officers heard it not. I talked more quickly—more vehemently ; but the noise steadily increased. I arose and argued about trifles, in a high key and with violent gesticulations ; but the noise steadily increased. Why *would* they not be gone ? I paced the floor to and fro with heavy strides, as if excited to fury by the observations of the men—but the noise steadily increased. O God ! what *could* I do ? I foamed—I raved—I swore ! I swung the chair upon which I had been sitting, and grated it upon the boards, but the noise arose over all and continually increased. It grew louder—louder—*louder !* And still the men chatted pleasantly, and smiled. Was it possible they heard not ? Almighty God !—no, no ! They heard !—they suspected !—they *knew !*—they were making a mockery of my horror !—this I thought, and this I think. But anything was better than this agony ! Anything was more tolerable than this derision ! I could bear those hypocritical smiles no longer ! I felt that I must scream or die !—and now—again !—hark ! louder ! louder ! louder ! *louder !*—

"Villains ! " I shrieked, " dissemble no more ! I admit the deed !—tear up the planks !—here, here !— it is the beating of his hideous heart ! "

X

A TALE OF THE RAGGED MOUNTAINS

DURING the fall of the year 1827, while residing near Charlottesville, Virginia, I casually made the acquaintance of Mr. Augustus Bedloe. This young gentleman was remarkable in every respect, and excited in me a profound interest and curiosity. I found it impossible to comprehend him either in his moral or his physical relations. Of his family I could obtain no satisfactory account. Whence he came, I never ascertained. Even about his age—although I call him a young gentleman—there was something which perplexed me in no little degree. He certainly *seemed* young—and he made a point of speaking about his youth—yet there were moments when I should have had little trouble in imagining him a hundred years of age. But in no regard was he more peculiar than in his personal appearance. He was singularly tall and thin. He stooped much. His limbs were exceedingly long and emaciated. His forehead was broad and low. His complexion was absolutely bloodless. His mouth was large and flexible, and his teeth were more widely uneven, although sound, than I had ever before seen teeth in a human head. The expression of his smile, however, was by no means unpleasing, as might be supposed ; but it had no variation whatever. It was one of profound melancholy—of a phaseless and unceasing gloom. His eyes were abnormally large, and round like those of a cat. The pupils, too, upon any accession or diminution of light, underwent contraction or dilation, just such as is observed in the feline tribe. In moments of excitement the orbs grew bright to a degree almost inconceivable ; seeming to emit luminous rays, not of a reflected, but of an intrinsic lustre, as does a candle or the sun ; yet their ordinary condition was so totally vapid, filmy, and dull, as to convey the idea of the eyes of a long-interred corpse.

These peculiarities of person appeared to cause him much annoyance, and he was continually alluding to them in a sort of half explanatory, half apologetic strain, which, when I first heard it, impressed me very painfully. I soon, however, grew accustomed to it, and my uneasiness wore off. It seemed to be his design rather to insinuate, than directly to assert that, physically, he had not always been what he was—that a long series of neuralgic attacks had reduced him from a condition of more than usual personal beauty, to that which I saw. For many years past he had been attended by a physician, named Templeton—an old gentleman, perhaps seventy years of age—whom he had first encountered at Saratoga, and from whose attention, while there, he either received, or fancied that he received, great benefit. The result was that Bedloe, who was wealthy, had made an arrangement with Doctor Templeton, by which the latter, in consideration of a liberal annual allowance, had consented to devote his time and medical experience exclusively to the care of the invalid.

Doctor Templeton had been a traveller in his

younger days, and, at Paris, had become a convert, in great measure, to the doctrines of Mesmer. It was altogether by means of magnetic remedies that he had succeeded in alleviating the acute pains of his patient ; and this success had very naturally inspired the latter with a certain degree of confidence in the opinions from which the remedies had been educed. The Doctor, however, like all enthusiasts, had struggled hard to make a thorough convert of his pupil, and finally so far gained his point as to induce the sufferer to submit to numerous experiments.—By a frequent repetition of these, a result had arisen, which of late days has become so common as to attract little or no attention, but which, at the period of which I write, had very rarely been known in America. I mean to say, that between Doctor Templeton and Bedloe there had grown up, little by little, a very distinct and strongly-marked *rapport*, or magnetic relation. I am not prepared to assert, however, that this *rapport* extended beyond the limits of the simple sleep-producing power ; but this power itself had attained great intensity. At the first attempt to induce the magnetic somnolency, the mesmerist entirely failed. In the fifth or sixth he succeeded very partially, and after long-continued effort. Only at the twelfth was the triumph complete. After this the will of the patient succumbed rapidly to that of the physician, so that, when I first became acquainted with the two, sleep was brought about almost instantaneously, by the mere volition of the operator, even when the invalid was unaware of his presence. It is only now, in the year 1845, when similar miracles are witnessed daily by thousands, that I dare venture to record this apparent impossibility as a matter of serious fact.

The temperament of Bedloe was, in the highest degree, sensitive, excitable, enthusiastic. His imagination was singularly vigorous and creative ; and no doubt it derived additional force from the habitual use of morphine, which he swallowed in great quantity, and without which he would have found it impossible to exist. It was his practice to take a very large dose of it immediately after breakfast, each morning—or rather immediately after a cup of strong coffee, for he ate nothing in the forenoon—and then set forth alone, or attended only by a dog, upon a long ramble among the chain of wild and dreary hills that lie westward and southward of Charlottesville, and are there dignified by the title of the Ragged Mountains.

Upon a dim, warm, misty day, towards the close of November, and during the strange *interregnum* of the seasons which in America is termed the Indian Summer, Mr. Bedloe departed as usual for the hills. The day passed, and still he did not return.

About eight o'clock at night, having become seriously alarmed at his protracted absence, we were about setting out in search of him, when he unexpectedly made his appearance, in health no worse than usual, and in rather more than ordinary spirits. The account which he gave of his expedition, and of the events which had detained him, was a singular one indeed.

" You will remember," said he, " that it was about nine in the morning when I left Charlottesville. I bent my steps immediately to the mountains, and, about ten, entered a gorge which was entirely new to me. I followed the windings of this pass with much interest. The scenery which presented itself on all sides, although scarcely entitled to be called grand, had about it an indescribable, and to me, a delicious aspect of dreary desolation. The solitude seemed absolutely virgin. I could not help believing that the green sods and the grey rocks upon which I trod had never before been trodden by the foot of a human being. So entirely secluded, and in fact inaccessible, except through a series of accidents, is the entrance of the ravine, that it is by no means impossible that I was indeed the first adventurer—the very first and sole adventurer—who had ever penetrated its recesses.

" The thick and peculiar mist or smoke which distinguishes the Indian Summer, and which now hung heavily over all objects, served no doubt to deepen the vague impressions which these objects created. So dense was this pleasant fog that I could at no time see more than a dozen yards of the path before me. This path was excessively sinuous, and as the sun could not be seen, I soon lost all idea of the direction in which I journeyed. In the meantime the morphine had its customary effect—that of enduing all the external world with an intensity of interest. In the quivering of a leaf—in the hue of a blade of grass— in the shape of a trefoil—in the humming of a bee— in the gleaming of a dew-drop—in the breathing of the wind—in the faint odours that came from the forest—there came a whole universe of suggestion— a gay and motley train of rhapsodical and immethodical thought.

"Busied in this, I walked on for several hours, during which the mist deepened around me to so great an extent that at length I was reduced to an absolute groping of the way. And now an indescribable uneasiness possessed me—a species of nervous hesitation and tremor,—I feared to tread, lest I should be precipitated into some abyss. I remembered, too, strange stories told about these Ragged Hills, and of the uncouth and fierce races of men who tenanted their groves and caverns. A thousand vague fancies oppressed and disconcerted me—fancies the more distressing because vague. Very suddenly my attention was arrested by the loud beating of a drum.

"My amazement was, of course, extreme. A drum in these hills was a thing unknown. I could not have been more surprised at the sound of the trump of the Archangel. But a new and still more astounding source of interest and perplexity arose. There came a wild rattling or jingling sound, as if of a bunch of large keys—and upon the instant a dusky-visaged and half-naked man rushed past me with a shriek. He came so close to my person that I felt his hot breath upon my face. He bore in one hand an instrument composed of an assemblage of steel rings, and shook them vigorously as he ran. Scarcely had he disappeared in the mist, before, panting after him, with open mouth and glaring eyes, there darted a huge beast. I could not be mistaken in its character. It was a hyena.

"The sight of this monster rather relieved than heightened my terrors—for I now made sure that I dreamed, and endeavoured to arouse myself to waking consciousness. I stepped boldly and briskly forward. I rubbed my eyes. I called aloud. I pinched my limbs. A small spring of water presented itself to my view, and here stooping, I bathed my hands and my head and neck. This seemed to dissipate the equivocal sensations which had hitherto annoyed me. I arose, as I thought, a new man, and proceeded steadily and complacently on my unknown way.

"At length, quite overcome by exertion, and by a certain oppressive closeness of the atmosphere, I seated myself beneath a tree. Presently there came a feeble gleam of sunshine, and the shadow of the leaves of the tree fell faintly but definitely upon the grass. At this shadow I gazed wanderingly for many minutes. Its character stupefied me with astonishment. I looked upward. The tree was a palm.

"I now arose hurriedly and in a state of fearful agitation—for the fancy that I dreamed would serve me no longer. I saw—I felt that I had perfect command of my senses—and these senses now brought to my soul a world of novel and singular sensation. The heat became all at once intolerable. A strange odour loaded the breeze.—A low continuous murmur, like that arising from a full but gently-flowing river, came to my ears, intermingled with the peculiar hum of multitudinous human voices.

"While I listened in an extremity of astonishment which I need not attempt to describe, a strong and brief gust of wind bore off the incumbent fog as if by the wand of an enchanter.

"I found myself at the foot of a high mountain, and looking down into a vast plain, through which wound a majestic river. On the margin of this river stood an Eastern-looking city, such as we read of in the Arabian Tales, but of a character even more singular than any there described. From my position, which was far above the level of the town, I could perceive its every nook and corner, as if delineated on a map. The streets seemed innumerable, and crossed each other irregularly, in all directions, but were rather long winding alleys than streets, and absolutely swarmed with inhabitants. The houses were wildly picturesque. On every hand was a wilderness of balconies, of verandahs, of minarets, of shrines, and fantastically carved oriels. Bazaars abounded ; and in these were displayed rich wares in infinite variety and profusion—silks, muslins, the most dazzling cutlery, the most magnificent jewels and gems. Besides these things, were seen on all sides, banners and palanquins, litters with stately dames close veiled, elephants gorgeously caparisoned, idols grotesquely hewn, drums, banners and gongs, spears, silver and gilded maces. And amid the crowd, and the clamour, and the general intricacy and confusion—amid the million of black and yellow men, turbaned and robed, and of flowing beard, there roamed a countless multitude of holy filleted bulls, while vast legions of the filthy but sacred ape clambered, chattering and shrieking, about the cornices of the mosques, or clung to the minarets and oriels. From the swarming streets to the banks of the river there descended innumerable flights of steps leading to bathing-places, while the river itself seemed to force a passage with difficulty through the vast fleets of deeply-burthened ships that far and wide encumbered its surface. Beyond the limits of the city arose, in frequent majestic groups, the palm and the cocoa, with other gigantic and weird trees of vast age ; and here and there might be seen a field of rice, the thatched hut of a peasant, a tank, a stray temple, a gipsy camp, or a solitary graceful maiden taking her way, with a pitcher upon her head, to the banks of the magnificent river.

" You will say now, of course, that I dreamed ; but not so. What I saw—what I heard—what I felt— what I thought—had about it nothing of the unmistakable idiosyncrasy of the dream. All was rigorously self-consistent. At first doubting that I was really awake, I entered into a series of tests which soon convinced me that I really was. Now, when one dreams, and in the dream suspects that he dreams, the suspicion *never fails to confirm itself*, and the sleeper is almost immediately aroused. Thus Novalis errs not in saying that ' we are near waking when we dream that we dream.' Had the vision occurred to me as I describe it, without my suspecting it as a dream, then a dream it might absolutely have been, but occurring as it did, and suspected and tested as it was, I am forced to class it among other phenomena."

" In this I am not sure that you are wrong," observed Doctor Templeton, " but proceed. You arose and descended into the city."

" I arose," continued Bedloe, regarding the Doctor with an air of profound astonishment, " I arose, as you say, and descended into the city. On my way, I fell in with an immense populace, crowding through every avenue, all in the same direction, and exhibiting in every action the wildest excitement. Very suddenly, and by some inconceivable impulse, I became intensely imbued with personal interest in what was going on. I seemed to feel that I had an important part to play, without exactly understanding what it was. Against the crowd which environed me, however, I experienced a deep sentiment of animosity. I shrank from amid them, and, swiftly, by a circuitous path, reached and entered the city. Here all was the wildest tumult and contention. A small party of men, clad in garments half Indian, half European, and officered by gentlemen in a uniform partly British, were engaged, at great odds, with the swarming rabble of the alleys. I joined the weaker party, arming myself with the weapons of a fallen officer, and fighting I knew not whom with the nervous ferocity of despair. We were soon overpowered by numbers, and driven to seek refuge in a species of kiosk. Here we barricaded ourselves, and, for the present, were secure. From a loop-hole near the summit of the kiosk, I perceived a vast crowd, in furious agitation, surrounding and assaulting a gay palace that overhung the river. Presently, from an upper window of this palace, there descended an effeminate-looking person, by means of a string made of the turbans of his attendants. A boat was at hand, in which he escaped to the opposite bank of the river.

And now a new object took possession of my soul. I spoke a few hurried but energetic words to my companions, and, having succeeded in gaining over a few of them to my purpose, made a frantic sally from the kiosk. We rushed amid the crowd that surrounded it. They retreated at first before us. They rallied, fought madly, and retreated again. In the meantime we were borne far from the kiosk, and became bewildered and entangled among the narrow streets of tall overhanging houses, into the recesses of which the sun had never been able to shine. The rabble pressed impetuously upon us, harassing us with their spears, and overwhelming us with flights of arrows. These latter were very remarkable, and resembled in some respects the writhing creese of the Malay. They were made to imitate the body of a creeping serpent, and were long and black, with a poisoned barb. One of them struck me upon the right temple. I reeled and fell. An instantaneous and dreadful sickness seized me. I struggled—I gasped—I died."

"You will hardly persist *now*," said I, smiling, "that the whole of your adventure was not a dream. You are not prepared to maintain that you are dead?"

When I said these words, I of course expected some lively sally from Bedloe in reply; but, to my astonishment, he hesitated, trembled, became fearfully pallid, and remained silent. I looked towards Templeton. He sat erect and rigid in his chair—his teeth chattered, and his eyes were starting from their sockets. "Proceed!" he at length said hoarsely to Bedloe.

"For many minutes," continued the latter, "my sole sentiment—my sole feeling—was that of darkness and nonentity, with the consciousness of death. At length there seemed to pass a violent and sudden shock through my soul, as if of electricity. With it came the sense of elasticity and of light. This latter

I felt—not saw. In an instant I seemed to rise from the ground. But I had no bodily, no visible, audible, or palpable presence. The crowd had departed. The tumult had ceased. The city was in comparative repose. Beneath me lay my corpse, with the arrow in my temple, the whole head greatly swollen and disfigured. But all these things I felt—not saw. I took interest in nothing. Even the corpse seemed a matter in which I had no concern. Volition I had none, but appeared to be impelled into motion, and flitted buoyantly out of the city, retracing the circuitous path by which I had entered it. When I had attained that point of the ravine in the mountains at which I had encountered the hyena, I again experienced a shock as of a galvanic battery ; the sense of weight, of volition, of substance, returned. I became my original self, and bent my steps eagerly homewards—but the past had not lost the vividness of the real—and not now, even for an instant, can I compel my understanding to regard it as a dream."

" Nor was it," said Templeton, with an air of deep solemnity, " yet it would be difficult to say how otherwise it should be termed. Let us suppose only, that the soul of the man of to-day is upon the verge of some stupendous psychal discoveries. Let us content ourselves with this supposition. For the rest I have some explanation to make. Here is a water-colour drawing which I should have shown you before, but which an unaccountable sentiment of horror has hitherto prevented me from showing."

We looked at the picture which he presented. I saw nothing in it of an extraordinary character ; but its effect upon Bedloe was prodigious. He nearly fainted as he gazed. And yet it was but a miniature portrait —a miraculously accurate one, to be sure—of his own very remarkable features. At least this was my thought as I regarded it.

"You will perceive," said Templeton, "the date of this picture—it is here, scarcely visible, in this corner—1780. In this year was the portrait taken. It is the likeness of a dead friend—a Mr. Oldeb—to whom I became much attached at Calcutta, during the administration of Warren Hastings. I was then only twenty years old. When I first saw you, Mr. Bedloe, at Saratoga, it was the miraculous similarity which existed between yourself and the painting which induced me to accost you, to seek your friendship, and to bring about those arrangements which resulted in my becoming your constant companion. In accomplishing this point I was urged partly, and perhaps principally, by a regretful memory of the deceased, but also, in part, by an uneasy and not altogether horrorless curiosity respecting yourself.

"In your detail of the vision which presented itself to you amid the hills, you have described, with the minutest accuracy, the Indian city of Benares upon the Holy River. The riots, the combats, the massacre, were the actual events of the insurrection of Cheyte Sing, which took place in 1780, when Hastings was put in imminent peril of his life. The man escaping by the string of turbans was Cheyte Sing himself. The party in the kiosk were sepoys and British officers headed by Hastings. Of this party I was one, and did all I could to prevent the rash and fatal sally of the officer who fell, in the crowded alleys, by the poisoned arrow of a Bengalee. That officer was my dearest friend. It was Oldeb. You will perceive by these manuscripts " (here the speaker produced a note-book in which several pages appeared to have been freshly written) " that at the very period in which you fancied these things amid the hills, I was engaged in detailing them upon paper here at home."

In about a week after this conversation, the following paragraphs appeared in a Charlottesville paper :

" We have the painful duty of announcing the death of Mr. AUGUSTUS BEDLO, a gentleman whose amiable manners and many virtues have long endeared him to the citizens of Charlottesville.

" Mr. B., for some years past, has been subject to neuralgia, which has often threatened to terminate fatally ; but this can be regarded only as the mediate cause of his decease. The proximate cause was one of especial singularity. In an excursion to the Ragged Mountains, a few days since, a slight cold and fever were contracted, attended with great determination of blood to the head. To relieve this, Doctor Templeton resorted to topical bleeding. Leeches were applied to the temples. In a fearfully brief period the patient died, when it appeared that, in the jar containing the leeches, had been introduced, by accident, one of the venomous vermicular sangsues which are now and then found in the neighbouring ponds. This creature fastened itself upon a small artery in the right temple. Its close resemblance to the medicinal leech caused the mistake to be overlooked until too late.

" *N.B.*—The poisonous sangsue of Charlottesville

may always be distinguished from the medicinal leech by its blackness, and especially by its writhing or vermicular motions, which very nearly resemble those of a snake."

I was speaking with the editor of the paper in question, upon the topic of this remarkable accident, when it occurred to me to ask how it happened that the name of the deceased had been given as Bedlo.

" I presume," said I, " you have authority for this spelling, but I have always supposed the name to be written with an *e* at the end."

" Authority ?—no," he replied. " It is a mere typographical error. The name is Bedlo with an *e*, all the world over, and I never knew it to be spelt otherwise in my life."

" Then," said I mutteringly, as I turned upon my heel, " then indeed has it come to pass that one truth is stranger than any fiction—for Bedlo without the *e*, what is it but Oldeb conversed ? And this man tells me it is a typographical error."

XI

THE PREMATURE BURIAL

THERE are certain themes of which the interest is all-absorbing, but which are too entirely horrible for the purposes of legitimate fiction. These the mere romanticist must eschew, if he do not wish to offend or to disgust. They are with propriety handled only when the severity and majesty of truth sanctify and sustain them. We thrill, for example, with the most intense of " pleasurable pain " over the accounts of the Passage of the Beresina, of the Earthquake at Lisbon, of the Plague at London, of the Massacre of St. Bartholomew, or of the stifling of the hundred and twenty-three prisoners in the Black Hole at Calcutta. But in these accounts it is the fact—it is the reality —it is the history which excites. As inventions, we should regard them with simple abhorrence.

I have mentioned some few of the more prominent and august calamities on record ; but in these it is the extent, not less than the character of the calamity, which so vividly impresses the fancy. I need not remind the reader that, from the long and weird catalogue of human miseries, I might have selected many individual instances more replete with essential suffering than any of these vast generalities of disaster. The true wretchedness, indeed—the ultimate woe— is particular, not diffuse. That the ghastly extremes of agony are endured by man the unit, and never by man the mass—for this let us thank a merciful God !

To be buried while alive is beyond question the most terrific of these extremes which has ever fallen to the lot of mere mortality. That it has frequently, very frequently, so fallen, will scarcely be denied by those who think. The boundaries which divide life from death are at best shadowy and vague. Who shall say where the one ends and where the other begins? We know that there are diseases in which occur total cessations of all the apparent functions of vitality, and yet in which these cessations are merely suspensions, properly so called. They are only temporary pauses in the incomprehensible mechanism. A certain period elapses, and some unseen mysterious principle again sets in motion the magic pinions and the wizard wheels. The silver cord was not for ever loosed, nor the golden bowl irreparably broken. But where meantime was the soul?

Apart, however, from the inevitable conclusion, *a priori*, that such causes must produce such effects —that the well-known occurrence of such cases of suspended animation must naturally give rise now and then to premature interments—apart from this consideration, we have the direct testimony of medical and ordinary experience to prove that a vast number of such interments have actually taken place. I might refer at once, if necessary, to a hundred well authenticated instances. One of very remarkable character, and of which the circumstances may be fresh in the memory of some of my readers, occurred not very long ago in the neighbouring city of Baltimore, where it occasioned a painful, intense, and widely-extended excitement. The wife of one of the most respectable citizens—a lawyer of eminence and a member of Congress—was seized with a sudden and unaccountable illness, which completely baffled the skill of her physicians. After much suffering she died, or was supposed to die. No one suspected, indeed, or had reason to suspect, that she was not actually dead. She presented all the ordinary appearances of death. The face assumed the usual pinched and sunken outline. The lips were of the usual marble pallor. The eyes were lustreless. There was no warmth. Pulsation had ceased. For three days the body was preserved unburied, during which it had acquired a stony rigidity. The funeral, in short, was hastened, on account of the rapid advance of what was supposed to be decomposition.

The lady was deposited in her family vault, which for three subsequent years was undisturbed. At the expiration of this term it was opened for the reception of a sarcophagus ;—but, alas ! how fearful a shock awaited the husband, who personally threw open the door. As its portals swung outwardly back, some white-apparelled object fell rattling within his arms. It was the skeleton of his wife in her yet unmouldered shroud.

A careful investigation rendered it evident that she had revived within two days after entombment—that her struggles within the coffin had caused it to fall from a ledge or shelf to the floor, where it was so broken as to permit her escape. A lamp which had been accidentally left full of oil within the tomb was found empty ; it might have been exhausted, however, by evaporation. On the uppermost of the steps which led down into the dread chamber was a large fragment of the coffin, with which it seemed that she had endeavoured to arrest attention by striking the iron door. While thus occupied she probably swooned, or possibly died, through sheer terror ; and, in falling, her shroud became entangled in some iron-work which projected interiorly. Thus she remained, and thus she rotted, erect.

In the year 1810, a case of living inhumation happened in France, attended with circumstances which go far to warrant the assertion that truth is indeed stranger than fiction. The heroine of the story was a Mademoiselle Victorine Lafourcade, a young girl of illustrious family, of wealth, and of great personal beauty. Among her numerous suitors was Julien Bossuet, a poor *littérateur*, or journalist, of Paris. His talents and general amiability had recommended him to the notice of the heiress, by whom he seems to have been truly beloved ; but her pride of birth decided her finally to reject him, and to wed a Monsieur Renelle, a banker, and a diplomatist of some eminence. After marriage, however, this gentleman neglected, and perhaps even more positively ill-treated her. Having passed with him some wretched years, she died,—at least her condition so closely resembled death as to deceive every one who saw her. She was buried—not in a vault—but in an ordinary grave in the village of her nativity. Filled with despair, and still inflamed by the memory of a profound attachment, the lover journeys from the capital to the remote province in which the village lies, with the romantic purpose of disinterring the corpse and possessing him-

self of its luxuriant tresses. He reaches the grave.
At midnight he unearths the coffin, opens it, and is
in the act of detaching the hair, when he is arrested
by the unclosing of the beloved eyes. In fact the lady
had been buried alive. Vitality had not altogether
departed ; and she was aroused by the caresses of her
lover from the lethargy which had been mistaken for
death. He bore her frantically to his lodgings in the
village. He employed certain powerful restoratives
suggested by no little medical learning. In fine, she
revived. She recognised her preserver. She remained
with him until by slow degrees she fully recovered
her original health. Her woman's heart was not
adamant, and this last lesson of love sufficed to soften
it. She bestowed it upon Bossuet. She returned no
more to her husband, but concealing from him her
resurrection, fled with her lover to America. Twenty
years afterwards the two returned to France, in the
persuasion that time had so greatly altered the lady's
appearance that her friends would be unable to recognise her. They were mistaken, however ; for at the
first meeting Monsieur Renelle did actually recognise
and make claim to his wife. This claim she resisted ;
and a judicial tribunal sustained her in her resistance,
deciding that the peculiar circumstances, with the
long lapse of years, had extinguished, not only equit-
ably but legally, the authority of the husband.

The " Chirurgical Journal " of Leipsic—a periodical
of high authority and merit, which some American
bookseller would do well to translate and republish—
records in a late number a very distressing event of
the character in question.

An officer of artillery, a man of gigantic stature and of robust health, being thrown from an unmanageable horse, received a very severe contusion upon the head, which rendered him insensible at once; the skull was slightly fractured, but no immediate danger was apprehended. Trepanning was accomplished successfully. He was bled, and many other of the ordinary means of relief were adopted. Gradually, however, he fell into a more and more hopeless state of stupor, and, finally, it was thought that he died.

The weather was warm, and he was buried with indecent haste in one of the public cemeteries. His funeral took place on Thursday. On the Sunday following the grounds of the cemetery were as usual much thronged with visitors; and about noon an intense excitement was created by the declaration of a peasant that, while sitting upon the grave of the officer, he had distinctly felt a commotion of the earth, as if occasioned by some one struggling beneath. At first little attention was paid to the man's asseveration; but his evident terror, and the dogged obstinacy with which he persisted in his story, had at length their natural effect upon the crowd. Spades were hurriedly procured, and the grave, which was shamefully shallow, was in a few minutes so far thrown open that the head of its occupant appeared. He was then seemingly dead, but he sat nearly erect within his coffin, the lid of which, in his furious struggles, he had partially uplifted.

He was forthwith conveyed to the nearest hospital, and there pronounced to be still living, although in an asphyctic condition. After some hours he revived, recognised individuals of his acquaintance, and in broken sentences spoke of his agonies in the grave.

From what he related it was clear that he must have been conscious of life for more than an hour, while inhumed, before lapsing into insensibility. The grave was carelessly and loosely filled with an exceedingly porous soil, and thus some air was necessarily admitted. He heard the footsteps of the crowd overhead, and endeavoured to make himself heard in turn. It was the tumult within the grounds of the cemetery, he said, which appeared to awaken him from a deep sleep, but no sooner was he awake than he became fully aware of the awful horrors of his position.

This patient, it is recorded, was doing well, and seemed to be in a fair way of ultimate recovery, but fell a victim to the quackeries of medical experiment. The galvanic battery was applied, and he suddenly expired in one of those ecstatic paroxysms which occasionally it superinduces.

The mention of the galvanic battery, nevertheless, recalls to my memory a well-known and very extraordinary case in point, where its action proved the means of restoring to animation a young attorney of London, who had been interred for two days. This occurred in 1831, and created at the time a very profound sensation wherever it was made the subject of converse.

The patient, Mr. Edward Stapleton, had died apparently of typhus fever, accompanied with some anomalous symptoms which had excited the curiosity of his medical attendants. Upon his seeming decease his friends were requested to sanction a *post-mortem* examination, but declined to permit it. As often happens when such refusals are made, the practitioners resolved to disinter the body and dissect it at leisure in private. Arrangements were easily effected with some of the numerous corps of body-snatchers with which London abounds ; and upon the third night after the funeral, the supposed corpse was unearthed from a grave eight feet deep, and deposited in the operating chamber of one of the private hospitals.

An incision of some extent had been actually made in the abdomen, when the fresh and undecayed appearance of the subject suggested an application of the battery. One experiment succeeded another, and the customary effects supervened, with nothing to characterise them in any respect except upon one or two occasions a more than ordinary degree of life-likeness in the convulsive action.

It grew late. The day was about to dawn, and it was thought expedient at length to proceed at once to the dissection. A student, however, was especially desirous of testing a theory of his own, and insisted upon applying the battery to one of the pectoral muscles. A rough gash was made, and a wire hastily brought in contact, when the patient with a hurried but quite unconvulsive movement, arose from the table, stepped into the middle of the floor, gazed about him uneasily for a few seconds, and then spoke. What he said was unintelligible ; but the words were uttered ; the syllabification was distinct. Having spoken, he fell heavily to the floor.

For some moments all were paralysed with awe— but the urgency of the case soon restored them to their presence of mind. It was seen that Mr. Stapleton was alive, although in a swoon. Upon exhibition of ether he revived and was rapidly restored to health, and to the society of his friends—from whom, however, all knowledge of his resuscitation was withheld, until a relapse was no longer to be apprehended. Their wonder—their rapturous astonishment—may be conceived.

The most thrilling peculiarity of this incident nevertheless, is involved in what Mr. S. himself asserts. He declares that at no period was he altogether insensible—that, dully and confusedly, he was aware of everything which happened to him, from the moment in which he was pronounced *dead* by his physicians, to that in which he fell swooning to the floor of the hospital. " I am alive," were the uncomprehended words which, upon recognising the locality of the dissecting-room, he had endeavoured in his extremity to utter.

It were an easy matter to multiply such histories as these, but I forbear, for, indeed, we have no need of such to establish the fact that premature interments occur. When we reflect how very rarely, from the nature of the case, we have it in our power to detect them, we must admit that they may *frequently* occur without our cognisance. Scarcely, in truth, is a graveyard encroached upon for any purpose, to any great extent, that skeletons are not found in postures which suggest the most fearful of suspicions.

Fearful indeed the suspicion, but more fearful the doom ! It may be asserted, without hesitation, that *no* event is so terribly well adapted to inspire the supremeness of bodily and of mental distress as is burial before death. The unendurable oppression of the lungs—the stifling fumes of the damp earth—the clinging to the death garments—the rigid embrace of the narrow house—the blackness of the absolute night—the silence like a sea that overwhelms—the unseen but palpable presence of the conqueror worm —these things, with thoughts of the air and grass above, with memory of dear friends who would fly to save us if but informed of our fate, and with consciousness that of this fate they can *never* be informed —that our hopeless portion is that of the really dead —these considerations, I say, carry into the heart which still palpitates a degree of appalling and intolerable horror from which the most daring imagination must recoil. We know of nothing so agonising upon earth—we can dream of nothing half so hideous in the realms of the nethermost hell ; and thus all narratives upon this topic have an interest so profound ; an interest, nevertheless, which, through the sacred awe of the topic itself, very properly and very peculiarly depends upon our conviction of the *truth* of the matter narrated. What I have now to tell is of my own actual knowledge—of my own positive and personal experience.

For several years I have been subject to attacks of the singular disorder which physicians have agreed to term catalepsy in default of a more definitive title. Although both the immediate and the predisposing causes, and even the actual diagnosis of this disease, are still mysterious, its obvious and apparent character is sufficiently well understood. Its variations

seem to be chiefly of degree. Sometimes the patient
lies for a day only, or even for a shorter period, in a
species of exaggerated lethargy. He is senseless and
externally motionless, but the pulsation of the heart
is still faintly perceptible ; some traces of warmth
remain ; a slight colour lingers within the centre of
the cheek ; and upon application of a mirror to the
lips we can detect a torpid, unequal, and vacillating
action of the lungs. Then again the duration of the
trance is for weeks—even for months ; while the
closest scrutiny, and the most rigorous medical tests,
fail to establish any material distinction between the
state of the sufferer and what we conceive of absolute
death. Very usually he is saved from premature interment solely by the knowledge of his friends that he
has been previously subject to catalepsy, by the consequent suspicion excited, and, above all, by the non-
appearance of decay. The advances of the malady
are, luckily, gradual. The first manifestations,
although marked, are unequivocal. The fits grow
successively more and more distinctive, and endure
each for a longer term than the preceding. In this
lies the principal security from inhumation. The
unfortunate whose *first* attack should be of the extreme
character which is occasionally seen would almost inevitably be consigned alive to the tomb.

My own case differed in no important particular
from those mentioned in medical books. Sometimes,
without any apparent cause, I sank, little by little,
into a condition of semi-syncope or half-swoon ; and
in this condition, without pain, without ability to
stir, or, strictly speaking, to think, but with a dull

lethargic consciousness of life and of the presence of those who surrounded my bed, I remained, until the crisis of the disease restored me, suddenly, to perfect sensation. At other times I was quickly and impetuously smitten. I grew sick, and numb, and chilly, and dizzy, and so fell prostrate at once. Then for weeks all was void, and black and silent, and Nothing became the universe. Total annihilation could be no more. From these latter attacks I awoke, however, with a gradation slow in proportion to the suddenness of the seizure. Just as the day dawns to the friendless and houseless beggar who roams the street throughout the long desolate winter night—just so tardily— just so wearily—just so cheerily came back the light of the soul to me.

Apart from the tendency to trance, however, my general health appeared to be good; nor could I perceive that it was at all affected by the one prevalent malady—unless, indeed, an idiosyncrasy in my ordinary *sleep* may be looked upon as superinduced. Upon awaking from slumber, I could never gain at once thorough possession of my senses, and always remained for many minutes in much bewilderment and perplexity; the mental faculties in general, but the memory in especial, being in a condition of absolute abeyance.

In all that I endured there was no physical suffering, but of moral distress an infinitude. My fancy grew charnel. I talked " of worms, of tombs, and epitaphs." I was lost in reveries of death, and the idea of premature burial held continual possession of my brain. The ghastly danger to which I was subjected haunted me day and night. In the former, the torture of meditation was excessive—in the latter, supreme. When the grim darkness overspread the earth, then, with very horror of thought, I shook—shook as the quivering plumes upon the hearse. When nature could endure wakefulness no longer, it was with a struggle that I consented to sleep—for I shuddered to reflect that upon awaking I might find myself the tenant of a grave. And when, finally, I sank into slumber, it was only to rush at once into a world of phantasms, above which, with vast, sable, over-shadowing wings, hovered predominant the one sepulchral idea.

From the innumerable images of gloom which thus oppressed me in dreams, I select for record but a solitary vision. Methought I was immersed in a cataleptic trance of more than usual duration and profundity. Suddenly there came an icy hand upon my forehead, and an impatient gibbering voice whispered the word " arise ! " within my ear.

I sat erect. The darkness was total. I could not see the figure of him who had aroused me. I could call to mind neither the period at which I had fallen into the trance, nor the locality in which I then lay. While I remained motionless, and busied in en-deavours to collect my thoughts, the cold hand grasped me fiercely by the wrist, shaking it petulantly, while the gibbering voice said again :

" Arise ! did I not bid thee arise ? "

" And who," I demanded, " art thou ? "

" I have no name in the regions which I inhabit," replied the voice, mournfully ; " I was mortal, but am fiend. I was merciless, but am pitiful. Thou dost feel that I shudder. My teeth chatter as I speak, yet it is not with the chilliness of the night—of the night without end. But this hideousness is insufferable. How canst *thou* tranquilly sleep? I cannot rest for the cry of these great agonies. These sights are more than I can bear. Get thee up! Come with me into the outer night, and let me unfold to thee the graves. Is not this a spectacle of woe!—Behold!"

I looked; and the unseen figure, which still grasped me by the wrist, had caused to be thrown open the graves of all mankind, and from each issued the faint phosphoric radiance of decay, so that I could see into the innermost recesses, and there view the shrouded bodies in their sad and solemn slumbers with the worm. But, alas! the real sleepers were fewer by many millions than those who slumbered not at all; and there was a feeble struggling; and there was a general sad unrest; and from out the depths of the countless pits there came a melancholy rustling from the garments of the buried; and of those who seemed tranquilly to repose I saw that a vast number had changed, in a greater or less degree, the rigid and uneasy position in which they had originally been entombed. And the voice again said to me as I gazed:

"Is it not—O, is it *not* a pitiful sight?" But before I could find word to reply, the figure had ceased to grasp my wrist, the phosphoric lights expired, and the graves were closed with a sudden violence, while from out them arose a tumult of despairing cries, saying again, "Is it not—O, God! is it *not* a very pitiful sight?"

Phantasies such as these presenting themselves at night extended their terrific influence far into my waking hours. My nerves became thoroughly unstrung, and I fell a prey to perpetual horror. I hesitated to ride, or to walk, or to indulge in any exercise that would carry me from home. In fact, I no longer dared trust myself out of the immediate presence of those who were aware of my proneness to catalepsy, lest, falling into one of my usual fits, I should be buried before my real condition could be ascertained. I doubted the care, the fidelity of my dearest friends. I dreaded that, in some trance of more than customary duration, they might be prevailed upon to regard me as irrecoverable. I even went so far as to fear that, as I occasioned much trouble, they might be glad to consider any very protracted attack as sufficient excuse for getting rid of me altogether. It was in vain they endeavoured to reassure me by the most solemn promises. I exacted the most sacred oaths that under no circumstances they would bury me until decomposition had so materially advanced as to render further preservation impossible ; and even then my mortal terrors would listen to no reason, would accept no consolation. I entered into a series of elaborate precautions. Among other things, I had the family vault so remodelled as to admit of being readily opened from within. The slightest pressure upon a long lever that extended far into the tomb would cause the iron portals to fly back. There were arrangements also for the free admission of air and light, and convenient receptacles for food and water, within immediate reach of the coffin in-

tended for my reception. This coffin was warmly
and softly padded, and was provided with a lid,
fashioned upon the principle of the vault-door, with
the addition of springs so contrived that the feeblest
movement of the body would be sufficient to set it
at liberty. Besides all this, there was suspended from
the roof of the tomb a large bell, the rope of which,
it was designed, should extend through a hole in the
coffin, and so be fastened to one of the hands of the
corpse. But, alas! what avails the vigilance against
the destiny of man? Not even these well-contrived
securities sufficed to save from the uttermost agonies
of living inhumation a wretch to these agonies fore-
doomed!

There arrived an epoch—as often before there had
arrived—in which I found myself emerging from total
unconsciousness into the first feeble and indefinite
sense of existence. Slowly—with a tortoise gradation
—approached the faint grey dawn of the psychal day.
A torpid uneasiness. An apathetic endurance of dull
pain. No care—no hope—no effort. Then, after long
interval, a ringing in the ears; then, after a lapse still
longer, a pricking or tingling sensation in the extremities; then a seemingly eternal period of pleasurable quiescence, during which the awakening feelings
are struggling into thought; then a brief re-sinking
into nonentity; then a sudden recovery. At length
the slight quivering of an eyelid, and immediately
thereupon an electric shock of a terror, deadly and
indefinite, which sends the blood in torrents from the
temples to the heart. And now the first positive effort
to think. And now the first endeavour to remember.

And now a partial and evanescent success. And now the memory has so far regained its dominion that, in some measure, I am cognisant of my state. I feel that I am not awaking from ordinary sleep. I recollect that I have been subject to catalepsy. And now, at last, as if by the rush of an ocean, my shuddering spirit is overwhelmed by the one grim danger—by the one spectral and ever-prevalent idea.

For some minutes after this fancy possessed me, I remained without motion. And why? I could not summon courage to move. I dared not make the effort which was to satisfy me of my fate; and yet there was something at my heart which whispered me *it was sure*. Despair—such as no other species of wretchedness ever calls into being—despair alone urged me after long irresolution to uplight the heavy lids of my eyes. I uplifted them. It was dark—all dark. I knew that the fit was over. I knew that the crisis of my disorder had long passed. I knew that I had now fully recovered the use of my visual faculties—and yet it was dark—all dark—the intense and utter raylessness of the night that endureth for evermore.

I endeavoured to shriek, and my lips and my parched tongue moved convulsively together in the attempt—but no voice issued from the cavernous lungs, which, oppressed as if by the weight of some incumbent mountain, gasped and palpitated, with the heart, at every elaborate and struggling inspiration.

The movement of the jaws in this effort to cry aloud showed me that they were bound up, as is usual with the dead. I felt too that I lay upon some hard substance; and by something similar my sides were also closely compressed. So far I had not ventured to stir any of my limbs—but now I violently threw up my arms, which had been lying at length with the wrists crossed. They struck a solid wooden substance which extended above my person at an elevation of not more than six inches from my face. I could no longer doubt that I reposed within a coffin at last.

And now amid all my infinite miseries came sweetly the cherub hope—for I thought of my precautions. I writhed and made spasmodic exertions to force open the lid ; it would not move. I felt my wrists for the bell-rope ; it was not to be found. And now the comforter fled for ever, and a still sterner despair reigned triumphant ; for I could not help perceiving the absence of the paddings which I had so carefully prepared ; and then too there came suddenly to my nostrils the strong peculiar odour of moist earth. The conclusion was irresistible. I was *not* within the vault. I had fallen into a trance while absent from home—while among strangers—when or how I could not remember ; and it was they who had buried me as a dog—nailed up in some common coffin—and thrust deep, deep, and for ever, into some ordinary and nameless *grave*.

As this awful conviction forced itself thus into the innermost chambers of my soul, I once again struggled to cry aloud ; and in this second endeavour I succeeded. A long, wild, and continuous shriek, or yell of agony resounded through the realms of the subterrene night.

" Hillo ! hillo, there ! " said a gruff voice, in reply.

" What the devil's the matter now ? " said a second

" Get out o' that ! " said a third.

" What do you mean by yowling in that ere kind of style like a cattymount ? " said a fourth ; and hereupon I was seized and shaken without ceremony for several minutes by a junto of very rough-looking individuals. They did not arouse me from my slumber —for I was wide awake when I screamed—but they restored me to the full possession of my memory.

This adventure occurred near Richmond, in Virginia. Accompanied by a friend I had proceeded upon a gunning expedition some miles down the banks of James River. Night approached, and we were over-taken by a storm. The cabin of a small sloop lying at anchor in the stream, and laden with garden mould, afforded us the only available shelter. We made the best of it, and passed the night on board. I slept in one of the only two berths in the vessel—and the berths of a sloop of sixty or seventy tons need scarcely be described. That which I occupied had no bedding of any kind. Its extreme width was eighteen inches. The distance of its bottom from the deck overhead was precisely the same. I found it a matter of exceed-ing difficulty to squeeze myself in. Nevertheless, I slept soundly ; and the whole of my vision—for it was no dream, and no nightmare—arose naturally from the circumstances of my position—from my ordinary bias of thought, and from the difficulty, to which I have alluded, of collecting my senses, and especially of regaining my memory for a long time after awaking from slumber. The men who shook me were the crew of the sloop and some labourers engaged to unload it. From the load itself came the earthy smell. The bandage about the jaws was a silk handkerchief in which I had bound up my head in default of my customary nightcap.

The tortures endured, however, were indubitably quite equal for the time to those of actual sepulture. They were fearfully—they were inconceivably hideous; but out of evil proceeded good, for their very excess wrought in my spirit an inevitable revulsion. My soul acquired tone—acquired temper. I went abroad. I took vigorous exercise. I breathed the free air of heaven. I thought upon other subjects than death. I discarded my medical books. " Buchan " I burned. I read no " Night Thoughts "—no fustian about churchyards—no bugaboo tales—*such as this*. In short I became a new man and lived a man's life. From that memorable night I dismissed for ever my charnel apprehensions, and with them vanished the cataleptic disorder, of which perhaps they had been less the consequence than the cause.

There are moments when, even to the sober eye of reason, the world of our sad humanity may assume the semblance of a hell ; but the imagination of man is no Carathis to explore with impunity its every cavern. Alas ! the grim legion of sepulchral terrors cannot be regarded as altogether fanciful ; but, like the demons in whose company Afrasiab made his voyage down the Oxus, they must sleep or they will devour us—they must be suffered to slumber or we perish.

XII

THE SYSTEM OF DOCTOR TARR AND PROFESSOR FETHER

DURING the autumn of 18—, while on a tour through the extreme southern provinces of France, my route led me within a few miles of a certain *Maison de Santé* or private Mad-house, about which I had heard much in Paris from my medical friends. As I had never visited a place of the kind, I thought the opportunity too good to be lost; and so proposed to my travelling companion (a gentleman with whom I had made casual acquaintance a few days before— that we should turn aside for an hour or so and look through the establishment. To this he objected— pleading haste in the first place, and in the second, a very usual horror at the sight of a lunatic. He begged me, however, not to let any mere courtesy towards himself interfere with the gratification of my curiosity, and said that he would ride on leisurely, so that I might overtake him during the day, or at all events during the next. As he bade me good-bye, I bethought me that there might be some difficulty in obtaining access to the premises, and mentioned my fears on this point. He replied that, in fact, unless I had personal knowledge of the superintendent, Monsieur Maillard, or some credential in the way of a letter, a difficulty might be found to exist, as the regulations of these private madhouses were more rigid than the public hospital laws. For himself, he added, he had some years since made the acquaintance of Maillard, and would so far assist me as to ride up to the door and introduce me, although his feelings on the subject of lunacy would not permit of his entering the house.

I thanked him, and turning from the main-road we entered a grass-grown by-path, which, in half-an-hour, nearly lost itself in a dense forest closing the base of a mountain. Through this dank and gloomy wood we rode some two miles, when the *Maison de Santé* came in view. It was a fantastic *château*, much dilapidated, and indeed scarcely tenantable through age and neglect. Its aspect inspired me with absolute dread, and, checking my horse, I half resolved to turn back. I soon, however, grew ashamed of my weakness and proceeded.

As we rode up to the gateway, I perceived it slightly open, and the visage of a man peering through. In an instant afterward, this man came forth, accosted my companion by name, shook him cordially by the hand, and begged him to alight. It was Monsieur Maillard himself. He was a portly, fine-looking gentleman of the old school, with a polished manner, and a certain air of gravity, dignity, and authority, which was very impressive.

My friend having presented me, mentioned my desire to inspect the establishment, and received Monsieur Maillard's assurance that he would show me all attention, now took leave, and I saw him no more.

When he had gone, the superintendent ushered me into a small and exceedingly neat parlour, containing among other indications of refined taste, many books, drawings, pots of flowers, and musical instruments. A cheerful fire blazed upon the hearth. At a piano, singing an aria from Bellini, sat a young and very beautiful woman, who, at my entrance, paused in her song, and received me with graceful courtesy. Her voice was low, and her whole manner subdued. I thought, too, that I perceived the traces of sorrow in her countenance, which was excessively, although to my taste, not unpleasingly pale. She was attired in deep mourning, and excited in my bosom a feeling of mingled respect, interest, and admiration.

I had heard, at Paris, that the institution of Monsieur Maillard was managed upon what is vulgarly termed the "system of soothing"—that all punishments were avoided—that even confinement was seldom resorted to—that the patients, while secretly watched, were left much apparent liberty, and that most of them were permitted to roam about the house and grounds in the ordinary apparel of persons in right mind.

Keeping these impressions in view, I was cautious in what I said before the young lady, for I could not be sure that she was sane; and in fact there was a certain restless brilliancy about her eyes which half led me to imagine she was not. I confined my remarks, therefore, to general topics, and to such as I thought would not be displeasing or exciting even to a lunatic. She replied in a perfectly rational manner to all that I said, and even her original observations were marked with the soundest good sense; but a long acquaintance with the metaphysics of *mania* had taught me to put no faith in such evidence of sanity, and I continued to practise, throughout the interview, the caution with which I commenced it.

Presently a smart footman in livery brought in a tray with fruit, wine, and other refreshments, of which I partook, the lady soon afterwards leaving the room. As she departed I turned my eyes in an inquiring manner towards my host.

" No," he said, " oh, no—a member of my family— my niece, and a most accomplished woman."

" I beg a thousand pardons for the suspicion," I replied, " but of course you will know how to excuse me. The excellent administration of your affairs here is well understood in Paris, and I thought it just possible, you know——"

" Yes, yes—say no more—or rather it is myself who should thank you for the commendable prudence you have displayed. We seldom find so much of forethought in young men, and, more than once, some unhappy *contretemps* has occurred in consequence of thoughtlessness on the part of our visitors. While my former system was in operation and my patients were permitted the privilege of roaming to and fro at will, they were often aroused to a dangerous frenzy by injudicious persons who called to inspect the house. Hence I was obliged to enforce a rigid system of exclusion ; and none obtained access to the premises upon whose discretion I could not rely."

" While your *former* system was in operation ! " I said, repeating his words—" do I understand you, then, to say that the ' soothing system ' of which I have heard so much, is no longer in force ? "

"It is now," he replied, "several weeks since we have concluded to renounce it for ever."

"Indeed! you astonish me!"

"We found it, sir," he said with a sigh, "absolutely necessary to return to the old usages. The *danger* of the soothing system was at all times appalling, and its advantages have been much over-rated. I believe, sir, that in this house it has been given a fair trial, if ever in any. We did everything that rational humanity could suggest. I am sorry that you could not have paid us a visit at an earlier period, that you might have judged for yourself. But I presume you are conversant with the soothing practice—with its details."

"Not altogether. What I have heard has been at third or fourth hand."

"I may state the system then, in general terms, as one in which the patients were *ménagés* humoured. We contradicted *no* fancies which entered the brains of the mad. On the contrary, we not only judged but encouraged them; and many of our most permanent cures have been thus effected. There is no argument which so touches the feeble reason of the madman as the *reductio ad absurdum*. We have had men, for example, who fancied themselves chickens. The cure was, to insist upon the thing as a fact— to accuse the patient of stupidity in not sufficiently perceiving it to be a fact—and thus to refuse him any other diet for a week than that which properly appertains to a chicken. In this manner a little corn and gravel were made to perform wonders."

"But was this species of acquiescence all?"

"By no means. We put much faith in amusements of a simple kind, such as music, dancing, gymnastic exercises generally, cards, certain classes of books, and so forth. We affected to treat each individual as if for some ordinary physical disorder, and the word 'lunacy' was never employed. A great point was to set each lunatic to guard the actions of all the others. To repose confidence in the understanding or discretion of a madman is to gain him body and soul. In this way we were enabled to dispense with an expensive body of keepers."

"And you had no punishments of any kind?"

"None."

"And you never confined your patients?"

"Very rarely. Now and then, the malady of some individual growing to a crisis, or taking a sudden turn of fury, we conveyed him to a secret cell, lest his disorder should infect the rest, and there kept him until we could dismiss him to his friends; for with the maniac raging we have nothing to do. He is usually removed to the public hospitals."

"And you have now changed all this—and you think for the better?"

"Decidedly. The system had its disadvantages, and even its dangers. It is now, happily, exploded throughout all the *Maisons de Santé* of France."

"I am very much surprised," I said, "at what you tell me; for I made sure that, at this moment, no other method of treatment for mania existed in any portion of the country."

"You are young yet, my friend," replied my host, "but the time will arrive when you will learn to judge for yourself of what is going on in the world, without trusting to the gossip of others :—Believe nothing you hear, and only one half that you see. Now, about our *Maisons de Santé*, it is clear that some ignoramus has misled you. After dinner, however, when you have sufficiently recovered from the fatigue of your ride, I will be happy to take you over the house, and introduce to you a system which, in my opinion, and in that of every one who has witnessed its operation, is incomparably the most effectual as yet devised."

" Your own ? " I inquired—" one of your own invention ? "

" I am proud," he replied, " to acknowledge that it is—at least in some measure."

In this manner I conversed with Monsieur Maillard for an hour or two, during which he showed me the gardens and conservatories of the place.

" I cannot let you see my patients," he said, " just at present. To a sensitive mind there is always more or less of the shocking in such exhibitions ; and I do not wish to spoil your appetite for dinner. We will dine. I can give you some veal *à la Sainte Ménéhould*, with cauliflowers in *velouté* sauce—after that a glass of *Clos Vougeot*—then your nerves will be sufficiently steadied."

At six dinner was announced ; and my host conducted me into a large *salle à manger*, where a very numerous company were assembled—twenty-five or thirty in all. They were, apparently, people of rank —certainly of high breeding—although their habiliments, I thought, were extravagantly rich, partaking somewhat too much of the ostentatious finery of the *vieille cour*. I noticed that at least two-thirds of these guests were ladies; and some of the latter were by no means accoutred in what a Parisian would consider good taste at the present day. Many females, for example, whose age could not have been less than seventy, were bedecked with a profusion of jewelry, such as rings, bracelets, and ear-rings, and wore their bosoms and arms shamefully bare. I observed, too, that very few of the dresses were well made—or, at least, that very few of them fitted the wearers. In looking about I discovered the interesting girl to whom Monsieur Maillard had presented me in the little parlour; but my surprise was great to see her wearing a hoop and farthingale, with high-heeled shoes, and a dirty cap of Brussels lace, so much too large for her that it gave her face a ridiculously diminutive expression. When I had first seen her she was attired, most becomingly, in deep mourning. There was an air of oddity, in short, about the dress of the whole party, which, at first, caused me to recur to my original idea of the " soothing system " and to fancy that Monsieur Maillard had been willing to deceive me until after dinner, that I might experience no uncomfortable feelings during the repast at finding myself dining with lunatics; but I remembered having been informed in Paris that the southern provincialists were a peculiarly eccentric people, with a vast number of antiquated notions; and then, too, upon conversing with several members of the company, my apprehensions were immediately and fully dispelled.

The dining-room itself, although perhaps sufficiently

comfortable and of good dimensions, had nothing too much of elegance about it. For example, the floor was uncarpeted; in France, however, a carpet is frequently dispensed with. The windows, too, were without curtains; the shutters, being shut, were securely fastened with iron bars, applied diagonally, after the fashion of our ordinary shop-shutters. The apartment, I observed, formed in itself a wing of the *château*, and thus the windows were on three sides of the parallelogram—the door being at the other. There were no less than ten windows in all.

The table was superbly set out. It was loaded with plate, and more than loaded with delicacies. The profusion was absolutely barbaric. There were meats enough to have feasted the Anakim. Never in all my life had I witnessed so lavish, so wasteful, an expenditure of the good things of life. There seemed very little taste, however, in the arrangements; and my eyes, accustomed to quiet lights, were sadly offended by the prodigious glare of a multitude of wax candles which, in silver *candelabra*, were deposited upon the table and all about the room, wherever it was possible to find a place. There were several active servants in attendance; and upon a large table at the farther end of the apartment were seated seven or eight people with fiddles, fifes, trombones, and a drum. These fellows annoyed me very much at intervals during the repast, by an infinite variety of noises, which were intended for music, and which appeared to afford much entertainment to all present with the exception of myself.

Upon the whole, I could not help thinking that

there was much of the *bizarre* about everything I saw
—but then the world is made up of all kinds of
persons, with all modes of thought, and all sorts of
conventional customs. I had travelled, too, so much
as to be quite an adept in the *nil admirari ;* so I
took my seat very coolly at the right hand of my host,
and having an excellent appetite, did justice to the
good cheer set before me.

The conversation in the meantime was spirited and
general. The ladies, as usual, talked a great deal. I
soon found that nearly all the company were well
educated ; and my host was a world of good-humoured
anecdote in himself. He seemed quite willing to speak
of his position as superintendent of a *Maison de
Santé ;* and, indeed, the topic of lunacy was, much to
my surprise, a favourite one with all present. A great
many amusing stories were told having reference to
the *whims* of the patients.

" We had a fellow here once," said a fat little
gentleman, who sat at my right—" a fellow that
fancied himself a tea-pot ; and, by the way, is it not
especially singular how often this particular crotchet
has entered the brain of the lunatic ? There is scarcely
an insane asylum in France which cannot supply a
human tea-pot. *Our* gentleman was a Britannia-ware
tea-pot, and was careful to polish himself every morning
with buckskin and whiting."

" And then," said a tall man, just opposite, " we
had here, not long ago, a person who had taken it
into his head that he was a donkey—which, alle-
gorically speaking, you will say, was quite true. He
was a troublesome patient ; and we had much ado to

keep him within bounds. For a long time he would eat nothing but thistles; but of this idea we soon cured him by insisting upon his eating nothing else. Then he was perpetually kicking out his heels—so— so——"

"Mr. De Kock! I will thank you to behave yourself!" here interrupted an old lady, who sat next to the speaker. "Please keep your feet to yourself! You have spoiled my brocade! Is it necessary, pray, to illustrate a remark in so practical a style? Our friend, here, can surely comprehend you without all this. Upon my word, you are nearly as great a donkey as the poor unfortunate imagined himself. Your acting is very natural, as I live."

"*Mille pardons! Ma'mselle!*" replied Monsieur De Kock, thus addressed—"a thousand pardons! I had no intention of offending. Ma'mselle Laplace— Monsieur De Kock will do himself the honour of taking wine with you."

Here Monsieur De Kock bowed low, kissed his hand with much ceremony, and took wine with Ma'mselle Laplace.

"Allow me, *mon ami*," now said Monsieur Maillard, addressing myself, "allow me to send you a morsel of this veal *à la Sainte Ménéhould*—you will find it particularly fine."

At this instant three sturdy waiters had just succeeded in depositing safely upon the table an enormous dish, or trencher, containing what I supposed to be the "*monstrum, horrendum, informe, ingens, cui lumen ademptum*." A closer scrutiny assured me, however, that it was only a small calf roasted whole, and set upon its knees, with an apple in its mouth, as is the English fashion of dressing a hare.

" Thank you, no," I replied ; " to say the truth, I am not particularly partial to veal *à la Sainte*—what is it ?—for I do not find that it altogether agrees with me. I will change my plate, however, and try some of the rabbit."

There were several side-dishes on the table containing what appeared to be the ordinary French rabbit— a very delicious *morceau*, which I can recommend.

" Pierre," cried the host, " change this gentleman's plate, and give him a side-piece of this rabbit *au chat*."

" This what ? "

" This rabbit *au chat*."

" Why, thank you—upon second thoughts, no. I will just help myself to some of the ham."

There is no knowing what one eats, thought I to myself, at the tables of these people of the province. I will have none of their rabbit *au chat*—and for the matter of that, none of their *cat au rabbit* either.

" And then," said a cadaverous-looking personage, near the foot of the table, taking up the thread of the conversation where it had been broken off—" and then, among other oddities, we had a patient once upon a time who very pertinaciously maintained himself to be a Cordova cheese, and went about with a knife in his hand soliciting his friends to try a small slice from the middle of his leg."

" He was a great fool, beyond doubt," interposed some one, " but not to be compared with a certain individual whom we all know, with the exception of this strange gentleman. I mean the man who took himself for a bottle of champagne, and always went off with a pop and a fizz, in this fashion."

Here the speaker, very rudely, as I thought, put his right thumb in his left cheek, withdrew it with a sound resembling the popping of a cork, and then, by a dexterous movement of the tongue upon the teeth, created a sharp hissing and fizzing which lasted for several minutes, in imitation of the frothing of champagne. This behaviour, I saw plainly, was not very pleasing to Monsieur Maillard; but that gentleman said nothing, and the conversation was resumed by a very lean little man in a big wig.

" And then there was an ignoramus," said he, " who mistook himself for a frog; which, by the way, he resembled in no little degree. I wish you could have seen him, sir,"—here the speaker addressed myself—" it would have done your heart good to see the natural airs that he put on. Sir, if that man was *not* a frog, I can only observe that it is a pity he was not. His croak thus—o-o-o-o-gh—o-o-o-o-gh! was the finest note in the world—B flat; and when he put his elbows upon the table thus—after taking a glass or two of wine—and distended his mouth thus, and rolled up his eyes thus, and winked them with excessive rapidity thus, why then, sir, I take it upon myself to say positively, that you would have been lost in admiration of the genius of the man."

" I have no doubt of it," I said.

" And then," said somebody else, " then there was Petit Gaillard, who thought himself a pinch of snuff, and was truly distressed because he could not take himself between his own finger and thumb."

" And then there was Jules Desoulières, who was a very singular genius indeed, and went mad with the idea that he was a pumpkin. He persecuted the cook to make him up into pies—a thing which the cook indignantly refused to do. For my part, I am by no means sure that a pumpkin pie *à la Desoulières* would not have been very capital eating indeed ! "

" You astonish me ! " said I ; and I looked inquisitively at Monsieur Maillard.

" Ha ! ha ! ha ! " said that gentleman—" he ! he ! he !—hi ! hi ! hi !—ho ! ho ! ho—hu ! hu ! hu !—very good indeed !—You must not be astonished, *mon ami ;* our friend here is a wit—a *drôle*—you must not understand him to the letter."

" And then," said some other one of the party, " then there was Bouffon le Grand—another extraordinary personage in his way. He grew deranged through love, and fancied himself possessed of two heads. One of these he maintained to be the head of Cicero ; the other he imagined a composite one, being Demosthenes from the top of the forehead to the mouth, and Lord Brougham from the mouth to the chin. It is not impossible that he was wrong ; but he would have convinced you of his being in the right ; for he was a man of great eloquence. He had an absolute passion for oratory, and could not refrain from display. For example, he used to leap upon the dinner-table thus, and—and——"

Here a friend, at the side of the speaker, put a hand upon his shoulder, and whispered a few words in his ear ; upon which he ceased talking with great suddenness, and sank back within his chair.

"And then," said the friend who had whispered, "there was Boullard, the tee-totum. I call him the tee-totum, because, in fact, he was seized with the droll, but not altogether irrational crotchet that he had been converted into a tee-totum. You would have roared with laughter to see him spin. He would turn round upon one heel by the hour, in this manner —so——"

Here the friend whom he had just interrupted by a whisper, performed an exactly similar office for himself.

"But then," cried an old lady, at the top of her voice, "your Monsieur Boullard was a madman, and a very silly madman at best ; for who, allow me to ask you, ever heard of a human tee-totum ? The thing is absurd. Madame Joyeuse was a more sensible person, as you know. She had a crotchet, but it was instinct with common sense, and gave pleasure to all who had the honour of her acquaintance. She found, upon mature deliberation, that by some accident she had been turned into a chicken-cock ; but, as such, she behaved with propriety. She flapped her wings, with prodigious effect—so—so—so—and as for her crow, it was delicious! Cock-a-doodle-doo!—cock-a-doodle-doo —cock-a-doodle-de-doo-doo-dooo-do-o-o-o-o-o-o- ! "

"Madame Joyeuse, I will thank you to behave yourself ! " here interrupted our host, very angrily. "You can either conduct yourself as a lady should do, or you can quit the table forthwith—take your choice."

The lady (whom I was much astonished to hear addressed as Madame Joyeuse, after the description

of Madame Joyeuse she had just given) blushed up
to the eyebrows, and seemed exceedingly abashed at
the reproof. She hung down her head, and said not
a syllable in reply. But another and younger lady
resumed the theme. It was my beautiful girl of the
little parlour !

" Oh, Madame Joyeuse *was* a fool ! " she exclaimed ;
" but there was really much sound sense, after all, in
the opinion of Eugénie Salsafette. She was a very
beautiful and painfully modest young lady, who
thought the ordinary mode of habiliment indecent,
and wished to dress herself, always, by getting outside, instead of inside of her clothes. It is a thing
very easily done, after all. You have only to do so—
and then so—so—so—and then so—so—so—and
then "——

" *Mon Dieu !* Ma'mselle Salsafette ! " here cried a
dozen voices at once. " What *are* you about ?—forbear !—that is sufficient !—we see, very plainly, how
it is done !—hold ! hold ! " and several persons were
already leaping from their seats to withhold Ma'mselle
Salsafette from putting herself upon a par with the
Medicean Venus, when the point was very effectually
and suddenly accomplished by a series of loud screams,
or yells, from some portion of the main body of the
château.

My nerves were very much affected indeed by these
yells ; but the rest of the company I really pitied. I
never saw any set of reasonable people so thoroughly
frightened in my life. They all grew as pale as so
many corpses, and, shrinking within their seats, sat
quivering and gibbering with terror, and listening for

a repetition of the sound. It came again—louder and seemingly nearer—and then a third time *very* loud, and then a fourth time with a vigour evidently diminished. At this apparent dying away of the noise, the spirits of the company were immediately regained, and all was life and anecdote as before. I now ventured to inquire the cause of the disturbance.

" A mere *bagatelle*," said Monsieur Maillard. " We are used to these things, and care really very little about them. The lunatics, every now and then, get up a howl in concert ; one starting another, as is sometimes the case with a bevy of dogs at night. It occasionally happens, however, that the *concerto* yells are succeeded by a simultaneous effort at breaking loose ; when, of course, some little danger is to be apprehended."

" And how many have you in charge ? "

" At present we have not more than ten altogether."

" Principally females, I presume ? "

" Oh, no—every one of them men, and stout fellows, too, I can tell you."

" Indeed ! I have always understood that the majority of lunatics were of the gentler sex."

" It is generally so, but not always. Some time ago there were about twenty-seven patients here, and of that number no less than eighteen were women ; but, lately, matters have changed very much, as you see."

" Yes—have changed very much, as you see," here interrupted the gentleman who had broken the shins of Ma'mselle Laplace.

" Yes—have changed very much, as you see ! " chimed in the whole company at once.

" Hold your tongues, every one of you ! " said my host, in a great rage. Whereupon the whole company maintained a dead silence for nearly a minute. As for one lady, she obeyed Monsieur Maillard to the letter, and thrusting out her tongue, which was an excessively long one, held it very resignedly, with both hands, until the end of the entertainment.

" And this gentlewoman," said I, to Monsieur Maillard, bending over and addressing him in a whisper— " this good lady who has just spoken, and who gives us the cock-a-doodle-de-doo—she, I presume, is harmless—quite harmless, eh ? "

" Harmless ! " ejaculated he, in unfeigned surprise, " why—why, what *can* you mean ? "

" Only slightly touched ? " said I, touching my head. " I take it for granted that she is not particularly—not dangerously affected, eh ? "

" *Mon Dieu !* what *is* it you imagine ? This lady, my particular old friend, Madame Joyeuse, is as absolutely sane as myself. She has her little eccentricities, to be sure—but then, you know, all old women —all *very* old women are more or less eccentric ! "

" To be sure," said I—" to be sure—and then the rest of these ladies and gentlemen——"

" Are my friends and keepers," interrupted Monsieur Maillard, drawing himself up with *hauteur*—" my very good friends and assistants."

" What ! all of them ? " I asked—" the women and all ? "

" Assuredly," he said—" we could not do at all without the women ; they are the best lunatic nurses in the world ; they have a way of their own, you

know ; their bright eyes have a marvellous effect ;—
something like the fascination of the snake, you
know."

"To be sure," said I—"to be sure ! They behave
a little odd, eh ?—they are a little *queer*, eh ?—don't
you think so ? "

"Odd !—queer !—why, do you *really* think so ?
We are not very prudish, to be sure, here in the South
—do pretty much as we please—enjoy life, and all
that sort of thing, you know——"

"To be sure," said I ; "to be sure."

"And then, perhaps, this *Clos Vougeot* is a little
heady, you know—a little *strong*—you understand,
eh ? "

"To be sure," said I ; "to be sure. By-the-by,
monsieur, did I understand you to say that the
system you have adopted, in place of the celebrated
soothing system, was one of very rigorous severity ? "

"By no means. Our confinement is necessarily
close ; but the treatment—the medical treatment, I
mean—is rather agreeable to the patients than
otherwise."

"And the new system is one of your own invention ? "

"Not altogether. Some portions of it are referable
to Professor Tarr, of whom you have necessarily
heard ; and, again, there are modifications in my plan
which I am happy to acknowledge as belonging of
right to the celebrated Fether, with whom, if I mistake
not, you have the honour of an intimate acquaintance."

"I am quite ashamed to confess," I replied, "that

I have never even heard the name of either gentleman before."

"Good heavens!" ejaculated my host, drawing back his chair abruptly, and uplifting his hands. "I surely do not hear you aright! You did not intend to say, eh? that you had never *heard* either of the learned Doctor Tarr, or of the celebrated Professor Fether?"

"I am forced to acknowledge my ignorance," I replied; "but the truth should be held inviolate above all things. Nevertheless, I feel humbled to the dust, not to be acquainted with the works of these, no doubt, extraordinary men. I will seek out their writings forthwith, and peruse them with deliberate care. Monsieur Maillard, you have really—I must confess it—you have *really*—made me ashamed of myself!"

And this was the fact.

"Say no more, my good young friend," he said kindly, pressing my hand—"join me now in a glass of Sauterne."

We drank. The company followed our example, without stint. They chatted—they jested—they laughed—they perpetrated a thousand absurdities— the fiddles shrieked—the drum row-de-dowed—the trombones bellowed like so many brazen bulls of Phalaris—and the whole scene, growing gradually worse and worse as the wines gained the ascendency, became at length a sort of Pandemonium *in petto*. In the meantime, Monsieur Maillard and myself, with some bottles of Sauterne and Clos Vougeot between us, continued our conversation at the top of the voice.

A word spoken in an ordinary key stood no more chance of being heard than the voice of a fish from the bottom of Niagara Falls.

"And, sir," said I, screaming in his ear, "you mentioned something before dinner about the danger incurred in the old system of soothing. How is that?"

"Yes," he replied, "there was occasionally very great danger indeed. There is no accounting for the caprices of madmen; and, in my opinion, as well as in that of Doctor Tarr and Professor Fether, it is *never* safe to permit them to run at large unattended. A lunatic may be 'soothed,' as it is called, for a time, but in the end he is very apt to become obstreperous. His cunning, too, is proverbial and great. If he has a project in view, he conceals his design with a marvellous wisdom; and the dexterity with which he counterfeits sanity, presents to the metaphysician one of the most singular problems in the study of mind. When a madman appears *thoroughly* sane, indeed, it is high time to put him in a strait jacket."

"But the *danger*, my dear sir, of which you were speaking—in your own experience—during your control of this house—have you had practical reason to think liberty hazardous in the case of a lunatic?"

"Here?—in my own experience?—why, I may say yes. For example:—no *very* long while ago, a singular circumstance occurred in this very house. The 'soothing system,' you know, was then in operation, and the patients were at large. They behaved remarkably well—especially so—any one of sense might have known that some devilish scheme was brewing from that particular fact, that the fellows behaved so *remarkably* well. And, sure enough, one fine morning the keepers found themselves pinioned hand and foot, and thrown into the cells, where they were attended, as if *they* were the lunatics, by the lunatics themselves, who had usurped the offices of the keepers.

" You don't tell me so ! I never heard of anything so absurd in my life ! "

" Fact—it all came to pass by means of a stupid fellow—a lunatic—who by some means had taken it into his head that he had invented a better system of government than any ever heard of before—of lunatic government, I mean. He wished to give his invention a trial, I suppose, and so he persuaded the rest of the patients to join him in a conspiracy for the over-throw of the reigning powers."

" And he really succeeded ? "

" No doubt of it. The keepers and kept were soon made to exchange places. Not that exactly either, for the madmen had been free, but the keepers were shut up in cells forthwith, and treated, I am sorry to say, in a very cavalier manner."

" But I presume a counter-revolution was soon effected. This condition of things could not have long existed. The country people in the neighbour-hood—visitors coming to see the establishment—would have given the alarm."

" There you are out. The head rebel was too cun-ning for that. He admitted no visitors at all—with the exception, one day, of a very stupid-looking young gentleman of whom he had no reason to be afraid. He let him in to see the place—just by way of variety—to have a little fun with him. As soon as he had gammoned him sufficiently, he let him out, and sent him about his business."

" And *how* long, then, did the madmen reign ? "

" Oh, a very long time, indeed—a month certainly—how much longer I can't precisely say. In the meantime, the lunatics had a jolly season of it—that you may swear. They doffed their own shabby clothes, and made free with the family wardrobe and jewels. The cellars of the *château* were well stocked with wine ; and these madmen are just the devils that know how to drink it. They lived well, I can tell you."

" And the treatment—what was the particular species of treatment which the leader of the rebels put into operation ? "

" Why, as for that, a madman is not necessarily a fool, as I have already observed ; and it is my honest opinion that his treatment was a much better treatment than that which it superseded. It was a very capital system indeed—simple—neat—no trouble at all, in fact it was delicious—it was——"

Here my host's observations were cut short by another series of yells, of the same character as those which had previously disconcerted us. This time, however, they seemed to proceed from persons rapidly approaching.

" Gracious heavens ! " I ejaculated—" the lunatics have most undoubtedly broken loose."

" I very much fear it is so," replied Monsieur Maillard, now becoming excessively pale. He had scarcely finished the sentence before loud shouts and imprecations were heard beneath the windows; and immediately afterwards it became evident that some persons outside were endeavouring to gain entrance into the room. The door was beaten with what appeared to be a sledge-hammer, and the shutters were wrenched and shaken with prodigious violence.

A scene of the most terrible confusion ensued. Monsieur Maillard, to my excessive astonishment, threw himself under the sideboard. I had expected more resolution at his hands. The members of the orchestra, who for the last fifteen minutes had been seemingly too much intoxicated to do duty, now sprang all at once to their feet and to their instruments, and, scrambling upon their table, broke out with one accord into " Yankee Doodle," which they performed, if not exactly in tune, at least with an energy super-human, during the whole of the uproar.

Meantime, upon the main dining-table, among the bottles and glasses, leaped the gentleman who with such difficulty had been restrained from leaping there before. As soon as he fairly settled himself he commenced an oration, which no doubt was a very capital one if it could only have been heard. At the same moment, the man with the tee-totum predilections set himself to spinning around the apartment with immense energy, and with arms outstretched at right angles with his body, so that he had all the air of a tee-totum in fact, and knocked everybody down that happened to get in his way. And now, too, hearing an incredible popping and fizzing of champagne, I discovered at length that it proceeded from the person who performed the bottle of that delicate drink during dinner. And then, again, the frogman croaked away as if the salvation of his soul depended upon every note that he uttered. And in the midst of all this, the continuous braying of a donkey arose over all. As for my old friend Madame Joyeuse, I really could have wept for the poor lady, she appeared so terribly perplexed. All she did, however, was to stand up in a corner by the fireplace, and sing out incessantly, at the top of her voice, " Cock-a-doodle-de-dooooooh ! "

And now came the climax—the catastrophe of the drama. As no resistance beyond whooping and yelling and cock-a-doodleing was offered to the encroachments of the party without, the ten windows were very speedily and almost simultaneously broken in. But I shall never forget the emotions of wonder and horror with which I gazed, when, leaping through these windows and down among us *pêle-mêle*, fighting, stamping, scratching, and howling, there rushed a perfect army of what I took to be Chimpanzees, Ourang-Outangs, or big black baboons of the Cape of Good Hope.

I received a terrible beating, after which I rolled under a sofa and lay still. After lying there some fifteen minutes, however, during which time I listened with all my ears to what was going on in the room, I came to some satisfactory *dénouement* of this tragedy. Monsieur Maillard, it appeared, in giving me the account of the lunatic who had excited his fellows to rebellion, had been merely relating his own exploits. This gentleman, had, indeed, some two or three years before been the superintendent of the establishment, but grew crazy himself, and so became a patient. This fact was unknown to the travelling companion who introduced me. The keepers, ten in number, having been suddenly overpowered, were first well tarred, then carefully feathered, and then shut up in underground cells. They had been so imprisoned for more than a month, during which period Monsieur Maillard had generously allowed them not only the tar and feathers (which constituted his " system "), but some bread and abundance of water. The latter was pumped on them daily. At length, one escaping through a sewer gave freedom to all the rest.

The " soothing system," with important modifications, has been resumed at the *château* ; yet I cannot help agreeing with Monsieur Maillard that his own " treatment " was a very capital one of its kind. As he justly observed, it was " simple, neat, and gave no trouble at all—not the least."

I have only to add that, although I have searched every library in Europe for the works of Doctor *Tarr* and Professor *Fether*, I have, up to the present day, utterly failed in my endeavours at procuring an edition.

XIII

THE CASK OF AMONTILLADO

THE thousand injuries of Fortunato I had borne as I best could, but when he ventured upon insult, I vowed revenge. You, who so well know the nature of my soul, will not suppose, however, that I gave utterance to a threat. *At length* I would be avenged ; this was a point definitely settled—but the very definiteness with which it was resolved precluded the idea of risk. I must not only punish, but punish with impunity. A wrong is unredressed when retribution overtakes its redresser. It is equally unredressed when the avenger fails to make himself felt as such to him who has done the wrong.

It must be understood that neither by word nor deed had I given Fortunato cause to doubt my good will. I continued, as was my wont, to smile in his face, and he did not perceive that my smile *now* was at the thought of his immolation.

He had a weak point—this Fortunato—although in other regards he was a man to be respected and even feared. He prided himself on his connoisseurship in wine. Few Italians have the true virtuoso spirit. For the most part their enthusiasm is adopted to suit the time and opportunity to practise imposture upon the British and Austrian *millionnaires*. In painting and gemmary Fortunato, like his countrymen, was a quack, but in the matter of old wines he was sincere. In this respect I did not differ from him materially ; I was skilful in the Italian vintages myself, and bought largely whenever I could.

It was about dusk, one evening during the supreme madness of the carnival season, that I encountered my friend. He accosted me with excessive warmth, for he had been drinking much. The man wore motley. He had on a tight-fitting parti-striped dress, and his head was surmounted by the conical cap and bells. I was so pleased to see him, that I thought I should never have done wringing his hand.

I said to him—" My dear Fortunato, you are luckily met. How remarkably well you are looking to-day ! But I have received a pipe of what passes for Amontillado, and I have my doubts."

" How ? " said he, " Amontillado ? A pipe ? Impossible ? And in the middle of the carnival ? "

" I have my doubts," I replied ; " and I was silly enough to pay the full Amontillado price without consulting you in the matter. You were not to be found, and I was fearful of losing a bargain."

" Amontillado ! "

" I have my doubts."

" Amontillado ! "

" And I must satisfy them."

" Amontillado ! "

" As you are engaged, I am on my way to Luchesi. If any one has a critical turn, it is he. He will tell me——"

" Luchesi cannot tell Amontillado from Sherry."

" And yet some fools will have it that his taste is a match for your own."

" Come, let us go."

" Whither ? "

" To your vaults."

" My friend, no ; I will not impose upon your good nature. I perceive you have an engagement. Luchesi——"

" I have no engagement ; come."

" My friend, no. It is not the engagement, but the severe cold with which I perceive you are afflicted. The vaults are insufferably damp. They are encrusted with nitre."

" Let us go, nevertheless. The cold is merely nothing. Amontillado ! You have been imposed upon ; and as for Luchesi, he cannot distinguish Sherry from Amontillado."

Thus speaking, Fortunato possessed himself of my arm. Putting on a mask of black silk, and drawing *a roquelaure* closely about my person, I suffered him to hurry me to my palazzo.

There were no attendants at home ; they had absconded to make merry in honour of the time. I had told them that I should not return until the morning, and had given them explicit orders not to stir from the house. These orders were sufficient, I well knew, to insure their immediate disappearance, one and all, as soon as my back was turned.

I took from their sconces two flambeaux, and giving one to Fortunato, bowed him through several suites of rooms to the archway that led into the vaults. I passed down a long and winding staircase, requesting him to be cautious as he followed. We came at length to the foot of the descent, and stood together on the damp ground of the catacombs of the Montresors.

The gait of my friend was unsteady and the bells upon his cap jingled as he strode.

" The pipe," said he.

" It is farther on," said I ; " but observe the white web-work which gleams from these cavern walls."

He turned towards me, and looked into my eyes with two filmy orbs that distilled the rheum of intoxication.

" Nitre ? " he asked, at length.

" Nitre," I replied. " How long have you had that cough ? "

" Ugh ! ugh ! ugh !—ugh ! ugh ! ugh !—ugh ! ugh ! ugh !—ugh ! ugh ! ugh !—ugh ! ugh ! ugh ! "

My poor friend found it impossible to reply for many minutes.

" It is nothing," he said, at last.

" Come," I said, with decision, " we will go back ; your health is precious. You are rich, respected, admired, beloved ; you are happy, as once I was. You are a man to be missed. For me it is no matter. We will go back ; you will be ill, and I cannot be responsible. Besides, there is Luchesi——"

" Enough," he said ; " the cough is a mere nothing ; it will not kill me. I shall not die of a cough."

" True—true," replied I ; " and, indeed, I had no intention of alarming you unnecessarily—but you should use all proper caution. A draught of this Medoc will defend us from the damps."

Here I knocked off the neck of a bottle which I drew from a long row of its fellows that lay upon the mould.

" Drink," I said, presenting him the wine.

He raised it to his lips with a leer. He paused and nodded to me familiarly, while his bells jingled.

" I drink," he said, " to the buried that repose around us."

" And I to your long life."

He again took my arm, and we proceeded.

" These vaults," he said, " are extensive."

" The Montresors," I replied, " were a great and numerous family."

" I forget your arms."

" A huge human foot d'or, in a field azure ; the foot crushes a serpent rampant whose fangs are imbedded in the heel."

" And the motto ? "

" *Nemo me impune lacessit.*"

" Good ! " he said.

The wine sparkled in his eyes and the bells jingled. My own fancy grew warm with the Medoc. We had passed through walls of piled bones, with casks and puncheons intermingling, into the inmost recesses of the catacombs. I paused again, and this time I made bold to seize Fortunato by an arm above the elbow.

" The nitre ! " I said ; " see, it increases. It hangs like moss upon the vaults. We are below the river's bed. The drops of moisture trickle among the bones. Come, we will go back ere it is too late. Your cough——"

" It is nothing," he said ; " let us go on. But first, another draught of the Medoc."

I broke and reached him a flaçon of De Grâve. He emptied it at a breath. His eyes flashed with a fierce light. He laughed and threw the bottle upwards with a gesticulation I did not understand.

I looked at him in surprise. He repeated the move ment—a grotesque one.

" You do not comprehend ? " he said.

" Not I," I replied.

" Then you are not of the brotherhood ? "

" How ? "

" You are not of the masons."

" Yes, yes," I said, " yes, yes."

" You ?   Impossible !   A mason ? "

" A mason," I replied.

" A sign," he said.

" It is this," I answered, producing a trowel from beneath the folds of my *roquelaure*.

" You jest," he exclaimed, recoiling a few paces. " But let us proceed to the Amontillado."

" Be it so," I said, replacing the tool beneath the cloak, and again offering him my arm. He leaned upon it heavily. We continued our route in search of the Amontillado. We passed through a range of low arches, descended, passed on, and descending again, arrived at a deep crypt, in which the foulness of the air caused our flambeaux rather to glow than flame.

At the most remote end of the crypt there appeared another less spacious. Its walls had been lined with human remains piled to the vault overhead, in the fashion of the great catacombs of Paris. Three sides of this interior crypt were still ornamented in this manner. From the fourth the bones had been thrown down, and lay promiscuously upon the earth, forming at one point a mound of some size. Within the wall thus exposed by the displacing of the bones, we perceived a still interior recess, in depth about four feet, in width three, in height six or seven. It seemed to have been constructed for no especial use within itself, but formed merely the interval between two of the colossal supports of the roof of the catacombs, and was backed by one of their circumscribing walls of solid granite.

It was in vain that Fortunato, uplifting his dull torch, endeavoured to pry into the depths of the recess. Its termination the feeble light did not enable us to see.

" Proceed," I said ; " herein is the Amontillado. As for Luchesi——"

" He is an ignoramus," interrupted my friend, as he stepped unsteadily forward, while I followed immediately at his heels. In an instant he had reached the extremity of the niche, and finding his progress arrested by the rock, stood stupidly bewildered. A moment more and I had fettered him to the granite. In its surface were two iron staples, distant from each other about two feet, horizontally. From one of these depended a short chain, from the other a padlock. Throwing the links about his waist, it was but the work of a few seconds to secure it. He was too much astounded to resist. Withdrawing the key I stepped back from the recess.

" Pass your hand," I said, " over the wall ; you cannot help feeling the nitre. Indeed it is *very* damp. Once more let me *implore* you to return. No ? Then I must positively leave you. But I must first render you all the attentions in my power."

" The Amontillado ! " ejaculated my friend, not yet recovered from his astonishment.

" True," I replied ; " the Amontillado."

As I said these words I busied myself among the pile of bones of which I have before spoken. Throwing them aside, I soon uncovered a quantity of building stone and mortar. With these materials and with the aid of my trowel, I began vigorously to wall up the entrance of the niche.

I had scarcely laid the first tier of the masonry when I discovered that the intoxication of Fortunato had in a great measure worn off. The earliest indication I had of this was a low moaning cry from the depth of the recess. It was *not* the cry of a drunken man. There was then a long and obstinate silence. I laid the second tier, and the third, and the fourth ; and then I hear the furious vibrations of the chain. The noise lasted for several minutes, during which, that I might hearken to it with the more satisfaction, I ceased my labours and sat down upon the bones. When at last the clanking subsided, I resumed the trowel, and finished without interruption the fifth, the sixth, and the seventh tier. The wall was now nearly upon a level with my breast. I again paused, and holding the flambeaux over the mason-work, threw a few feeble rays upon the figure within.

A succession of loud and shrill screams, bursting suddenly from the throat of the chained form, seemed to thrust me violently back. For a brief moment I hesitated—I trembled. Unsheathing my rapier, I began to grope with it about the recess ; but the thought of an instant reassured me. I placed my hand upon the solid fabric of the catacombs, and felt satisfied. I reapproached the wall. I replied to the yells of him who clamoured. I re-echoed—I aided—I surpassed them in volume and in strength. I did this, and the clamourer grew still.

It was now midnight, and my task was drawing to a close. I had completed the eighth, the ninth, and the tenth tier. I had finished a portion of the last and the eleventh ; there remained but a single stone to be fitted and plastered in. I struggled with its weight ; I placed it partially in its destined position. But now there came from out the niche a low laugh that erected the hairs upon my head. It was succeeded by a sad voice, which I had difficulty in recognising as that of the noble Fortunato. The voice said—

" Ha ! ha ! ha !—he ! he !—a very good joke indeed —an excellent jest. We will have many a rich laugh about it at the palazzo—he ! he ! he !—over our wine —he ! he ! he ! "

" The Amontillado ! " I said.

" He ! he ! he !—he ! he ! he !—yes, the Amontillado. But is it not getting late ? Will not they be awaiting us at the palazzo, the Lady Fortunato and the rest ? Let us be gone."

" Yes," I said, " let us be gone."

" *For the love of God, Montresor !* "

" Yes," I said, " for the love of God ! "

But to these words I hearkened in vain for a reply. I grew impatient. I called aloud—

" Fortunato ! "

No answer. I called again—

" Fortunato ! "

No answer still. I thrust a torch through the remaining aperture and let it fall within. There came forth in return only a jingling of the bells. My heart grew sick—on account of the dampness of the catacombs. I hastened to make an end of my labour. I forced the last stone into its position; I plastered it up. Against the new masonry I re-erected the old rampart of bones. For the half of a century no mortal has disturbed them. *In pace requiescat!*

THE END